HOPE AND RED

THE EMPIRE OF STORMS: BOOK ONE

JON SKOVRON

orbit

www.orbitbooks.net

ORBIT

First published in Great Britain in 2016 by Orbit

1 3 5 7 9 10 8 6 4 2

A CIP catalogue record for this book is available from the British Library.

ISBN 978-0-356-50712-5

Typeset in Times New Roman MT by Hewer Text UK Ltd, Edinburgh
Printed and bound in Great Britain by Clays Ltd, St Ives plc

Papers used by Orbit are from well-managed forests and other responsible sources.

MIX
Paper from
responsible sources
FSC
www.fsc.org
FSC® C104740

Orbit
An imprint of
Little, Brown Book Group
Carmelite House
50 Victoria Embankment
London EC4Y 0DZ

An Hachette UK Company www.hachette.co.uk
www.orbitbooks.net

HOPE
AND RED

'I'll ask you again, girl,' he said, although his tone was still gentle. 'What's yer name?'

She only stared at him.

'Where'd you come from?'

Still she stared.

'Are you . . .' He couldn't believe he was even thinking it, much less asking it. 'Are you from Bleak Hope?'

She blinked then, as if coming out of a trance. 'Bleak Hope.' Her voice was hoarse from lack of use. 'Yes. That's me.' There was something about the way she spoke that made Toa suppress a shudder. Her voice was as empty as her eyes.

'How did you come to be on my ship?'

'That happened after,' she said.

'After what?' he asked.

She looked at him then, and her eyes were no longer empty. They were full. So full that Toa's salty old heart felt like it might twist up like a rag in his chest.

'I will tell you,' she said, her voice as wet and full as her eyes. 'I will tell *only* you. Then I won't ever say it aloud ever again.'

For my father, Rick Skovron, who gave me my first fantasy novel. See what you started?

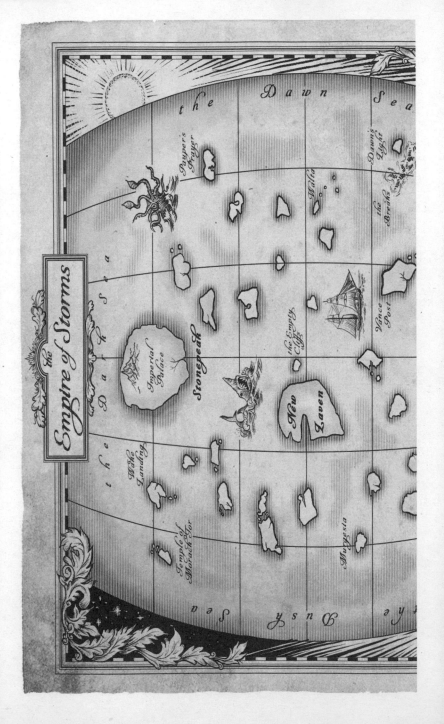

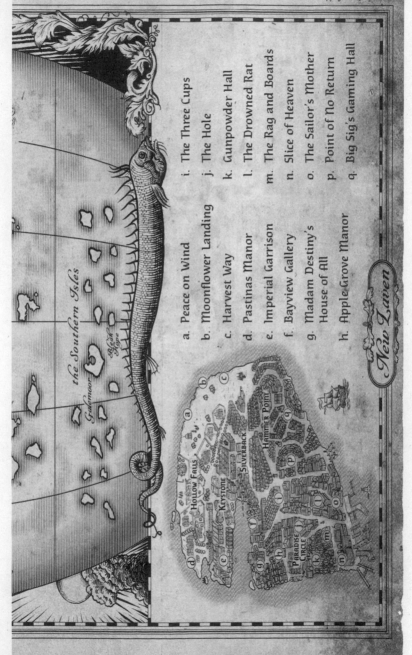

the Southern Isles

New Laven

a. Peace on Wind
b. Moonflower Landing
c. Harvest Way
d. Pastinas Manor
e. Imperial Garrison
f. Bayview Gallery
g. Madam Destiny's House of All
h. Apple Grove Manor

i. The Three Cups
j. The Hole
k. Gunpowder Hall
l. The Drowned Rat
m. The Rag and Boards
n. Slice of Heaven
o. The Sailor's Mother
p. Point of No Return
q. Big Sig's Gaming Hall

PART ONE

Those who have lost everything are free to become anyone. It is a steep price to pay, but greatness is ever thus.

– from *The Book of Storms*

1

Captain Sin Toa had been a trader on these seas for many years, and he'd seen something like this before. But that didn't make it any easier.

The village of Bleak Hope was a small community in the cold Southern islands at the edge of the empire. Captain Toa was one of the few traders who came this far south, and even then, only once a year. The ice that formed on the water made it nearly impossible to reach during the winter months.

Still, the dried fish, whalebone, and the crude lamp oil they pressed from whale blubber were all good cargo that fetched a nice price in Stonepeak or New Laven. The villagers had always been polite and accommodating, in their taciturn Southern way. And it was a community that had survived in these harsh conditions for centuries, a quality that Toa respected a great deal.

So it was with a pang of sadness that he gazed out at what remained of the village. As his ship glided into the narrow harbor, he scanned the dirt paths and stone huts, and saw no sign of life.

'What's the matter, sir?' asked Crayton, his first mate. Good fellow. Loyal in his own way, if a bit dishonest about doing his fair share of work.

'This place is dead,' said Toa quietly. 'We'll not land here.'

'Dead, sir?'

'Not a soul in the place.'

'Maybe they're at some sort of local religious gathering,' said Crayton. 'Folks this far south have their own ways and customs.'

''Fraid that's not it.'

Toa pointed one thick, scarred finger toward the dock. A tall sign had been driven into the wood. On the sign was painted a black oval with eight black lines trailing down from it.

'God save them,' whispered Crayton, taking off his wool knit cap.

'That's the trouble,' said Toa. 'He didn't.'

The two men stood there staring at the sign. There was no sound except the cold wind that pulled at Toa's long wool coat and beard.

'What do we do, sir?' asked Crayton.

'Not come ashore, that's for certain. Tell the wags to lay anchor. It's getting late. I don't want to navigate these shallow waters in the dark, so we'll stay the night. But make no mistake, we're heading back to sea at first light and never coming near Bleak Hope again.'

They set sail the next morning. Toa hoped they'd reach the island of Galemoor in three days and that the monks there would have enough good ale to sell that it would cover his losses.

It was on the second night that they found the stowaway.

Toa was woken in his bunk by a fist pounding on his cabin door.

'Captain!' called Crayton. 'The night watch. They found . . . a little girl.'

Toa groaned. He'd had a bit too much grog before he went to sleep, and the spike of pain had already set in behind his eyes.

'A girl?' he asked after a moment.

'Y-y-yes, sir.'

'Hells' waters,' he muttered, climbing out of his hammock. He pulled on cold, damp trousers, a coat, and boots. A girl on board, even a little one, was bad luck in these Southern seas. Everybody knew that. As he pondered how he was going to get rid of this stowaway, he opened the door and was surprised to find Crayton alone, turning his wool cap over and over again in his hands.

'Well? Where's the girl?'

'She's aft, sir,' said Crayton.

'Why didn't you bring her to me?'

'We, uh . . . That is, the men can't get her out from behind the stowed rigging.'

'Can't get her . . .' Toa heaved a sigh, wondering why no one had just reached in and clubbed her unconscious, then dragged her out. It wasn't like his men to get soft because of a little girl. Maybe it was on account of Bleak Hope. Maybe the terrible fate of that village had made them a bit more conscious than usual of their own prospects for Heaven.

'Fine,' he said. 'Lead me to her.'

'Aye, sir,' said Crayton, clearly relieved that he wasn't going to bear the brunt of the captain's frustration.

Toa found his men gathered around the cargo hold where the spare rigging was stored. The hatch was open and they stared down into the darkness, muttering to each other and making signs to ward off curses. Toa took a lantern from one of them and shone the light down into the hole, wondering why a little girl had his men so spooked.

'Look, girlie. You better . . .'

She was wedged in tight behind the piles of heavy line. She looked filthy and starved, but otherwise a normal enough girl of about eight years. Pretty, even, in the Southern way, with pale skin, freckles, and hair so blond it looked almost white. But there was something about her eyes when she looked at you. They felt empty, or worse than empty. They were pools of ice that crushed any warmth you had in you. They were ancient eyes. Broken eyes. Eyes that had seen too much.

'We tried to pull her out, Captain,' said one of the men. 'But she's packed in there tight. And well . . . she's . . .'

'Aye,' said Toa.

He knelt down next to the opening and forced himself to keep looking at her, even though he wanted to turn away.

'What's your name, girl?' he asked, much quieter now.

She stared at him.

'I'm the captain of this ship, girl,' he said. 'Do you know what that means?'

Slowly, she nodded once.

'It means everyone on this ship has to do what I say. That includes you. Understand?'

Again, she nodded once.

He reached one brown, hairy hand down into the hold.

'Now, girl. I want you to come out from behind there and take my hand. I swear no harm will come to you on this ship.'

For a long moment, no one moved. Then, tentatively, the girl reached out her bone-thin hand and let it be engulfed in Toa's.

Toa and the girl were back in his quarters. He suspected the girl might start talking if there weren't a dozen hard-bitten sailors staring at her. He gave her a blanket and a cup of hot grog. He knew grog wasn't the sort of thing you gave to little girls, but it was the only thing he had on board except fresh water, and that was far too precious to waste.

Now he sat at his desk and she sat on his bunk, the blanket wrapped tightly around her shoulders, the steaming cup of grog in her tiny hands. She took a sip, and Toa expected her to flinch at the pungent flavor, but she only swallowed and continued to stare at him with those empty, broken eyes of hers. They were the coldest blue he had ever seen, deeper than the sea itself.

'I'll ask you again, girl,' he said, although his tone was still gentle. 'What's yer name?'

She only stared at him.

'Where'd you come from?'

Still she stared.

'Are you . . .' He couldn't believe he was even thinking it, much less asking it. 'Are you from Bleak Hope?'

She blinked then, as if coming out of a trance. 'Bleak Hope.' Her voice was hoarse from lack of use. 'Yes. That's me.' There was something about the way she spoke that made Toa suppress a shudder. Her voice was as empty as her eyes.

'How did you come to be on my ship?'

'That happened after,' she said.

'After what?' he asked.

She looked at him then, and her eyes were no longer empty. They were full. So full that Toa's salty old heart felt like it might twist up like a rag in his chest.

'I will tell you,' she said, her voice as wet and full as her eyes. 'I will tell *only* you. Then I won't ever say it aloud ever again.'

*   *   *

She had been off at the rocks. That was how they'd missed her.

She loved the rocks. Great big jagged black boulders she could climb above the crashing waves. It terrified her mother the way she jumped from one to the next. 'You'll hurt yourself!' her mother would say. And she did hurt herself. Often. Her shins and knees were peppered with scabs and scars from the rough-edged rock. But she didn't care. She loved them anyway. And when the tide went out, they always had treasures at their bases, half-buried in the gray sand. Crab shells, fish bones, seashells, and sometimes, if she was very lucky, a bit of sea glass. That she prized above all else.

'What is it?' she'd asked her mother one night as they sat by the fire after dinner, her belly warm and full of fish stew. She held up a piece of red sea glass to the light so that the color shone on the stone wall of their hut.

'It's glass, my little gull,' said her mother, fingers working quickly as she mended a fishing net for Father. 'Broken bits of glass polished by the sea.'

'But why's it colored?'

'To make it prettier, I suppose.'

'Why don't *we* have any glass that's colored?'

'Oh, it's just fancy Northland frippery,' said her mother. 'We've no use for it down here.'

That made her love the sea glass all the more. She collected them until she had enough to string together with a bit of hemp rope to make a necklace. She presented it to her father, a gruff fisherman who rarely spoke, on his birthday. He held the necklace in his leathery hand, eyeing the bright red, blue, and green chunks of sea glass warily. But then he looked into her eyes and saw how proud she was, how much she loved this thing. His weather-lined face folded up into a smile as he carefully tied it around his neck. The other fishermen teased him for weeks about it, but he would only touch his calloused fingertips to the sea glass and smile again.

When *they* came on that day, the tide had just gone out, and she was searching the base of her rocks for new treasures. She'd seen the top of their ship masts off in the distance, but she was far too focused on her hunt for sea glass to investigate. It wasn't until she finally clambered back on top of one of the rocks to sift through her collection of shells and bones that she noticed how strange the ship was. A big boxy thing with a full three sails and cannon ports all along the sides. Very different from the trade ships. She didn't like the look of it at all. And that was before she noticed the thick cloud of smoke rising from her village.

She ran, her skinny little legs churning in the sand and tall grass as she made her way through the scraggly trees toward her village. If there was a fire, her mother wouldn't bother to save the treasures stowed away in the wooden chest under her bed. That was all she could think about. She'd spent too much time and effort collecting her treasures to lose them. They were the most precious thing to her. Or so she thought.

As she neared the village, she saw that the fire had spread across the whole village. There were men she didn't recognize dressed in white-and-gold uniforms with helmets and armored chest plates. She wondered if they were soldiers. But soldiers were supposed to protect the people. These men herded everyone into a big clump in the center of the village, waving swords and guns at them.

She jerked to a stop when she saw the guns. She'd seen only one other gun. It was owned by Shamka, the village elder. Every winter on the eve of the New Year, he fired it up at the moon to wake it from its slumber and bring back the sun. The guns these soldiers had looked different. In addition to the wooden handle, iron tube, and hammer, they had a round cylinder.

She was trying to decide whether to get closer or run and hide, when Shamka emerged from his hut, gave an angry bellow, and fired his gun at the nearest soldier. The soldier's face caved in as the shot struck him, and he fell back into the mud. One of the other soldiers raised his pistol and fired at Shamka, but missed. Shamka laughed triumphantly. But then the intruder fired a second time without reloading. Shamka's face was wide with surprise as he clutched at his chest and toppled over.

The girl nearly cried out then. But she bit her lip as hard as she could to stop herself, and dropped into the tall grass.

She lay hidden there in the cold, muddy field for hours. She had to clench her jaw to keep her teeth from chattering. She heard the soldiers shouting to each other, and there were strange hammering and flapping sounds. Occasionally, she would hear one of the villagers beg to know what they had done to displease the emperor. The only reply was a loud smack.

It was dark, and the fires had all flickered out before she moved her numb limbs up into a crouch and took another look.

In the center of the town, a huge brown canvas tent had been erected, easily five times larger than any hut in the village. The soldiers stood in a circle around it, holding torches. She couldn't see her fellow villagers anywhere. Cautiously, she crept a little closer.

A tall man who wore a long, hooded white cloak instead of a uniform stood at the entrance to the tent. In his hands, he held a large wooden box. One of the soldiers opened the flap of the tent entrance. The cloaked man went into the tent, accompanied by a soldier. Some moments later, they both emerged, but the man no longer had the box. The soldier tied the flap so that the entrance remained open, then covered the opening with a net so fine not even the smallest bird could have slipped through.

The cloaked man took a notebook from his pocket as soldiers brought out a small table and chair and placed them before him. He sat at the table and a soldier handed him a quill and ink. The man immediately began to write, pausing frequently to peer through the netting into the tent.

Screams began to come from inside the tent. She realized then that all the villagers were inside. She didn't know why they screamed, but it terrified her so much that she dropped back into the mud and held her hands over her ears to block out the sound. The screams lasted only a few minutes, but it was a long time before she could bring herself to look again.

It was completely dark now except for one lantern at the tent entrance. The soldiers had gone and only the cloaked man remained, still scribbling away in his notebook. Occasionally, he would glance into the tent, look at his pocket watch, and frown. She wondered where the soldiers were, but then noticed that the strange boxy ship tied at the dock was lit up, and when she strained her hearing, she could make out the sound of rowdy male voices.

The girl snuck through the tall grass toward the side of the tent that was the farthest from the man. Not that he would have seen her. He seemed so intent on his writing that she probably could have walked right past him, and he wouldn't have noticed. Even so, her heart raced as she crept across the small stretch of open ground between the tall grass and the tent wall. When she finally reached the tent, she found that the bottom had been staked down so tightly that she had to pull out several of them before she could slip under.

It was even darker inside, the air thick and hot. The villagers all lay on the ground, eyes closed, chained to each other and to the thick tent poles. In the center sat the wooden box, the lid off. Scattered on the ground were dead wasps as big as birds.

Far over in the corner, she saw her mother and father, motionless like all the rest. She moved quickly to them, a sick fear shooting through her stomach.

But then her father moved weakly, and relief flooded through her. Maybe she could still rescue them. She gently shook her mother, but she didn't respond. She shook her father, but he only groaned, his eyes fluttering a moment but not opening.

She searched around, looking to see if she could unfasten their chains. There was a loud buzzing close to her ear. She turned and saw a giant wasp hovering over her shoulder. Before it could sting her, a hand shot past her face and slapped it aside. The wasp spun wildly around, one wing broken, then dropped to the ground. She turned and saw her father, his face screwed up in pain.

He grabbed her wrist. 'Go!' he grunted. 'Away.' Then he shoved her so hard, she fell backward onto her rear.

She stared at him, terrified, but wanting to do something that would take the awful look of pain away from his face. Around her, others were stirring, their own faces etched in the same agony as her father.

Then she saw her father's sea glass necklace give an odd little jump. She looked closer. It happened again. Her father arched his back. His eyes and mouth opened wide, as if screaming, but only a wet gurgle came out. A white worm as thick as a finger burst from his neck. Blood streamed from him as other worms burrowed out of his chest and gut.

Her mother woke with a gasp, her eyes staring around wildly. Her skin was already shifting. She reached out and called her daughter's name.

All around her, the other villagers thrashed against their chains as the worms ripped free. Before long, the ground was covered in a writhing mass of white.

She wanted to run. Instead, she held her mother's hand and watched her writhe and jerk as the worms ate her from the inside. She did not move, did not look away until her mother grew still. Only then did she stumble to her feet, slip under the tent wall, and run back into the tall grass.

She watched from afar as the soldiers returned at dawn with large burlap sacks. The cloaked man went inside the tent for a while, then came back out and wrote more in his notebook. He did this two more times, then said something to one of the soldiers. The soldier nodded, gave a signal, and the group with sacks filed into the tent. When they came back out, their sacks were filled with writhing bulges that she guessed were the worms. They carried them to the ship while the remaining soldiers struck the tent, exposing the bodies that had been inside.

The cloaked man watched as the soldiers unfastened the chains from the pile of corpses. As he stood there, the little girl fixed his face in her memory. Brown hair, weak chin, pointed ratlike face marked with a burn scar on his left cheek.

At last they sailed off in their big boxy ship, leaving a strange sign driven into the dock. When they were no longer in sight, she crept back down into the village. It took her many days. Perhaps weeks. But she buried them all.

Captain Sin Toa stared down at the girl. During her tale, her expression had remained fixed in a look of wide-eyed horror. But now it settled back into the cold emptiness he'd seen when he first coaxed her out of the hold.

'How long ago was that?' he asked.

'Don't know,' she said.

'How did you get aboard?' he asked. 'We never docked.'

'I swam.'

'Quite a distance.'

'Yes.'

'And what should I do with you now?'

She shrugged.

'A ship is no place for a little girl.'

'I have to stay alive,' she said. 'So I can find that man.'

'Do you know who that was? What that sign meant?'

She shook her head.

'That was the crest of the emperor's biomancers. You haven't got a prayer of ever getting close to that man.'

'I will,' she said quietly. 'Someday. If it takes my whole life. I'll find him. And kill him.'

Captain Sin Toa knew he couldn't keep her aboard. It was said maidens, even eight-year-old ones, could draw the attention of the sea serpents in these waters as sure as a bucketful of blood. The crew might very well mutiny at the idea of keeping a girl on board. But he wasn't about to throw her overboard or dump her on some empty piece of rock either. When they landed the next day at Galemoor, he approached the head of the Vinchen order, a wizened old monk named Hurlo.

'Girl's seen things nobody should have to see,' he said. The two of them stood in the stone courtyard of the monastery, the tall, black stone temple looming over them. 'She's a broken thing. Could be a monastic life is the only option left to her.'

Hurlo slipped his hands into the sleeves of his black robe. 'I sympathize, Captain. Truly, I do. But the Vinchen order is for men only.'

'But surely you could use a servant around,' said Toa. 'She's a peasant, accustomed to hard work.'

Hurlo nodded. 'We could. But what happens when she comes of age and begins to blossom? She will become too great a distraction for my brothers, particularly the younger ones.'

'So keep her till then. At least you'll have sheltered her a few years. Kept her alive long enough for her to make her own way.'

Hurlo closed his eyes. 'It will not be an easy life for her here.'

'Don't think she'd know what to do with an easy life if you gave her one anyway.'

Hurlo looked at Toa. And to Toa's surprise, he suddenly smiled, his old eyes sparkling. 'We will take in this broken child you have found. A bit of chaos in the order brings change. Perhaps for the better.'

Toa shrugged. He'd never fully understood Hurlo or the Vinchen order. 'If you say so, Grandteacher.'

'What is the child's name?' asked Hurlo.

'She won't say for some reason. I half think she doesn't remember.'

'What shall we call her, then, this child born of nightmare? As her unlikely guardians, I suppose it is now up to us to name her.'

Captain Sin Toa thought about it a moment, tugging at his beard. 'Maybe after the village she survived. Keep something of it in memory, at least. Call her Bleak Hope.'

2

Sadie was drunk that night. Far too drunk to make it back to her bed. But she couldn't stay where she was either.

'Closing down the bar, Sadie,' said Bracers Madge.

Sadie looked up at Madge, struggling to keep the double vision at bay. Bracers Madge was the bouncer and order-keeper of the Drowned Rat Tavern. She was over six feet tall and got the nickname Bracers because she was so large, she had to wear suspenders to keep her skirts up. Madge was one of the most feared and respected persons in the slums of New Laven. It was known throughout Paradise Circle, Silverback, and Hammer Point that she kept order in her tavern. Anyone foolish or reckless enough to cause trouble would have their ear torn off and would be barred from the tavern and marked with shame for the rest of their life. Madge kept her collection of ears in little pickling jars behind the bar.

'Sadie,' said Madge. 'Time to go.'

Sadie nodded and lurched to her feet.

'You got a place to stay?' asked Madge.

Sadie waved her hand as she dragged her feet across the sawdust floor. 'I can take care of myself.'

Madge shrugged and started putting chairs up on tables.

Sadie stumbled out of the Drowned Rat. She scanned the block for anyone she knew who might put her up for the

night, squinting in the dim light of the flickering street lamps.
But the street was practically empty, which meant the police
had either just come through or were just about to.

'Piss'ell,' she cursed, scratching at her dirty, matted hair.

She shuffled down the street a ways until she caught sight
of the plain wooden sign for an inn called the Sailor's
Mother. It was a notorious crimp house. But she was Sadie
the Goat, known in Paradise Circle, Silverback, and Hammer
Point as one of the most accomplished thieves, mercenaries,
and artists of mayhem currently breathing. She had a rep.
Nobody was stupid enough to southend her.

She wove her way unsteadily into the inn, where she
ordered a room for the night. The innkeeper, a thin, pouchy
gaf named Backus, eyed her speculatively.

'And no funny business,' she said, poking her finger on his
forehead hard enough to leave a mark.

'Naturally not.' Backus smiled a thin, pouchy smile. 'I'll
take care of you myself. Wouldn't want no . . . misunderstandings, right?'

'Sunny,' said Sadie. 'Lead on, then, innkeeper.'

Backus took her up broken wooden stairs and down a
dingy hallway that echoed with laughter, sobs, and some
bastard playing his fiddle at this ungodly hour. Backus
unlocked the last door on the left, and Sadie shoved past him
toward the filthy mattress that lay on the ground.

'Want I should get you a nightcap?' asked Backus.

'That'd be real sunny, Backus,' said Sadie. 'Maybe I had
you figured wrong.'

'I'm willing to bet you did,' said Backus, giving the smile
again.

Sadie dropped to the mattress, not bothering to take off
skirts, boots, or knives. She watched the cracked ceiling spin
unpleasantly for a few minutes until Backus returned with a
cold mug of something nice.

Had she not been so drunk, she would have smelled the traces of black rose before she'd even had a sip. But as it was, she downed the whole thing in one go, and a few minutes later everything went dark.

When Sadie woke up, she wasn't on a mattress in a flophouse anymore. She was lying facedown on a wooden deck. It took her a second to realize that the deck was rocking back and forth. A small shaft of sunlight came in through a round portal that brightened things up just enough for her to see that she was in a ship's cargo hold.

'Piss'ell.' She struggled to stand, but her hands and feet were tied with grimy rope, so the best she could manage was to sit up. She tried to untie her wrists, but it was hard to get a grip at that angle and it was some sailor knot so bewilderingly complex, she didn't even know where to start.

She leaned back against something that gave a light grunt. She turned and saw a young boy next to her, also tied up. He was ragged and filthy, probably some street urchin that had been picked up same as her.

'Eh, boy.' She poked him hard in the ribs with her boney elbow. 'Wake up.'

'Get off, Filler,' the boy muttered. 'I ain't got nothing for you.'

'Stupid,' she said and jabbed him again. 'We've been pissing southended!'

'What?' The boy's eyes opened. They were bright red, like rubies. It was the sign of a kid who'd been born to a mother addicted to coral spice. Nasty drug, very hooky and slowly ate the brain right out of your head. Most kids who were born coral-hooked didn't last past the first month. Sadie figured there must be some hidden mettle in this kid for him to have survived. Hidden, because she sure as piss couldn't see it now. The boy was blubbering and whining like a whipped puppy, tears falling from red eyes beneath a ragged curtain of brown hair as he cried, 'W-w-w-where am I? W-w-w-what happened?'

'I just told you, didn't I?' said Sadie. 'We've been southended.'

'W-w-w-what's that mean?'

'Are you a complete cunt-dropping?' said Sadie. 'Never heard of southending? How'd you live on the streets and not know such a thing?'

The boy's lip quivered like he was starting a fresh bout of the weeps. But he surprised her by drawing in a shaky breath and saying, 'I only just landed on the street about a month ago. I don't know much. So please, lady. Please tell me what's going on.'

She looked at him and he looked back at her and maybe it was the first sign of soft old age setting in, but rather than laugh or spit, she just sighed. 'What's your name, kid?'

'Rixidenteron.'

'Piss'ell, that's a mouthful.'

'My mom was a painter. She named me after the great lyrical romantic painter Rixidenteron the Third.'

'She dead then, your mom?'

'Yeah.'

They were quiet for a minute, with only the occasional sniffle from the boy, the wooden creak of the ship, and the gentle hiss as the prow broke the water. They must be sailing at a pretty good clip.

Finally, she said, 'So this is the length of it. We've been taken aboard a ship bound for the Southern Isles. Press-ganged into service. They'll let us sit down here awhile and stew, then they'll come down, maybe bloody us up a bit to let us know they mean business. Then they'll give us the choice:

Join the crew or be declared a stowaway and thrown overboard.'

The boy's eyes had grown wider and wider until they looked like big red-and-white dinner plates.

'But . . .' His lip quivered again. 'But I can't swim.'

'That's the general idea. And even if you could swim, we'd be so far from shore, there'd be no way you could make it that far, even if you managed to escape the sharks and seals.'

'I-I-I don't want to go to the Southern Isles,' he whimpered. 'They say it's full of monsters and there's no food and no light and nobody ever comes back, that you *can't* come back, that once – you go – you're trapped there – *forever*!' His voice was coming out in spasms now as the sobs overwhelmed him.

Sadie had heard just about enough of it. She thought about giving him a nice kick to the head. That would shut him up. And she doubted he'd be much help when she made her escape anyway. He wasn't even a proper neighborhood wag. He was some artist's kid, probably suckled at the teat till he was five. How he'd even managed to survive a month on the streets was beyond her.

But he *had* survived. And didn't seem to be starving either. So there had to be something going for him. She wondered what it was.

The boy's sobs had quieted back to sniffles. As much to stop him making that annoying sound as anything else, she said, 'So tell me, Rixi-whatever your name is. What was your mom like? What happened to her?'

He gave one last sniffle and wiped his teary red eyes with his shoulder. 'You really want to know?'

'Course I do,' she said, nestling her back into a burlap sack of potatoes and making herself as comfortable as she could with her wrists and ankles tied up. It could be hours yet before anyone came down to the cargo hold and she'd be able to make her move. A dreary story of an artist's son was better than no entertainment at all.

'Okay.' His expression was earnest. 'But you got to promise you won't tell anyone.'

'I swear on my father's purple prick,' said Sadie.

Rixidenteron's mother, Gulia Pastinas, came from one of the well-to-do families that lived in the north end of New Laven, far away from the grime and violence of Paradise Circle, Silverback, and Hammer Point. She was the second daughter, and pretty enough, but so headstrong and fiercely independent that her father despaired of ever getting her married off. It was frowned upon in the wealthy families to let the women work, which meant he would have to support her.

He was thrilled when she told him that she was joining an artist group down in Silverback. It was fashionable at the time for the children of wealthy families to dabble in bohemian culture. That was all he thought it would be. A nice break from his troublesome baby girl.

But it turned out that she was an immensely talented artist, and that she would not be coming back within a year with her tail between her legs. That, in fact, she would not be coming back at all. First, because she was far too busy being the toast of the downtown New Laven arts community.

Later, because she was far too sick to return to him. Not that she would have returned even if she could.

Rixidenteron's father was a whore, descended from a long line of whores, male and female. It never occurred to him that there was a problem with his profession until he was at a party and met a beautiful, dark-eyed artist who, after talking to him for ten minutes, declared she would rescue him from his life of misery. She was flush from the sale of a new batch of paintings, and bold from a recently acquired coral spice addiction. She took him home that night and insisted that he give up his life in the sex trade. He smiled his soft, warm smile and nodded agreeably, so smitten with her poised charm and fiery passion that he would have done just about anything she'd asked.

So she would paint and he would cook and clean, and for a while, they were happy. Then Rixidenteron was born and everything changed, as it always does when people become parents. Their son was born with the telltale red eyes of a coral addict's child, and friends told them he wouldn't last more than a week. But perhaps he did have some hidden strength. Or perhaps it was because his parents spent every waking moment caring for him, doing everything they could think of to keep him alive. They went without food so that they could afford the medicine her sister brought down from the uptown apothecary. It got so bad that Rixidenteron's father offered to go back to work. But she refused and instead painted so much and so fiercely that her hands were perpetually stained with color. Years later, art critics would call this her finest period.

And Rixidenteron did survive against all odds. When they celebrated his first birthday, they figured the worst was behind them.

Except his mother's paints contained a jellyfish toxin, harmless in small doses, but it had been seeping into her skin for years now and was beginning to attack her nerves. Between that and the coral addiction, it was increasingly difficult for her to paint. By the time Rixidenteron was two, she could no longer hold a brush steady. Again his father offered to go back to work. Again she refused. Instead, she taught Rixidenteron to paint for her. She had him wear a pair of leather gloves so he wouldn't suffer the same fate. Then she put him to work. By the time he was four, he could create any image described to him with breathtaking precision. Rixidenteron flicked away at the canvas for hours a day while his mother lay on the battered blue couch in their apartment, trembling hands covering her eyes as she whispered the images in her head. And he would make them real.

He cherished this time they spent together and was proud that he could help his mother, the great painter, with her art. But as time went on, it got harder. Rather than steering her away from the coral spice, Rixidenteron's illness and her subsequent infirmity pushed her deeper into addiction. By the time he was six, her descriptions were nonsensical, and he was making up most of the images himself. But while he had her dexterity, he did not yet have her vision. And the paintings made that evident. People said she was through.

This time, his father did not ask. He just went back to work. He was older, and life had taken its toll on him. But he was still reasonably handsome and able to make enough money to anonymously buy his love's paintings. So she continued to think she was supporting her family. Rixidenteron knew the truth, but by the time he'd worked up the courage to tell her, she was too far gone to understand what he was saying. Or so it seemed. He always wondered. Because the night that he told her, she overdosed on coral spice and died.

For a while, Rixidenteron and his father continued to live on in the same way. But by the end of another year, his father had become thin and pale. Rixidenteron didn't know whether it was illness or the loss of his mother. Either way, his father did not seem interested in getting better.

A week shy of his eighth birthday, Rixidenteron found his father had died in his sleep. He cleaned the shit and blood from his father's body, burned the bedsheets, then left.

*   *   *

'But how did you live on the streets?' asked Sadie. 'How in all hells did you survive when you clearly knew nothing about nothing?'

He shrugged. 'I met some other boys, and they let me join them. Because I'm good at taking stuff.'

'What do you mean, good at taking stuff?'

'My hands are quicker than other people's. Maybe because of all the painting. I don't know. But taking wallets, watches, and the like is easy for me. They never notice.'

Sadie's eyes sparkled. 'That is a rare and useful gift.' She looked down at the complex knot that held her hands together. 'I don't suppose those hands of yours could work this out.'

'Probably,' he said.

'Even with your own hands tied?'

'I can try,' he said.

'Why don't you,' she said.

When a sailor finally came down into the hold to check on them, the sun had gone down and only faint moonlight spilled in through the portal. They heard the sailor before they saw him, his boots stumping down the steep wooden steps as he muttered to himself.

'Girls and kids as crew. What a rotten voyage this is shaping up to be.'

He was an older gaf, lots of white mixed in with his greasy black hair and beard. He wore a wool sweater stretched across a vast paunch, and he limped a little. Sadie and the boy were sitting next to each other on the floor, rope visibly wrapped around their wrists. She forced her face to remain blank as the sailor squinted at her with eyes that looked bleary with drink.

'Listen up, you two,' he said. 'You've been volunteered to work on the crew of this here ship, the *Savage Wind*. If you follow orders and do just as the captain and I say, you're free to go when we return to port at New Laven. We might even pay you. If you don't follow orders, you'll be flayed within a breath of dying. It'll be like this.' He slammed his great big slab of a hand into the side of Sadie's face so hard, her lip split. 'Only a lot worse. Do we have an understanding?'

Sadie smiled, letting the blood dribble out the side of her mouth. 'Do you know why they call me Sadie the Goat?'

He leaned in close, his breath stinking of grog. 'Because of the beard?'

She slammed her forehead into his face. While he gaped at her, blood gushing from his broken nose, she shook off the rope that had been loosely coiled around her wrists, pulled the dagger from his boot, and shoved it up into the soft skin beneath his chin. She slowly twisted, and he convulsed against her, blood spattering her face. Then she jerked the blade, opening a vertical slit in his neck that went all the way down to his collarbone. She pulled out the knife and let the still-shuddering body drop to the deck.

She wiped her face with her sleeve, then leaned over and drew the sailor's sword.

'Here.' She handed the knife to the boy. 'There's bound to be more of them topside. Most like we'll need to kill them all.'

The boy stared at the knife, still wet with blood, that lay in his hand.

'Red,' she said. When he didn't respond, she gave him a swat across the back of his head. 'Look at me when I'm talking to you.'

He blinked stupidly at her.

'Red. That's your name now. You're my sidekick. Sunny?'

His eyes grew wide, and he nodded.

'Now, let's go explain to these gafs how we ain't interested in being southended.'

It was dark out on the deck, with only a sliver of moon. The sailor who stood watch topside was so surprised to see them that she planted her sword in his eye before he could even say a word. He fell twitching, and it took her a moment to wrench the blade free from his skull. Most of the sailors were drunk or asleep or both. Sadie didn't care. This was what they deserved. She was no swordsman, so it was all hack and slash as they made their way through the ship. By the time they reached the captain's quarters, she was breathing hard, her arm ached, and she was covered in the blood of six men. The cabin door was locked, so she pounded on the wood with the pommel of her sword. 'Come out, you fish-bellied scum!'

'Sadie!' came Red's shrill voice.

She turned just in time to see a man in a wide-brimmed hat about ten feet away leveling a pistol at her. But instead of firing, the gun fell from his hand as he clutched the knife handle that protruded from his chest.

Red's hand was empty. He smiled a bit sheepishly, his ruby eyes glimmering in the moonlight. 'I was aiming for the gun.'

Sadie grinned and slapped him on the back. 'Well done, Red. I knew you had some mettle under all that artsy softness. Now, let's turn this tub around. There's one more gaf back on New Laven who needs it explained to him nice and slow why nobody southends Sadie the Goat.'

Getting the boat back to downtown New Laven was tricky with only Sadie and Red, neither of them knowing what they were doing. But the wind was in their favor and they reached the docks eventually. They probably would have crashed into the docks, but luckily, Sadie knew a few of the wags in port who helped guide them in without sinking themselves or someone else.

Sadie gave the sailors a terse grunt of thanks, then stomped down the docks, her blood-encrusted saber still in hand. Red scurried behind, eager to see how his new hero exacted her revenge.

It was too early in the day for Backus to be working at the Sailor's Mother, so Sadie headed for the Drowned Rat. When they reached the tavern, she threw the door wide. 'Backus! You shifty assworm!'

Backus lifted his thin, pouchy face up from his mug of ale and looked across the tavern. Every patron of the Drowned Rat went quiet, and all eyes bounced from him to Sadie and back again.

'If it ain't Sadie the Goat.' His calm tone sounded forced. 'I didn't expect to see you again. Too ugly for sailors even, is that it?'

'I'm about to make you a whole lot uglier than I left them.' Then Sadie lifted her sword and charged.

Backus looked at first incredulous. Everybody knew you didn't start trouble in the Drowned Rat. But as she drew near, his expression turned to terror.

Then Bracers Madge rose up, seemingly out of nowhere, and caught Sadie's sword arm. She yanked hard enough to lift Sadie off her feet, a snarl on her thick lips. She slammed Sadie's hand down hard on the nearest table, sending tankards of ale flying and forcing Sadie to let go of the sword.

'You know better'n to start trouble here, Sadie.' Her voice was a throaty growl.

'He's gotta know!' said Sadie, trying to twist her hand free of Madge's iron grip. 'Everybody's gotta know they can't southend Sadie the Goat!'

'I understand you,' said Madge. 'But everybody's got to know, *even you*, that nobody kills nobody in my bar. Now get the hells out of here.'

Everybody knew that Madge liked Sadie. She was giving her an out right then. Sadie could have taken it, and that would have been the end of it. But she didn't.

'Not till I show them all!' She lunged toward Backus with sudden strength.

Bracers Madge only grunted, her hand still tight around Sadie's wrist. She reeled Sadie back in close, grabbed her head with her other hand, leaned down, and with a wet tear and a spurt of blood, bit off Sadie's ear.

The wail that came from Sadie's throat was loud enough to rattle the glass behind the bar, as much from rage as it was pain. Sadie clutched at the bleeding side of her head. Madge held the ear between her teeth, along with a tuft of hair that had gotten in the way. Sadie ran out of the bar, choking back the sobs of shame.

All eyes were riveted to Madge as she walked calmly to the bar, took out an empty jar, spit the ear into it, and added it to the rest of her collection.

Red saw Sadie's bloody sword still on the table. He didn't know what would happen next, but he knew Sadie would probably need that sword. He sprinted across the tavern, just as Backus was turning toward it. Red snatched it up before Backus could lift a hand. Then he dashed out of the tavern after Sadie.

He found her stumbling back toward the docks. She was cursing and crying as she held the side of her head, blood leaking out from between her fingers.

'What happened?' His voice was shrill.

'I'm through,' she howled. 'Sadie the Goat, shamed in front of everybody. Bracers Madge has my ear in her collection and I can never show my face there again.'

'What do we do now?' he asked.

'We?' she snarled. 'What do *we* do?' She looked like she was about to haul off and smack him. But then she stopped and stood there, frowning. 'We,' she said again, this time a little quieter. She looked out at the docks. The *Savage Wind* was still tied up where they'd left her. 'We,' she almost whispered. Then she grinned at Red.

'*We* are entering a new business enterprise, my best wag. Who needs the filth of Paradise Circle, Silverback, or Hammer Point when so many other points of interest lie waiting for us, just begging to be plundered? Sadie the Goat may be through. But Sadie the Pirate Queen is just getting started.'

3

*T*he coast of Galemoor was comprised of jagged black rock worn smooth by the constant crash of icy waves. Further inland, the dark soil was hard but, when churned properly, rich and nourishing enough to grow an abundance of crops, particularly the barley and hops the Vinchen monks used to brew the brown ale that was prized all through the empire.

Most of the island was given over to agriculture, but in the center was the Vinchen monastery, hewn centuries ago from the black rock of the island by the disciples of Manay the True, one of the wisest grandteachers in the history of the empire. The long, rectangular buildings formed a large closed square around a courtyard, and in the center was the temple. The south side of the monastery contained the communal living quarters for the monks, and a separate – but still humble – dwelling for the grandteacher. The north side contained the kitchens, and the west side contained the brewery.

Grandteacher Hurlo had seen many boys arrive at the black iron gates of the monastery with looks of horror in their eyes. Most of them were rich, spoiled, and likely sent to become Vinchen because their parents found them difficult to manage at home. Hurlo remembered a time when being a

Vinchen had been desirable. Fashionable, even. But those brought to him now took years to appreciate what he and the other sworn monks were trying to give them. Still, he had grown to accept that it was the way of things now.

He didn't know what to expect of the girl, though. She was something completely new, both for him and for the order. Captain Toa brought her to the gates dressed in filthy rags. Her dark blue eyes took in everything around her, yet gave nothing away.

'Hello, child,' Hurlo said to her. 'I am Grandteacher Hurlo. Welcome to the Vinchen monastery.'

'Thank you,' she said in a barely audible voice.

'Good luck, then, Hurlo.' Sin Toa offered his thick, hairy hand.

'Good travels,' said Hurlo, taking it warmly.

Once Toa had left, Hurlo gathered all the monks and students in the courtyard. They eyed the little girl beside Hurlo with varying mixtures of surprise, confusion, and distaste.

'This is Bleak Hope, a child left orphaned and homeless because of the actions of a biomancer,' he said. 'She will be staying with us, helping with chores and other menial tasks until she is old enough and strong enough to depart.'

None of the monks were disrespectful enough to speak out, but Hurlo heard several gasp audibly. This didn't surprise him. No female of any age had ever stepped inside the monastery. Now they would be living with one every day, possibly for years.

'You may return to your duties,' he said calmly. As he watched them slowly disperse, casting frequent glances at him and Hope, he decided it would be interesting to observe how they handled this adjustment.

The Book of Storms said that there was only one Heaven, but many hells. Each hell was unique, but just as cruel as the next. This, the book said, was because there was no limit to human suffering, and no end to the number of ways the world could inflict it.

Grandteacher Hurlo thought often of that passage. He suspected that to the young boys who had recently joined the Vinchen order, Galemoor itself might be a hell. Far from the large cities and luxurious northern estates of their child-hoods, it was located in the center of the Southern Isles, as far from the warm, sunny capital of Stonepeak as one could get.

For many of the older brothers, change alone was a kind of hell. Adding one unexpected element to a routine that had become rigid from years of repetition sent these men into something like panic. They seemed not to mind the girl as long as she didn't affect their day in any way. But if she cleaned their rooms, they complained to Hurlo, sometimes even that their rooms were too clean. If she spooned food onto their trays at mealtime, they complained to Hurlo, even if it was that she had put too much on their plates.

For other brothers, hell was the sudden presence of a female in their midst. When she drifted past in the baggy, hemmed old black monk robe that hung down to her ankles, silent and pale as a wraith, her eyes lost in the shadow of her hood, Hurlo could not have even said that she was female. Yet, somehow, these brothers seemed unable to focus on even the simplest tasks when she was in the room.

The Book of Storms said that a man's hell told a great deal about him. So, too, did his reaction to that suffering. Hurlo found it interesting that while some complained about Hope, and others ignored her, still others tried to befriend the tiny blond agent of their suffering. But after a few attempts at flattery or gifts of sweets, those well-mean-ing brothers faltered under her unfathomable blue gaze, and slunk away.

After a few days of observation, Hurlo's attention drifted back to his studies and meditation. So he didn't notice at first when yet another reaction began to surface among his brothers. Cruelty.

It had been a week since Bleak Hope had entered the Vinchen monastery. She would not say she was happy. She was not sure she would ever be able to say that again. But she was comfortable. She had a warm place to sleep and three meals a day.

She didn't really understand what the Vinchen brothers did. They meditated, they read, and they exercised. Every evening just before dinner, they gathered in the temple for prayer. None of those activities had been popular in her village. In many ways, this life among the quiet monks was even more unfamiliar to her than those raucous few days aboard Captain Toa's ship.

She understood her work, though. Small rooms that needed to be kept neat, plain food that needed to be served, simple clothes that needed to be washed and mended. She took no pleasure in the work, but there was a certain peace to getting lost in the monotony of it. She treasured that peace, because the rest of the time, her thoughts were weighted with death and a dark hunger for revenge. Night was the worst time. She lay on her straw mat in the kitchen, and the thoughts pressed down on her until she could barely breathe. When sleep finally came, it was restless and full of nightmares.

'You there. Peasant girl.'

Hope stopped. She had been walking back to the kitchen from cleaning the outhouse. She turned and saw Crunta leaning in the doorway of the building where the brothers slept. Crunta was one of the younger brothers, about thirteen, and still in training.

When Hurlo had first given her the list of tasks, he had mentioned that most of her chores would be for the older brothers. That the younger ones must perform chores for themselves. So she was surprised that Crunta was calling to her.

'Me?' she asked.

'Yes, you, stupid,' he said, and waved her over.

Not sure how to handle the situation, she went over to him.

'Come in.' He turned and went inside.

Hope followed him. The inside of the building was all one room. The smooth wooden floors were lined with neatly spaced straw sleeping mats and small, cylindrical pillows. Hope watched as Crunta pulled his black monk robe off. Underneath he wore a small undergarment that left his upper body and most of his legs bare. His body was lean and tightly muscled with almost no hair on his chest.

He balled up his robe and shoved it into her arms. 'Wash this and bring it back to me right away.'

Hope was sure the younger brothers were supposed to do their own washing, but she was afraid to say so. 'Yes, brother.'

His hand flew out and smacked the side of her face. 'I'm not your brother. Call me master.'

Bleak Hope stared up at him, a dark rage spreading through her body. She imagined him screaming in agony as worms ripped through his skin. But she knew she could do nothing. She was just a weak little girl. So she swallowed her anger and said, 'Yes, master.'

He sauntered over to his mat and lay down. Then he picked up a book. 'Hurry back.'

Hope carried the robe, which stank of sweat and stale beer, over to the washtub outside the kitchen. As she scrubbed the cloth hard against the ridges of the washboard, she imagined that it was Crunta's face.

As she stretched the robe across the smoldering coals in the kitchen to dry, she imagined the coals searing into Crunta's bare chest. She knew these thoughts were wrong, but they gave her some relief. Even so, the feeling of helpless rage ate at her as she walked back across the courtyard with the robe neatly folded in her arms.

She found him still lounging on his mat in his undergarments. She laid the robe at his feet. 'Is there anything else, master?'

He looked at her over the top of his book for a moment, then stood. Ignoring the robe, he walked over to her. He stood several feet taller than her so that her face was level with his chest. She stared at it now because she liked the look in his eye even less. She didn't understand his gaze, but something about it made her skin crawl.

He pushed her hood back. She watched the rise and fall of his chest quicken as she felt his hand close on a lock of her hair. Her entire body shook, though from fear or loathing, she couldn't say.

'Brother Crunta!'

Hope turned her head, pulling her hair loose from Crunta's fingers. One of the older brothers, Wentu, stood in the doorway, a frown on his lined face. 'Do not stand before the girl in your undergarments! It's indecent!'

Crunta took a slow, leisurely step back, a smirk on his face. 'Yes, brother.' He leaned over and picked up his robe, then pulled it over his head.

His brow knit together and he pressed the cloth to his nose. 'Ugh, this stinks of the kitchens! Do you want me to smell like a servant?'

'S-s-s-sorry, master,' stammered Hope. 'You wanted me to be quick, so I dried it over the coals. I didn't—'

He slapped her across the face again.

'Young brother . . .' said Wentu disapprovingly.

'You're lucky I don't beat you senseless!' Crunta said to Hope, his fist raised. 'Get out of my sight, you filthy peasant.'

Hope ran to her straw mat in the back of the kitchen and curled up into a ball. She felt like crying, but no tears came. Only black thoughts of violence and revenge. She thought Crunta must be the cruelest brother in the monastery.

But she hadn't yet encountered Racklock.

Bleak Hope's favorite job was to care for the temple. The floor, walls, and altar were all made of the smooth black rock on the island, but in this place, it had been polished to a shine that made it feel at once solemn and bright. She loved the smell of the prayer candles, which gave a hint of jasmine as they burned. Most of all, she loved the tall stained glass windows at the top of the temple. She didn't understand the pictures they showed, strange creatures and black-armored warriors, but the colors reminded her of the necklace she had made for her father. She had supposed that she could never enjoy such things again. But there was a tiny ember that remained, and grew slightly warmer at the sight of sunlight streaming in through those colored windows.

'So here is where you shirk your duties,' came a deep voice.

Hope tore her gaze from the windows and looked at the short, powerfully built brother known as Racklock. He stood with his arms folded, his face hard. Hope knew Racklock was second in the order only to Hurlo, and all the other brothers feared him.

'It's my duty to clean the temple every day, master,' said Hope.

'I saw no cleaning.' Racklock took a step toward her. 'Only idling. We feed you, clothe you, give you a place when the world surely would have been rid of you. And this is how you repay us?'

Hope had learned from Crunta that defending oneself could be dangerous. So she only bowed her head and said, 'Sorry, master.'

'You are not a woman yet, but already your forked tongue tries to aid you.' He said it with calm disdain as he walked over to a cabinet. He opened the cabinet, which was filled with an assortment of items, and pulled out a long, wooden cane. As he examined it, he said, 'Others may be fooled, but I see what you truly are. A vile sickness that seeks to destroy this order from the inside. An evil to be purged.'

It was on that sun-dappled afternoon in early fall that Hurlo was shaken from a deep meditation by the sound of a little girl's screams. He rushed from his tiny room, across the sunny courtyard, and into the temple. There he found Bleak Hope cowering on the ground, her face pressed against the cold stone floor, her black robe wet with blood. Racklock loomed over her. His thick shoulders surged as he brought the cane hard against her back and she screamed again.

That was the moment Hurlo understood that he had not rescued the girl. He had merely moved her from one hell to another. That was also when he discovered a new hell of his own. The hell of allowing an innocent to suffer. True, he did not wield the cane, nor did he ask that the girl be brought to him in the first place. But as he looked down at her ashen face, he knew he could not stay in this hell a moment longer.

Racklock brought the cane down again, but this time Hurlo was there, little more than a black blur as he took the cane from his brother's grip, then knocked him forward so that he tripped over the prostrate girl. Racklock landed on his hands, then vaulted forward into a summersault so that he landed on his feet. But as he spun to face Hurlo, the grandteacher poked him in the throat with the tip of the cane just hard enough to leave him choking and temporarily unable to speak.

Hurlo watched him retch and wheeze for a moment, then said mildly, 'Did you have something to say? No? Then allow me to inform you that henceforth you will not harm this girl. Her cries disturb my meditation, and the smell of her blood in the temple vexes me. Nod once if you understand, twice if you wish me to strike you again.'

Racklock's face darkened with a reddish-purple color, but his lips pressed together in a hard line as he nodded once, then turned on his heel and stalked out of the temple.

Hurlo looked down at the shuddering little girl at his feet. He had a sudden urge to comfort her. To scoop her up in his arms and rock her to a sweet, dreamless sleep. But it was only a momentary flash. He was not, after all, some peace-loving, gentle old man. He was grandteacher of the Vinchen order, and one of the greatest warriors the empire had ever known. So instead, he walked quietly over to the meditation mat that lay before the black stone altar, and knelt down.

They stayed like that for some time, the girl prostrate on the floor, the old monk kneeling, silent, his back to her.

Finally she said in little more than a whisper, 'Master . . . thank you for saving me.'

'I am no master, child. I am a teacher.'

She paused to consider that a moment. Then he heard her shuffle a little closer on hands and knees. 'What do you teach?'

'Many things. Although I am not always successful. I tried to teach Racklock restraint, and it appears I failed in that.'

'He was punishing me.'

'A punishment should fit the crime. What did you do that warranted such a beating?'

'I . . . don't know. He said I was evil.'

'I see. And do you feel evil?'

She did not answer.

'Come and kneel facing me,' he said.

She shuffled around him cautiously, still on hands and knees. He could see where her black robes stuck to her back from the drying blood, but she did not flinch or wince at the pain. She knelt as he did, facing him, but with her head bowed.

'Look at me, child,' he said.

She looked up at him and he allowed himself to look deeply into those haunting eyes in a way he had not done before.

'I do see darkness in you,' he said. 'That is not surprising. Darkness begets darkness.'

Still she didn't answer, but only continued to look at him.

'Does it frighten you? This darkness within yourself?'

Her expression remained fixed, but tears welled up in her eyes.

'What if I could teach you how to control that darkness? How to use it to become a great and powerful warrior?' The moment he said those words, his heart began to race. What he proposed was forbidden by both *The Book of Storms* and the codes of the Vinchen order. But as he said it, he saw the light that broke on the little girl's face like the first dawn of a new world, and he knew that fulfilling such a promise was worth any risk. 'Would you like me to teach you this?'

'Oh, yes, please!' she said, the tears now freely coursing down her cheeks.

'Yes, Grandteacher,' he corrected her.

'Yes, Grandteacher.'

'It will not be easy. In fact, you will suffer a great deal along the way. There may even be times when you hate me. When you think me nearly as cruel as Racklock. Do you still wish to learn?'

'Oh yes, Grandteacher!' she shouted, her face wet and flushed.

'Good. Then let us begin your first lesson.'

'I am ready, Grandteacher!' Her body tensed, as if she could barely restrain herself from leaping to her feet.

'Your first lesson is to breathe.'

She cocked her head slightly and paused. 'Only to breathe, Grandteacher?'

'Breath is the most important thing. It is life itself. Until you master it, you can do nothing. A warrior can no more afford unrestrained joy than he can unbridled terror, and while it is true we cannot stop ourselves from having emotions, we can choose not to be swept away by them. We do this with the anchor of breath. So right now, you must breathe slow and deep until this tempest of emotion passes, and you return to calmness.'

'Yes, Grandteacher,' said Bleak Hope.

The old man and the little girl knelt facing each other, and the temple was silent except for their breath.

4

*S*adie knew she couldn't sail a ship, even a small sloop like the *Savage Wind*, with just herself and an eight-year-old boy. The trouble was, now that she'd been shamed at the Drowned Rat, none of her previous associates would have anything to do with her. In order to gather a crew, she had to look further afield and bring on people she didn't know as well from outside Paradise Circle.

She had a few connections over in Hammer Point, where they didn't give a piss about Bracers Madge or the Drowned Rat, or shame, for that matter. Bull Mackey was a square-jawed fighter she'd done some time with on the Empty Cliffs. He brought along a tall, thin wag with sunken eyes, named Spinner, who was either his cousin or his boyfriend, or maybe both. She also knew some people up in Silverback, from when she'd been a drug mule for Jix the Lift. Avery Birdhouse was an actor who was nearly as handsome as he thought he was. Wergishaw was mute but good in a scrap, and played a hell of a fine tune on a fiddle.

It had been a long time since Sadie had to convince a man that she was every bit as capable as him, and probably more. Sadie the Goat's reputation had spoken for her. It was why she'd been so desperate to keep it. Now she was back at the beginning. But she'd done it once before and if anything, she was even better at it the second time around. So it was only a week before she'd gathered herself a crew. There was only one problem. Not a one of them knew how to sail. That is, until Finn showed up.

It was a rare sunny morning in New Laven. Sadie stood on the deck of the *Savage Wind*, which was still tied at the same dock. She held up a line and glared at her crew. 'Nobody knows where this rope goes?'

'I thought it went up front somewhere,' said Bull Mackey.

'Nah, I saw it was tied on the right side,' said Spinner.

'Who even took it off in the first place?' asked Sadie.

'Sorry, I tripped over it,' said Avery Birdhouse.

Sadie glared at him. 'I thought actors were supposed to be graceful.'

'It's actually called a line, not a rope,' said a new voice, rough but cheerful. 'Also, the front of a boat is called the bow, and the right side when facing the bow is called starboard.'

A man stood on the dock, smiling up at them. His skin was deeply tanned, like he'd spent a lot of time under the sun, and he wore the loose-fitting linen shirt of a sailor. He also wore a black patch over one eye.

'That so?' asked Sadie, shifting her glare to this stranger. 'And I suppose you'd know.'

The man seemed unfazed by her tone. 'You don't remember me, do you?'

Sadie squinted at him. 'Should I?'

'Me and you tossed a few times in the alley behind Gunpowder Hall.' He waited expectantly. After a moment, he added, 'I had both eyes back then.'

Sadie scratched at her matted hair, then shook her head. 'Nope. I bent a lot of cocks in that alley. Can't say I remember you.'

His smile faltered.

'But you're a proper wag of the Circle, then?'

His smile returned. 'Born and raised. Lucky for you, I came down to the docks a while back and started working on ships.'

'Why's that lucky for me?'

'I heard there was a molly calling herself Captain Sadie who was putting together a crew for a new business venture. Looks like you have some solid wags here, but what you need is someone who really knows their way around a ship.'

'And that's you, is it?'

'It is.'

Sadie considered it a moment. 'What's your name?'

'On these docks, they call me Mister Finn.'

'Yeah, well I'm calling you *Missing* Finn.'

'On account of my eye?' he asked.

'On account of where in hells have you been this whole week I've been trying to get this tub fixed up?' She held out her hand to him. 'Welcome aboard the *Savage Wind*.'

His smile grew even broader as he took her hand and climbed aboard. 'What sort of business venture is this, anyway?'

'Oh, didn't I say?' asked Sadie. 'Piracy. We'll be plundering the coast.'

'Piracy?' asked Missing Finn. 'On New Laven? It's never been done.'

Sadie slapped his back. 'And that, my wag, is why it's going to work.'

True to his word, Missing Finn knew his way around a ship and had them fit to sail in a few hours. He instructed each member of the crew on their tasks and helped Sadie plot their course along the coast.

'That's it, then.' Finn rolled up the map. 'We're ready to set sail.'

'Not quite.' Sadie tapped her finger on one of the chart divider's points. 'My best wag is out doing a little job for me. He should be back anytime now.'

Red had been sitting outside the Sailor's Mother all day, posing as a beggar while he waited for a suitable mark. He'd even made a few coppers by the time the sun began to set and at last he saw what he'd been looking for. A man on the small side, wearing a broad captain's hat and fine black leather boots that went almost to the knee.

Red waited until he'd entered the inn, then quickly pocketed his begged coppers and followed. He stepped inside in time to see the black boots stomp up the stairs to the rooms.

'Hey, boy. What are you doing?'

Backus leaned across the front desk, eyeing him suspiciously.

'Oh, uh . . .' Red realized he should have thought of an alibi ahead of time. 'That's my, uh, uncle, and—'

'No, I remember you. That red-eyed boy following Sadie around. What are you up to?' He stepped out from behind his desk and started to roll up his sleeves. 'You better not be making mischief for my customers.'

Red had been on the streets long enough to see a beating coming. Without another word, he ran through the doors and out into the safety of the crowded street. He hid himself behind a cart and watched through the spokes to see if Backus would come after him. He waited a few minutes before deciding the danger had passed. But now what was Red supposed to do? There was no way he could sneak past the front desk with Backus looking out for him. But he couldn't go back to the ship either.

Sadie had told him she wanted a proper captain's hat and boots. This was his chance to prove he was good enough to belong on her crew. That he wasn't a charity case.

'Whatcha doing, Rixie?'

Red glanced up and saw Filler, the boy from his old pick-pocket gang. Filler had been a terrible pickpocket, and didn't seem all that smart either. But he was a head taller than any other kid his age, so they'd all done what he told them.

'It's Red now,' he said self-importantly.

'Who says?' asked Filler.

'Sadie the Goat.'

'Oh.' Filler looked impressed. He was keen enough to know the name, but thankfully not so keen as to know she was recently shamed. 'You with her now?'

'Yeah, so I don't have time to . . .' He trailed off as an idea came to him. He looked at Filler appraisingly and a smile slowly grew on his face. 'Say, Filler, my wag.' He put his hand on Filler's shoulder, attempting that casual swag-ger Sadie had whenever she wanted Red to do something for her. 'How's about you help me out with this job for Sadie?'

'Me?' Filler's eyes got wide. 'Helping out Sadie the Goat?'

'That's right,' said Red. 'I'll tell her what a true wag you are.'

'Okay, what do I have to do?'

'Follow me.' He led Filler back across the street to the Sailor's Mother, then into the side alley and around to the back of the inn. The sun had set by then, and the alley was dark except for the light that came from occupied rooms.

'It's awful dark back here,' said Filler.

'It's not even,' Red said absently as he scanned the lit windows. He saw his mark on the second floor, one window to the left of center. He watched the old sailor take off his hat and coat, then the light went out. 'Alright, Filler. Stand here.' He positioned Filler directly beneath the window. 'And put your hands together like this.' He showed his own hands with fingers interlocked.

Filler locked his hands together. 'Now what?'

'I'm going to run at you, and you're going to give me a boost up to the window.'

Filler looked up at the window. 'I don't know if I can throw you that high.'

'Fine, then how about to that little ledge below it?'

Filler squinted. 'I don't see any ledge.'

'You wouldn't see a flaming pile of horseshit if it was hurled at you.'

'Yes, I would.'

'Just trust me. It's there. Give me a heave and I'll catch it.'

Filler shrugged and held out his hands.

Red stepped as far back as the narrow alley allowed, then ran forward and jumped into Filler's waiting hands. At the same moment Filler pulled up, Red pushed off and was launched into the air.

Filler had been right about the window being too high, but Red overshot the ledge beneath it, slamming into a flat, empty section of wall. He bit down on his own whimper as he scrabbled for any purchase. His stomach lurched as he felt himself drop for a moment. Then his toes found the ledge. There was a sickening moment when his body started to tilt back into empty air, but he widened his stance and bent his knees out, like he'd seen lizards do when they clung to walls, and he found his balance.

'Guess there *was* a ledge,' observed Filler below him. 'But how are you going to reach the window above you?'

Red hadn't actually gotten that far into his plan. He craned his head up and tried to gauge the distance. It looked like it was close enough to reach if he jumped. But if he missed, it didn't seem likely he'd be able to land back on the ledge. He couldn't get a clear angle to see exactly how far of a fall it was, which was probably for the best. He wasn't going to let Sadie down. He had to do this. So he bent his knees even lower, his stomach and the insides of his thighs pressed against the gritty wall.

'You're not going to—' began Filler.

Before he could finish, Red launched himself up into the air, his arms stretched as high as they would go, fingers straining toward the windowsill. And he caught it.

'Piss'ell,' Filler said, his voice somewhere near awe.

Red hung from the sill by his fingers, his boots scratching at the wall as he tried to find even a momentary purchase so he could get a better grip. His fingers were already burning with fatigue and he didn't think he could hold on much longer. Doubt and fear began to creep up his spine. But then he remembered the day he first started painting for his mother. He'd looked up at her pleadingly through snot and tears of frustration. 'I can't draw like you!' She'd looked down at him with that knowing smirk of hers and said, 'If you believe you will succeed, there is always a chance you might. But if you believe that you will fail, then you will always fail. Never allow yourself to lose before you begin.'

Red hadn't fallen yet. He hadn't failed yet. But the specter of doubt continued to press down on him. He needed to think about something else. His fingers were on fire, throbbing with so much pain he was near tears. Then a new image came to his mind. Sadie grinning at him, her face streaked with the blood of dead sailors. *I knew there was something under all that artsy softness.* Artsy softness like hells. He'd watched one parent die, then the other. He'd survived on the streets of Silverback, then New Laven. He would show her there was not an inch of softness in him. He clenched his teeth and pulled himself up slowly to the window ledge.

'You did it, Rix – I mean Red!' said Filler.

'Shut it or you'll give me away,' hissed Red, covering his own shaky exuberance with a confidence he didn't feel. Then he looked through the window and saw a new problem. When the window had gone dark, he'd assumed the captain had gone to sleep. But now that he was able to see into the room by the faint rays of moonlight, he realized that the captain was in bed, but still awake. There was also a woman with him, and the two were bouncing against each other.

Red knew about sex, of course. The son of a whore doesn't go long in life before learning that bit of truth. He'd asked why the neighborhood alley cat had gotten so fat, and his father had casually explained that she was pregnant. Red was an inquisitive child, firing a battery of questions at his father until they arrived at the human act of sex. The way his father had explained it led Red to believe it was a quiet, gentle act that involved a great deal of affectionately whispered words. But that wasn't at all what Red was seeing through the window now.

The captain held himself up by his arms, his bald head gleaming with sweat and the skin of his hairy shoulders leached of color in the moonlight. He was facing the window, but his eyes were squeezed shut, like he was in pain. He rocked his lower body against the woman beneath him. Because of the angle, Red could only see the back of her head, one large, pillowy breast, and her arm, which dangled listlessly at the side of the bed. For a moment, he wondered if she was even conscious. But when he pressed his ear to the window, he could hear, along with the harsh grunts of the captain, a thin, screechy female voice saying, 'Oh yeah, tommy, gimme that big, fat cock!'

All in all, Red decided that sex was pretty gross. Still, with all the noise and commotion, there was a good chance he could get in and out of there without being noticed.

He turned his head back. 'Get ready to help me down in a minute.'

'How?' asked Filler.

'Just . . . be ready to do what I tell you,' said Red, because he had no idea yet how he would get down. Then he carefully eased open the window. He slipped into the room and crawled across the floor to the side of the bed where the captain's boots and hat had been dropped in a heap along with the rest of his clothes. The sex yells were getting even louder and the bed was starting to creak in protest as the captain's movements began to get more frantic. Red put the boots and hat in the coat, then rolled it up into an easy-to-carry bundle. Once he was ready to escape, he chanced one look up at the bed. Now he could see the woman's face, round-cheeked and flushed. But she stared up at the ceiling with a look of absolute indifference even as she moaned and yelled, like she was an actress bored with her part. His father had always talked about the passion and tenderness in sex. Had he lied? Red had noticed adults did that in an effort to protect him. Or they did until he got to Paradise Circle. Maybe that's why he liked it here so much. It was hard and mean, but nobody treated him like he was made of glass.

Then the woman's bored gaze shifted from the ceiling down to Red. He had waited too long. Her eyes went wide and she yelled, this time with genuine feeling. 'A kid! There's a pissing kid in the room!'

Red leapt for the window, the bundle cradled against his chest. If the captain had been more alert, he could have easily caught Red by the leg or even the back of his shirt, and that would have been the end of it. But the man was right in the middle of orgasm and seemed oblivious to just about everything. Until the woman smacked him in the side of the head and yelled, 'He's stealing your pissing clothes, you bludgeon!'

Red was halfway out the window by then. The captain's face crumpled up in rage as he lunged for Red, but his legs got tangled up in the blankets and he fell to the floor, naked and cursing.

'Catch me!' yelled Red as he launched himself out the window.

'What?' Filler instinctively held out his arms, and watched dumbfounded as Red came hurtling down and slammed into him. They fell to the cobblestones in a heap and both of them lay there, stunned, until the captain, his hairy chest heaving, started cursing at them from the window.

Red struggled to his feet. He held his bundle under one arm while he helped Filler up.

'Anything broke?' he demanded.

Filler shook his head, still looking dazed.

'Then pissing *run!*'

The two boys took off down the alley, leaving the sounds of the raving captain behind them. They ran for several blocks before they stopped at a corner, panting and grinning at each other like mad people.

'You.' Filler shook his finger in Red's face. 'Are completely slippy.'

Red decided he liked Filler calling him slippy, so his grin only grew broader. 'That may be, but the prize is mine!' He held up the bundle proudly.

'What do you even need that for?'

'It's for Sadie. We're leaving Paradise Circle.'

'Leaving the Circle?' Filler stared at him uncomprehendingly.

'Sadie's got herself a ship and we're going to be pirates!'

'Pirates? Like Dire Bane?'

'Of course like Dire Bane,' said Red, looking very pleased with himself. He shook Filler's hand. 'Well, my wag. You've been a great help, and I'll be sure to tell Sadie. See you around sometime.' Then he took off toward the docks, the bundle tucked under his arm.

When he got to the *Savage Wind*, he saw that the rigging

was set and the sails were fastened to the mast, ready to be unfurled.

''Bout time you showed up,' Sadie said as she helped him aboard. 'I was starting to wonder if the job I gave you was too hard.'

Red presented Sadie with the bundle. 'Look, I got you a hat, boots, *and* a coat!'

'Well, now.' Sadie unrolled the bundle and examined the contents. 'These are mighty fine and worth the wait. You done good, Red. I guess I had you right after all.'

Red beamed with pleasure.

'Any trouble in it?'

Red's face fell and he blushed. 'Oh, uh . . .'

Sadie frowned. 'There better not be a squad of imps about to come down on us.'

'No, nothing like that,' Red said quickly. 'It's just . . . when I was stealing this stuff, the captain was having sex with some lady. It weren't anything like my dad said it was. It was loud, and ugly, and not even friendly.'

Sadie laughed. 'Don't worry too much about that, my wag. There's as many ways to stretch a cunt as there is to pick a pocket. I'll explain it to you properly when you're a bit older. Now get some sleep. We set sail at first light.'

While the red light of dawn still lingered on the water, the *Savage Wind* set sail up the coast of New Laven. Missing Finn was at the wheel and Sadie the Pirate Queen strode across the deck in her captain's finery. Her boots had to be tightened at the ankle with leather thongs to keep them from sliding off, the feather of the wide-brimmed hat had been bent during its liberation, and the coat was much too large. But none of the crew said a word.

'You look pat as paws, Captain,' said Missing Finn when she came strutting over to him at the helm.

'Don't I, though,' she agreed. 'How soon do I get to show it off?'

'We're coming up soon on Joiner's Bay in Silverback. Between there and Hollow Falls we'll find a lot of lacies in little pleasure boats out for an afternoon cruise.'

'Keystown's also in between there,' said Sadie.

'True, but the military garrison at Keystown is mostly land-based. They have a few ships out looking for smugglers, but nothing we can't outrun.'

'Then let's catch us some lacies!'

It was shortly after midday when they spotted their first victim, a yacht gliding parallel to the coast.

'Get ready, wags!' called Sadie as they bore down on the small boat. She pulled out her spyglass and saw three men in fine white shirts and artfully embroidered coats, their hair carefully curled, their fine clear faces looking utterly bewildered as they stared at the *Savage Wind*.

Missing Finn turned the wheel so that they came about in a wide arc until they were side by side with the yacht.

'Cast the grapples!' called Sadie.

Avery Birdhouse at the bow and Spinner at the stern each threw a hook with a line tied to it. The hooks sank into the soft wood of the yacht's deck.

'Reel 'em in!' called Sadie.

Avery Birdhouse and Spinner pulled in their lines until the yacht's port side hit the *Savage Wind*'s starboard with a hard crack.

'We'll need to get some fenders,' muttered Missing Finn.

'Bull Mackey and Wergishaw, with me,' said Sadie as she drew her cutlass and stepped onto the yacht.

'I say, fronzies,' said one lacy to another. 'I think we've been boarded by pirates.'

'Took you long enough,' said Sadie as she leveled the point of her cutlass at the man's throat. 'Thought I'd have to explain it to you myself.'

'Miss, you can't just come aboard a man's ship like this!' said the lacy.

'I reckon you don't seem to have a grasp of the situation after all.' Sadie snapped her blade down, cutting open his shirt and leaving a thin red line that quickly began to seep blood. The man's face went from petulance to terror. 'I'm Captain Sadie the Pirate Queen. These are *my* waters and I'll go where I please and take what I like. Keen?'

'You didn't have to *hurt* me,' whined the lacy as he clutched at his bleeding chest.

'Somebody shut this cock-dribble up before I lose my generous spirit,' said Sadie.

Wergishaw calmly hit the lacy on the head with his club. The lacy's eyes rolled back in his head and he fell to the deck.

'Any other complaints?' Sadie asked the other two lacies.

It wasn't long before they had stripped the yacht of valuables and were under way. Red had been told to stay back on the ship during the boarding. But after, Sadie let him help sort through their loot. He sat on the floor of her tiny captain's cabin and sorted the silver from the gold, the stuff that could easily be bartered from the stuff of questionable value that might need to be appraised.

'I didn't know men wore jewelry,' he said as he held a gold ring with a glistening opal up to the sunlight that streamed through the portal.

'Lacy men.' Sadie lounged on her bunk, not bothering to take off her coat or boots.

'They seem pretty useless,' said Red.

'You should see the women. Don't even work. Just sit at home all day idle. Makes me sick just to think about.'

'Why do you know so much about lacies?' asked Red.

'Back when I was a girl, they used to come down to Paradise Circle all the time. You could roll one every day for coins and never run out of the fools.'

'What were they doing in Paradise Circle?'

'This was back when Yorey Satin ran the Circle. He had all these dance halls and theaters. Real pat places that the lacies just loved.'

'What happened to them all?'

'Yorey got himself murdered. Jix the Lift took over, and he wouldn't know a pat dance hall if it pissed in his mouth. He and his boots turned the Circle into what it is today. He'll get himself murdered one day, too, and someone else will take over. All we can do is hope that whoever it is, they're better and not worse.'

'Why don't *you* take over, Sadie?' asked Red.

Sadie laughed. 'Maybe I will. First the coast, then the Circle.'

Red looked at her solemnly. 'Will I still be your best wag?'

'Here now.' She leaned over and flicked his nose hard.

'Ow!' He rubbed at it.

'Don't talk bludgeon,' said Sadie. 'You're my best wag till death.'

5

The library at Galemoor was one of the greatest in the empire. But that was of little use until Bleak Hope learned to read.

'Do you think I'll be able to learn this skill, Grandteacher?' asked Hope as the two stood in the library. The room was no larger than Hurlo's sleeping quarters, but it was packed from floor to ceiling with scrolls, books, and stacks of parchment.

'Why wouldn't you?' asked Hurlo as he pulled down a thick bound volume.

'No one in my village could read. Not even Shamka, our elder. And I'm only a girl.'

Hurlo looked at her sharply. 'You will not utter the phrase "only a girl" ever again. You are my student. You will do as I say and learn what I teach you. No excuses. Do you understand?'

Hope dropped her gaze to the floor. 'Yes, Grandteacher.'

He smiled. 'Excellent. Then we will begin with this.' He held up the book. '*The History of Selk the Brave, Founder of the Vinchen Order*, volume one.'

It was slow going at first. Hurlo found it was lack of confidence rather than lack of intelligence that made reading a struggle for Hope. But once she crossed that threshold and no longer had to labor over individual words, her appetite for knowledge proved boundless. She consumed the five-volume history of Selk the Brave, followed quickly by the three-volume set of Manay the True. She finished the entire ten-volume *A Brief History of the Empire* in less than a month.

Once Hurlo was satisfied that she had a sense of history, he assigned her books on geography and biology. It was this last field of study that really seemed to spark her passion.

'Grandteacher!' She burst into his room one afternoon holding a ragged book, the binding nearly undone. Her eyes were wide.

Hurlo had been meditating. Rather than break from it, startled and off balance, he simply allowed her into his meditation. He closed his eyes again, and said softly, 'Yes, child?'

'Did you know,' she said, 'that *no one* knows how snakes move?'

'Yes, child.'

'It can't be magic, can it?'

'It's unlikely.'

'Then there must be a *reason*. It just hasn't been discovered yet.'

'Yes, child.'

'Do we have any snakes on the island, Grand-teacher? Maybe *I* could be the one to discover it!'

Hurlo smiled faintly, his eyes still closed. 'You are welcome to try.' Because what good was book knowledge without practical application? And when she did finally catch a snake and study it, she may not have discovered how it moved, but she did learn how to treat a snakebite.

The other monks did not understand Hurlo's sudden interest in educating the girl. By this time, they had accepted her as a part of their lives, but only in a servant capacity. Nearly all Vinchen came from upper-class families who employed servants, so it wasn't a difficult stretch for them. But the idea of educating a servant was baffling. Some thought him kind, some thought him indulgent, some thought him slipping into senility, and others suspected him of ulterior motives, such as lechery. None of them actually expected him to succeed. So it was with quite a bit of shock when old Brother Wentu discovered her on a cold winter afternoon curled up next to the oven with a copy of *The History of Economic Trade During the Reign of Emperor Bastelinus*.

Hurlo did not mind their shock, speculation, or gossip. While it did create a little unrest in the monastery, it also distracted them from the much graver crime he was committing. Not even his authority extended to sanctioning the training of a female in the ways of the Vinchen warrior. So while he openly trained her mind during the day, it was at night, while the rest of the order were in their beds, that he trained her body.

Hope learned that it was in the east side of the monastery that the Vinchen warrior monks trained. It had an armory, a smithy, and a small tannery. But the largest building was a long, rectangular sparring hall. The walls of the hall were sliding canvas doors that could be opened in the warm months. The floor was a smooth pine, much softer than the hard black stone that comprised most of the floors in the monastery.

At night, when the other monks were asleep, Hurlo took Hope to the sparring hall, where he put her through a battery of exercises to increase her strength, stamina, and agility.

For several months, that was all they did, because by the end
of it, she was too exhausted to do anything else.

Once she could perform the exercises to Hurlo's satisfaction and still have energy left to move, he began to teach her
close combat. At first, this involved mostly punching and
kicking a padded wooden dummy. But as her technique grew
more assured, he began to spar with her directly. She was
amazed at how nimble the old man was. She sparred with
him every night for hours, and it was almost a month before
he even needed to block one of her strikes.

As valuable as she knew this training was, there was something else she hungered for even more. So one night, when
they had finished sparring and Hope was mopping the sweat
from her body with a thick rag, she said, 'Grandteacher,
when will I be able to use a sword?'

He stood looking through a window at the night sky. Not
once in their months of sparring had he broken a sweat.
'Why do you ask?'

'I don't know.' She opened and closed her hand, unable to
put into words her longing to feel a weapon in her grasp. 'I
just . . . think about it a lot.'

He turned from the window to regard her for a moment.
'Come with me.'

She followed him from the sparring hall into the courtyard. The night air quickly dried her sweat and sent a chill
straight down her spine. He led her into the temple. The
lamps were not kept burning at night, but the candles on the
altar continued their flickering dance. By this light, she saw
him gesture to the meditation mat in front of the altar. She
knelt silently on the mat while he continued behind the altar
and opened the same cabinet that Racklock had taken the
cane from. Hope felt a ripple of fear when she saw that, but
quickly admonished herself. Grandteacher Hurlo would
never beat her simply for asking a question.

Instead of a cane, Hurlo took a sheathed sword from the cabinet. He held it reverently in two hands, parallel to the ground, as he brought it to the front of the altar and knelt in front of Hope. The sheath was black lacquered wood carved with inlaid gold designs. The handle was intercrossed with black-and-white fabric, while the hilt and pommel were gold.

He slowly pulled the sword from its sheath. As he did, the blade hummed softly.

'This sword is called the Song of Sorrows. It is one of the greatest swords ever made.' He moved the sword slowly through the air, and again the blade hummed.

Hope's eyes were wide as she took in the cold, beautiful gleam of the blade. 'Why does it make that sound?'

'It was forged by the biomancer Xunera Ray for Manay the True, back when biomancers and Vinchen still worked together for the good of the empire. The method of its creation has been lost, but it is said that the Song of Sorrows remembers every life it takes, and the sound you hear . . .' He swept the blade through the air again, faster this time, and the hum came louder, with a solemn, mournful air. 'It is the loss it feels at every death.'

'Can a sword truly remember and feel?' asked Hope.

'I don't know,' said Hurlo. 'My teacher, Shilgo the Wise, believed so, although he also admitted to me, when I asked him, that he had no proof. All we know for certain is that there is no logical reason for it to make such a sound.' He sheathed the blade, and the hum abruptly cut off. 'Now, you asked when you would learn to use a sword.' He held out the Song of Sorrows to Hope.

'I . . . can touch it?'

'Take it in your hands.'

She took the sword from him. It was much heavier than she expected.

'Hold it by the handle,' instructed Hurlo.

Hope shifted her hands to the black-and-white grip. The tip of the sword immediately sank to the ground.

'When you can hold this sword upright, we will begin your training with it.'

It seemed impossibly heavy, and Hope's heart sank as low as the sword. 'Yes, Grandteacher.'

'You doubt this is possible?'

She looked away, embarrassed. Vinchen warriors did not doubt themselves or their teacher. 'It is very heavy, Grandteacher.'

'It is indeed. And it will take a long time for you to get strong enough. Years, I expect. But I promise you, Bleak Hope. When you are finally able to wield a blade such as this, you will be a fearsome warrior indeed.'

A fearsome warrior. Hope hardly thought it possible, but as she stared down at the sword in her hands, she knew that was exactly what she needed to become. No matter how long it took, or how difficult the journey.

After a few months, Hurlo realized that Bleak Hope was beginning to show signs of training, particularly in strength and muscle tone. To allay suspicion, he assigned her a strenuous regimen of morning chores that included as much manual labor as he could find. She moved ale barrels and repaired furniture. She stretched hides for the tanner, and even assisted the brother responsible for the smithy. Some days, when there was nothing else to be done, he would have her move a pile of rocks from one side of a building to the other.

Many of the brothers saw Hope's increased task load as a sign that Hurlo had begun to dislike her as much as they did. He allowed them to think that. But not all the brothers were so easily fooled.

Hurlo was in the sparring hall alone one afternoon. The sunlight streamed in through the open sliding doors, casting the grandteacher in silhouette as he moved slowly and steadily with a heavy wooden sword, his breath perfectly in time with the motion. Hurlo saw no difference between sword training and meditation.

'May I spar with you, Grandteacher?' Racklock stood with his thick shoulders filling the doorway. He held a wooden sword in his hand.

'You may,' said Hurlo as he finished his final form. He came to stillness, his sword held upright before him, and allowed himself one last peaceful breath. Then he angled his body to face Racklock. 'Come.'

Racklock moved in swiftly with an overhead blow, but Hurlo knocked it aside, the wooden swords giving a sharp *clack* as they met.

Hurlo smiled. 'Always trying to catch me off guard with that first blow.'

'One day it will work, Grandteacher,' said Racklock. 'That is when I will know that my time has come to lead the order.' He swung again.

Hurlo parried again. 'And what will you do, that you are so eager to lead the order?'

Racklock executed a series of attacks, all of which Hurlo blocked or dodged. 'I will take us out of exile on this cold rock. I will make us once again a respected and feared order in the empire.'

'If respect and fear is what you desire, you have that already from your own brothers,' said Hurlo.

Racklock attacked again, striking as he said, 'I also want power. And renown.'

'Power, I can understand,' said Hurlo, blocking each strike. 'All men crave power, if only to protect what they cherish. But renown? That will bring you nothing but unhappiness.'

'That is easy for *you* to say, Hurlo the Cunning. Your place among the great stories is assured. I wonder, though, do you keep us all here so that none of us have the opportunity to eclipse you?'

Hurlo's gaze hardened and he switched to the offensive, delivering a succession of blows that Racklock was barely able to counter. 'You know why it is we remain here. As long as we are at cross-purpose with the emperor, our only options are self-exile or insurrection. Would you have us clash directly with the emperor and his biomancers? That would tear the empire apart.'

Racklock struck back harder. 'Or we could join them. The world has changed, old man. We must change as well, or perish.'

Hurlo smiled mischievously. 'You do not think we are changing?'

They traded a few more blows without speaking. The crack of wood on wood echoed through the training hall.

'You have been punishing the girl hard with work lately,' said Racklock. 'The others think it is because you dislike her. But I know different, Grandteacher.'

'A heavy load in the hands forgets a heavy load in the heart,' said Hurlo. 'I believe she finds peace in the work.'

'You have grown soft in your old age.'

'I have grown kind,' said Hurlo. 'There is a difference.'

Racklock stepped back from Hurlo and lowered his sword. 'You have some other plan at work, Hurlo the Cunning. And it has something to do with that girl.'

'You are right,' said Hurlo. 'That plan is the rehabilitation of my soul.'

Hurlo had always been one to speak from the heart. Many times, he would say things and not know that they were true until he said them. His famous cunning came in part from his ability to surprise even himself. So when he told Racklock that Bleak Hope was the rehabilitation of his soul, he had not considered it at all before then. And yet, the moment he spoke it, he knew it to be true.

That night, he took her down to the rocky shoreline. The wind howled fiercely, pulling at their black robes as they stood on the narrow spit of gray sand in slippered feet. Before them, hard waves crashed against the ragged black rocks that lay half-submerged in the dark water.

'It is so *cold*, Grandteacher!' Bleak Hope's arms hugged her torso, and her entire body shivered. Her blue eyes were so comically wide that Hurlo laughed.

'Yes, child, it is. And why is that?'

Hope's pale brow furrowed. 'What do you mean, Grandteacher?'

'Why is it so cold here, now, in this place?'

'Oh, because it is winter and we are in the Southern Isles, which are the coldest in the empire.'

'Correct. And what would happen if we traveled north by boat?'

'It would get slowly warmer?'

'Yes. Your studies are coming along well. Now, if we were to travel by boat, how would we know which way is north?'

'By the sun, which rises in the east and sets in the west.'

'What if we were to travel by night?' He gestured up at the black-and-purple sky.

'I . . . don't know, Grandteacher.'

'By the stars. Have you not read that astronomy book?'

'I have not yet,' admitted Hope. 'I thought it was . . . unimportant. What difference do the stars make to us down here?'

'When you read it, you will learn about the constellations. Pictures in the sky that never change. There.' He pointed up to a five-point cluster. 'That is the Fist of Selk the Brave.

And there.' He pointed to a small cluster of stars with a thin line of stars trailing behind it. 'That is the Great Serpent. And there.' He pointed to a large cluster of stars. 'That is the Kraken.' He turned back to her. 'Learn these shapes. Memorize them. They will help guide you on your way.'

'*Us*, Grandteacher,' corrected Hope. 'You mean they will help guide *us*.'

'Of course,' said Hurlo.

Hope stared up at the dark, twinkling sky for a while. Hurlo could tell she was working something out for herself, so he waited.

'I have seen a symbol, Grandteacher. A black oval with eight trailing lines. It looks like a squid or kraken. The captain who brought me here. He said it was the symbol of the biomancers.'

'He is correct,' Hurlo said quietly.

Hope nodded, still staring up at the sky. 'What *are* the biomancers, Grandteacher? They are mentioned frequently in histories of the empire, yet it is never clear who they are exactly. Are they sorcerers? Or holy men?'

'They are scientists, of a sort. Mystics of biology. They can take living creatures and change them.'

'Change them how?'

'Make them bigger or smaller. For example, mole rats used to be tiny things no bigger than mice, once upon a time. Did you know that?'

Hope shook her head.

'A biomancer may make a living thing grow, or decay, or make it into something else completely.'

'Are biomancers good or bad?'

'They serve the emperor, for good or bad.'

'Don't the Vinchen serve the emperor?' asked Hope.

'We serve the *empire*. That is why we live and train far from the palace and its corrupting influence and power. A single emperor may be flawed or cruel. But the empire is bigger than one man. And it is always worth fighting for. Perhaps when the time comes, you will be the one to correct its course.'

Hope looked at him then. Her gaze had softened over the months of their training. But now it looked again as it did that night Toa brought her to him. 'A biomancer killed my parents and everyone in my village.'

'I know,' said Hurlo.

'Is it wrong that I want to kill a servant of the emperor?'

'What does the Vinchen code say about vengeance?'

Bleak Hope closed her eyes, as if reading it on the backs of her eyelids. 'Vengeance is one of the most sacred duties of a warrior. It may be swift or slow, but it must be done with honor. When a warrior confronts his offender, he must give his name and ask the offender for his. The warrior must state clearly his reason for vengeance and allow the offender the chance to arm himself. The only true vengeance is the death of the offender. If the warrior fails in this, better that he die than live in such dishonor.'

'Will you abide by this code?' asked Hurlo.

The wind lashed at Hope's hair as she stood with her eyes still closed. 'Yes, Grandteacher.'

'Then you have your answer.'

6

*A*fter a month of raiding lacy yachts along the coast, word started to spread of Sadie the Pirate Queen. The yachts got scarce and imperial patrols started to appear. The naval ships were large and slow compared to the *Savage Wind*, so they were easy to avoid. But now Sadie and her crew needed to find new targets.

'There's merchant ships,' Missing Finn said doubtfully one night. He and Sadie sat at the bow, watching the sun set red on the horizon and passing a bottle back and forth.

'Yeah, big old cargo ships,' Sadie said eagerly. 'That'll be easy.'

'Easy to catch,' said Finn. 'But where are we going to put their cargo? Besides, to get to those ships, we have to stop hugging the coast and head out into deeper waters. And that's where the imp navy can get us.'

'Alright. So aren't there smaller cargo ships? Ones that come in close?'

'Further north we might have some luck. A lot of luxury items come through Radiant Harbor in Hollow Falls. But I don't know those waters as well. Who knows what else we'll find that way.'

'It was boldness that got us this far,' said Sadie. 'It's boldness that will take us further.'

They made their way up the coast the next day. The morning was tense, what with the uniform military barracks of Keystown looming to the east, and large imperial frigates lurking along the horizon to the west. But they had a favorable wind and made good time. By the afternoon, they had cleared the thickest concentration of imperial power and made it north to Hollow Falls, a peaceful, wealthy region where the lacies lived on sprawling estates in glorious mansions. Most of the homes were set too far back from the water to see, but every now and then, one was built right on the water. Sadie couldn't resist pulling out her spyglass and having a closer look at the turrets that jutted out over the water.

'Wouldn't mind having a view like that in my home,' said Missing Finn from his usual post at the helm. 'Sunsets must be real nice from there.'

Sadie collapsed her spyglass and shrugged. 'They look nice from here, too. I was looking to see if there was anything worth stealing in them.'

'Is there?'

'Sure, but there's bars on everything. And the way they hang out over the water, it would be a trick to even get to them.'

'Probably household guards, too,' said Finn.

'True. We need more modest targets than that for now.'

They reached Radiant Harbor by nightfall. Rather than dock in the harbor, they anchored in a small, concealed inlet just north.

'Thought you said you didn't know these waters,' said Sadie.

'I said I didn't know them as *well*,' replied Missing Finn. 'I've sailed on some ships that had goods to unload in Hollow Falls but didn't want any imp harbor inspections.'

The next morning, Avery Birdhouse spotted a merchant

ship only slightly larger than the *Savage Wind* heading north from Radiant Bay.

'Weigh anchor and set sail,' said Sadie. 'We'll keep at a distance till we get a bit further from the harbor.'

The ship continued to head north along the coast until it reached the top of New Laven, then it changed course to north-northeast.

'She's heading out into open waters,' said Missing Finn. 'Better close soon, or we'll be vulnerable to the imp frigates. Wouldn't take more than a few of those cannons to sink this boat.'

'Let out the jib!' called Sadie, who had been learning the proper names of sails from Finn.

Spinner unfurled the front sail. It snapped taut and the ship picked up speed.

Sadie watched the merchant ship with her spyglass. 'They let out their jib, too. Looks like they've made us.'

Finn grinned. 'Should we give chase, Captain Sadie?'

'Oh, yes, Missing Finn.'

They chased the merchant ship for nearly an hour, going so far out to sea that New Laven was only a dark smudge on the horizon. But even though the two ships were around the same size, the merchant ship was weighed down with cargo. Bit by bit, the *Savage Wind* gained on them until they were close enough to grapple. What they found on that ship was not the hysterical lacies they were accustomed to, but hardened sailors armed with knives, clubs, and pikes of their own.

'Finally.' Sadie drew her cutlass. 'A decent fight. Missing Finn, I leave the ship to you. Red, stay in the cabin. Everyone else with me.'

It was short and ugly. Wergishaw lay about him with his club, cracking heads and kneecaps. Avery Birdhouse, a knife in each hand, darted in and out as he went for soft spots like necks, bellies, and groins.

Bull Mackey hacked off hands and the tops of heads with his ax. Spinner ran them through with his pike. And in the center of it all, Sadie swung her cutlass again and again. No matter how hardened those merchant sailors might be, they were still no match for a bunch of wags from Paradise Circle, Hammer Point, and Silverback.

'You'll hang for this!' screamed the captain, a short man with a red face and a wispy beard. Bull Mackey and Spinner had found him hiding in the cargo hold and dragged him before Sadie.

'That so?' asked Sadie.

'These spices are bound for Stonepeak! For the emperor himself!'

'The emperor, you say?' Sadie looked impressed. 'Well, then, do me a favor and give your emperor a message from Sadie the Pirate Queen.' She looked at Bull Mackey and Spinner. 'Hold him down.'

The two grinned at each other as they stretched him out on the deck. He thrashed desperately, but couldn't get loose.

Sadie straddled him and began to hike up her skirts.

'What in hells are you doing?' demanded the captain.

'Here's my message to the emperor.' Sadie squatted and pissed all over the captain, while he cursed, and her crew howled with laughter.

The celebration that night was particularly rowdy. Red was used to seeing the crew of the *Savage Wind* drunk, including Sadie. But that night it was so loud and chaotic, it made him nervous, so he retreated to the stern, where Missing Finn sat and stared up at the starry sky.

'Why aren't you celebrating with the rest of the crew?' asked Red.

'A sailor learns that out here in open water, anything is liable to happen at any time. Always best to have someone keep a sober watch.'

Several of the crew hollered something incoherent. Both Finn and Red turned to see Sadie punch Avery Birdhouse so hard that his nose began to gush blood. Then she grabbed him by the shirt collar and kissed him hard, his blood smearing all over her face.

'Do you wish you didn't have to keep watch?' asked Red.

Missing Finn shrugged and turned back to look at the stars.

'You in love with Sadie?' asked Red.

Missing Finn smiled faintly. 'What do you know of love, boy?'

'My dad loved my mom.'

'That so?'

'It is. Everything he did was for her.'

'He tell you that?'

'Nah. It was easy to see.'

'It's a good thing to grow up seeing that.'

'Why?'

'It means you know there's something more than . . .' He nodded to the celebration. 'That.'

Red didn't know much about Missing Finn, other than that he had sailed more than anyone else on the ship. 'What happened to your eye?'

'Ain't a pleasant story.'

'I didn't think it would be,' said Red.

Finn grinned and ruffled Red's hair. 'You got a sharp tongue on you. Hope that doesn't get you into more trouble than you can handle.'

'So you're really not going to tell me?'

'What'll you give me in return?'

Red thought about it. 'A secret for a secret?'

'How do you know my story's a secret?'

'Because you ain't told anyone on this ship about it. Not even Sadie.'

'It's not a secret, exactly. Just real personal.'

'All secrets are personal. That's why they're secret.'

Finn smiled again. 'I'm starting to see why Sadie keeps you around. Clever as claws, you are.'

'So it's a deal?' pressed Red.

'I suppose. But you first.'

Red had already thought of his secret, so he jumped in eagerly. 'After my mom died, it was just me and my dad. He used to leave a lot to go work. He was a whore. That meant people paid him to have sex with them.'

'I know what a whore is, boy.'

'You ever pay someone to have sex with you?'

'Of course. I reckon most people in Paradise Circle have.'

'I never will,' said Red. Despite Sadie's assurance that not all sex was like the kind he'd witnessed, the whole idea still seemed unappealing.

'That your secret?' asked Missing Finn.

'Of course not. So when my dad went to work, he left me with our neighbor, Old Yammy. She was a nice lady. Taught me things like juggling and playing stones.'

'You play stones?'

'I'd beat you, I bet.'

'I'd like to see you try.'

'We can play if you like, but you'll have to put down some coppers. Old Yammy told me never play for free.'

Missing Finn laughed. 'Maybe I will, just to see you lose. Now, what was that secret of yours, then?'

Red leaned in close. He could feel a flush of embarrassment creep up on his cheeks. 'She was so nice and taught me stuff, and what did I do? I stole from her. She had a big bowl of fruit on her table and every time I came over, I would take a piece, even if I wasn't hungry.'

'You stole that captain's clothes,' pointed out Finn. 'And what do you think we're doing every day on this ship but stealing?'

'There's right stealing and wrong stealing,' said Red. 'Don't think I don't know the difference.'

Missing Finn looked at him for a moment, then nodded. 'I guess you've got a point.'

'Anyway, I went to look for her after my dad died, but the imps locked her up on the Empty Cliffs. I don't know why. And I never got a chance to say sorry.' Red thought about that for a moment, wishing he could see her again. Then he shook his head. That was soft artsy stuff. 'Now it's your turn. How'd you lose your eye?'

Missing Finn turned to look back out across the water. 'I was older than you, but didn't have any real talents or trade to speak of. As you might expect, things weren't going so well for me, and somehow I ended up sleeping down on the piers. That's where a captain by the name of Brek Frayd found me and offered me food and a place to sleep as long as I put in an honest day's work on his ship.'

'That's when you became a sailor?'

'That's when I started learning how to sail.'

'What's the difference?'

'Patience, boy. See, it wasn't a good fit, at first. I got terrible seasick whenever the wind was high. And I wasn't mindful of my work. So many times Captain Frayd had to tell me to go back and secure a line better after I'd just wrapped it around a cleat a few times. That is until one time, during a real bad luffer, a line I was supposed to secure came undone. The pulley whipped into the air, and the hook end caught me right in the face.'

Red examined the oval-shaped wooden pulleys in the

nearby rigging. Each one had an iron hook on the end that was as thick as his thumb. He imagined something like that going into his eye and shuddered.

'You know what Captain Frayd told me after that?' asked Missing Finn. 'He said, "The sea's a terrible cruel mistress, Finny, and she'll always take her due. You done paid in advance with that eye, my boy, and the sea will always welcome you now as her own."' Finn turned to Red, and his one good eye gleamed wetly in the moonlight. 'I been sailing these seas ever since. I never got sick again, and I never again left a line unsecured.'

'That's how you became a sailor,' Red said quietly.

Finn nodded. 'I been thinking about what that captain said ever since. Took me years to really understand what he gave me that day.'

'Gave you?'

'After something like that, I could've avoided ships the rest of my life. Nobody would have blamed me for being afraid the sea might take the other eye. But I didn't think of it that way, because of the way he explained it to me. He didn't try to make what happened any less terrible. He just made it worth something. And if you ask me, you can endure any kind of suffering, as long as it has a purpose.'

'My parents died,' Red said quietly. 'Did that have a purpose?'

'That's for you to decide. If they hadn't died, would you have met Sadie? Would you have even come to Paradise Circle?'

Red shook his head.

'So that suffering made you into who you are now. A clever boy and a damn fine thief who knows good from bad.' He grinned. 'Maybe it will make you into the greatest thief New Laven has ever seen.'

'How do I know if it does?'

'You'll never know for certain, but nobody's ever going to be able to prove otherwise, so you might as well just say it does.'

A smile slowly spread across Red's face. His ruby eyes twinkled. 'Hey, yeah.'

'It doesn't bring your parents back. But at least it means their deaths were not for nothing.'

Red stared up into the night sky. 'The greatest thief New Laven has ever seen,' he said quietly, for the first of many times.

That first successful raid on a merchant ship made Sadie hungry for another. They prowled the northern coast, looking for more than the bits of jewelry and coin they had been taking from lacy yachts. But perhaps that captain's threats hadn't been idle, because within a few weeks' time, the coastal waters were teeming with imperial ships from Stonepeak.

'Not a good time for us to be out,' Finn said as he and Sadie shared a bottle in her cabin. 'We should lay low until those imps get tired of circling New Laven like a pack of goblin sharks.'

'Nah, we just need a new mark,' said Sadie.

'Like what?'

Sadie took a pull on the bottle. 'Them little villages we see all along the northeast coast. They've got to have something worth plundering.'

'Food and lamp oil is about all.'

'We need those things, don't we?'

'I suppose.' Missing Finn thought of what Red had said. There was right stealing and there was wrong stealing. 'But Sadie, those folks are no better off than us. Some of them probably worse.'

'Oh, don't go all soft on me. I get enough of that from the boy. I promise not to kill anybody unless they force my hand. Does that appease your delicate conscience?'

The next day, the *Savage Wind* began its reign of terror on the villages along the northeast coast of New Laven. They were tiny places, usually only one dirt road. The people wore plain wool smocks. Many didn't even have shoes. And they were completely unprepared for the small whirlwind of violence that descended on them. When Sadie came at them with her cutlass, most simply ran.

'Easier than getting a slap from my father,' said Sadie as she watched a man nearly twice her size take off down the road.

Sadie left Red to mind the ship at the dock, and the rest of the crew fanned out to look for anything worth taking. Avery Birdhouse located the large storage shed near the docks. Sadie had Bull Mackey and Wergişhaw break the lock on the door. Inside, they discovered not only food and lamp oil, but several large barrels of ale.

'I'd say this was worth the taking.' Sadie turned to Missing Finn. 'Sometimes it's not about the money, but about a finer quality of living.'

They continued to ravage the coast for a few more weeks, going from village to village. Then one day they landed at a village with a sign that proudly proclaimed, MOONFLOWER LANDING, POPULATION 50. Except when she and her crew entered, not one of the fifty could be found.

'I don't like this one bit,' said Missing Finn, his one eye narrowed suspiciously.

'Maybe they already ran away?' said Avery Birdhouse.

'How would they know to run unless someone tipped them?' asked Finn.

'Who would do that?' asked Spinner.

'One of the other villages maybe. Who's to say they don't all know each other. Not that much distance between them.'

'Let's find where they keep the loot and be off before this goes leeward, then,' said Sadie.

There were several small storage sheds. Every one of them lay open and empty except one all the way on the other side of the village. Bull Mackey broke the lock easily, since it was old and corroded with rust. But there was nothing inside.

'Why lock an empty shed?' said Finn.

Sadie grunted and turned back in the direction of the ship. The mast of the *Savage Wind* was visible above the village rooftops, and she could see an oily black smoke twining around it.

'The ship!' said Missing Finn.

'Red!' Sadie charged back toward the ship, her tall captain's boots churning up the dirt, her cutlass held high like she could use it to frighten off the fire as easily as she'd frightened the villagers. But by the time she reached the dock, the sails were ashes, the charred mast had collapsed, and water was fighting with the fire to consume the remainder of the ship. The saboteurs, most likely villagers, had already slipped away.

'Oh God, Red!' Sadie threw aside her hat and cutlass, jerked off her boots, and threw aside her coat. She was just about to dive into the wreckage when she heard a boyish voice at the far end of the dock.

'Right here, Sadie!' Red popped up from inside an empty barrel.

'Piss'ell, boy! You had me worried!' She stalked over to him, her fists clenched.

He gave her a surprised look. 'You didn't think I had enough sense to get off a burning boat?'

She jerked to a halt and thought about that. 'I guess I didn't. Sorry, you got that much sense.'

Red gave her a sly smile. 'Would you say I have enough sense to grab a bit of money on my way out?' He held up a small sack and shook it so that it jingled softly.

'You really are my best wag!' Sadie pulled him out of the barrel and into a crushing embrace.

The rest of the crew had reached the dock by then. They stared morosely as the last bit of burnt lumber sank.

'Well, that's everything,' said Missing Finn.

'Not everything,' said Sadie, her arms still around Red. 'We still got our health, our wags, and enough money to get us home.'

'Home?' asked Red.

'That's right. Back to Paradise Circle for you and me.' Then in a singsong voice she said:

Where it's dismal and wet,
And the sun never gets.
But still it's my home.
Bless the Circle!

Backus was having a quiet drink at the Drowned Rat when he looked up and saw a shape darken the doorway.

'Not again . . .' he whimpered.

Sadie the Goat stood there, much as she had a few months ago, with that same red-eyed kid in tow. At first Backus thought his eyes were fooling him. After all, she'd been shamed in front of everyone in this very tavern. And yet, there she was, looking tired and dirty, but still a far sight better than the last time he'd seen her. The entire tavern went quiet as she walked calmly into the tavern, pat as you please.

'Hiya, Backus,' she said as she passed him. Then she winked.

She was halfway to the bar before Bracers Madge appeared. Backus was never sure how such a big woman could appear so suddenly, but there she was, looming over Sadie, her thumbs in her suspenders.

The boy looked terrified and shrank back, but Sadie just nodded. 'Hi, Madge.'

'What you doing here, Sadie?'

'I come to beg your forgiveness,' Sadie said loud and clear so the whole place could hear her.

'My *what*?' asked Madge, looking confused.

Sadie dropped down on one knee. 'You've always been good to me, Madge. Fair and true and a damn sight kinder than most. When I came in here, hells-bent on revenge, I spit on everything good you done me. It was wrong as things can be and I'm forever sorry I did it. All I want to know is, will you forgive me?'

Bracers Madge stood over Sadie, her arms crossed, her face expressionless. There was not a whisper in the tavern as everyone waited to see what she would say. But she didn't say anything. After a moment, she turned and walked behind the bar. She picked up the little pickling jar that contained Sadie's ear. Then she came back around to the front of the bar and solemnly handed the jar to Sadie.

Sadie stared down at the jar in her hand, her expression full of wonder. Never had Bracers Madge given one of her prize ears back to its owner. It was a thing unheard of in Paradise Circle.

Madge nodded to her, then walked back behind the bar and poured herself a whiskey.

Sadie slowly stood, the jar clutched in her fist.

'Well, now. This calls for some celebrating. And I think I have just enough money from my pirating adventure to buy a round for the house.'

The tavern erupted in hoots and cheers, fists pounding on the tables.

Sadie looked over at Backus. 'See you around, old pot.' Then she gave an evil chuckle.

That was to be Backus's last relaxing drink in the Drowned Rat for many years.

Sadie basked in appreciation and ale that night.

'Time you started drinking.' She slid a foamy tankard to Red as she sat down at their table.

Red's eyes went wide as he looked down at it.

'Go on, take a sip.'

He took a gulp, and shuddered. 'I thought it would taste *good*.'

She laughed. 'It tastes as it tastes. I've had better and I've had worse. Now, my best wag, what are your plans?'

'Plans?' he asked as he sniffed at his tankard, wondering if he could take another sip without throwing up, afraid that Sadie would make him anyway.

'We're back in the Circle and everything true as trouble again. We're older and wiser and a bit more keen. So what do you plan to do?'

'I thought . . .' Red's pulse sped up in alarm. 'I thought I was still with you.'

'Oh God, you can't be hanging from my teat all the time. I'm still here and you're still my best wag. But I'm not your captain anymore, and it's time you started to make your own decisions.'

'I don't really know what to do.'

'Well, what do you want to be?'

'The greatest thief New Laven has ever seen,' he said immediately.

Sadie had been in the midst of drinking from her tankard. When she heard that, ale sprayed from her nose and she laughed so hard, she nearly fell out of her chair.

Red clutched his own tankard, looking embarrassed. He took a tiny sip. 'It's stupid, I guess.'

'Stupid?' said Sadie. 'It's the sunniest thing I ever heard. And I don't doubt that if you apply yourself, someday it will be said.'

PART TWO

*As youth and innocence give way to experi-
ence, doubt clouds the mind. Those who find
renewed purpose in the complexity will thrive
instead of falter.*

– from *The Book of Storms*

7

'D o you know how I fall asleep so easily each night?'
asked Grandteacher Hurlo.

He sat cross-legged before the candlelit black stone altar.
These last few years, age had prevented him from kneeling.
But there was a peaceful smile on his old face, and a gentle
look in his filmy eyes.

'No, teacher, I don't.' Bleak Hope found it difficult to
concentrate on what he was saying because she had been
sitting in a suspended middle split for the last hour. Her heels
balanced on the tops of narrow poles on either side, which
kept her raised above a glowing pile of hot coals. But she
knew these were the moments when her teacher chose to
impart his most important knowledge. He said when the
body was strained, the mind was relaxed. So she pressed her
palms together, breathed through the ache in her legs and
lower back, and focused on the sound of his soft, dusty
voice.

'What I do,' said the grandteacher, 'is lie down on my
mat, close my eyes, and ask myself if I have done something truly worthwhile in my life. I think about everything I
have done, and when I come to one deed in particular, I say
to myself, "Yes, I have done something." And then I sleep
soundly.'

'The sleep of the righteous, Grandteacher?'

'I suppose. Do you know what deed it was that comforts me?'

Over her years of training, the grandteacher had shared with Hope many of his youthful exploits. As she continued to balance between the two poles, she considered the most impressive ones. 'Was it the time you saved the emperor from being assassinated by the Jackal Lords?'

'That was a memorable day,' agreed the grandteacher. 'But no, that is not the deed that I consider most worthwhile.'

Hope frowned, her blue eyes lost in thought. 'Was it . . . when you rescued Archlady Maldious from the horde of giant mole rats?'

'Another momentous event. But that is not what sends me peacefully off to sleep each night.'

'It wasn't when you slew the pirate Dire Bane in the Painted Caves, was it?'

He shook his head. 'You are following the wrong path of reasoning. While all of those deeds were important and even courageous, none of them mattered in a way that gives much comfort in my old age.'

'Then . . . I am sorry, teacher.' She bowed her head. 'I don't know.'

His smile was still gentle and warm, his eyes closed as he said, 'In truth, I doubted you would. That was why I asked you the question. No, my child. The thing that gives me tranquility every night is thinking of the day I offered to train you.'

'*Me*, teacher? But—'

'Despite the risks, I knew I must. And it is that courageous decision which gives me peace. That, and knowing someday this night would come, and when it did, we would be ready.'

'Ready for what, teacher?' asked Hope, her pale face frowning. 'Is tonight special?'

'The night itself is like any other. It is the events of tonight which will be special.'

'What will happen tonight?'

The grandteacher opened his eyes, and his smile faded. 'Come before me, Bleak Hope.'

'Yes, teacher.' She flexed her legs and pushed herself up so that she flipped over the hot coals and landed on one knee directly in front of the grandteacher.

'Sit with me,' he said.

She nodded and folded her legs in front of her.

'Close your eyes,' he said. 'And tell me, what do you hear?'

'The crackle of burning coals, teacher.'

'Beyond that?'

She concentrated for a moment. 'I hear the wind blowing strong from the north against the windows near the ceiling of this temple.'

'Good. And beyond that?'

'I hear . . .' It took her a moment, but as she listened, the sounds grew stronger. Voices. Angry voices outside in the courtyard. Boots stomping on flagstone. Swords sliding from scabbards. Her eyes snapped open. 'Teacher! They are coming for us! They mean to harm us!'

'Yes.'

'But your own brothers!'

'Perhaps if I had sent you away a few years ago, we could have avoided it. But I did not have the heart to cut you off from your training just when you were beginning to show your true potential.'

'They *know*, teacher?'

'Yes.'

Hope pressed her face on the cold, hard stone. 'I have

failed you, teacher. It was my responsibility to keep my training hidden from them.'

'No, child. It was not failure that showed our hand, but success. I have trained you every night these past eight years in the way of the Vinchen order, knowing that a day would come when your skills would grow so exceptional that even your most casual movements would betray us. You no longer walk through this world like a servant, but like a warrior. And there is no shame in that. However, we have broken one of the oldest laws of our order. There must be consequences.'

The sound of angry voices out in the courtyard grew steadily louder.

Hope snapped up into a crouch. 'I will face them, teacher. I am not afraid.'

The truth was, she hungered for it. Eight years she had washed their clothes, cooked their food, oiled their armor, polished their weapons, and done a hundred other stupid, meaningless tasks. Some had treated her courteously. But most had treated her no better than a workhorse, and a few had gone out of their way to be cruel. Those, the world would not miss. If she was to die this night, she would take them with her.

'Not so fast, my most beloved pupil,' Hurlo said. 'First you must do something for me.'

'Anything, Grandteacher.'

He reached behind the altar and picked up a sheathed sword.

'Do you know this blade?'

'Of course, teacher. It is the Song of Sorrows, one of the finest blades in the world.'

Fists pounded on the temple door. Voices shouted, demanding that 'the girl' be released to them.

'Swear on the Song of Sorrows that you will not confront our brothers tonight or seek vengeance on them in the future.

Instead, you must flee this place and go seek your path in the world. There is a small boat waiting for you at the dock with enough supplies to get you to the nearest port.'

'But teacher, I—'

'Swear it!'

Hope reluctantly laid her hand on top of the grandteacher's. She looked into his tired gray eyes and said, 'I swear it.'

His serene smile returned. 'Good. Now, so that you don't forget, take this sword with you.'

'I can't take the Song of Sorrows!'

The pounding changed to a slow methodical slam. They were using something to batter down the door.

'This is my final command to you as your teacher,' Hurlo said. 'Do you understand?'

She bowed her head. 'Yes, Grandteacher.'

He let go of the sword, and it stayed in her hand.

'I have done all I can for you,' he said. 'This knowledge gives me peace.'

The sharp crack of wood echoed through the temple as the door gave way.

'Blasphemer!' came a shout from the open doorway as men in the black leather armor of the Vinchen warrior charged into the temple.

'Now, go!' said Hurlo.

His words brought forth a memory of Hope's father, his face etched in pain as he told her to go, to run. And she didn't want to. Couldn't leave him. It was happening all over again. The shouts of warriors mingled in her head with the sounds of men and women dying all around her as the worms of the biomancer burst from them . . .

'Hope!' Grandteacher Hurlo's voice cracked like a whip, shaking her out of her memories. 'You must go now!'

'Teacher, not again.' Her eyes filled with tears. 'Please, don't make me be the one to survive again.'

He placed his withered hand on her cheek and smiled sadly. 'I am sorry, my child. You must endure.'

Bleak Hope blinked back the tears and nodded.

She tucked the Song of Sorrows under her arm just as the men began to surround them. She jumped first to one wall, then across to the other, working her way up until she reached the windows near the ceiling of the temple. She broke the glass with the pommel of the sword, and swung out and up onto the roof.

'Follow her!' shouted one of the men.

He leapt after her, but the grandteacher sprang up, grabbed his ankle, and yanked him back down.

'Hurlo! You have disgraced yourself, your title as grand-teacher, and this order,' said Racklock, his massive shoulders heaving with exaltation. 'You *should* be given a fair trial before your peers. But if you do not step aside, I will cut you down where you stand.' He pointed his sword forward, and the other monks followed suit until Hurlo was surrounded by a ring of sharp steel.

The old grandteacher stood there, alone, no sword in his hand, with nothing but a smile on his lips.

'You are welcome to try.'

Hope ran along the rooftop, crouched low, her black robes flapping in the cold night air. She heard the shouts of pain and the clash of steel on rock and stopped. She could take down at least three, maybe four, before they overwhelmed her. But the sword weighed heavy in her grasp, and therefore so did her promise. If she returned, the look of disappoint-ment on her teacher's face would wound her far worse than any blade. She kept moving.

When she reached the edge of the temple roof, she jumped, letting the momentum carry her to a nearby treetop. She dropped from branch to branch with her slippered feet and free hand until she landed softly on the ground. She scanned the courtyard and saw no one, so she left the cover of the trees and sprinted across the open space toward the front gate. She had almost reached it when she heard the *hiss* of a sword leaving its sheath. She dodged to the side, at the same time bringing up her own still-sheathed sword. The *thock* of blade on wooden scabbard echoed in the empty courtyard. Hope continued from her dodge into a roll, twisting as she did into a protective crouch, and brought her sheathed sword up to guard herself.

Crunta stood before her, his sword raised, blocking her way to the gate. No doubt he had lagged behind the others, suspecting the grandteacher's loyalty to Hope went deep enough that he would help her escape. Of all the brothers, he had been one of the most cruel. Because she was a girl? Because she was a servant? It didn't really matter.

But she had sworn to Grandteacher Hurlo that she would not confront her brothers.

'Let me pass, Crunta.'

'Do not think because you have been playing at battle in the midnight hours with a foolish old man that you are a match for me. Throw down your toy sword and return to the temple for judgment, or I will leave your pretty guts strewn across the flagstones.'

'Toy sword?' Hope slowly straightened from her crouch. 'I know it is dark and the moonlight is faint, but do you truly not recognize this blade?' She held it out horizontally, one hand on the sheath, one on the handle.

Crunta's eyes widened. 'No . . . how could he . . .' He shook his head. 'This only makes your crimes more terrible. Surrender or die.'

Hope nodded. 'If that is your choice.' She had obeyed her teacher and sought not to confront this brother. But now he was preventing her from fulfilling the second part of her oath. So he must be removed.

She pulled the Song of Sorrows from its sheath, and the blade sang as it moved through the air. Crunta lifted his own sword to parry, but not quickly enough. It was a short song, and by the time it ended, it was his guts that lay strewn on the flagstones.

Hope stood for a moment, sword extended past her body as she watched Crunta drop heavily to his knees and try to stuff his intestines back into his body for a moment before finally toppling over. Her blade gleamed red in the moonlight. This was the first blood she had ever spilled. She had expected to feel something. Satisfaction. Regret. But all she felt was the same old darkness. Except now it did not frighten her. It strengthened her.

Grandteacher Hurlo had taught Bleak Hope many things. Unfortunately, long-distance sea navigation had mostly been theoretical training, with very little practical application. She had never sailed more than a few miles from Galemoor. She had studied maps, of course. She knew the general layout of the surrounding islands, and theoretically, she knew the course she would need to keep in order to reach the closest port before the supplies on her little boat ran out. But after two days at sea with no land in sight and less than a day's rations remaining, she had to admit that she was lost.

She scanned the empty horizon, sunlight sparkling so hard on the surface of the water that she had to squint. A cold wind whipped through her long blond hair, giving some relief from the heat that was turning her pale skin into an angry red.

She should be less than a half-day from port, but the whole world seemed empty – of land, of humanity, of anything. The only indication of life was an odd cluster of bubbles that rose to the surface now and then.

She opened the bag that contained the remaining food and water. The grandteacher had not packed a map. That might have helped. Or perhaps not. The sunlight beat down hard directly above, and she couldn't even be certain she was traveling in the right direction. A compass would have been helpful, she decided. But he hadn't packed one of those either.

What the grandteacher *had* packed was a suit of the black leather armor worn by Vinchen warriors. The boots, leggings, and jacket were thick enough to slow down an arrow or bullet but not so heavy that they impeded movement. They had straps with buckles evenly spaced up the arms and legs, which could be used to hold additional weapons or as tourniquets if the warrior were seriously wounded.

When Hope had discovered the armor on the first morning, she hadn't immediately understood that it was hers. After all, only a true brother of the order was allowed to don the black armor. It was something that she had assumed, even in the deepest part of her training, would always be beyond her reach. Yet here was the smallest armor she had ever seen. She remembered a night when the grandteacher had taken careful measurements of her. He had not given a reason, and it would have been presumptuous of her to ask. He must have cut and bound the armor himself, since the tanner would have been suspicious of the size. The grandteacher must have also oiled and polished it himself. She held it up to the sun and watched admiringly as the light gleamed off the black creases. She imagined him working the polish slowly into the leather with his wrinkled old hands, just for her.

She wished she hadn't left him there to be murdered by his own brothers, promises and duty be damned. But of course now it was too late. And she had sworn not to take vengeance on them, so she did not even have that comfort. She hugged the armor to her chest and swore that she would wear it with honor in his name. It was all she had.

Hope pulled off her soft monk's robes and stuffed them into the sack with the food. She paused a moment, staring at the water. Another cluster of bubbles rose to the surface. She wondered what made them. A gust of wind blew past, chilling her skin beneath her thin undergarments. She shivered and pulled on the black leather armor. It fit perfectly.

She was ready for battle.

Or so she thought at the time. It was now a day later, and she was lost and alone. She had one of the greatest blades ever forged and some of the finest armor ever crafted by one of the wisest men who ever lived. But in this battle, there was no one to fight but the sea.

What now? Hope didn't know where she was going. And that was true not just in terms of navigating this stretch of water. She could just as easily have asked *What now?* of her whole life. Hurlo had told her she must endure. But why?

There was one reason she knew. Somewhere out there was a man who had murdered her parents and her village. She would have vengeance on that man. But she didn't know who he was, only that he was a biomancer. Now she was on her own in a world she knew almost nothing about other than what she had read in books. How could she possibly find one man?

As she stared at the horizon, she realized there was something out there. At first, it was little more than a black dot and she thought it might be a small island. But it grew rapidly larger, and she understood that it was moving toward her. Before long, she could make out the details of a merchant ship. Sails billowed from the two tall masts, and the sun gleamed wetly from the feminine figurehead on the bow. She caught a flash near the top of the front mast and realized someone had a spyglass trained on her. There were faint shouts as the sailors called to each other. The sails went slack and the ship slowed as it neared her.

A tall man with a broad blue hat and a wool sea coat leaned over the rail. What little of his face could be seen behind his curly black and gray beard was a darker brown than she had ever seen.

'Ahoy!' he called. 'I'm Captain Carmichael, and this is my ship. Maritime law expects any captain registered under imperial trade to assist a ship in distress. Do you require assistance?'

'I'm lost,' she called up. 'Can you point me in the direction of the nearest port?'

'Aye, but in a vessel like that it's many days off.'

'Many? I only have rations for another day or so.'

Another sailor with a long mustache said something to the captain that she couldn't hear. The captain turned to him, regarding him without expression. Then he turned back to her.

'I could spare you some rations,' he said. 'But you're in deep waters and in a little boat like that, like as not the oarfish will get you.'

'Oarfish?'

'Great big sea serpents,' called the man with the long mustache. 'They swim vertical beneath the surface, gazing up at the dark shadows above them until they see or smell something that looks like prey. And, as everyone knows, sea serpents of all kinds are drawn to the scent of womenfolk. They're probably tracking you as we speak.' He turned to the rest of the crew. 'We shouldn't have even stopped. Now she's put us *all* in danger.'

'You best shut your mouth, Ranking,' said Captain Carmichael calmly.

'Or what?' retorted Ranking. 'You've already doomed us with this showy bit of sentimentality.' He eyed the surface of the water warily. 'I tell you, they could be on us at any time.' Then he turned back to the other sailors. 'And don't think we're safe up here! Oarfish can—'

Hope's small sailboat vibrated beneath her feet, and the water surrounding her began to bubble, then boil. She vaulted into the air and landed on the larger ship's rail, balancing on the balls of her feet. A moment later, the smaller boat smashed to pieces as a mouth with teeth as long as her forearm shot up from beneath it. The oarfish rose ten feet into the air with no sign of where it ended. Its snakelike body was as thick around as a man's chest and a dark mottled green. It curved its head around and fixed her with its black glassy eyes, then dropped back below the surface.

The sailors ran to the cabins and the rigging, shouts, curses, and prayers filling the air.

'He ain't done yet,' Captain Carmichael said as he looked up at Hope, who was still balanced on the rail. 'You might want to get down from there.'

She smiled slightly as she looked down at him from her perch. 'You might want to clear to one side.'

The oarfish burst from the water again, this time angled so that it came directly at Hope. At the last instant, she darted to one side and the oarfish flew past her. The Song of Sorrows slid from its sheath, sunlight glinting on the blade as it hummed through the air and came down just past the gills, slicing cleanly through. The head continued on its trajectory, the gaping maw still open, until it slammed into the main mast, the teeth embedding into the wood. The headless body slammed onto the deck, spraying blood and seawater as it slid to the starboard rail before coming to a halt. Only then did Bleak Hope jump from the port rail to land soundlessly beside the captain.

'You see?' shouted Ranking. 'She brought in an oarfish as sure as anything. I was right!'

'Whether she brought it in or not,' said Carmichael, 'she sure as piss took it out.' He turned to her. 'Are you retained?'

'Retained?' she asked.

'Do you swear loyalty to anyone? Does someone pay you?' She shook her head.

'You aren't thinking of bringing her on board, Captain?' said Ranking. 'A woman? That's the worst kind of luck!'

Carmichael looked from Ranking to Hope, then to the headless oarfish. Finally, he addressed the whole crew. 'Man, woman. Don't see how that makes a whole lot of difference. What I do see is a *warrior*, the like of which you don't come across too often in your life.' He turned back to Hope. 'How about it? Care to join my crew for a spell?'

Hope considered it. The captain had stopped to offer her assistance. He had called her a warrior. He seemed to be a somewhat honorable man. 'Do you travel a great deal? All over the empire?'

'We do.'

She looked around at the ship. It was true she didn't know much about the world. But she couldn't think of a better place to learn.

'Very well, Captain,' she said. 'You have my sword for a time. Until I feel I must move on.'

'Fair enough,' he said. 'Doubt I could keep you from going anyway.'

'Captain, no—' Ranking stepped toward them, but he jerked to a halt when Hope whipped her blade around, setting the point an inch from his throat.

'Contradicting the captain could be considered mutiny, punishable by death,' she said quietly.

'She has the right of it,' Carmichael said. 'So you want to tell me how you planned to end that sentence?'

'Uh . . .' Sweat trickled down Ranking's temple as he eyed the blade that was still wet with the dark blood of the oarfish. 'I was saying, Captain, no, please let me be the first to welcome her aboard, seeing as how I was so rude to her at first.'

Carmichael grinned, showing yellow teeth in his black beard. 'Anyone else with an objection?'

The ship was silent.

Captain Carmichael nodded approvingly, then turned back to Hope. 'What's your name, warrior?'

'My name is Bleak Hope.'

'Well, Hope, welcome aboard the *Lady's Gambit*.'

8

*I*t was the grand opening of the Three Cups dance hall, and Red had no intention of sleeping that night. The sun had just set, and already the floor was packed with young toms and mollies hoping for a little flash in their otherwise muddy existence.

'It's awful crowded,' observed Filler, who stood next to him at their spot against the wall. Eight years later and Filler was still the tallest wag Red knew, and thanks to his recent apprenticeship at the smithy, also one of the strongest. He kept his hair close cropped, and had the wispy beginnings of a beard on his chin.

'Crowded is good,' said Red, brushing his dark hair out of his ruby eyes as he scanned the room. The band sat off in the corner: a guitar, horn, flute, and drums. They were playing nice and fast, but despite that and the crowds, no one was dancing. The toms and mollies stood on opposite sides of the room, eyeing each other, not quite sure how to proceed. He remembered Sadie had said that back before Jix the Lift ran Paradise Circle, dance halls were common. Jix had turned them all into brothels and drug dens. Red's generation never had the opportunity to experience a dance hall. But now Jix was gone, and it was a new era. The era of Deadface Drem.

Red saw Drem over by the bar. A bit on the tall side, with a long face, pale, almost colorless eyes, and thinning, carefully combed hair. He wore a pat gray jacket and a black cravat like the kind lacies wore. You wouldn't know it to look at him, but Deadface Drem was the most powerful gang lord in Paradise Circle and notorious throughout all the neighborhoods for being a cold, unscrupulous smuggler, pimp, murderer, and even occasional police informant when it suited him. He'd started running a rival drug operation to Jix a few years back. It had been a long time since anyone had tested Jix, and maybe his reaction was a little excessive. One night when Drem and his molly were walking home from a tavern, Jix and a group of his wags cornered them in an alley. Jix said he would let Drem go if he could watch his girl get tortured, raped, and murdered without getting upset. Drem watched the whole thing, his face dead calm, and that's how he got his nickname. True to his word, when they all had their fun, Jix let Drem go. But every night after, one of Jix's men was found dead, brutally mutilated, until finally it was Jix they found one morning, strangled with his own guts. That was how Drem got his reputation.

That night, Deadface Drem sat at the bar of his new dance hall and looked out at all the people not dancing in it. He did not look pleased.

'Let's do old Deadface a favor and get the dancing started,' said Red.

'What?' The look on Filler's face was absolute panic. Ever since Red had gotten back from his pirating adventures with Sadie, Filler had fallen in behind Red as if it was the most natural thing in the world. He had followed Red into many dangerous, potentially deadly situations since then. But Red could tell at a glance that asking him to dance in front of people was too much a test of even his loyalty.

Red patted his best wag on the shoulder. 'Alright, then. Wish me luck.' He scanned the line of mollies on the opposite side, looking for a likely candidate. Someone attractive, of course. But she also had to be bold enough to join him in the first dance this hall had ever seen. Then he saw her. Long curly dark hair and smoldering brown eyes. High, perfect cheekbones and full lips. She wore a short wool jacket and breeches instead of a dress, but that seemed to accentuate her curves even more. Her high leather boots were set in a square stance that said she was not taking any nonsense from anybody. Red had seen her around and had thought about approaching her. Now was the perfect opportunity. Two loops in the knot.

The hall didn't go silent as Red crossed the empty dance zone between the two groups, but he felt like maybe the general volume of conversation dipped a little. And maybe it seemed like the guitarist was giving him a grateful look. Red imagined there were a lot of people depending on the success of this club, and this could be his way of helping them out. Make that three loops in the knot.

He crossed the rest of the empty space and now stood in front of the dangerous, dark-eyed molly he'd spotted. She had watched him approach with a cool, studied expression. He flashed a grin and said, 'Good evening.'

'What's wrong with your eyes?' she asked.

'Terrible sad story. Just now, when they witnessed your otherworldly beauty, they went fiery red with passion. I fear it might be permanent unless I'm allowed to dance with you.'

'That so?' she said. 'Never had that effect on a leaky tom before.'

'That's because you never met a tom like me before. What's your name?'

'They call me Nettles.'

'Who does?'

'Anyone smart enough to realize they better call me what I pissing well want to be called. And you must be Red.'

'You heard of me?' Red was pleased.

'Mostly that you're a thief, liar, and cheat.'

'It's more fanciful embroidering than actual lies,' said Red.

'Some of the mollies say you ain't a real person. That Sadie the Goat made a deal with a necromancer and raised you up from some hell, and that's why you've got red eyes.'

Red felt like this conversation was rapidly going leeward, and he fought to keep his grin intact. 'Some mollies will always say things.'

'I also heard trouble follows you as loyally as that big ox of a wag you always have with you. That you'd steal from your own grandmom if you had one, that the imps use your portrait for target practice, and let's see . . . oh yeah, that your dad was a whore.'

Red thought about trying to refute those accusations, but he had to admit, at least to himself, that most of them were true. He could try to keep pushing, but at a certain point, there was more dignity in a graceful retreat.

'Well, Nettles. I guess you must know me pretty well for never having met me.' Then he turned and steeled himself for the slow, sad walk back to his side of the room.

'I didn't say any of that bothered me,' said Nettles.

His smile slowly returned as he looked back over his shoulder at her. 'Not even the bit about being from hell?'

She shrugged. 'Depends on how good of a dancer you are.'

He turned back and held out his hand to her. 'The best in Paradisc Circle. Care to verify it?'

'Might as well. I was getting bored just standing here anyway.'

The two walked out into that great big empty space, and this time he was sure the musicians were smiling at him as their tune suddenly surged with energy. They danced for a while. Red was as good as he said, but Nettles was slightly better. She moved like water, a constant flow that never missed a beat. She was not shy about getting close either. They pressed together, hip to hip, her breasts against him, her warm breath on his neck. She smelled like sandalwood and spice. Then she slid her hand between them and pushed him back, keeping her hand pressed flat against his abdomen, a wicked smile on her face. Then she let him ease back in for a little while, so close her thick eyelashes brushed his chin. She pushed him away again, but not so far that he was out of reach. It became a game of sorts. How close could he get? And for how long?

Red fought through the heat of his leaky brain. He was getting distracted. The main plan was working. Other couples were stepping out onto the dance floor. He glanced at Deadface Drem by the bar and saw that he looked, if not happy, at least satisfied.

Nettles pulled him in close and pressed her soft lips to his ear. 'Why do I feel like you've got a whole 'nother thing in play here?'

'I'm a complicated wag,' he said. 'I've always got a few things in play. But you are by far the prettiest.'

She slipped her fingers into his waistband and tugged gently. 'Oh, I'm part of one of your schemes, am I?'

'The centerpiece.'

'What if you're part of one of my schemes?'

'As long as they don't conflict, I have no problem with that.' The floor was full of dancers now. He wouldn't attract attention if he left. But there was still the matter of this molly tugging at his pants. He was tempted to save his plan for another night and pursue this beauty tonight. But if he was going to roll this place, tonight was his best chance of success. 'Tell you what, Nettles. If you let me slip away quietly right now without any fuss, I swear I will commit myself whole-heartedly to whatever scheme you have in mind at another time.'

'Interesting proposition.' She considered it for a moment. 'Yeah, alright. Tomorrow at noon. Outside Gunpowder Hall.'

'I'll be there.'

'I know you will.' She released him, a slight smile on her face. Red felt like she had one on him. He wasn't used to that feeling, and decided he didn't like it at all. Well, he mostly didn't like it. There was a tiny part of him that liked it quite a lot. He gave her one last look, then slipped into the crowd.

Filler still stood against the wall with a couple of other toms. He was a full head taller than anyone else in the room. Sometimes Red wished his best wag didn't stick out so much. But his size was helpful as often as not. Especially if things went leeward, which, Red was the first to admit, sometimes they did. But this wouldn't be one of those times. This plan was solid.

'You ready?' he quietly asked Filler.

Filler nodded, and the two made their way through the crowds toward the exit. Then, at the last moment, they veered off down a side hallway, the staff entrance that led toward the back of the bar. Had they tried that move earlier when no one was dancing, it would have been in plain view of the guards on the floor. But now there was a wall of people between them. Filler still had to hunch down, but soon they were moving quickly down the service hallway to the back of the bar. Both bartenders were over by Drem, ready to get him anything he needed. All three were still watching the dancing.

Crouching again so their heads couldn't be seen above the bar, Red and Filler eased past them to the stockroom. There was a large door at the back of the stockroom that led to the alley behind the building, where casks of spirits and barrels of ale were delivered. There was also a large wooden hatch in the floor of the stockroom. Filler popped it open and they followed the sturdy wooden steps to the cellar. The space stretched under most of the building, with hard-packed dirt floors, casks and barrels stacked neatly on either side. The ceiling was high enough that Red could stand up straight, but Filler had to stoop a little. There was a narrow aisle in the center that stretched the length of the cellar. At the far end, barely visible in the dim lamplight, was a massive safe. Red knew the wag who had installed the thing, which was why he knew it existed. He also knew it was where Deadface Drem kept all his money.

They walked noiselessly on the dirt floor to the safe. It was the largest Red had ever seen, spanning from floor to ceiling and just as wide. It was impressive. But a lock was a lock. If anything, the size of the keyhole might make it even easier to pick.

Filler kept an eye on the steps while Red took out his lock-picking tools and went to work. It was new and well oiled. That and its size made it the easiest lock he had ever picked. Within minutes he heard the satisfying *click* of a job well done.

As the massive door began to swing slowly open, he said, 'Filler, my old pot, we've got—'

He stopped when he saw what was in the safe. His informant had been right. There was more money in that safe than Red had ever seen in one place. What the informant hadn't known about was the armed guard inside with it.

'Hello, boys,' said Brackson, Drem's number two. He pointed his rifle at Red's face. 'Drem had a hunch someone stupid might try something like this.'

Red held his hands up. 'Would you believe I was looking for a place to piss?'

'Turn around,' said Brackson.

Red turned back toward the steps and joined Filler, who also had his hands up.

'Now, up to the stockroom,' said Brackson.

Red and Filler walked side by side up the steps.

'Hey, Red,' said Filler.

'Shut up or I'll shoot that pathetic attempt at a beard right off your face,' said Brackson.

Once they reached the main floor, Brackson had them stand in front of the door that led to the alley.

'Drem don't want no commotion on his grand opening, so we're going to go out back to . . . discuss this.'

'Sounds reasonable.' Red was confident that once they were out in the open, dodging this boot wouldn't be that difficult.

'Oh yeah?' Brackson sounded amused. 'Why don't you go ahead and open the door, then.'

When Red opened the door, he saw why Brackson was amused. Seven more of Drem's boots sat in the alley, playing stones and looking bored. But when they saw Red and Filler with their hands up, they stood, looking a lot less bored.

'Got us a couple of safe-picking gafs here,' Brackson called to them.

'I don't actually pick safes,' said Filler.

'Move forward or you'll be picking lead out of your skull.' Brackson jammed his rifle into Filler's back, then Red's. The two lurched forward into the alley. Red noticed that Brackson was the only one armed with a gun. The rest had knives and clubs. If he could just come up with a way to take out Brackson, he thought they could handle the rest. He slowly moved his hand down toward the back of his neck.

'Oh, now,' said Brackson. 'You wouldn't happen to have a blade back there.'

Red felt cold metal on his sweaty neck.

'Nah, just had an itch, old pot,' Red said with forced cheer.

'Here, let me scratch it with—'

There was a jangle of chain and Brackson dropped to the cobblestones. Behind him stood Nettles, a thick chain coiled around her fist. 'I don't think much of your plan,' she told Red.

Red pulled the knife strapped to his back and threw it at one of the boots. The blade went through his eye and he dropped to the ground. 'Are you kidding? It's going perfectly.'

Nettles snapped her chain out like a whip and caught another boot in the face. She watched as the man clutched a mouth full of blood and broken teeth. 'Oh, I'm still your centerpiece?'

Red pulled a second knife from his boot and whipped it at a third man, catching him in the heart. 'A centerpiece this lovely should last the whole meal.'

Nettles coiled her chain around her fist again and slammed it into the fourth boot's stomach. She quickly stepped to one side to avoid the vomit that gushed from his mouth. 'Don't act like you knew I was going to help you out of this stupidity.'

'And how should I act?' Red drew his last knife from his belt, dodged under the swing of the fifth boot's club, then spun and stabbed him in the back.

'A bit of honest surprise, maybe.' Nettles smashed her chain-wrapped fist on the vomiting boot's head, knocking him to the street.

'Does a wag act surprised when the glorious sun suddenly shines through dark and cloudy skies?' asked Red as he finished off his boot by slicing his throat. 'No, he simply smiles with gratitude and gets on with his business.'

Nettles shook her head, but smiled a little. 'Do you ever run out of those lines?'

'Haven't yet.' He turned to Filler, who had the last two boots, one in each hand, and was bashing their heads together repeatedly. 'You about done?'

Filler slammed their heads together one last time, then let them drop. 'Yeah.'

'Then I suggest we make ourselves scarce before Drem gets wind of this.'

The three of them ran through the streets of Paradise Circle. It was a late-spring evening. It had rained a little earlier and the air still held a whiff of freshness – a rare thing in downtown New Laven. Their boots slapped against the wet cobblestones as they put some distance between themselves and the Three Cups.

Red should have felt disappointed. He'd been planning this scheme all week and he was coming away with nothing. Less than nothing, since Brackson would probably remember him, and that meant Red could never show his face at the first and only dance hall in Paradise Circle. So then why did he feel so sunny?

He glanced over at Nettles. Maybe the evening wasn't a total loss. She was a good wag to have on his side. Smart, good in a fight, and nice to look at as well.

After they'd run ten blocks, they stopped to catch their breath.

'So, any plans for the rest of the evening?' Red asked Nettles.

'The original plan had been to dance at Drem's new hall, but clearly that's not happening.'

'Sorry.'

Nettles shrugged. 'My curiosity. It gets to me sometimes. I had to know what you two were up to.' She gave him a speculative look. 'Still, if you feel responsible, I suppose I could let you make it up to me.'

'Oh? And how would I go about doing that?'

She reached out and hooked her finger on his waistband like she had at the dance hall, and drew him close. 'Finish where we left off. Have somewhere private we can go?'

'Yeah, um, sure I do.' Red gave Filler a pleading look.

Filler looked questioningly at him for a moment, then understanding broke on his face. 'Oh, right. I'll just spend the night at Henny and the Twins' place.'

'I owe you one, Fill!' said Red.

'You do,' agreed Filler. 'Night, then.' He turned and walked off down the street.

'Well, then, I supposed we . . .' Red trailed off as Nettles leaned in and pressed her lips to his neck. The words just left. A first for him, really. All that remained was heat and hunger. His body was suddenly filled with it. He looked down at her as her lips parted slightly and her tongue darted out to wet them. His hands gripped her upper arms, which were smooth and taut with muscle, and he kissed her hard. She grabbed a fistful of his hair and pressed their mouths together even tighter. It was like they were two starving people, eating each other's heat, unable to get enough.

Finally she broke the kiss. Her soft lips brushed his cheek as she said, 'How about that someplace private?'

Red was only dimly aware of the walk home. Even though he'd been on these streets for eight years now, they seemed strangely unfamiliar. It felt as if the world had been put under a spell. All the confusion and complexity had been stripped away, and there was only this one need he had for this beautiful molly. He kept his arm around her shoulder, and she kept her arm around his waist. It wasn't a very practical way to walk, but he worried that if he let go of her, the magic would end.

Somehow in this state they made it to his building, up the rickety stairs, and into the tiny room that he and Filler shared. The moment the door was closed, they were grabbing each other, clumsily pulling each other's clothes off. The sound of heavy breathing and belts unbuckling, of the *thump* of bodies hitting the wooden floorboards, of sweaty skin pressing against skin, peeling off, then slapping together again.

Red had held on to his distaste for sex longer than most boys. He'd done his share of kissing and groping, but the spectral memory of that hairy old captain had always stopped him from more. Now that memory burned in a puff of smoke from his hunger for this girl. He wanted her so badly that his hands shook. Her perfect face, her taut neck, her smooth shoulders, her firm breasts, her flat stomach, her strong legs. Hells, even the backs of her knees looked like works of art to him. He wanted all of her. He pressed down on her, covering her whole body with his so that their heat combined until it was a furnace. Then she guided him inside her, and all his clever words were reduced to one endless, 'Yes, yes, yes, yes.'

'Red, why's there a naked lady in your bed? And where's Filler?'

Red opened his eyes. Feeble light streamed in through the one window. Nettles lay next to him on his sleeping mat, the blanket more or less covering them both. Little Bee, the neighbor's six-year-old daughter, stood over them, her skinny little arms crossed.

'Piss'ell, Bee,' he groaned, trying to spread the blanket out so it better covered him and Nettles. 'Didn't I tell you to knock?'

'I did knock. You didn't answer.'

'Maybe it was because I didn't want visitors.'

Little Bee squinted at him like he wasn't making sense.

'Who in all hells is that?' Sunlight filtered through Nettles's mussed hair in a way that Red found very pleasing to look at, but her frown was like a thundercloud.

'My name is Jilly, but everybody calls me Little Bee, because I'm so busy. I live next door and I come visit Red and Filler all the time. Who are you?'

Nettles glared at Red. 'Why did you let her in?'

'I didn't,' he said wearily.

'She has a key?'

'Worse. I taught her how to pick locks.'

'Why in hells did you do that?'

'I don't know. She'd been bugging me nonstop about something.'

'I wanted him to show me how to throw a knife properly,' said Little Bee.

'There, see?' said Red. 'Lock picking doesn't sound so bad as an alternative, does it?' He turned back to Little Bee. 'Alright, you little mole rat. I need some privacy. You go on home.'

'My mom's gone missing. I think the Jackal Lords took her.'

Red sighed. Little Bee's mom, Jacey, drank too much and had terrible taste in men. She was not the most reliable parent, and this would not be the first time she hadn't come home. There'd been many a day that Little Bee wouldn't have eaten if Red and Filler didn't see to it.

'I'm sure it wasn't the Jackal Lords, Bee. Why don't you go down to the Drowned Rat and see if Prin will give you a few coppers to help her scrub the tankards. I'll meet you there later and we'll ask around if anyone's seen your mom.'

'Why don't I help you, and then you give me some coppers?'

'Because I don't need your help right now, and I haven't got any coppers. Now go.'

Little Bee stuck her tongue out at him and left, slamming the door behind her.

Red turned to see Nettles regarding him strangely. 'What?'

'All the rumors and gossip about you in the Circle. None of it lets on what a sugar lump you are underneath.'

'We all have our flaws.' He reached under the blanket and laid his hand on her bare hip. 'Now how's about another toss?'

She thought about it a moment, her full lips pursed. 'Nah. You still owe me a wholehearted commitment to my plan after cutting out on me on the dance floor.'

'Oh, yeah . . .'

'Forgot your promise so easily?'

'I have a terrible memory.' He smiled innocently. 'It's another one of my flaws.'

It was a typically cool, gray, windy day in Paradise Circle. The streets were bustling with people, horses, wagons, and the occasional carriage. Red and Nettles walked at a leisurely pace, comparing all the friends they had in common. Paradise Circle was small enough that if you didn't know someone, you knew someone who did.

'Do you know Tosh?' asked Nettles.

'Sure. She and I kissed under the docks a few times,' said Red.

'She started whoring a few months back. Works down at Slice of Heaven.'

'Really? I hope she's better at bending cocks than she was at kissing. She did this weird smacking thing.' Red made a sour face.

'The customers love her.'

'Are you a whore there, too?' asked Red.

Nettles glared at him. 'Do I pissing look like a whore?'

Red held up his hands placatingly. 'I didn't know whores had a look.'

'Of course. They're all delicate little pissing flowers who can't do a thing for themselves and never stop complaining.'

'So . . . you work security there, then?'

She looked surprised. 'How'd you know?'

The only time Red remembered his dad complaining about being a whore was not because of a client, but because of the harsh, insensitive manner of the brothel security. 'Lucky guess. So, do you know Handsome Henny?' he asked.

'Henny? Haven't seen him for years,' said Nettles. 'He's handsome now?'

'Nah. Last year he was breaking into a warehouse and a guard dog bit off his nose. Now everybody calls him Handsome Henny.'

Nettles let out a dark, rich chuckle. 'How'd you meet Henny, anyway? Doesn't seem your type of wag.'

'He was in the same pickpocket gang with me and Filler back when I first came to the Circle.'

'What do you mean, first came?'

'I was born in Silverback. My parents died when I was eight and I sort of ended up down here.'

'Oh,' said Nettles.

'Why?'

She shrugged. 'Just didn't realize you weren't a true wag of the Circle is all.'

'So . . .' said Red, trying to shake off the hurt that Nettles didn't consider him a true wag. 'What's this plan of yours anyway?'

By this time, they had arrived at Gunpowder Hall. It was the largest building in Paradise Circle and the most popular place for wags of all kinds to congregate. It was one of the oldest buildings in the Circle as well, with dingy, yellowed marble archways. The outside of the building was ringed with merchant tents that sold food, fabric, clothing, and an assortment of items like tools and small weapons, nearly all of it stolen goods. There were other things that could be purchased at Gunpowder Hall, such as sex, drugs, or murder, but those transactions were handled inside.

'You're well connected around here,' said Nettles. 'Find me a smithy who'll make some custom modifications to my chain. And for cheap.'

'That's simple as sideways,' Red said, eager to show just how well connected he was. 'My best wag, Filler, is an apprentice blacksmith.'

'The one I saved along with you last night?'

'That's him.'

'Hm, I should have gone home with *him*, then.'

'Nah. Wouldn't have done you any good,' he said, again hiding the hurt in his voice. 'Filler prefers the toms.'

'Oh well,' she said. 'He should at least give me some sort of discount for helping out last night.'

Red led her along the line of tents. Merchants called out to them, trying to sell fruit, knives, clothes, even old rusty guns. Down at the end was the smithy tent, about twice the size of the others. It was made of leather instead of canvas to prevent a stray spark from burning it down.

The master smith considered Red a huge distraction for his star apprentice. Red was the first to admit this was mostly true. He'd never understood why Filler wanted a respectable profession when money could be gotten much more easily by other means. The best Filler had been able to explain it was simply that he liked doing it. Red found it hard to argue with that.

Red was in luck that day. When he and Nettles stepped into the tent, he saw that the master smith had left Filler to mind the shop. He was shirtless except for the leather apron and thick leather gloves, pounding an ax head into shape on an anvil.

'Hey,' he said, his face streaming sweat. 'Almost finished with this.' Then he continued to hammer.

It was stifling hot as they waited, and the ring of the hammer made Red's jaw clench. He had no idea how Filler found this experience enjoyable. Nettles seemed less bothered by it. She stood and calmly examined the many finished pieces that hung from the walls of the tent.

Finally, Filler dropped the ax head into a tub of water, which filled the room with steam and made it feel even hotter. But at least the hammering had stopped.

'What's going on?' Filler asked as he mopped his face and neck with a towel.

'You remember Nettles here from last night?' asked Red.

'Sure.'

'She's looking to make some improvements to that chain of hers.'

'It is pretty crude.' He turned to her. 'What kind of improvements?'

'I want something more . . . efficient on the end.' She placed her chain on the small table. 'Maybe a weight or something.'

Filler picked up one end of the chain. 'You want to do more damage?'

'Exactly.'

'You want them dead?'

'Only sometimes. Can't kill every customer because they start acting up. Sometimes a gaf just needs a swift crack on the head to help him remember his manners. But there are other times when dead would be good.'

Filler picked up the other end of the chain. He looked at both ends carefully. 'What if we put a weight on one end, and a blade on the other?'

'A blade?' asked Nettles.

'A small one. Like a knife blade.'

'Filler, that's brilliant!' said Red.

'I don't know . . .' said Nettles. 'It's hard enough to throw. Not sure I'd be accurate enough to make a blade useful.'

Filler nodded. 'It would be better with a much smaller and lighter chain.'

'But then you're talking about a whole new weapon.' Nettles's eyes narrowed. 'How much is that going to cost?'

'Figure I owe you for last night. You get me the material, I'll do the work for free.'

'Linking fine chain and all?' asked Nettles.

'Sure. That's worth me and Red's life, right?'

'And then some,' said Nettles. 'Tell you what, I'll throw in a free toss at the Slice of Heaven. We got plenty of toms there, too, you know.' She held out her hand. 'What do you say?'

'Yeah, sure.' He shook her hand. 'Real generous of you.'

Filler got back to work and Red and Nettles left the sweltering tent.

When they stepped outside, Red sighed with relief. 'I don't know how he can stand it in there for so long.'

'Me neither,' said Nettles, her dark eyes bright and focused. 'Alright, I'll see you around.'

'What? Where you going?' asked Red.

'To get the materials, obviously.'

'Oh. Need any help?'

'Nah, I'll manage. Besides, don't you have to meet that Little Bee of yours to help find her mom?'

'Yeah, I guess,' admitted Red. 'I'll see you later, though?'

'You'll be seeing a lot of me.'

'Really?'

'Sure. Your best wag is making the weapon of my dreams for free. Until it's done, I'll be hovering near him constantly.'

'Oh. Right.'

'Hey now, don't get all poncey and sotted on me, Silverback art boy.'

'I'm not sotted,' Red protested. 'I just . . . like you, is all.'

Nettles reached up and put her hand on the side of his face. 'You're cute. This was fun. I reckon we'll be doing it again soon. That make you feel better?'

Red grinned. 'Sunny.'

She smacked his cheek playfully. 'Good. Now go and help that poor little girl, you softy.'

As Red walked to the Drowned Rat, he wondered if maybe he *was* a little sotted with Nettles. Was that such a bad thing? Sure there were things she said that sounded a bit mean. But they were also kind of funny. And there was something about her, like an invisible pull that made him want to touch her all the time.

One thing was clear: She seemed to think it was a bad thing. So unless he wanted her to slide, he would have to play it pat, no matter how intense he felt. This wasn't a new problem for him, though. Most people in Paradise Circle kept their feelings close and hidden. The fact that Red couldn't always do that, Sadie blamed on his 'soft artsy' childhood.

When he entered the tavern, he saw Little Bee behind the bar, scrubbing at the ale tankards with a coarse brush. Prin, the barkeep, stood nearby watching her.

'Hey, Prinny,' said Red. 'Letting the kid do all the work, I see.'

Prin shrugged. 'I told her five and I'd help, or ten if she did them all herself. Not my fault she's greedy.'

Red motioned for her to come to the other end of the bar, out of earshot. Prin frowned and followed him down.

'You work last night?' he asked quietly.

'If you can call it that,' said Prin. 'Place was near dead on account of the Three Cups opening. By the way, did you hear? Some bludgeon tried to roll the place.'

'Hadn't heard that,' said Red carelessly.

Prin's eyes narrowed. 'It was you, wasn't it? I swear, Red, if you ever try to roll this place, I'll—'

'Prinny, my sweet provider of ale, I would never!' said Red. 'The Drowned Rat is like a second home to me.'

'True enough.'

'That's not what I wanted to talk to you about, though. Since it was so slow last night, maybe you remember seeing Little Bee's mom?'

Prin thought about it for a moment. 'Yeah, she was in, but not long. Came in here already drunk, yelling about Deadface Drem being a snake and a liar or something. I told her she'd had enough to drink and should probably watch what she said besides. She and Brackson have history, but I figured it wasn't smart to go cursing his boss like that.'

'Then she left?'

'After cursing me out a bit, thanks. Then I saw her through the window talking to an imp patrol on the street. Well, yelling at them more like.'

'Then what?'

She shrugged. 'I stopped watching. Had a customer and anyway she wasn't my problem anymore. I figured the imps would handle her.'

'Probably brought her down to the Hole to dry out,' said Red. 'Bet she's still there.' He leaned over the bar and called, 'Hey, Bee. When you're done with that, we'll go down and collect your mom from the Hole.'

She stopped scrubbing for a moment and sighed dramatically. 'Again? I guess I don't need to hurry, then.'

*   *   *

There was a saying in Paradise Circle: *Every circle has a hole*.
Over time, it came to mean no place was perfect. But the
original meaning was a specific reference to the Hole, a nickname for the large jail cell at the imperial police station in the
center of Paradise Circle. Red found this sort of history
fascinating. No one else he knew did, though, except Little
Bee. Maybe that was why they got along, despite their many
differences.

'How do you know all this historical stuff?' she asked him
as they walked to the imp station.

'I read it in books,' said Red.

'You read? How'd you learn to do that?'

'My mom taught me when I was about your age.'

'Could you teach me?'

'Maybe. It's not an easy thing to learn like lock picking.'

'I'm pretty smart, though, Red.'

He smiled. 'You are at that, Little Bee.'

The imperial police station in Paradise Circle was not a
large or impressive building. Supposedly it had been both
once. But it had been burned down so many times, it seemed
they gave up and just put up the cheapest, most unassuming
building they could. No one had tried to burn it down since.

Red and Little Bee walked through the main entrance.
The front room was small. One lone imp sat at a table, looking bored, his white-and-gold uniform unbuttoned and
wrinkled.

'Good afternoon, sir,' Red said cheerfully.

The imp eyed him suspiciously. 'Don't I know you?'

'I doubt it,' Red said blandly. It was entirely possible they
had met, and probably not under good circumstances. 'We're
just here to pick up this girl's mother from the Hole.'

The imp reached for a piece of paper on his desk. 'Name?'

'My name is Jilly, but everyone calls me Little Bee because
I'm so busy.'

'Your mom's name,' he said with irritation.

'Oh, her name is Jacey.'

The imp scanned down his list of names. When he reached the bottom, Red noticed his eyebrows gave a little jump. 'You sure it's Jacey?'

'Of course I know my own mom's name,' said Little Bee in a snotty tone.

But it didn't seem to bother the imp. All the irritation had left him, to be replaced with something that looked a lot like pity. He cleared his throat and looked fixedly at Red. 'She, uh, volunteered for imperial service.'

'She *what*?' asked Red.

The imp glanced at Little Bee, but only for a moment. Then he was back to Red. 'If this girl has any family anywhere, she should go live with them.' He swallowed. 'Until her mom is done with her service, of course.'

'Have you met Jacey?' demanded Red. 'Do you have any idea how slippy that sounds?'

The imp's face was tense. 'I don't know her. That's what the paper says. That's all I know.'

'Don't give me that balls and pricks. You know more than that.'

The imp pulled out a pistol. 'That's all I can tell you. Now you need to leave. And don't talk about this anymore. To anyone. For your own good and hers. Do you understand?'

Red stood there and glared at him, his fists balled up.

'Red, he's pointing a gun at you,' said Little Bee.

'I know, Bee.'

'We should go,' she said.

'You heard her.' The imp was trying to look stern, but there was something almost pleading behind it. 'Go.'

Red took Little Bee's hand, then turned and stalked out of the station.

'That's pretty weird, huh?' said Little Bee.

'It is,' agreed Red.

'I guess she wanted to make the empire a safer place, huh? That's what they do when they become imp soldiers.'

'That so?' asked Red, his expression still dark.

'Better an imp than a stinky old drunk, right, Red?'

Red didn't think Jacey had enlisted in the imperial army. She would never do it and they wouldn't have accepted her anyway. About the only thing she would be accepted for was as a test subject for some biomancer experiment. And nobody 'volunteered' for that. But what good would it do telling Little Bee? Jacey was dead or worse now. Better that Bee think her mom was off marching around in a uniform somewhere. So he just said, 'Right, Little Bee.'

That's how it was in the Circle. Now and then, someone was taken by the biomancers. He was supposed to just accept it.

9

*T*he *Lady's Gambit* was a midsize, two-mast brig that bought and sold cargo all over the empire. Captain Carmichael employed a crew of ten men, although Hope wasn't sure why, since only half of them seemed to be working at any given time. The rest lounged on the deck, drinking grog and playing a game with little numbered stones.

'It's true that when the weather is fair, she only needs a crew of four or five,' said Carmichael when Hope asked. He held the wheel easily in his calloused hands, his dark brown eyes gazing to the horizon. 'A steady breeze and a clear sky makes it look easy enough. But the sea can be fickle, and she'll turn on you in a single breath of wind. When the weather's foul, the extra hands at the rigging could mean the difference between life and a watery grave.'

'Killed by the weather?' Hope asked skeptically.

He gave her a knowing smile. 'You'll see soon enough, if my nose is right. And it usually is.'

'You can smell a storm?'

'There's a certain taste to the air, and an unnatural calmness to the water. Look there.' He pointed to the dark green stippled water that stretched before them. 'Can you see it there, holding its breath, like it's ready to pounce?'

Hope shook her head.

'You only just came aboard. You'll get the hang of it in time. Now go tell Ranking we best batten down. This one's going to be bad.'

The only clouds Hope could see were far off on the horizon. It seemed unlikely that they would reach the ship soon, if at all. But she made her way across the deck to the fore of the ship, where most of the crew was gathered. The sun was shining down hard and the wind had been faint all day, so the sailors were all stripped down to the waist, their thin, sinewy shoulders tan and gleaming with sweat. Two of them were arguing about the stones game they were playing, and the others were chiming in with their opinions. As Hope walked past them, the argument broke out into a fistfight. The two sailors punched and kicked and bit each other with brutish savagery, while the rest sat and cheered for one or the other. Ranking leaned against the rail and watched the fight with an amused smile.

When Hope reached him, she said, 'The captain said you—'

'Leave off until they've finished.' Ranking waved his hand in her direction, not bothering to look away from the fight.

Things had not improved in the few days since their first meeting. But Ranking was first mate, and his authority extended to everyone on the crew except Hope. The rest of the crew would not listen to her. She could do nothing except wait until the fight was over.

As she watched the crude exchange, she keenly missed the quiet calm of the monastery. Racklock and Crunta had been cruel, but they had at least been predictable. She had learned how to manage or avoid them years ago. On this ship, drunken bouts of violence were liable to erupt at any time, with no purpose except to relieve boredom. These sailors lacked any decorum, discipline, or as far as she could tell, sobriety. At first, she had found it difficult to tell who was drunk, until she realized that they were all drunk, all the time. There was a passage in the Vinchen code that cautioned against excessive consumption of strong drink. She had never understood the concern before. The monks brewed ale, and they drank it in moderation, savoring each sip. But these sailors poured grog down their throats as if it were water, and if they remarked on the taste at all, it was only to wince at the unpleasantness. At any given time, half the crew seemed barely able to stand, much less sail a ship. She wondered how they even made it from one port to the next.

'Well, Southie,' said Ranking as the two fighters dropped to the deck in exhaustion with no clear victor, 'what was it you wanted?' He glared at Hope impatiently, as if he had been the one waiting on her.

'The captain said to batten down. There's a bad storm coming.'

Ranking's eyes went wide. 'Piss'ell, why didn't you say so before?'

'I tried—'

'No time to be getting into pointless arguments with the likes of you.' Ranking blew shrilly on a tin whistle he had on a string around his neck. 'Listen up, you bludgeon toms! We've got a luffer coming down our throats before this sun sets. The captain ain't never been wrong about a storm and I don't expect this one will be any different. So unless you want to be bedding down with the crabs tonight, I suggest you batten down and get to your stations.'

He blew his whistle again and the crew instantly got to their feet, looking alert and clear-headed, as if the whistle had cast a magic spell over them all. They split off into different directions, their faces full of purpose.

Hope turned to Ranking, a little awed by the sudden change he had wrought on the men. 'What can I do?'

'Unless you Vinchen have figured out how to stab a storm in its eye, just stay the hells out of the way.'

Hope watched as the sailors went about their work, still marveling at their transformation. They sealed all the port-holes, latched the doors, secured the lines, and stowed any loose items in little wooden compartments that had been built into the deck at certain points along the ship. And then they waited.

Under normal circumstances, waiting would have included a great deal of drinking, yelling, and violence among the sailors. But now they stood quietly at their stations, some on the deck, some up in the rigging. Their eyes remained alert, and their expressions grave. As the skies darkened, one of them began to hum in a low voice. Two others began to hum as well, a ghostly harmony carried on the strengthening wind. Then from up in the rigging, the smallest and youngest member of the crew besides Hope, a man named Mayfield, started singing in a clear tenor:

> No matter which way the wind goes,
> It never blows for me.
> A sailor's life is never fair,
> But for the beauty of the sea.

The clouds, which had seemed far away before, rolled in so quickly, it looked as though a giant blanket had been thrown across the sky. The dark green waters turned a choppy, white-flecked gray. Lightning snaked across the sky, followed by peals of thunder.

> No matter who I love or hate,
> Or if I married be.
> None of it can hold my heart,
> Like the freedom of the sea.

The sailors stopped singing. The whole world seemed to hold its breath. Then the dark gray sky cracked open. The rain came down in a hissing torrent, hammering Hope's head, shoulders, and back. She made her way across the suddenly slick deck as waves slammed into the side of the ship, sending sheets of seawater across her path. *One hand for the ship, one hand for yourself.* Words Carmichael had spoken to her on the day she arrived now came to her mind. They hadn't made much sense before. But as the ankle-deep waves threatened to pull her feet out from under her and take her over the side, she understood. One hand at all times holding on to something, while the other was at the ready to fend off a line or a boom as it swung past.

Eventually, she reached the helm, where the captain stood, his head held high despite the pounding rain.

'Look lively, my wags! Take in the trysail!' he shouted over the storm.

The ship rode up and down the waves. Soon they grew so high that when the ship dropped down in the valley, Hope couldn't see the sky at all, just a wall of curling dark water. When they crested again, the wind slammed into the white sails so hard, it sounded like a drum.

'Haul in those sails before they're ripped to tatters!' roared Carmichael.

Hope watched through her curtain of streaming blond hair as the sailors climbed the rigging and began to gather in the sails and tie them to the yards. The wind jerked at the wet lines they clung to, and it amazed Hope that they weren't flung out to sea. They slowly worked sail by sail up the masts, which swayed dangerously in the gale.

'Are the masts *bending*?' Hope yelled to Carmichael.

'They have to be supple, or they'd snap like dry twigs in a storm like this,' he shouted back.

The sailors had taken in nearly all the sails. Only the top back sail, which Hope had learned was called the main royal, remained, looking taut as a drum. Then suddenly the sail split and the wind tore at it like an eager beggar, raking through the hole and twisting the sail almost sideways. The sailors slid quickly back down to the deck just as the mast began to bow to the side so low, the top was nearly a forty-five-degree angle to the water.

'Cut that sail loose or it'll rip the mast clean out by the roots!' shouted Carmichael.

Ranking, the ends of his long mustache dripping with water, nodded grimly to the captain. He pulled a knife from his belt and held it between his teeth. Then he began to climb the mainmast, as it whipped back and forth like a switch.

'How is he even holding on?' yelled Hope.

Carmichael laughed. 'Say what you will about Ranking, he's a true sailor, with fishhooks for fingers!'

Ranking slowly made his way up the mainmast. Every time the ship crested a swell, a fresh blast of wind slammed into him. He held on, waiting for the ship to drop back into the valley where they were somewhat sheltered so he could continue his ascent. Finally he reached the top and cut the lines. The sail flew off into the air, then darted down into the water, where it disappeared quickly in the churning gray. The mast eased back into an upright position. Ranking slid down to the deck and into the waiting arms of the crew, who cheered and lustily sang a new tune over the roar of the waves and thunder:

> *A sailor in the storm,*
> *Is small as Old Wrink's prick.*
> *Better know,*
> *Which way to go,*
> *Or the sea will take you quick!*

The storm finally passed near sunset. The sea evened out, the wind and rain tapered off, and the clouds parted to reveal a yellow sunset that turned the water to molten gold. The sunlight filtered through the still-dripping rigging, casting small patches of rainbow through the ship. The sailors, who had been working continuously to keep everything secure, stopped and lifted their faces to the sun, their eyes closed and faces smiling.

'How about it, Hope?' asked Carmichael. 'Still scoff at the weather?'

'Never again.' And she meant not just the weather, but these men. When it was necessary, they had shown a bold courage and reckless tenacity unlike any she had ever seen, even among the Vinchen warriors. Both the sea and the sailors earned her respect that day.

'Hey, Southie!' called Ranking. 'Thanks for not being a meddling slice and letting us get on with our jobs!'

Even Ranking, Hope was surprised to discover, had earned a little of her respect. Although she wondered how long it would be before he squandered that away.

That night, the sailors got drunker than ever. They ate and drank and sang for hours. On the previous nights, Hope had kept her distance, made uneasy by their coarse, frequently lewd behavior. But that night as she watched them, she began to understand the camaraderie and true fondness for each other that lay beneath their rude speech and rough action. She had agreed to stay on this ship awhile, learning about the world and the people in it. It occurred to her that standing aloofly as she had these past few nights was not the way to go about that. But could she ever call such men comrades?

'They can be filthy as sturgeons and loud as a pack of gulls.' Captain Carmichael sat next to her. 'But they're a damn fine crew in a pinch.'

'Shouldn't you be celebrating with them?' asked Hope.

'A captain must maintain a certain distance. Can't let his crew get too familiar, or they stop respecting his leadership.'

'It sounds lonely,' said Hope.

'I suppose it might.' Carmichael stared out at the dark water, which glittered with starlight. 'But a man's never truly alone when he has the sea.'

'You talk about the sea as if it was a living thing.'

'It is.'

'But it's just water.'

'The sea is more than just water. It's the plants and the weather. It's creatures in it and on it. It's all those things. You and me, we're part of the sea.'

'I don't feel part of anything,' Hope said quietly.

'What about that Vinchen order you come from?' asked Carmichael. 'Aren't you a part of that?'

Hope didn't know the answer to that question. She was not, nor could she ever be, a true Vinchen warrior. Her gender made that impossible. She knew that. Yet Hurlo had never said so, and the fact that he had made her armor said louder than any words that he considered her a warrior. The thought of him brought a mixture of fondness and pain. The world had lost a great man. She would not want to join the brothers who had murdered him, even if they were to change their minds and allow it.

She wondered if perhaps she could be a part of the sea, and its people. Did she want that? And if she did, would they accept her?

*   *   *

They made port the next day. As Captain Carmichael eased the ship into the docks, Hope stared with wonder at the cluster of buildings, some two-storied, that ran along a clean grid. It was larger than her home village and the monastery of Galemoor combined.

'What city is this?' she asked.

'Wouldn't call Vance Post a city,' said Carmichael. 'More like an oversize trading station.'

'Cities are even bigger than this?'

Carmichael smiled. 'Much.' He cleared his throat and addressed the whole crew. 'Let's get this cargo unloaded so we can get paid.'

The crew were back to their drunken idle selves, but mention of getting paid brought new life to their eyes, and they quickly secured the ship to the pier and unloaded the cargo onto the dock. The dockmaster inspected the cargo, then signed the shipping paper Carmichael gave him.

Carmichael held up the signed paper for Hope to see. 'Now we take this down to the Imperial Trade Commission and exchange it for money.'

The streets of Vance Post were crowded with merchants, some in fine dress, others in simple dress, but all neat and clean. After several days aboard the *Lady's Gambit*, where bathing was too high a luxury to afford, Hope knew how grimy she must look to them, her skin streaked with tar and salt, her yellow hair clumped together in spikes from repeated soakings in seawater. She pushed those self-conscious thoughts to the back of her mind, though. Her primary responsibility was the safety of her captain, so she scanned the streets carefully, her hand close to the pommel of her sword.

'You can relax a little, Southie,' said Ranking. 'I don't reckon we'll see a lot of action in this place.'

'It does seem very orderly,' admitted Hope.

'It's a place where people do business, and not much else,' said Carmichael. 'The only people who live here are merchants and their families. It's the largest port of call in the southeastern part of the empire. If you're trading in this region, you're coming through Vance Post.'

'In other words, this is where the money is,' said Ranking.

'That would seem to make it a tempting target to thieves,' said Hope.

'It might,' said Carmichael. 'If it weren't for the fleet of imperial naval ships stationed here at all times.' He gestured to a large square building across the street from them. Above the dark wood door hung a sign that read IMPERIAL TRADE COMMISSION. It was fixed with the imperial crest, a bolt of lightning colliding with a wave. 'It may not be as impressive as Stonepeak or New Laven, but Vance Post is one of the most important ports of call in the empire. Now, come on. Time to do business. My least favorite part of being a captain.'

He led them through the front doors of the Imperial Trade Commission. The room inside was lit by dim sunlight that filtered in through the windows. Several men lounged idly on benches that lined the walls. On the far side of the room, an imperial officer in a white-and-gold coat sat at a large wooden desk with a small oil lamp. A man stood in front of the desk, his hat in his hands as he talked quietly to the imperial officer. Carmichael stopped a respectful distance from them and waited.

The desk was flanked on either side by an imperial soldier, their gold chest plates glinting dimly from the lamp on the desk. Hope unconsciously tensed up at the sight of the uniforms. It was the first time she had seen those colors since the massacre of her village, and they hadn't changed in the slightest detail. She felt the dark hunger of vengeance beginning to spread and took a deep breath to anchor herself against it.

'Not fond of the imps, eh?' Ranking whispered to her as they waited.

'Imps?' Hope whispered back.

'Imperial soldiers. Thought you Vinchen would be all cozy with them, but your jaw just turned steel, so I reckon you've got a grind.'

'I do not trust imperial soldiers,' she admitted.

'Maybe we do have something in common, then.'

Hope wanted to ask him what he meant, but the man in front of them was gone and the desk was now open, so Carmichael stepped forward.

'Captain Carmichael of the *Lady's Gambit* with a delivery.' He placed the rumpled, salt-stained, signed paper on the clean desk, awkwardly smoothing it out with his rough hands.

The officer held up the sheet with one thumb and forefinger, squinting as he tried to make out the sun-bleached ink. 'Lamp oil, whale bone, salted meat . . . and lumber.'

'Aye,' said Carmichael.

The officer nodded, reached into his desk, and counted out a small stack of coins. 'One gold, twenty silver,' he said as he slid the stack to Carmichael.

'Thank you, sir,' said Carmichael. 'Any new cargo we can pick up?'

'It's been a slow week,' said the officer, nodding to the sailors sitting on the benches. 'Some of them have been waiting days for decent cargo.' He moved a few sheets of paper around on his desk, then held one up. 'The only thing I have right now is a shipment of food and spirits bound for Dawn's Light.'

'Dawn's Light?' asked Ranking. 'But that's—'

'I'll take it,' said Carmichael.

Ranking clamped his mouth shut, but Hope could tell something about the destination alarmed him. The officer seemed surprised as well.

'You can handle the voyage?' he asked.

'I can,' said Carmichael.

The officer shrugged, wrote something on the sheet, and handed it to Carmichael. 'Take this down to the dockmaster and he'll see your cargo gets loaded.'

'Thanks kindly, sir.' Carmichael turned and headed for the door, Hope and Ranking following behind.

As soon as they were back on the street, Ranking said, 'Piss'ell, Captain. Dawn's pissing Light?'

'I've never heard of that island,' said Hope.

'Military outpost way out on the eastern edge of the empire,' said Carmichael. 'Last spit of land before the Dawn Sea.'

'It's pissing no-man's-land,' said Ranking. 'You run into trouble out there, you're on your own.' His eyes were wide and he kept looking around as though the mere mention of the place might somehow magically transport him there instantly.

'I don't plan on us getting into trouble,' said Carmichael.

'You know it's out past the Breaks,' said Ranking.

'I can handle the Breaks.'

'I hear there's pirates lurking in the Breaks.'

'I've heard the same,' admitted Carmichael.

'Pirates? Like Dire Bane?' asked Hope. The infamous pirate that her teacher brought to justice was the only one she was familiar with.

Ranking spat. 'This lot is nothing like Dire Bane. No honor, no mercy. They're barely more than animals. I hear when they raid a ship, they kill the entire crew. And then instead of dumping the bodies overboard, they eat them.'

'Dawn's Light is a risk,' admitted Carmichael. 'But we need a new main royal, which is going to eat up a fair chunk of what we just made. And like as not, soon we'll need a new mainmast entirely. We need the money. We could be there and back by the time any other cargo shows up here. Otherwise we'll just be lolling around like the rest of them, losing money to those ridiculous overnight dock fees. Besides, Hope can take care of any pirate trouble we run into, isn't that right?'

'Of course, Captain,' said Hope, because that was what he wanted her to say. But she wondered if it were true. Her skills were still so untested. Her only real combat experience had been with one lone, overconfident Vinchen warrior and a big stupid fish. She felt a cold prickle of trepidation at the idea of a new adversary. But even stronger, she felt a yearning to meet the challenge and know herself as a true warrior.

The code said a Vinchen should never crave battle, so as they returned to the ship, she tried to put those thoughts aside. But the feeling chased her the rest of the day as they waited for their cargo, and even into her dreams, where she cut down pirates dressed in white and gold.

10

*W*hen Brigga Lin arrived at the temple of Morack Tor, he'd expected to find more than a pile of wind-worn rubble. It was said Morack Tor, one of the first true biomancers, built it centuries before the birth of the empire, and it had been a repository of knowledge for the order. But in the early days of the empire, long after Morack Tor was dead, the head of the biomancer council, Burness Vee, had it destroyed at the urging of Selk the Brave of the Vinchen order. Some knowledge, they said, was simply too dangerous to exist. But that was exactly the sort of knowledge Brigga Lin sought.

For the last decade, the biomancer council had grown increasingly alarmed by the threat of invasion from the north, beyond the Dark Sea. Every biomancer in the empire had been desperately searching for some new weapon that would show the emperor's dominance over the encroaching foreigners. But typical of the old, their thinking was too narrow and conventional. Not Brigga Lin. While he had been completing his novitiate at Stonepeak, he learned that the ruins of Morack Tor still existed, untouched since the time of the Dark Mage. He suggested to his mentor that they should explore the ruins. Surely, if the Dark Mage had found something worthwhile, so might they. His mentor had said it was a waste of time. That it was only a pile of rubble now. Despite those words, Brigga Lin had expected to find more. But as he dragged his small boat onto the beach, that was all he saw.

It was a small island, roughly rectangular, and barely a quarter-mile across. It was fringed in gray sand that gave way in the center to a dark green moss that covered the piles of carved stone that had once been the temple. That was all there was.

Brigga Lin sighed and sat on one of the moss-covered pillars. The council had refused his request to bring a squad of imperial guards, and he was glad of it now. They would have mocked him soundly for this disappointment. The imperial guards held the older biomancers in a reverence that bordered on fear. But they held no such respect for a newly ordained biomancer, especially one with such a lackluster reputation. It was true that Brigga Lin had not been the most adept at transformation, and that even his scholarly endeavors had been unimpressive. But what he lacked in talent, he made up for in resolve. He would find something among these ruins, or he would die trying.

So he began his search among the ruins of Morack Tor. And he nearly did die. Though he carefully rationed his supplies, they ran out after ten days. Still he searched, keeping himself alive by drinking the rainwater he squeezed out of the foul green moss. When he got hungry enough, he ate the moss as well. Unfortunately, the moss caused mild hallucinations. But even that did not stop him. Finally, one afternoon, while the clouds above seemed to pulse angrily and the stones seemed to melt into each other with agonized expressions, he found an underground passage.

It took him some time to make sure he was not hallucinating. But the visions came and went in waves, so in one of his lucid moments, he was able to verify that there was a square stone piece on the ground with a large metal ring. A diet of nothing but rainwater and hallucinogenic moss made him weak, but by using the wooden rudder of his ship, he was able to fashion a lever and pry the hatch open. He climbed down into the dark, underground room, muttering to himself about how they would all rue the day they doubted him. But then he thought perhaps he'd spoken too soon. There was nothing in the room. It was lined with bookshelves, but they were filled only with ash. There were also char marks on the stone floor and ceiling, as if someone had lit the entire library ablaze.

Brigga Lin dropped to his knees. He stared down at his white biomancer robe, now stained with mud and moss. Waves of dizziness rolled through his body as the toxic moss ran its course. He wondered if the moss would kill him. He hadn't even considered that until this moment. They were *all* right. His parents, his mentor, the council. He was nothing but an arrogant fool.

Then he noticed a perfectly round hole in the stone floor. He'd thought it strange that the floor was stone. Why not just leave it dirt? Unless there was something hidden beneath it.

There was text etched into the stone near the hole. He leaned over, fighting to read with his moss-poisoned vision. The letters seemed to ripple and undulate, so it took him a while to read the simple message, and longer before he thought he understood it.

He who is brave enough to reach blindly into the darkness will be lost to the darkness, and the darkness lost to him.

It didn't sound very promising. It was common knowledge that traps had been laid in many of the old biomancer temples, and being lost to the darkness sounded like a threat. But it was that last phrase that made him pause. How could the darkness be lost to someone? Perhaps it was the moss that clouded his thinking, but that didn't make sense to him. He sat and pondered it a long time, but came to no conclusion. Twice he stood as if to go, only to remember that this was his last hope. He either reached into the hole or returned empty-handed to Stonepeak and the rancor of his mentor and peers.

'Damn it to all the hells in this life and the next,' he muttered, then knelt down and shoved his hand into the hole.

11

Little Bee had an aunt in Hammer Point who took her in. Red didn't feel right about letting her leave the Circle for a neighborhood that everyone knew wasn't near as nice. But as Filler pointed out, there weren't any other options. When Red had suggested they take her in, Filler just stared at him like he'd gone slippy. Red had to admit that they were probably not ideal choices to care for a little girl, and it was fortunate that Little Bee had anyone at all. Or Jilly. Nobody would call her Little Bee now, Red realized. That idea troubled him perhaps more than any other part. In Paradise Circle, a name meant something, whether you chose it, or more often, it was chosen for you. And in the Circle, a name stuck.

But Red's doubts about Little Bee didn't linger, especially once she was gone. Because more and more, his thoughts and energy were spent trying to figure out how he could see Nettles as much as possible.

She wanted to be near Filler while he worked on her chainblade, as she'd started calling it, but didn't want to be a pest. So she spent a lot of time in Gunpowder Hall. The inside of the hall was one big open space with tables, benches, and tents scattered here and there. It was a popular spot for gamblers to get a game of stones, for whores to bring their clients, and murderers to dump their bodies. There was no judgment at Gunpowder Hall, and no imps either. The authorities had tried to raid the place a few years back, and after five days and heavy losses, gave up. Some places just couldn't be ruled.

'I was thinking I might want a custom weapon of my own,' Red said by way of greeting when he sat down next to her.

'Mmf?' she said, her mouth around the roasted fish on a stick she'd picked up at one of the tents outside.

He pulled out one of his throwing knives and held it up, looking at it thoughtfully. 'Sometimes when I throw one of these, they accidentally strike with the handle. Now, if I'm aiming for the head, it's still enough to stun them or even knock them out. But if I'm aiming elsewhere, say the chest, all it does is make them mad. So I was thinking, why not have a blade at either end, so I don't have that problem anymore?'

'Because where would you hold it, you salthead?' said Nettles.

'I thought of that, too.' He gave her a smug grin. 'See, I don't need to hold it, I just need a way to fling it. If there was like a loop or something in the middle I could get my finger through, I could hook it and whip it out right from the sheath.'

'Even if the loop was stiff leather, you'd risk it being flat and closed up when you needed it,' Nettles said. 'Better to make it metal. Like a ring of metal you can easily get your finger through.'

Red's eyes widened. 'That's a sunny idea, Nettie! What if the ring was actually what joined the two blades? Three pieces, easily joined. I bet Filler could whip me up some in no time.'

'After he's done with my chainblade,' said Nettles.

Once he'd met up with her, he would try to extend their time together beyond the initial conversation.

He would show her some strange little place he'd found in the neighborhood, like the underground pond in Apple Grove Manor. Or he'd get her over to the Drowned Rat for a pint and a game of stones. Or he would take her down to the docks and get Missing Finn to lend them some fishing poles. Sometimes she went along with his plan. Sometimes she said, 'Nah, let's go back to your place and toss instead.' And sometimes she just said she wasn't interested. Red tried not to show the sting he felt when that happened. He knew she would think him soft for it, call him artsy or a ponce. About the only time he could count on her to come along with him, no matter what, was when it was a job.

'What's this one, then?' asked Nettles as she sat down with Red at a table in the corner of the Drowned Rat. She coiled her shiny new chainblade around her hand. Filler had done a fine job. The chain was thin and light, but linked so tightly that it wasn't brittle. The blade was double-sided and a little longer than her forefinger.

'It's like this.' There were few things Red enjoyed more than sharing a new plan. 'You know the wrink who owns that butcher shop down on Manay Street? Calls himself Neepman?'

'I know the shop,' said Nettles. 'Never met the old man.'

'Because you're not a people person, Nettie. You have to talk to folks. Smile and make nice.'

She made a sour face. 'Too much work.'

'Work brings work, though,' said Red. 'I got to talking with Neepman, and find out he also owns the bakery over on Tide Lane. He was complaining what a chore it was to have his shops so far apart, transporting things between them. I couldn't help but wonder what things he might be transporting. An afternoon of friendly talk over at the bakery, and a few nights of careful observation on the route between the two shops led me to the discovery that there is no safe at the bakery. Not enough room, what with the ovens. So old Neepman has the day's earnings transported to the butcher's after closing by one of his shopgirls.'

'You can handle rolling a shopgirl,' said Nettles. 'So what do you need me for?'

'Because a day's earnings at a bakery is barely worth my time. No, we're going to use this to get to the bigger prize, which is the safe in the butcher's.'

'How do we do that?'

'Like I said, they let this shopgirl in after closing. Unlock the doors and lead her straight to wherever the safe is hidden. And this girl just happens to be about your height and have similar hair.'

'You want to roll the shopgirl, then have me pose as her to find the safe and get in it.'

'I'll trail you to the shop. Then when it's time for you to make the grab, I'll step in and help with whatever muscle they've got there. In and out. Simple as sideways.'

'It's never as simple as you say,' said Nettles.

He grinned at her. 'I wouldn't want you to get bored.'

That night, they spotted the shopgirl halfway between the shops. On one hand, it seemed an odd, not very safe way to transport money. On the other hand, most people wouldn't think of a mousy little shopgirl like her having anything worth stealing. She played it well, too. Walking at a leisurely pace, not giving anything away that she might have something worth taking or that she was going somewhere important. If Red hadn't stumbled across the knowledge, he wouldn't have been the wiser. But over the years, he had learned that, more than throwing a knife or picking a lock, finding things out was the skill most useful to thriving in Paradise Circle.

Nettles positioned herself in an alley ahead of the girl, and Red was on the street a block beyond that. Red started walking toward the girl and timed it so that she crossed the alley just as he was about to walk past her. Nettles threw out the blunt, weighted end of her chainblade, striking the girl in the temple. Red was there to catch her before she hit the ground. He quickly moved her into the alley where Nettles waited. Nettles put on the girl's ragged scarf and hat, then took the small purse of coins meant to be transported to the butcher's.

'Better not take any yet,' said Red. 'They'll expect to see it when they open the safe.'

Nettles looked doubtfully down at the unconscious shopgirl. 'Tell me true, do I really look like her?'

'Sure you do, Nettie. Except prettier.' He winked.

She frowned. 'Let's find out just how full of piss you and this plan are, then.'

Nettles walked the rest of the way to the butcher's with Red trailing cautiously behind, staying in the shadows or blending in with small clusters of people. The sun was setting and the imp patrols who lit the street lamps hadn't reached that part of the neighborhood yet, so there was plenty of dark to hide in. Red was pleased to see that Nettles had adopted the same leisurely pace as the shopgirl. He knew it wasn't easy to act relaxed when you were about to pull a job like this.

Finally they reached the butcher shop. Nettles knocked on the door with the rhythm Red had observed the shopgirl use, and a tense minute later, the door opened. A tall, thick man wearing a bloody apron looked down at her.

'Where's the usual girl?'

Nettles only hesitated a moment, probably to silently curse Red in her thoughts. 'Burned her hand on the oven today, so they sent me instead.'

The man looked at her a moment and Red held his breath,
ready to jump in and pull Nettles out if things went leeward.
But then the man just nodded.

'Yeah, alright.' He stepped aside and motioned Nettles to
come in. As she passed, he said, 'Tell the boss he should send
you more often,' and swatted her rear.

Nettles paused, and again Red held his breath. She might
gut the tom right then and there. It was certainly in her rights
to do so. But it would foul the whole job.

'Yeah, alright, maybe I will,' she said and smiled at him.
He seemed pleased by the smile, but Red recognized it immediately as the *not only will I kill you, I will make it painful*
smile, and shuddered. He made a mental note to leave that
one to her.

Once they were inside, the man pulled the door closed. At
the last second, Red threw one of his new two-sided blades,
keeping the door slightly ajar. The man pulled the latch to
lock it. He might normally have noticed the additional resist-
ance in fastening it, but his eyes were now locked on Nettles.

Once Red could no longer see them in the window, he
moved swiftly toward the door. The blade left a small crack
between the door and the lintel just wide enough for him to
get one of his slim lock picks through to pop the latch. As
the door swung open, he retrieved the throwing blade stuck
in the lintel and slipped inside.

The front area where customers ordered their cuts was
dark. He could hear voices from a doorway on the other side
of the counter. He crept forward cautiously, following the
sound. The doorway opened into the back room, where sides
of meat hung on hooks. There was a big table in the center,
stained with years of blood, and buckets with congealed
blood beneath. The safe was all the way in the back. In addition to the tom with Nettles, there were two others just as
big.

'What's your name, molly?' one of them asked.

'Ell,' she said, giving her best attempt at a shy smile. It didn't look very convincing to Red, but the toms seemed to buy it.

As Red waited for them to open the safe, he became aware of a stinging pain in his hand. He looked down and saw his palm was sliced open, a trickle of blood coming out. He must have cut himself when he threw his blade. Clearly his technique needed some refinement.

Finally, the toms stopped flirting long enough to open the safe.

'So, what are you doing later—' one of them began. But then a thrown blade embedded itself in his neck. He grabbed at it, which only made him slice up his hands as well. The one on the other side went down a moment later. That left only the one from the entrance. He stared in shock at his two fellows, who lay choking on their own blood.

'You treacherous slice!' He took a swing at her with his big fist. She dodged to one side and threw her chain so that the blade embedded itself in his wrist. She yanked hard, pulling him off balance as the blade came loose. He stumbled, and she kicked him in the side of his head. He reeled back, swinging wildly with his good hand. Nettles waited for an opening, then threw the weighted end of her chain at his cock. He gave a feeble whimper and dropped to his knees.

Nettles loomed over him. 'I'm going to let you live so that you can tell every tom you meet the important lesson of never touching a molly's ass without her say-so. Keen?' Then she grabbed his head with both hands and slammed her knee into his face. He flopped to the floor, unconscious.

'Nicely done,' said Red.

As they scooped the contents of the safe into a sack, Nettles said, 'Why are your hands bleeding?'

'I haven't figured out how to throw my blades yet without catching myself,' Red admitted.

'Well, until you do, you might want to wear some gloves so you don't bleed out before the end of a job.'

Red shook his head. 'Wouldn't be able to get gloved fingers through the rings.'

'So cut off the fingers. That would still protect your palms, wouldn't it?'

'Good idea,' said Red, looking at his sliced-up hands.

'So was this,' said Nettles, nodding to the safe.

He beamed at her. 'You think so?'

'Yeah. Good haul, minimum risk. Who knew an artsy ponce from Silverback could work the Circle so well?'

Red chose to view that as a compliment. Nettles was usually extra leaky after a successful job, so he didn't want to ruin the mood.

The top floor of Slice of Heaven was where the employees who weren't whores lived. Nettles shared a room with the cleaning woman, Ipsy. Ipsy's tom was a sailor and often out on the water. When he was in port, she always stayed with him at the Sailor's Mother, which wasn't a crimp house anymore, just an inn. She'd been gone the past week, so Red and Nettles had the place all to themselves. This led to a great deal of sex, and that night was no exception.

If you'd asked Red if the sex was good, he'd have said yes, even though he didn't have any basis of comparison. No tom wanted to admit he didn't enjoy a toss. It just wasn't a thing to say. But right after, still sweaty and panting, when he reached for her and she pushed him off, there was always a moment that struck him with a cold and lonely shot to the gut. In those moments, he would try anything to bridge that gap. Nettles didn't cuddle. She'd made that perfectly clear. Even holding hands irritated her. So he would use words to bridge that gap. Most of the time, as they lay in the dark, he would just rabbit on about whatever popped into his head, and she would respond with noncommittal grunts. But the night they robbed the butcher's, when he was going on about how he'd ingratiated himself with Neepman to find out the information that helped them succeed that night, she interrupted him.

'Your parents were from Silverback, then?'

'My dad was a whore there, as was his mom, and her dad before him. Long proud line of Silverback whores who served the artistic community for generations. Some call the whores in Silverback the Muses, since they are, on the whole, uncommonly attractive and have inspired many a painter or musician. My dad included.'

'What about your mom?'

At another place and time, Red would have answered more cautiously. He was not completely bludgeon. But in that moment, he was still on a high from the plan and the fight and the money and the sex, and he was so very desperate to close the gap he couldn't quite admit to himself that he felt. So he spoke crystal.

'My mom was from Hollow Falls.'

'Balls and pricks she was.'

'No, really. That's how I know how to read. I can paint, too, though I don't do that much these days.'

'Must be nice, coming from all that privilege.'

'What does *that* mean?'

'Nothing. So your mom was one of those lacy girls who came down to Silverback with dreams of being a famous painter?'

'She *was* a famous painter, actually. Until she got sick.'

'From the coral spice, you mean? Your red eyes give that away. Though I never seen 'em on anyone other than a baby.'

'Not just the spice. She had this other problem from the paints. She was real sick toward the end.'

'What was her name?'

'Gulia Pastinas.'

'Lacies always have such fancy names.'

'Lyrical names,' he said absently.

'Odd thing for a proper lacy like her to have a son named Red. Especially with the eyes. It's a bit pointed, isn't it?'

'Red is the name Sadie gave me when she took me in.'

'What's your birth name, then?'

'Promise you won't laugh?'

'Why would I laugh?'

'I don't know. Just promise.'

'Sure, fine, I promise.'

'My birth name is Rixidenteron.'

There was a long silence.

'Nettie?'

He heard a small rustling, and through the blanket he could feel her shaking. Then she suddenly burst out into the loudest laugh he'd ever heard from her.

'Sorry, sorry!' she gasped between bursts. 'I just didn't expect!' Another burst of laughter. 'Something like that!'

'Uh-huh.' Red felt the heat of shame rise in him.

'You're serious? Really?'

'Yes, that's my birth name. You can ask Filler. He's . . .' He wondered whether it was a good idea to share any more truth that night. But maybe it would help her see what a big deal it was and how much she was hurting him. 'He's the only person I've told that to, besides you.'

'I can see why!' Nettles said, and erupted into a fresh burst of laughter.

*   *   *

The next night, Red and Filler sat in their room and shared a jug of ale that Prin had given them for clearing off some rowdy drunks at the Drowned Rat earlier that day. Summer heat had descended on New Laven like a blanket drenched in boiling water, and they sat side by side under the open window, trying to keep cool.

'Nettie came by the shop today to get a few adjustments to her chainblade. Said she gave it a good test last night while you two were on a job.'

'She did,' agreed Red. 'My throwing blades worked well, too. Except they cut up my palms.'

'That why you got those leather gloves today from Brimmer?'

'Yeah.'

Filler took a long swallow on the jug. 'Today, also. She asked me if it was true about your birth name.'

'Yeah, I told her last night.'

Filler handed Red the jug as he said, 'She laughed, you know. When I told her it was true, she about choked on the gad.'

Red took a pull on the jug. 'Yeah.' He took another pull, then handed it back to him. 'She laughed last night, too.'

'You're getting sotted with her,' said Filler.

'Am not,' said Red automatically.

Filler gave him a skeptical look and took another swig.

'So what if I am, then?' asked Red. 'It's not a bad thing, you know.'

'It is if she's not sotted with you.' He handed the jug back to Red.

Red frowned and stuck his thumb in the jug mouth, popping it in and out so it made a hollow noise. He had plenty of doubts himself. But sometimes doubts only made a person want to fight harder to believe. 'I think she *is* sotted with me.'

'Nah. She likes you. And she likes tossing you. But she's not sotted.'

'How would you know?' Red couldn't help the defensive tone that was creeping into his voice.

'She don't look at you the same way you look at her.'

All Red's fancy talk and agile thinking sometimes just allowed him to run circles around himself faster than most. Sometimes it was Filler, with his simple way, who laid things bare and direct. Said like that from the wag Red knew and trusted above all others, there was nothing to be done but acknowledge it.

He looked at Filler plaintively. 'What do I do?'

'Ask her. Maybe I'm wrong. Either way, then you'll know.'

'But what if we're supposed to be together? Like fate. Don't you think we're perfect for each other?'

'No,' said Filler. 'Not really.'

Red looked over at him, his ruby eyes wide with surprise. 'I thought you liked Nettles.'

'I like her fine. But she don't understand you the way you deserve to be understood.'

'You talk like I'm some sort of artsy ponce,' Red said bitterly.

Filler sighed. 'Just promise me. When you talk to her, if things go leeward, promise you'll go see Sadie after.'

Red took a long swallow on the jug, then leaned his head back to rest on the open windowsill so the night winds blew across his sweaty forehead. 'Fine. But it won't come to that. You'll see. She keeps it close, like any true wag of the Circle. But she's just as sotted as me.'

Red loved Paradise Circle. More than Silverback, where he'd spent his early childhood. More than the *Savage Wind*, though those were some of his favorite memories. And certainly more than Hollow Falls, which he'd never set eyes on. Granted, there had been times in his life, especially when he was younger, when he'd wished his aunt Minara would suddenly appear and take him to her uptown lacy mansion. He remembered her a little from the few times she'd come to visit while his mother was alive. Older and more conservative than his mother, but nearly identical in looks and far more gentle in speech and touch. Particularly in those months before he'd met Sadie, he'd longed for that touch. But now he knew those had been the dreams of a weak and frightened child. These days, if he thought about his aunt at all, it was to wonder why she'd never come, and mostly to be glad she hadn't.

Red loved Paradise Circle, but there were days when the clouds were low and gray, and rain fell not to clean the grimy streets, but only to turn the mud and trash and shit into a fetid soup. Days when every face in the street looked pinched with hunger and hostility, babies wailed for mothers that would never come, and children played listless games next to the bloated, rotting corpse of a horse. It was on days like that Red escaped to the rooftops.

He could see the whole neighborhood up there, and occasionally farther, if the clouds weren't too low. The air tasted different up there, unspoiled by the sewage that ran down the open gutters along the sides of the streets. And it was quiet up there. The sounds of the neighborhood receded to a murmur beneath the winds that rose up from the sea. For a little while, Red could pretend he was untouched by it all.

The rooftops had always been Red's alone. Filler wouldn't have admitted it outright, but he wasn't fond of heights. And there was no one else he wanted to share this temporary escape with. Until he met Nettles. He'd been trying to decide when the best time would be, and now he knew that it was where he would ask if she wanted him as her tom and she as his molly, forever and always.

Most of the roofs in Paradise Circle were slanted, but Red knew every one that was flat and wide enough to comfortably stand. And as it happened, one of them was a perfect place. Well, perfect symbolically. Just not easy to reach.

'We're doing what?' asked Nettles as they stood in a side street. She looked up skeptically at the awning above the door.

'If you need help, I can get up there first and throw down a rope.' He'd brought one, just in case.

'I don't need help, you salthead. I just don't know why we're doing it.'

'You'll see.' Red bounced his eyebrows mysteriously.

Nettles sighed. 'Fine.'

They scrambled up onto the awning. From there, they shimmied along a ledge to a windowsill. From the windowsill it was a short jump to a clothesline pulley. Once one of them had the pulley, they had to swing their legs up to hook their heels on the rain gutter, then curl up to reach their hands on the gutter, and pull themselves up to the roof.

'Piss'ell.' Nettles massaged her hands. 'How did you even figure that out?'

'It took a bit of doing,' said Red. 'But if it were easy, everybody would be up here, right? Look at this view and tell me it wasn't worth it.'

He gestured with both hands to the rooftops that stretched out in all directions. The old temple and some of the other building tops were shrouded in the mist, which Red thought added a nicely magical touch. Even though it was still a while before sunset, the street lamps had already been lit in this section of the neighborhood, which made the fog luminescent.

'Huh,' said Nettles.

'And of course, when you look down there, you'll see why I chose this particular rooftop.' He pointed down to the intersection below with a flourish and a sly smile.

Nettles looked down at it, her expression unreadable.

Red waited.

Finally, Nettles shook her head. 'Sorry. Not getting it. Why this rooftop?'

'Because it overlooks the intersection where we first kissed!' he said.

'Oh yeah. I guess it was.' Nettles looked around again, then rubbed her hands together. 'A bit chilly. Why are we up here again?'

'Well, I just . . .' The reason seemed so obvious to Red that he had a hard time putting it into words. 'It's sort of special. For us.'

She nodded.

'And . . .' Red's heart picked up speed. His hands were already sweating. His mouth was suddenly dry. He was actually nervous. Maybe it was Filler planting doubts in his head. Maybe it was the fact that Nettles clearly wasn't getting the whole romantic rooftop thing. Whatever the reason, he found his words catching in his throat as he looked at her.

She gazed at him through narrowed eyes, her arms crossed. 'You're acting a bit slippy. What's going on?'

'I know – I – Sorry,' he sputtered. Then he took a deep breath and tried again. 'You are the finest molly I've ever met. Won't you be mine for keeps?' He reached his hand out to her.

She stared at his extended hand like it was something she didn't recognize. The longer she stared, the lower Red's stomach sank.

'I like you, Red,' she said quietly. 'I like being with you. I like tossing with you. I would go far enough to say that I like you better than anyone I know. Except myself. I like me best of all. I ain't nobody's molly, and never will be. If that's what you want, you'll have to look elsewhere.'

Red stared at her. He was still standing, but on the inside he felt himself collapsing.

'You keen?' she asked.

'Yeah,' he said numbly. 'My mistake.' He turned and started to walk away.

'Now, don't get all poncey on me, Rixie,' she said teasingly.

It was the worst thing she could have said, and his walk turned into a run.

'Red? Come on, I was only joking!'

But he jumped to the next roof and kept running. He'd spent months trying to get as close as possible to this molly, and now he couldn't stand to be anywhere near her. He kept running from roof to roof, sliding on the treacherous angles of some of them, but never stopping until he came to a space too wide to jump. Below him was a long line of tents. He had reached Gunpowder Hall. He hadn't come here on purpose. But maybe there was a part of him deep down that had been drawn to this place. Or more specifically, to a person in this place.

Off to one side in Gunpowder Hall was a small cluster of tables where the old wrinks congregated. Red saw Sadie among them, leaning back against a table, her legs stretched out into the aisle. Life was hard in the Circle, and the last eight years had taken their toll on her. Her matted hair was mostly gray, her skin sagged a great deal, and she was missing more than a few teeth. But her eyes were still sharp and her mind was still quick. Most importantly, she was alive, which was better than many of her contemporaries. Few people were savvy enough to make it to old age in Paradise

Circle. So anyone who did was given a measure of respect and generally left alone to reminisce, or whatever it was the old wrinks did in their corner.

'Well, don't you look pissed and peppered,' Sadie observed.

Red sat down next to her with an ungraceful flop. 'I'm a bludgeon cock-dribble.'

'Damned if you are,' said Sadie. 'What's this all about?'

'There's this girl . . .'

'Oh, we're there, are we?' she asked gravely. 'Out with it. Who did what?'

'She doesn't want me to be her tom. She – she didn't even say why.'

'Like as not, she did. Just wasn't something you could understand, or maybe didn't want to hear.'

'Maybe I'm ugly.'

'You don't even believe that.'

'Maybe she doesn't like my eyes. Some people think I'm evil, you know. On account of my red eyes.'

'There's a lot of stupid people in the world. This molly you're sotted with, she stupid?'

Red shook his head.

'Then she don't think you're evil.'

'Maybe it's because I'm not a proper wag of the Circle.'

'Why'd you even say a thing like that?'

'She said it. When I told her I was from Silverback.'

'Now that is a load of balls and pricks. Do you look out for your wags?'

Red nodded.

'Do you stand for your freedom and the Circle in the face of the imps and any who would take it from us?'

'Of course.'

'That's all you need, then.'

'So you don't think I'm privileged, coming from Silverback and having family in Hollow Falls?'

'Oh, I do,' she said. 'But that don't mean you ain't a true wag of the Circle. To my mind, it just means you have more to do. You're smart with all them books you read. You understand better than most how it is, and more importantly what might be done to fix it. As long as you stick with that and always show your quality, I'd say you earned your place in the Circle.'

Red left Gunpowder Hall with Sadie's words still singing in his head. It didn't make Nettles's rejection sting any less, but at least it gave him some hope that he did fit here after all.

There was something off about the market outside the hall. It was late afternoon, still before sunset. The tents should have been crowded. But everything was shut up, as if ready for a hurricane. Except the breeze was far too light for a storm.

Then he saw that this storm was not natural, but imperial. A squad of imps were working their way down the line of tents, harassing those who hadn't been fast enough or smart enough to close in time. While it was true that the imps had never infiltrated Gunpowder Hall, they occasionally made raids on the market, like rattling the bars to remind people that a safe haven could just as easily be a cage. That's how it was in the Circle, and the best thing for Red to do was move on, grateful it wasn't him getting the beating.

But then he stopped. It might be how it was, but Red knew it shouldn't be. This was what Sadie had been telling him. He should know better. This was all wrong. *He* was all wrong. Letting the imps pound on other wags. Stealing from other wags like poor Neepman, or even Deadface Drem. Sure, Drem was a drug-peddling, murderous scum. But he was doing things for this community. He was part of this community. It was these invaders, these boots of the emperor, who were the real enemy. And they needed to understand how it was in the Circle, just like everyone else.

Rcd pulled on his new fingerless gloves as he silently wove between the tents. When he drew near the imps, he saw who it was they were harassing and in that moment, he knew that no matter how things went, he'd be forever glad he made the choice to not pass this by. Because they were at the smithy tent, and they had Filler on his knees in front of the tent. Blood trickled from the corner of his mouth, and his eye had already begun to swell.

'Making weapons so your wags can kill imps, is that it?' one of them sneered, then kicked Filler in the stomach.

Filler doubled over, then slowly rose up again, his face folded in absolute hatred. He'd lost a more respectable smithy apprenticeship because he'd refused to do work for an imp officer. Now they'd followed him to Gunpowder Hall. No doubt, when they'd stepped into that smithy tent, they hadn't expected him to put up a fight. But imps had killed Filler's parents, and he never could show restraint around them after that.

One of the imps came out of the smithy tent, wearing one of the thick leather smithy gloves and holding a glowing poker hot from the forge. 'I don't think you'll be making any more weapons once we've put out your eyes.'

Red's throwing blade embedded in the imp's arm, causing his hand to spasm and the poker to drop onto his boot, searing quickly through the thin leather. Three more blades found exposed necks. Filler grabbed the fifth imp's head and twisted hard enough to break his neck.

'You're all murderous, thieving filth!' screamed the imp with the throwing blade in his arm. Blood dripped from it as he trained his rifle on Red. 'Your deaths make this place a tiny bit better.'

Red was out of throwing blades and Filler was too far away to help. The imp cocked his rifle, wincing at the pain in his arm. But the barrel remained steady as he took aim.

Then a metal jingle rang through the air as Nettles's chainblade shot out, the blade burying itself in the imp's ear. She yanked hard on the chain, his shot went wide, and he fell twitching into the mud.

'Thanks, Nettie!' said Filler.

Red remained silent, eyeing her warily. He wasn't sure at all what to make of this or how he felt about it.

'When you ran off like that, I figured you'd find trouble of some kind,' said Nettles as she coiled her chain and wiped the blade clean.

Still Red said nothing as he walked from body to body, retrieving his throwing blades.

'Look,' she said. 'I wanted a fun, easy toss. You wanted romance. I'm sorry we couldn't give each other what we wanted. But whatever else we were or are, I will always be there to pull you out of a bind. Keen?'

She held out her hand.

It wasn't what he wanted exactly. But that, too, was how it was in the Circle. You didn't often get what you wanted exactly. Nettles wouldn't be the molly he wanted. But she was one hell of a fighter, and in the Circle, you were bludgeon if you didn't accept an alliance when it was offered.

So even though there was a small part of him that still ached, he took her hand and gripped it hard. 'Yeah, alright. Likewise, I guess.'

12

*I*t was a four-day voyage to Dawn's Light. Hope tried to fill her time with meditation and exercise, but there was only so much of that one person could do, even a Vinchen. While every other person on the ship had a number of jobs and responsibilities, Hope's only true responsibility was to wait around for something everyone else on the ship hoped wouldn't happen. Something not even Hope herself was sure she could do.

'You seem restless,' said Carmichael in the sunny afternoon of the second day. He held the wheel loose in his hands, his brown face tilted up toward the light. 'Even your footsteps sound impatient.'

'I wish I could be more useful,' she said. 'But I know nothing of ships or sailing.'

'You could learn,' said Carmichael.

'How?'

'Start simple. Go ask one of the crew what they do and why. Ask Ticks about the rigging, for example. He knows the lines of this ship better than just about anyone. You learn each piece from each man on the crew, and soon enough, you'll be a better sailor than me.'

'I doubt I could ever be as good as you, Captain,' said Hope. 'But I'll try your suggestion.'

He smiled faintly. 'Good luck.'

Hope searched the ship for Ticks and found him by the foremast, securing a thick line of rope. Ticks was a short man with a bald head and eyebrows like squashed hairy spiders.

'Can you explain to me what you're doing?' she asked him.

He gave her a guarded look. 'Why's that, miss?'

'I want to learn about sailing.'

One of his hairy spiders rose up. 'Nothing you need to concern yourself with, miss. Now, if you'll excuse me, I have to tend to another line.'

She tried Sankack next. Sankack was a tall man with a droopy face and almost no chin. She found him back in the stern of the ship, sitting on a stool, a sail in his lap, a large needle and thread in his hands.

'Are you mending that sail?' she asked.

'Hmm,' he grunted, not looking up.

'Was it torn in the storm?'

'Hmm.'

'Would you mind showing me how you do it?'

'Hmm.'

Hope tried several more times, but never got anything more than that sound out of him. Finally she gave up and went looking for the captain. Ranking was taking his shift at the helm, so Hope went back to the captain's quarters. She knocked quietly on the door.

'Who is it?'

'Hope, sir.'

'Ah. Come in.'

She found Carmichael seated at a small table, a quill in one hand and a logbook open in front of him.

'Well?' The faint smile came back to his bearded lips.

'It's like they don't trust me,' she burst out.

'They don't.'

'They don't think I can pull on a rope? Stitch up a sail?'

'None of them have ever seen a female on board a ship except maybe a captain's wife, who never does anything useful except berate the captain for being a lousy, brutish drunk. They seen you kill that oarfish, sure. And the next time there's an oarfish troubling them, they'll go straight to you. But the idea that you could do what they do has barely even brushed the tops of their thick skulls. A few will come around eventually, then the rest will follow.'

'How do you know?'

'I don't. But it's the captain's job to always say something he wants to happen like he knows it's *going* to happen.' His smile broadened into a wide grin. 'There, see? I'm teaching you my part, at least.'

Hope tried again the following day, moving from one crew member to the next. She was either ignored or brushed off by each in turn, except Ranking, who laughed right to her face. After a discouraging few hours, she again retreated to Carmichael's company at the helm.

'You're not helping any by sticking close to me,' he told her. 'They need to get accustomed to your presence. And the only way that will happen is if you're actually present.'

So Hope reluctantly returned to the crew that afternoon. She didn't push or pry this time, though, but simply watched and listened. They looked uncomfortable with her presence for the first hour or so. But then it seemed they forgot she was there, and went about their work. Some things she was able to pick up by observing. She learned other things by listening to them talk to each other. They spoke with no regard for courtesy or decorum. At first it made her uncomfortable. But over time she grew accustomed to it just as they had grown accustomed to her.

On the morning of the fourth day, the *Lady's Gambit* reached the Breaks. Hope stood with Ranking, Ticks, and Sankack at the port bow and gazed at the distant line of jagged gray reefs that stretched north to south for a mile. They jutted up from the water into the cloudless blue sky, fighting against the prevailing current so that the water around the base churned an endless frothy white.

'I hear them reefs rose up from a burning hell beneath the ground, carrying the heat up with them, and that's why the water boils,' said Ticks.

'I hear a biomancer was the one who made them, as a shield against invading demons,' said Sankack. 'And it's the frustrated rage of the demons on the other side that makes it boil.'

At the mere mention of the word *biomancer*, Hope's pulse jumped, but still she kept her silence.

'Don't be bludgeon,' said Ranking. 'Biomancers can't change rock, only *living* things. Everybody knows that.'

'Oh yeah?' Sankack scowled at him. 'And you're an expert on biomancers? Bet you never even seen one.'

Ranking stared coldly at him for a moment before speaking. 'Once. Back when I was still in New Laven.'

There was a moment of silence as Ticks and Sankack exchanged looks. Then Ticks cleared his throat. 'So, are they as bad as people say?'

Ranking smiled bitterly. 'Well, I chose to be out here on the edge of the world with you sorry wags instead, so what does that tell you?'

Once they were within a hundred yards of the Breaks, Carmichael pointed the ship so they ran parallel to the reefs, heading for the north end. As they came around the northern edge of the Breaks, Carmichael called out, 'I need eyes up high!'

The *Lady's Gambit* didn't have a proper crow's nest, but Mayfield scrambled quickly up the ratlines of the foremast until he reached the topgallant yard about three-fourths of the way up the mast. Once there, he straddled the mast, hooked his legs over the yard, and pulled out a spyglass.

With Mayfield in place, the captain turned the ship and they headed east, the northern end of the Breaks on their port side. Once they were past, Hope and the others were able to see the far eastern side of the Breaks for the first time.

'It's a pissing ship's graveyard,' Ticks said quietly.

Dashed all along the line of ragged, frothing gray reefs were ships of every shape and size, from tiny one-mast sloops to massive three-mast imperial frigates. There were even some strange ships Hope didn't recognize that seemed made more of metal than wood.

'Why so many?' she asked, but no one answered.

Then their ship gave a lurch and began to shudder. A low, wooden groan came from deep within the hull.

'Something pulling on the keel . . .' Ranking leaned over the rail and stared down at the water, then looked back at the reefs. When he turned back to them, his face was pale. 'The current's pulling us in toward the rocks.'

'All hands!' roared Carmichael at the helm. He was fighting to keep the wheel still. 'Get ready to jibe hard!'

'Ticks, go help the captain turn the ship,' said Ranking. 'If we stay at this angle for long, the keel will snap and we're as good as dead. Sankack, go rouse anyone below deck. We'll need all hands if we have any chance of pulling free from this current.'

Ranking blew a shrill note on his whistle and the crew sprang into action, moving smoothly from one task to the next. Hope felt again that pang of uselessness, unable to do

anything except watch as everyone else worked desperately
to turn the ship and get away from the Breaks.

The ship rotated with painful slowness, the sails snapping
as they turned in the wind. Finally they came about so the
stern faced the reefs and the sails went taut again.

'I want every inch of canvas we have flying!' bellowed
Carmichael.

The sailors scrambled to unfurl additional sails, letting
out the trysail in the stern and several jibs in the bow. Hope
moved to port stern and stared at the reefs, trying to gauge if
they were making any headway. At first, it seemed as though
they were locked into place, the wind and current in perfect
balance. But then, almost imperceptibly, the ship began to
move forward.

'That's it, my wags!' said Carmichael. 'Keep on it and
we'll be clear in no time!'

That was when Mayfield called down from his perch,
'Ship off the starboard side!'

Hope ran to the other side of the ship, Ranking right at
her heels. A small, one-mast sloop was headed straight
toward them.

'Pirates,' Ranking said. 'I pissing warned him. And they've
got us by the pricks. Stuck here in this current, we can't make
a run for it.'

'Then we fight,' said Hope.

'With what?' sneered Ranking as he continued to stare out
at the incoming ship. 'Maybe you noticed that we don't have
a single pissing cannon on this boat?'

'Why not?'

'Only imperial navy are permitted to sail with cannons,
and you know our captain wouldn't break the law even if it
meant the death of him and his entire crew. Why do you
think that imp asked if we could handle the voyage? Because
usually, only off-duty military take it on. But our captain,

he wants a little extra money so's he can start saving up to retire. Mark my words, that old man will be the death of us all!'

Hope attributed this sudden burst of mutinous talk to panic. 'Calm yourself,' she told him coldly. 'Do you have a spyglass so I can assess these pirates?'

Ranking shook his head, his eyes fixed on the pirate ship. 'The captain does.'

Hope moved quickly to the helm, where the captain still held the wheel, his expression grim.

'Can I use your spyglass, Captain?' She held out her hand.

Carmichael nodded, pulled it out of his coat, and handed to it her.

Hope expanded it out to its full length and took a bead on the ship. She counted thirty heads on the small ship.

'It's packed with men,' she reported. 'Swivel cannons fore and aft.'

'Aye,' said Carmichael. 'They'll not bother with the cannons, since we don't have any ourselves and they have a chance of taking the ship undamaged. Instead they'll come alongside, throw over grappling hooks, reel themselves in, and board us.'

Hope continued to scan the ship. The men, most of them dressed in rags, looked half-starved and sick with scurvy. The captain was armed with an old flintlock pistol. A few had swords or knives. The majority were armed only with clubs, hammers, or wrenches.

'They don't look very impressive,' said Hope.

'They don't need to. They've got us outnumbered three to one, and they'll just swarm over us like a wave of locusts. My men are better armed, but truth be told, probably no better skilled at close fighting.'

Hope's eyes followed the length of the foremast up to where Mayfield still sat perched on the topgallant yard. She recalled how the mast had bent in the wind to keep from snapping during the storm.

'Captain, if we were to shift the cargo all to starboard and have the crew lean on the starboard rail, would it be enough weight to tilt the ship so that the masts were angled over the water?'

Carmichael's eyes narrowed. 'I think so. Why?'

'If you do this for me, I swear on my life that not a single member of your crew will need to fight pirates this day.'

He regarded her silently for a moment, his bearded face giving no indication of his thoughts. 'Fine. It's what I hired you for anyway.'

'Thank you, Captain.'

Carmichael lifted his face up and bellowed, 'All hands into the hold to shift every inch of cargo to the starboard side, then back up and lining the starboard rail, armed and ready to fight.' More quietly to Hope, he said, 'Just in case.'

'Of course. And you should tell Mayfield he'll want to get clear of the path.'

Carmichael's eyes widened. 'The path?'

The crew looked troubled with the order, but complied. In a situation like this, balking at the captain's orders could lose the ship. The cargo was quickly shifted, and the ship tilted to the starboard side. The crew came back up on deck, spreading out across the starboard rail, and the ship tilted even further.

Hope stood a few feet back from the base of the foremast and watched as the pirate ship veered out into a wide arc, then came about so that their port side was parallel with the *Lady's Gambit*'s starboard side. Just as the two bows came in line, Hope ran up the tilted mast. As she neared the top, she spotted two pirates with grappling hooks, one fore and one aft, getting ready to throw. The ships were still roughly twenty feet apart. Those hooks would bring them together so the pirates could board. Hope couldn't let that happen.

When she reached the end of the mast, she slammed her weight down hard so that the tip bowed down for a moment, then snapped back, catapulting her across the gap. She summersaulted in the air so that her feet slammed into the man with the grapple on the pirate ship's bow. The shouts of surprise and confusion from the pirates were so loud, they nearly drowned out the cold hum as she drew the Song of Sorrows from its sheath.

All during the four-day voyage, Hope had continued to harbor doubts about her ability in true combat situations. But the moment the first pirate came at her with an ax, so slow and clumsy that she barely needed to shift her weight in order to avoid his attack, she realized that this battle was already won. She understood for the first time what a privilege Hurlo's years of training had been. As she moved through the ship, swift and cutting as an icy Southern wind, it was not arrogance or bloodlust or rage that filled her heart. It was gratitude to the man who had not only given her a life, but had surrendered his own to save her. Every day, she would strive to be worthy of that.

Over the wet *thwack* of steel on flesh and the screams of pain, she heard the captain's flintlock pistol cock behind her. She spun, bringing her sword around as the shot was fired, and slapped the bullet from the air. The pirate captain stared at her, his mouth open as he clutched the smoking pistol in his hand. Hope moved toward him, cutting through the slowly loosening knot of men until she stood before him. He fumbled for his own sword, but she knocked it away the moment he drew it. She held the point of her sword at his throat.

'Ask for quarter, and it will be given,' she said.

Because with privilege came responsibility, and there was no honor in killing any more of these starved and desperate men than necessary. It was as Hurlo would have wanted.

His face folded in rage. 'I'd sooner die, Southie slice!'

She ran her sword smoothly through his neck, because also as Hurlo would have wanted, there were no second chances at mercy. Then she whipped the sword out, flinging the captain's blood in the faces of his crew. As the body dropped to the deck, she regarded the remaining eleven men. 'How many more die today?'

'Please, miss,' one of them said. 'Give us quarter.'

The pirates had little of value. Carmichael took their small chest of coins, had them stow their rigging, then towed them the rest of the way to Dawn's Light. When they docked at the military outpost, they were met by a hard-eyed soldier in white and gold.

'Ahoy,' said Carmichael. 'We've a shipment of cargo for you. And what's left of a pirate raiding crew.'

'We will take them both,' the soldier said flatly. He signaled to a squat building at the end of the dock, and a small garrison of soldiers emerged. The soldier in charge gave them a few terse commands, and they set about securing the small pirate sloop to the dock, and leading the pirates away in chains.

Once the cargo had been offloaded and payment made, Carmichael turned to his crew.

'No point in staying ashore here. Not even a tavern on this spit of land. Let's make ready to sail.'

As the crew began to climb back aboard the ship, Hope said to Carmichael, 'I don't like the idea of giving those men over to the soldiers. What will they do with them? It doesn't look like they have a jail.'

'That's the law, Hope. We do our best to honor it.' He sighed and rubbed his temples with the thumb and forefinger of one hand. 'Although it seems harder to do that the longer I live.'

Once everyone was aboard, Carmichael looked around at them, then in a voice loud enough for them all to hear, he said, 'By the way, Hope. You broke your promise to me.'

'Captain?' asked Hope, her stomach suddenly cold.

'You said none of my crew would have to fight pirates today. But I saw one of them take on an entire ship of the bloodthirsty wretches, putting herself in harm's way in a most spectacular fashion, all to save the rest of us from injury or worse.'

The welter of emotions that swept through Hope made it difficult to speak. Relief, confusion, embarrassment, pleasure. 'Captain, I—'

'Let no man say,' continued Captain Carmichael, as his gaze swept the rest of the group, 'that Bleak Hope is not a true member of this crew.' He turned back to her, flashing a yellow smile in his beard. 'Come here, you deadly little thing.' Then he pulled her into a rough embrace.

It had been a very long time since anyone had embraced Hope, and she had to resist the automatic impulse to snap his neck. Hurlo had been many wonderful things, but demonstratively affectionate was not one of them. This warm contact was something she had not felt since her parents were alive. To be part of this crew, to be part of the sea. He was giving her a place to belong. And she found that for now, she not only wanted it, but needed it.

'Thank you,' she said quietly to him.

He chuckled, then stepped away and said to the whole crew, 'Let's get under way, then! This pirate money doesn't sit well in my pocket. The sooner we reach Vance Post, the sooner I can spend it all on drinks for my crew!'

The men all cheered and got to their stations. Hope stood and watched wistfully as they began their work.

'Here, Miss Hope,' called Ticks over by the mainmast rigging. 'Give me a hand with this line, will you?'

Hope smiled. 'It would be my pleasure, Mr. Ticks.'

13

*B*rigga Lin did not know where he was exactly, or how he'd gotten there. But one thing he was certain of: He would change the world with his discovery.

He'd woken up in a simple cot, still wearing his stained white biomancer robe. It seemed to be a military barracks of some kind, with twenty cots evenly spaced throughout the room. All the other cots were empty and the sun streamed in through the windows.

He was terribly weak, but there was a jug of fresh water and some hard bread on the table next to him. He ate and drank the simple fare with a relish he had never known.

'Feeling better, then, sir?' asked an imperial soldier as he entered the room, his helmet held under one arm. The gold tassels on his shoulders indicated that he was a captain.

'Yes, Captain,' said Brigga Lin, wiping the crumbs from his mouth. He was still struggling to piece his memory back together, most likely thanks to that damned moss. 'How long have I been out?'

''Bout two days, sir. Washed ashore in a rudderless boat, nearly dead. Fisherman found you, recognized the robes, and came running to us.'

He had a vague memory of climbing out of the underground passage, laughing hysterically. Then he'd stumbled to his boat, pushed it out into open water, and set the sail. He had no idea how long he'd been adrift, but it couldn't have been more than a few days or he would have starved. It was luck he'd drifted ashore on an inhabited island. Or perhaps fate.

'Thank you for taking me under your care, Captain,' he said. 'I will make sure you are amply rewarded.'

'Sorry we didn't get you cleaned up better, sir.' The captain indicated Brigga Lin's torn and muddy robes. 'But you were clinging to that book with such a desperation, when someone tried to take it from you, you got . . . uh, real unhappy.' He coughed. 'So I thought it best to leave it alone.'

The memories snapped into place like a puzzle. 'The book! Captain, where is it!'

'Right there, sir.' The captain pointed to a large black tome on the floor next to the cot. 'Looks like you dropped it while you were unconscious.'

Brigga Lin leaned over and snatched up the book. He was not ready for such a sudden movement, and the world spun for a moment. He held the book tightly to his chest until it passed.

'You did exactly right, Captain,' he said at last. 'This book will protect the empire from a grave threat.'

'Glad to be of service, sir.'

Brigga Lin stared down at the book. It had to be five hundred years old, perhaps more. It was a treasure beyond worth with knowledge that would make the biomancers more powerful than they had ever been.

'Where am I, exactly?' he asked.

'Wake Landing, sir,' said the captain.

'I see.' It made sense. Wake Landing was one of the closest neighboring islands. A bit removed from the center of the empire, but that might actually suit his purposes. 'Is there a temple on Wake Landing?'

'Yes, sir. But it's a bit small and nobody's been in it for years.'

'That will do just fine, Captain.'

The book Brigga Lin had discovered was the *Biomancery Praxis* that every biomancer studied as a novitiate. However, this older version included a final chapter that had been removed from later editions. This lost chapter spoke of the dual nature of biomancery. To create as well as destroy. It spoke of the interconnected threads of all life, not just solid matter, but liquid, and even the air itself. But to harness such power required a specific kind of biomancer. Namely, a female one.

There were no female biomancers, of course. *The Book of Storms* very clearly forbade either the biomancery or Vinchen orders from allowing female members. So if Brigga Lin wanted to test this newly discovered idea, he would have to secretly train a girl in the biomancer tradition, but not at Stonepeak. Was such a thing even possible? Even if it were, it would take him at least a decade. And he wondered, was the female mind strong enough to comprehend the know-ledge that was required? After all that time and effort, he might find she was not even capable of biomancery. He might find that the entire idea was impossible. It would explain why subsequent editions of the book had omitted the chapter.

But there was another way he could test it. A way that would take significantly less time. It would be unorthodox, certainly. But so was training a female biomancer. And with threat of invasion looming from the north, did the empire even have the luxury of a decade-long experiment? No, he suspected it did not. So once again, for the good of the empire, he would have to thrust his hand blindly into the darkness.

It took another day before he was healthy enough to move

around. Then the captain had a few soldiers take him through
Wake Landing to the temple. The town was even smaller
than he'd realized. Most of the island was given over to agriculture. He wondered why it warranted a full imperial squad.
Perhaps because it was in the northwest corner of the empire,
set equally between the Dusk Sea and the Dark Sea. If the
forces of Aukbontar were to get a foothold such as Wake
Landing, it was possible not even the Guardian would be
able to protect Stonepeak from a direct assault.

The captain had been right. It was the smallest temple
Brigga Lin had ever seen. Just one room with an altar no
bigger than a table. But it would be enough.

He turned to the two soldiers who had guided him to the
temple. 'Bring me food and fresh water once a day, but leave
them outside the temple. No one is to enter without my leave.
Do you understand?'

'Yes, sir,' said one of the soldiers nervously. This far from
the capital, they feared all biomancers equally. That would
also suit his purposes.

'Good. Then leave me.'

The soldiers hurried away, carefully closing the temple
door behind them.

Brigga Lin laid the book open on the altar. Then he
stripped off his dirty robe and undergarments. He stood
naked, the colored sunlight that leaked in through the
stained glass creating random patterns on his bare flesh. He
stared down at his penis. He would never have admitted it,
but he found it a strangely repulsive little worm, wrinkled
and venous. He'd never had sex, and even the idea of
masturbation – of jerking the little worm up and down –
filled him with distaste.

He'd always been concerned about that, well aware that he
was not normal in that way. But perhaps it really was fate,
preparing him for this moment.

He gathered his thoughts together, then reached down and touched his penis. For a moment, nothing happened, and he wondered if he'd gotten the focus wrong. It wouldn't have been the first time. But then a cord of pain shot up through his abdomen that brought him to his hands and knees. He hunched there on all fours as the pain rippled through him. He hoped the walls of this temple were thick enough to mute the noise. Because if he was already in this much pain, it was very likely he'd soon be screaming.

He felt dizzy as the blood drained from his brain and engorged his penis. It stood warm, erect, and quivering, throbbing with his pulse. But it didn't stop there. He moaned piteously as the warmth turned to searing heat, the throbbing to an unrelenting pressure. His genitals continued to expand until his penis looked more like a bloated sausage, and his scrotum like a small fruit. That was when he shrieked, like an animal.

Then his penis exploded in a gush of blood and semen while his scrotum shriveled into an empty sack. He collapsed to the floor, shuddering as the tattered shreds of his penis and his empty scrotum withered and withdrew into his body. Just as that pain began to subside, he felt new pains. His chest pulsed and swelled, the skin rippling as it changed into the shape of breasts. He also felt a deep wrenching in his body as ovaries and uterus formed, shoving the rest of his internal organs into new positions to make room. Then the remains of his genitals began to come together and reshape themselves into a concave form.

Brigga Lin wasn't sure how long the transformation took. But by the time she was finally able to stand and make her way gingerly to the door, she found two meals sitting outside. She ate the food slowly, her insides still tender. She slept for a long time. When she woke again, there were two more meals. She ate those more quickly.

She wandered the small space of the temple until she
found a small silver platter that was shiny enough to see her
reflection. She held up the platter at arm's length and looked
at herself. Something in her mind clicked into place and she
thought, *Yes*. It took her a little by surprise. She hadn't realized it until now, but whenever she'd looked at herself before,
she'd always thought, *No*, as if the reflection had seemed
wrong somehow. But this was right. For the first time in her
life, she felt whole.

Satisfied, Brigga Lin walked over to the altar and looked
down at the open book.

Now it was time to begin the experiment.

PART THREE

In its uncaring majesty, the storm may give as easily as it takes. Do not grieve so heavily for what is lost that you do not see what can be gained.

— from The Book of Storms

14

*H*ey, Red.' Sadie's voice was dry and muted. 'Tell me about when we was pirates.'

Red gazed down at her. She looked shriveled up as a raisin as she lay on the filthy straw mat, clutching a wool blanket. Her hair was like dry corn silk, and her skin was stretched painfully thin across her bones. She hadn't left this room in weeks. She would probably die here. Very soon.

But there was no hint of that in Red's expression as he knelt beside her. He raked his fingers through his hair and smiled, his ruby eyes gleaming from the light of the small oil lamp he had brought with him.

'The tale of Sadie the Pirate Queen,' he said quietly. 'That's one of my favorites. Where should I begin?'

Sadie's gnarled, bent hands groped for his and when he gave it to her, she squeezed it. Her wrinkled lips worked silently for a moment. 'From . . . from when I lose my ear.'

'Temporarily,' said Red.

She gave a toothless grin. 'Temporarily.'

'So.' His voice became intense, theatrical. 'Sadie had just had her ear torn off by Bracers Madge. It now lived in a pickling jar behind the bar of the Drowned Rat, along with a great many others. More than the pain of losing that ear was the shame of being turned out from the hall where thieves conspired, murderers were hired, and a dangerous girl with an unhealthy reputation could make a good living. But how could Sadie do that now? She was like to starve if she didn't do something bold. Fortunately . . .' He paused and looked down at her expectantly.

'Fortunately,' said Sadie, who had heard him tell this tale many times. 'She was twice as bold as any other wag in Paradise Circle, Silverback, or Hammer Point.'

'Right you are,' said Red. 'She conceived of a daring new business venture: piracy! She still had the commandeered ship, the *Savage Wind*. So she and her trusty first mate, Red, set about turning it into a proper pirate vessel, with a proper pirate crew. And it wasn't long before the *Savage Wind* could be seen cruising up and down the coast, its fierce captain pacing the bridge in a broad, feathered hat and long boots, looking for her next unlucky victim. Indeed, the docks of New Laven lived in constant fear of her sudden appearance. They said she gave no quarter, that if you were unlucky enough to be taken alive, she'd make you walk the plank over the reefs so that you'd fall and break yourself on them, spending hours half-submerged and bleeding out on the sharp coral before the cold waters of the deep finally claimed you. They said she once overtook and boarded a spice trader bound for the private docks of the emperor himself. When the captain rudely informed her that she would swing for it, she laughed, then had her crew pin him to the deck while she pissed all over him.'

Sadie laughed at that, a deep wet sound that ended in a spastic hacking cough that left blood on her lips.

'She became one of the most famous pirates who ever sailed,' continued Red, 'second only to Dire Bane, scourge of the empire. Other pirates kept clear of New Laven completely, leaving Captain Sadie free to terrorize the coasts of the city with impunity. Oh, to be sure, the emperor's ships tried to catch her. But she knew secret ways and hidden inlets. Their dreary military methods were no match for her wily cunning.

'But all streaks must end, and so it was with the glorious reign of Captain Sadie the Pirate Queen. It was the poor honest peasants who finally banded together one night. As she made port to pillage a small coastal village, they appeared out of nowhere and launched burning pitch onto her ship from makeshift catapults. Within minutes, the *Savage Wind* was ablaze, and within the hour, Sadie was left once again with nothing but the clothes on her back.'

Red paused to look down at her. He brushed a few stray white hairs out of her face. 'But was she ready to give up on this rotten old life?' he asked in a more subdued tone.

'No . . .' whispered Sadie.

'Of course not!' he said, returning to his previous intensity. 'She marched right back to Paradise Circle, faithful Red still in tow, walked into the Drowned Rat, and threw herself at the mercy of Bracers Madge. Sadie owned that she had been in the wrong to try and kill Backus in Madge's establishment, that it had been disrespectful and unprofessional, and she was forever sorry she'd done it. And Bracers Madge, it was said, was so moved by Sadie's declaration and humility, that she gave Sadie the jar that contained her long-lost ear, the first and only time Madge ever returned one of her prize souvenirs. From that night on, Sadie wore the small jar on a leather strap around her neck, and she was welcomed back to the neighborhood with open arms. Because that's how it is in the Circle.'

'That's how it is in the Circle . . .' echoed Sadie.

Her withered hand drifted to her throat, where the small jar rested on her boney chest.

'Where it's dismal and wet,' said Red.

'And the sun never gets,' responded Sadie.

'But still it's my home, bless the Circle,' finished Red.

Sadie smiled peacefully, and her eyes slowly closed. A moment later, she began to snore.

Red laid a gentle hand on her forehead and whispered, 'Sleep well, you old goat.' Then he stretched his long legs and brushed the dirt from his pants.

'Is that how it really was?' asked a satiny female voice.

Red turned toward the doorway and saw Nettles leaning against the frame, her arms crossed, her long dark hair falling across her face in a dramatic way that Red knew was entirely on purpose.

'What, the story of Sadie the Pirate Queen?' He shrugged on his brown leather longcoat. 'Close enough. Maybe I took a few harmless liberties. She never threw anybody onto a bed of coral. She did piss on that gaf, though. Funniest thing I've ever seen, him wailing and cursing the whole time.'

Nettles smirked. She'd taken to painting her full lips a dark mulberry lately. Red had to admit that it suited her well.

'How long was it really?' she asked. 'The time you two plundered the coasts?'

'Only about three months.' Red picked up the small lantern he'd brought down with him. The light cast shadows across his lean face as he grinned. 'But it was a sunny three months.'

He paused at the doorway and looked back into the room. Dirt floor, no windows. He hated leaving her here, alone. Still, underground hole or not, it was better than her dying in the street like a dog or a broken-legged horse.

'She's lucky to have you,' said Nettles.

'Hm,' said Red.

'We should all have some handsome young scoundrel to care for us in our final days.'

'Who said these are her final days?' Red asked sharply, although of course he knew they were.

'Sorry. Nobody.' Nettles was a good friend like that, usually.

Red looked at her then, the lantern playing off her smooth forehead and high cheekbones, her dark eyes sparkling with mystery. He wondered, not for the first time, why it hadn't worked out between them a couple of years back.

Then she squinted and plucked at his leather longcoat. 'What in piss'ell are you *wearing*? Looks like a mole rat climbed onto your back and died.'

Oh yeah. Now he remembered why.

'It happens to be deer leather, finely tanned and cured, soft as velvet,' Red replied loftily. 'You'll never find better.'

'Who'd you steal it from?'

'I won it in a game of stones.'

'That's what I just said.'

Red sighed. 'What are you doing here, Nettie?'

'I was coming to the hall to take care of some personal matters, and Filler asked me to pop down and tell you it's on for tonight.'

'He got a horse?' Red's ruby eyes shone eagerly in the lantern light.

'I don't know what he does or doesn't got,' said Nettles. 'I only know the message and that's *all* I want to know. You boys been getting too serious lately.'

'Like you don't know trouble.'

'Trouble, I know. But what you wags are doing?' She shook her head. 'It's only a matter of time before you swing. Or worse.'

'It's not *that* bad,' said Red. 'We just—'

'Like I said, that's all I want to know!'

Sadie groaned in her sleep.

'Come on, we're making too much noise,' said Red.

Nettles nodded and the two left the room, their boots tracking softly in the dirt as they passed other doorways, some quiet, some full of moans or cries, and some stinking of death. At the end of the hallway, they climbed the narrow wooden ladder up to the ground level of Gunpowder Hall.

As Red and Nettles picked their way through the crowds, a voice called, 'Red! Hey, Red!'

A thin, pouchy-faced old man was making his way over to them.

'Backus.' Red met him halfway and clasped his hand. 'How are things?'

'Things are as they are,' said the old man. 'But thought I should tell you, I'm out of Sadie's medicine. I been bringing it to her regular, like you said, and it's all used up.'

'Oh,' said Red.

'You . . . uh . . . think that'll do?' asked Backus. 'I mean . . . Red, it don't seem to be doing nothing, and I know however you get it, it ain't cheap.'

Red shook his head. 'No.'

'Sadie wouldn't want you spending all your money on her. You know that.'

'Well, she'll just have to get well enough to tell me that herself,' said Red.

Backus looked at him a moment, his sagging face unreadable. Finally, his mouth worked up into a half-smile. 'She raised you a proper man of the Circle. Alright, you get me that medicine, I'll keep giving it to her.'

Red put his hand on Backus's boney shoulder. 'Thank you.'

Backus shrugged. 'It's the only thing to do. You'll understand someday. If you're lucky enough to be one of the few that makes it into old age, the folks of your youth, be they friend or foe, become the ones you treasure most.'

Red watched as Backus made his way back to the corner of the hall where the old wrinks congregated.

'I can't believe he's not scamming you somehow,' said Nettles. 'Selling off that medicine or something.'

'I know,' said Red. 'But I asked around, and everybody says he gives her the meds every day like clock. Old people are funny like that.'

'Soft is what it is,' said Nettles. 'Hope I die first.'

Red grinned at her. 'Nettie, you haven't got an ounce of romance in you.'

'And a good thing, too. Romance is for ponces and halfwits.'

And that, thought Red, was the other reason things hadn't worked out between them.

'Well.' He pulled on his thick leather fingerless gloves. 'I best see if Filler has really come through.'

Nettles eyed his gloves. 'Going to work, then?'

'There is a city out there with wealth in desperate need of redistribution,' he said, smiling.

She roughly clasped his hand. 'You better come back alive, is all. Or else.'

'Or else what?'

'Or else I will get a necromancer and pissing summon you, just so I can kick you in your ghostly balls.'

He bowed mockingly to her and left Gunpowder Hall, wondering if maybe she did have an ounce or so of romance after all.

'And you're *sure* about this, Red?' asked Filler, scratching his scruffy short beard as he eyed the horse. Although he'd been the one to score the big animal, he didn't seem to like being around it.

'Of course.' Red patted the horse's large pink-and-white nose with his gloved hand. The two stood with the horse in a narrow alley off Central Street.

'And to steer, all I have to do is move these reins to the right or to the left?' Filler squinted skeptically.

'Filler, my best wag,' said Red. 'If I didn't know better, I'd say you were scared of this dumb animal.'

'Not scared,' said Filler.

'Of course not,' agreed Red.

'Only . . . my cousin, Brig. He got his head kicked in by a horse, and now all he does is sing nursery songs and shit his pants.'

'Ah,' said Red, nodding seriously. He reached up to put his arm around Filler's shoulders. 'So, it's like this, old pot. One of us needs to ride the horse, and one of us needs to pick the lock. Now, tell me. Are you any good at picking locks?'

Filler shook his head.

'Well then, *I* need to be doing that bit, don't I?'

'I suppose.'

'And if I'm picking the lock, I can't very well ride the horse, too, can I? So the only other option would be to bring in a third party to this venture. Someone who isn't haunted by the memories of horse-kicked cousins. Who doesn't mind riding a fine steed such as this one. Someone like, oh, I dunno, Handsome Henny, maybe. Or perhaps Nettles, seeing as how you practically invited her on the job anyway.'

'I swear, Red, I didn't tell her nothing about it.'

'Even so, if we *did* bring in a third party, that would mean splitting the take three ways instead of two. Now, I know you aren't too fond of maths, so to give you a sense of it, we'd each have to give *half* of our take to make a third equal share. Does that sound like something you want to do?'

'No,' said Filler, his nervousness already deflating into defeat.

'Agreed. So, Filler, my wag, swallow the fear and let's be men about this.'

He nodded gloomily, still eyeing the horse.

'If you'd like, we can club an imp for his helmet,' offered Red. 'Don't know what good it would do against horse hooves, but—'

'I ain't wearing no pissing imp hat,' said Filler, his expression hardening.

'That's the spirit!' Red slapped him on the back. 'Now, that cart should be along here soon, so let's get ourselves ready.'

They'd been watching it for weeks now. A horse-drawn cart that came through every morning escorted by two imps in full riot armor – one in front, one in the rear – plus a driver. The riot armor prevented Red from solving the whole problem with a few quick throwing blades. What's more, the cart itself was really just a strongbox on wheels, black iron secured by a key lock. He'd learned from reliable sources that the key was kept by another mounted imp who took a separate route through the city. Red thought that was a nice touch. Inside the strongbox were the imperial taxes on the previous day's earnings from gambling houses and dance halls. Those earnings also included the money from the quiet back-room sale of coral spice. In general, Red tried to be an open-minded sort of wag. But for personal reasons, he was not fond of coral spice dealers or those who profited from them.

Filler had taken the horse off to his post, and Red stood alone in a narrow alley, his back pressed against the wall as he listened to the splash of hooves out on the muddy street. A few moments later, the lead imp on horseback trotted past, his studded leather police helmet gleaming faintly in the sickly morning light. His gold-and-white riot armor stuck out in the drab city streets. A few moments after him came the horse-drawn strongbox cart, the driver looking half-asleep. A few more moments, and the cart was followed by the rear guard.

Red held his breath, listening to the steady clop of hooves as the rear guard passed. When they came to a halt, Red let out his breath and smiled.

He peeked around the corner. Filler sat astride the horse, silent and brooding as he blocked the road. His height and broad shoulders always made him an intimidating presence. On horseback, the effect was magnified. The rear guard moved to the front, and together the two imps approached him cautiously.

'Step aside,' said one of the imps, pushing his gold uniform jacket aside to show the pistol at his hip.

Filler did not respond.

'We'll give you to the count of three.' The second imp drew his pistol and the other followed suit.

By this time, Red had already snuck to the back of the cart and was working at the lock.

'One,' said the imp.

As he worked the pins, Red noted that this lock had not been well maintained.

'Two.'

Red wondered how they even opened the damn thing with a key, it was such a disaster.

'Thr—'

Filler slapped his horse's flank and took off down the next alley before they finished the word.

'You continue with the cart!' shouted the rear guard imp to the other. Then he took off after Filler.

The front guard moved forward. The cart driver snapped his reins, and the cart followed.

Red silently mouthed a curse. There wasn't anywhere to sit on the cart, so he hooked his legs on the struts and straddled the strongbox, praying that the driver didn't turn around. He had never tried to pick a lock that bumped and shook. He found that it was impossible. He was almost there, but he needed the cart to stop, just for a moment, so he could get the last pin.

He pulled himself up as far forward as he could go, only a few feet from the back of the driver's head. He took a deep breath, then at the top of his lungs, shouted, 'Stop in the name of the emperor!'

The driver started and instinctually yanked back on the reins. The horse and wagon came to a sudden halt. Red slid his pick into the lock, heard a satisfying click. The door popped open and he grabbed the bag of coins inside. The driver turned in his seat, fumbling with his pistol. Red jumped to the ground, then took a single coin from the sack of money he had just rescued and flicked it at the horse's flank. The horse surged forward. The driver pitched back and slammed into the strongbox, dropping his pistol into the mud.

'Guard!' shouted the driver.

But by the time the imp wheeled his mount around, Red had ducked down the alley. From there, he climbed the gutters and pulled himself up onto the roof. He lingered long enough to watch the imp try to coax his horse into the narrow alley. But when Red laughed out loud, the imp saw him and fired his pistol. The shot glanced off the edge of the gutter, and Red took off across the rooftops, still laughing.

'Stop in the name of the emperor?' asked Handsome Henny.

Red had made it safely to the Drowned Rat and met up with Filler to split the money. Now he sat comfortably at his usual table with his usual drinking wags. Filler, of course; noseless Handsome Henny; and the Twins, Brimmer and Stin, who weren't actually twins, or even brothers, but whose ginger-colored hair was so out of place in the predominately dark-haired population that everyone initially assumed they must be related. By the time anyone realized they weren't brothers, the name had already stuck. In the Circle, a name always stuck.

Red grinned at Henny. 'You sore Filler and I didn't invite you on this one?'

'Are you kidding?' Henny leaned back in his chair. 'That was a suicide attempt, plain and simple. You got lucky, as you do more often than any man should. But one of these days, an imp is going to shoot you right between those pretty red eyes of yours. That is, if they don't hand you over to a biomancer for some unspeakable experiment.'

'They don't ever do that,' said Brimmer. Then he looked uncertainly at Stin. 'Do they?'

'I hear they do,' said Stin. 'My aunt? She said her nephew got taken once because he was on some citizen protest group. And when they brought his body back a month later for burial, it didn't even look human anymore.'

'Your aunt's nephew, huh?' Red sighed and shook his head. 'You wags are worse than a bunch of wrinks, you know that? Fact is, don't matter what they would have done to me if they caught me. Because they didn't catch me.'

'They almost caught Filler,' said Henny. 'What'd you have done then, I wonder? It's all fine to risk yourself, I suppose. But what about your best wag?'

'They didn't almost catch Filler.' Red turned to the large man. 'Did they?'

Filler shrugged. 'He was good with his horse. I wasn't. Only reason I got away was because he heard the shot the other imp took at you and realized I was just the decoy.'

'Just as I'd planned,' said Red.

'Liar,' said Henny.

'Look, how's about I buy us all a drink, and we let it wash away this bad taste you all seem to have.' He signaled to Prin. 'A round of dark for the table, Prinny. On me.'

Prin raised an eyebrow at him. 'You got coin for that?'

Red gave her a hurt look. 'Why of course, Prinny. How could you doubt me?'

'Experience, that's how,' said Prin. 'Show me.'

Red held up his hand, a shining coin between each finger. Prin's eyes widened. 'That'll set you the rest of the night.'

'Then you'd better start 'em coming!'

'Seriously, Red,' said Henny. 'Anytime you want to knock over a grocery or roll a lacy from uptown, you know I'm your wag. And even if you've got a grind with someone like Big Sig and his crew, I'll back you right up. But messing with the pissing imps in broad daylight? That's bringing unwanted attention to the whole neighborhood. That's making it harder for all of us.'

'But don't you see, Hen, it's the pissing imps who *deserve* it,' said Red. 'Robbing some poor wrink's grocery is just balls and pricks. That kind of inside violence is what really hurts the neighborhood. Instead of picking on each other, we should join together. Strength in numbers.'

'Except Big Sig,' said Stin. 'We can't never join up with him.'

'Rot and damnation to Big Sig and the whole of Hammer Point,' agreed Brimmer. 'May all their cocks and cunts drop off from the blight.'

'If I thought it would give us an edge against the imps, I would work with Big Sig in a drop,' said Red.

'Balls and pricks, you don't mean that,' said Henny.

'I do,' said Red. 'Look, they're just like us. Maybe not as smart or good-looking. But they're just as poor, and just as put down by the imps.'

'But—' said Henny.

'Let it go, Handsome,' said Filler. 'You're only getting him more wound up. It's that uptown blood of his. He can't help it, he just gets ideas.'

'It's gonna get him and maybe us killed one of these days,' muttered Henny.

'But until then . . .' Red gestured grandly as Prin brought over five metal tankards of foamy dark ale. 'Let's drink!'

The evening wore on, and Prin refilled those tankards many times. Although Red was paying, his was refilled the least. That's the way he liked it. To be the sharpest one at the table. So he nursed one drink most of the night, playing stones with Henny and beating him more easily with each round. Other wags came and enjoyed his hospitality here and there, and he'd tell them of that morning's adventure, the number of imps increasing with each telling. He never said where the bulk of his score had gone and nobody asked, which was for the best. It was okay that Nettles knew he was taking care of Sadie, but he doubted any of those other salt-heads would understand or respect it. Red was used to being alone in that. He liked it that way, too.

As evening set in, and Prin came out from behind the bar to light the oil lamps around the tavern, Red put his mud-encrusted black boots on the table.

'Filler, old wag,' he said. 'Would you say you're content?'

'Eh?' said Filler, blinking through his drunken haze.

'Happy. Are you happy?'

Filler shrugged. 'I s'pose. Never really thought about it.'

'That's the key, I suspect.' Red held up one of the gaming stones, a smooth rectangle with a painted number four on it, watching the glaze catch the lamplight. 'Not to think about it so much.'

He flicked the stone and it popped into Brimmer's mouth just as he was yawning. Brimmer started hacking as Stin pounded on his back, while Henny let loose with a high-pitched giggle, and Filler gave one of his rumbling guffaws.

Red smiled. 'Me? I don't think there's a thing more in the world that I need than this.'

Later, he would think back ruefully on that statement and admit that he had more or less asked for what came next.

An older man walked into the Drowned Rat with the roll-ing gait and wool coat that marked him as a seaman. He had a broad blue hat, a curly black beard, and skin nearly as dark. Red barely paid him any mind, but what he saw next made him sit up and put his boots squarely on the floor.

Behind the seaman walked a woman around Red's age, with the golden hair and pale, freckled skin of a Southerner. Red had always considered Southies to be somewhat sickly-looking. But there was nothing sickly about this woman. She moved like liquid steel, each step confident and utterly precise. And her eyes . . . they were like the frozen depths of the sea, forged into tiny daggers that stabbed him in the chest when her gaze swept every patron in the bar, assessing them.

'Who . . .' he hissed, grabbing Henny's arm hard. 'Who is that wondrous creature?'

Henny followed his gaze and smirked. 'That molly? I heard about her. Landed a few days ago with Captain Carmichael, the gaf she's with there. He's made port here times before, brings down fruit from Murgesia. Apparently, she's his bodyguard.'

Red sighed. 'She's a pissing angel in black leather.'

'You know what that leather suit is, right?' asked Stin. 'It's a pissing Vinchen uniform.'

'Girl Vinchen?' asked Brimmer. 'That's not even allowed, I don't think.'

'Tell that to *her*,' said Henny.

Captain Carmichael and his bodyguard walked to the table all the way at the back of the hall, where Deadface Drem sat with his crew.

'I thought you said this captain traded in fruit,' said Red.

'Maybe he traded *up* for something more lucrative.'

'But Drem? That's serious.'

'Maybe why he got himself that ice-maiden bodyguard.'

Red watched Drem look up from his table at the sea captain, frowning slightly. He looked at the angel bodyguard, and his frown deepened even more.

Another sailor came into the hall, this one with a long mustache. He hurried over to the captain and the ice maiden. When Deadface Drem saw this latecomer, his face went blank.

'Piss'ell,' Red muttered.

'I think your molly is about to be in a world of trouble,' said Henny.

15

*W*hen they first arrived at Murgesia on a sunny afternoon, Hope thought it was the prettiest island they'd
ever made port during her two years aboard the *Lady's
Gambit*. Curling palm trees and smooth, white sand beaches,
so different from the rocky quays that she grew up with.
They'd come to Murgesia to buy citrus fruit. Captain
Carmichael said they should be able to sell it for double the
price on New Laven.

Hope and Ranking accompanied him into the village to
meet with the merchant. It was a small but neat community,
with simple wood and mortar buildings. The narrow dirt
paths bustled with villagers who watched them curiously but
were quick to give a friendly smile when Hope caught them
staring.

The fruit storehouse was at the center of the village. It was
the largest building on the island. Out front, a man lounged
in a wooden chair with an umbrella to shield him from the
sun. When he saw them approach, he smiled warmly.

'Captain Carmichael!' he said, getting to his feet and
walking over to them. 'So good to see you. Seems like it's
been ages!'

'I hope you've been keeping well, Ontelli.' Carmichael
clasped his hand.

'Oh, sure, keeping.' Ontelli nodded. 'It's been an interesting couple of years.'

'Sorry to hear that,' said Carmichael. 'Personally, I like to keep my years nice, dull, and predictable. Helps a person live longer.'

Ontelli kept nodding and smiling. 'Right enough. Well, I hate to do this to you, Captain, but do you suppose you could come back later?'

'Oh?' asked Carmichael.

'I'm just so busy right now.' Ontelli gestured vaguely to the storehouse behind him.

'Busy?' asked Carmichael, his black-and-gray eyebrows rising. There didn't seem to be any activity at the storehouse.

'Yes,' said Ontelli. 'I don't suppose you could come back later? Perhaps a little after sunset? I should have your cargo packed by then. Same as last time, right? And we can do it all in one smooth transaction.'

'I suppose . . .' said Carmichael.

'I realize I'm putting you out a bit,' said Ontelli, his smile still firmly in place. 'Tell you what, if you humor me and come back after sunset, I'll take an extra ten percent off the price for you.'

Carmichael shrugged. 'Well, now, that is friendly of you. Sure, we'll be back after dark with a few extra wags to help haul the cargo back to the ship.'

'Wonderful!' said Ontelli. 'Thanks for being flexible, Captain. I'll see you tonight.' He hurried to the storehouse and went inside.

'I don't like it, sir,' said Hope. 'That whole exchange seemed off to me.'

'I agree,' said Carmichael. 'But we need the cargo.'

So they returned to the ship and waited. After nightfall, they set out again for the storehouse. Hope took the lead this time, followed by Carmichael.

Behind him came Ranking and after that, Sankack and Ticks pulling an empty cart that would be used to haul the fruit back to the ship.

There were no lights in the village. No torches to mark the paths or intersections, and strangely, no lights were coming from inside any of the houses. The only light in the entire village was the lantern that hung from the cart pulled by Sankack and Ticks. It was as if the entire place was deserted.

Except it wasn't. Hope caught glimpses of figures lurking in the darkness, creeping outside the reach of the lantern light with jerky, unnatural movements.

'Captain,' she said quietly, her hand going to her hilt.

'I see 'em,' he said.

'What are they?' Ranking asked. 'Don't move like people.'

'Long as they keep their distance, I don't much care what they are,' said Carmichael. 'Let's move. Once we reach the village center, we should be safe enough.'

But when they reached the center of the village, it was as dark as the rest. A small group of people were clustered in front of the storehouse, waiting for them.

'Alright, Ontelli,' said Carmichael. 'We came at night. Just like you asked. And now you want to do business in pitch-black? What in the hells are you playing at? Last time I was here, this was a nice, easy, profitable deal for both of us. I hope you don't plan to screw that up.'

The gathered figures were still and silent.

'Ah, but Captain Carmichael,' came Ontelli's voice, sounding strained. 'I don't have plans anymore. Not really. Not like I used to. There's no point. You see, we had a visitor to Murgesia a while back. And now things are a bit different. We have different priorities. Different . . . needs.'

Hope sensed the shadowy figures creeping in closer from all directions. 'Captain, we're surrounded.'

'Damn you, Ontelli,' said Carmichael, sounding almost tired. 'You think you're going to roll us, do you? Take the money *and* the cargo? I'm telling you, that's not happening. If you won't trade, let us back to our ship and we'll be on our way. Otherwise, a lot of your people are going to die.'

'You misunderstand, Captain,' said Ontelli.

He stepped into the lantern light, and there was a strange, wild look in his eyes. He was drenched in sweat, and his mouth was curled up into an expression somewhere between a smile and a painful grimace. The other figures began moving into the light. Ranking had been right. They weren't people. They were unnaturally thin, with round heads, huge eyes, and short curved beaks where their mouths and noses had once been. Mottled feathers poked out of their skin in clumps instead of hair, and instead of arms they had scrawny, feathered wings.

'It's not your money we want,' said Ontelli. 'It's your flesh.' He shuddered. A beak emerged from between his lips as his whole face peeled back like a sack, exposing wet feathers and sharp owl eyes.

Sankack screamed, dropped his end of the cart, and bolted. He didn't make it far. One of the owl creatures jumped, flapping its wings. It didn't fly, but it got enough lift to reach Sankack. It dug its talons into his back as it knocked him face-first into the ground. A group of them swarmed in and pecked at him, tearing away chunks of meat as he thrashed and screamed.

Captain Carmichael drew his pistol and leveled it at the thing that had once been Ontelli. 'May God grant mercy to your soul, because he sure as piss didn't grant it to your life.'

The thing stretched its curved black beak wide and lunged at the captain, but its face exploded in a cloud of bloody feathers as the pistol fired.

'Captain?' asked Hope.

'Clear us a path back to the ship,' he said as he slammed the butt of his pistol into the side of another creature's head.

Hope drew the Song of Sorrows and lopped off the head of the nearest creature in one smooth motion.

'Ranking and Ticks,' said the captain. 'Leave the cart. Follow behind Hope and keep them off her back.'

Ranking drew his cutlass and Ticks a short mace. Once they were behind her, Hope worked her way forward. She twisted first one way, then the other, her sword flashing in the moonlight amid the hoots and screams of the creatures. The blade swam like a porpoise through the dense cluster of feathers, down and up, as it hewed through the spindly limbs. Hope's feet pivoted smoothly, her muscles taut and buzzing with warmth as she worked. She could almost hear Grandteacher Hurlo's crackling voice in her ear, saying, *Faster on the outside, quieter on the inside*, as she made her way through the throng.

'God, they just keep coming!' shouted Ranking. 'We'll never make it!'

'Shut up and fight,' said the captain.

Hope couldn't stop to see if he did, though. They were nearly through the densest part. It was all one continuous blur of motion. She felt as if she were disappearing, and there was nothing except the Song of Sorrows humming its terrible melody. The owl creatures may not have understood human speech, but they clearly knew the language of that sword and began shying away from it even before it came near.

Finally, she was through the mass of creatures. Before them was the unlit street that led to the ship.

'Go!' yelled Carmichael.

The group took off at a run, with the creatures close behind. They couldn't run as fast, but occasionally, one would get enough momentum to vault off the side of a building and drop down on them. But Ticks would knock it to one side with his mace, and its light bird bones would shatter on impact.

The ship came into view, her twinkling lanterns shining like a beacon.

'Captain, nearly there!' Hope chanced a glance back and saw what Carmichael did not. An owl creature jumped at Ranking. Rather than face it, he dodged behind Ticks, who was busy fending off one from the other side. Ranking stayed clear while Ticks was brought down with rending talons and beaks.

'Coward!' screamed Hope, lifting her sword to strike Ranking. But Carmichael grabbed her arm.

'The ship!' he shouted in her face. 'Now!'

Hope gritted her teeth and spun back to the front. A small pack of the creatures had outflanked them and circled around. She was glad of it and lashed out so hard their twitching bodies flew several feet back and crashed into a stack of old crates on the dock. The crates toppled over, revealing a large sign driven into the wood. On the sign was painted a black oval with eight black lines trailing down from it. The symbol of the biomancers.

Hope jerked to a halt. The shock of recognition constricted her chest as old memories came flooding to the surface. She could not catch her breath and she staggered forward, clawing at the air in front of her, her vision beginning to narrow.

'What now?' barked Carmichael.

She could only gasp and point at the sign. When he saw it, his eyes narrowed.

'I might have known.' He lifted his head to the ship and bellowed, 'All hands! All hands on deck! Prepare to cut and run!'

He leapt aboard as some of the crew scrambled for their weapons to fend off the attackers, while others hurriedly prepared to make sail.

Hope didn't follow. Instead she stood on the dock, gasping and shaking, feeling like a little girl again. The old darkness rose up inside and she heard her mother calling to her as she was ripped apart from the inside. She could smell the piles of dead bodies left to rot. She could feel the ache of endless days spent digging graves in the frozen, rocky soil. When it had come time to bury her father, she saw his face still twisted in the agony he felt at the moment of his death, like his soul would feel that pain for eternity. She had looked down at the sea glass necklace, and for a moment she had considered keeping it, as a way to remember him. But its beauty no longer held any appeal to her. The warmth, the color, it had been crushed out of her. It was better off with him, buried there in that cold, dead place . . .

'What in hells is wrong with you?' Ranking grabbed her shoulder as he stared fearfully at the swarm of descending owl creatures. But then he turned to her and seemed to recognize her expression. He paused, as if deciding something. Then he slapped her hard across the face.

The shock of it brought her back. He pulled her arm, and the two stumbled aboard the ship as the crew closed ranks after them, allowing them both to catch their breath.

Ranking stuck his finger in her face. 'You don't say anything about Ticks, and I won't say anything about this. Keen?'

Her face hardened, but she nodded.

'Sunny. Now, let's get the hells off this cursed rock.'

The owl creatures seemed endless as they boiled out of the darkness and across the docks. Hope and Ranking rejoined the crew and together fought the creatures off until the sails were ready, the lines were cut, and the *Lady's Gambit* made her way swiftly out into open waters.

'Thank God they can't properly fly,' said Ranking as the island shrank rapidly in the distance. He winked at her, like they were friends who shared a secret.

A little later, Carmichael summoned Hope and Ranking to his quarters. The three sat around the small table that was bolted to the floor. Carmichael and Ranking passed a bottle of dark rum back and forth while the captain laid out their situation.

'Losing that cargo has put us in a bad way,' said Carmichael. 'The ship is in need of repairs. I was counting on selling the cargo we picked up here in New Laven to pay for those repairs.'

'Can't we pick up cargo somewhere else?' asked Hope.

The captain shook his head. 'We'll barely make it to New Laven. We can't risk going any further out. One strong storm on open water, and we go down.'

'What if we picked up cargo in New Laven and made a quick run up the coast?' asked Ranking. 'No risk of open water. Just up and back for a nice bit of cash.'

Carmichael sighed and scratched at his curly beard. 'Smuggling?'

'I know a wag in Paradise Circle who's always looking for freelancers. Ships that the imperial police don't know on sight.'

The captain took a pull on the bottle of rum and sat for a moment, lost in thought. 'I don't see much choice. We'll try this contact of yours. Set course for New Laven. We'll sail straight through.'

'Aye, Captain,' said Ranking, a broad grin beneath his mustache as he left.

Hope stood up to go.

'Wait a moment,' said the captain. 'You okay?'

'Of course, sir.'

'You seemed pretty shaken back there when you saw the biomancer sign.'

'It . . . reminded me of something. From my childhood. I have seen that sign once before.'

'When a biomancer does something like what they did on Murgesia – when they change a whole island like that – they leave a sign to warn others off, to let them know the place isn't safe anymore. The people in Murgesia seemed to have had enough presence of mind to hide the sign.' He took another pull at the bottle. 'They were once good people. A nice, friendly little port.'

'Why do they do it?' she asked. 'The biomancers. Why do they do that to people?'

'Why? Because the emperor commands it, I suppose. No greater reason in all the lands.' He took another drink. 'Or so they say.'

'That's not a real reason.'

'No,' he agreed. 'It isn't.'

Later that night, Hope lay in her hammock for hours before she could fall asleep. When she closed her eyes, she saw that sign. Black oval with eight black lines trailing down. Like the silhouette of a kraken. Murgesia was many leagues away from her own village. She wondered just how many villages had suffered from the cruelty of biomancers. Perhaps she had been too narrow-minded. Too self-centered in her longing for vengeance. The more she thought of it, killing one biomancer was not enough. She would take vengeance for all those poor souls who had suffered from their 'experiments.' She would kill all the biomancers.

A haze hung over New Laven so thick that Hope wondered if the inhabitants could even see the sun. She stood at the ship railing with Captain Carmichael and looked out at the city before them. It was the biggest thing she'd ever seen. The docks alone stretched over more area than the village of

Murgesia. Beyond that lay a collection of buildings so vast she could not guess where it ended.

'This must be the greatest city in the world,' she said.

Carmichael smiled. 'No, Hope. It's impressive, I'll grant you. And has character to spare. But there are larger cities than this one. Stonepeak, the capital, is half again as big as this. And I've heard tell that past the Dark Sea are cities that span leagues.'

'I didn't realize there was anything past the Dark Sea,' admitted Hope.

'You thought the world just ended beyond the borders of the empire? My father came from a land called Aukbontar beyond that sea. He told my mother that his homeland was bigger than all the islands of the empire put together. Just one giant mass of land.'

'Is such a thing possible?'

'The world is far more vast than you or I could even conceive of. We are so very small, like minnows.'

'I already feel that way, being in a city like this,' she said.

Carmichael nodded. 'New Laven might not be the biggest city in the world, but it may well be the hardest and meanest. This city will chew you up and spit you out, make no mistake. It takes the kindness right out of a person and leaves behind a cold, scheming eye.'

They stood there in silence for a moment, watching the dockworkers unload crates from other ships.

Finally, Hope said, 'Captain, with respect, it seems like something has been bothering you since we made port.'

'Trying to understand how it is I ended up here.'

'Sir?'

'If you'd asked me five years ago whether I fancied becoming a smuggler running guns and drugs along the coasts of New Laven, I would have laughed in your face. Or maybe punched you. I tried to play by the rules, do the right thing. But life . . .' He shook his head. 'It has a way of wearing you down so that one day you look around at the choices before you, and drug running don't even secm all that bad anymore.'

'How do you know it'll be drugs? Ranking said he'd find us whatever he could. I don't think drugs would be his first choice.'

'He's been looking for days,' said Carmichael. 'I'm guessing there aren't a lot of choices. And anyway, what else would need smuggling? They make the drugs here and they sell them uptown where the paying customers live. Those lacies need something to while away the hours.'

'Lacies?'

'Rich folk. Like all cities, most people in New Laven don't have much, and a few people have most.'

'That doesn't seem right.'

'Add it to the list, Hope, my girl.'

'Still, we don't need to contribute to it.'

'I suppose not.'

'The Vinchen say it is better to fail with honor than succeed with dishonor. Because the victor's cup would be tainted and taste foul in your mouth.'

He turned to her and suddenly smiled. 'Maybe after two years with you, that Vinchen code stuff is rubbing off on me, because that actually made sense. I've been so worried about losing this ship. But if keeping her means turning her into a drug runner, then maybe she's not worth keeping.'

Ranking returned later that day with news that he'd found them a cargo.

'What kind of cargo?' Carmichael had asked.

'The kind that pays. I didn't ask for details.'

Ranking led Carmichael and Hope through the docks, which were still bustling with activity, even though it was nearing twilight. Then he took them into the city proper.

Hope had walked the docks and wharfs for the past few days, but this was the first occasion she'd had to see more of the city. It was even more crowded than the docks, and it was filthy. The streets were at times ankle deep in a mixture of mud, garbage, and feces. The whole place smelled worse than anything Hope had ever experienced. Her simple fishing village had been poor, perhaps even impoverished. It probably hadn't seemed like much to the few traders who came through. But the people had taken care of it. This city seemed so magnificent at a distance, but up close, it was rotting at the core.

'How do people live like this?' she asked.

'Most of them are born to it and don't know any different,' said the captain.

'And those that do, take to sea the first chance they get,' said Ranking.

'I forgot you're from here,' said Hope. 'I didn't mean any offense.'

'None taken,' he said. 'Come on, it's this way.'

Hope and Carmichael followed Ranking through the winding streets, deeper into the city. As the skies continued to darken, Hope expected to see fewer people. But when night set in, an imperial officer began lighting street lamps, and people continued with their activities, whether it was selling, buying, drinking, or fighting. The darkness hid much of the squalor, and the lights twinkled merrily in a line that stretched as far down the street as she could see.

'It has a certain beauty at night,' she said.

'You should see uptown.' There was a strange note of pride in Ranking's voice. 'Gas lighting piped right into the homes.'

'Does *anyone* in this city sleep?' asked Hope.

'It's a different rhythm, living in a large city,' said Carmichael. 'Always seemed to me a bit too hard on a person.'

'That last scenic, secluded island didn't seem all that healthy either,' said Ranking.

'Point taken,' said the captain.

They walked on a little farther until they came to a tavern with a weathered old sign out front showing a large, angry-looking rodent and the name THE DROWNED RAT painted on it.

'This is the place,' said Ranking.

'This?' asked Hope. Through the grimy window, she could see a ragged and shifty-looking crowd swilling ale and shouting at one another. 'I find it hard to believe we'll find someone with a good job in there.'

'I didn't say "good,"' said Ranking. 'I said *paying*. His name is Deadface Drem, and he'll be waiting at the table in the back.'

'Aren't you coming?' asked Hope.

'Sure, of course.' Ranking nodded, but he was looking around distractedly. 'I saw this girl I knew go past just now. I'll catch up with you. Only be a moment.' Then he hurried off down a side alley.

'Let's see what questionable cargo Ranking thinks he's found for us,' said Carmichael. 'Keep your sword close.'

'My sword is always close,' said Hope.

The inside of the tavern was about what she'd expected. Crowded, loud, and stinking of sweat and stale beer. The patrons looked like an unpleasant bunch of pickpockets and murderers. Off in one corner was a group of boys about her age, staring at her and whispering to each other. She imagined they were debating whether to follow her when she left and try to rob her. She almost wished they would, so she could teach them a lesson.

She followed the captain to the large table in the back of
the tavern. The three men at the table looked only slightly
more well off than the other patrons. They were playing a
game of stones. When Carmichael and Hope stepped up to
the table, all three looked up at them. The man in the middle
assessed them in a way that seemed predatory.

A moment later Ranking took his place on the other
side of the captain. Hope glared at him, wondering why
he'd felt the need to reunite with an old girlfriend right
then. Surely he realized how critical it was for them to
secure a job of some kind. When she turned back to look
at the man at the table, his face had assumed a strangely
blank expression.

'I judge you are the captain that Rank here was telling me
about,' the man said in a flat, rough voice.

'My name's Carmichael, and I captain the *Lady's Gambit*,'
he said, offering his hand.

'Name's Drem.' He ignored the offered hand. 'And I run
this neighborhood. You understand what that means?'

'Well enough,' said Carmichael.

'Sunny.' Drem's face was still eerily expressionless. 'I've
got goods that need to be moved up the coast to Radiant Bay
in Hollow Falls without inspection or any imperial contact.
We'll have them loaded before daybreak so you can set off at
first light.'

'And what is the cargo?' asked the captain.

'None of your business,' said Drem.

'My ship, my business.'

'That how it is?'

''Fraid so.'

'I'm a little confused, then,' said Drem. 'You said you
understood when I told you I run this neighborhood.
That includes the docks and any ship tied to them.' He
looked back down at the smooth, numbered stones on the

table in front of him as if he'd suddenly lost interest in the conversation. 'Rank, explain to the man how it is in the Circle.'

Hope had been focused on Drem and his men, ready if one of them made a move. She never would have expected one of Carmichael's own men to betray him. Not even Ranking. So when Ranking drew a pistol, it threw her for a second. And in that second, he fired a bullet into the side of Captain Carmichael's head. In the next second, the Song of Sorrows whistled from its sheath and removed Ranking's arm at the elbow while the captain's lifeless body dropped to the ground.

The two men at Drem's table stood and drew their guns. Hope lunged across the table and buried her blade in one man's neck before he could pull back the hammer on his gun. She turned to take down the other gunman, but found him drowning in his own blood as he clutched at a strange bladed object in his neck. She followed the trajectory and saw one of the boys who had been sitting in the corner. His dark hair fell partially across eyes that were oddly red-colored. He inclined his head and gave her a smug grin. She disliked him immediately.

She turned her attention back to Drem, who was getting to his feet, fumbling for his gun, his face no longer coolly blank, but a creased mask of rage. She leveled her sword at his chest. He froze.

'You can't kill me,' he snarled. 'I *run* this neighborhood.'

She glanced around the tavern. Except for Ranking groaning on the floor, and the red-eyed boy, the place was now empty.

'Your neighborhood appears to have abandoned you,' she said.

'They just know what's coming, and they're smart enough to get out of the way,' said Drem.

Several men burst through the front door of the tavern, guns blazing. A bullet grazed her side, allowing Drem to dive behind a nearby table.

The new gunmen continued to fire. They had those pistols that allowed six shots before reloading. She was surprised that street thugs could afford such expensive weapons, but there wasn't time to consider that now. She flipped the table on its side and took cover behind it.

Someone moved next to her, and she whipped her blade around, thinking it was Drem. But it was the boy who'd helped her.

'Whoa!' he shouted over the roar of gunfire. 'I'm on your side.'

'How do I know that?' she asked.

'Uh, because I just saved your life?'

'Hardly,' she said. 'I would have killed him before he had a chance to shoot.'

'Okay, then I'm saving your life right now,' said the boy. 'Because I'm getting us out of here.'

Hope glanced at him suspiciously, wondering why he was so bent on helping her. She'd already misplaced her trust once today. And yet, other than his general irritating smugness, she had a sense that he was genuine. Besides, the gunmen were staggering their shots and reloads, and the table wouldn't hold up much longer. Chunks were already splintering off around the edges.

'Do you have an exit strategy?' she asked.

'I *always* have one of those,' he said with that grin he probably thought was charming. He turned toward the bar. 'Prin!' he yelled over the gunfire.

The top of a girl's head peeped out from behind the bar.

'Toss me the keys to the cellar!'

She shook her head.

'Come on, Prin! I'll leave them down there for you to get

later. I promise. And . . .' He hesitated. 'And I'll leave this, too.' He held up a bag of coins.

Her eyes went wide at the sight of the bag, but then narrowed suspiciously.

'I will make sure he does as he says,' said Hope. 'You have my word as a warrior.'

She seemed to consider that, then her head disappeared behind the bar. A moment later, a key sailed over the bar and landed on the ground next to them.

'Say,' said the boy, 'having a trustworthy person around really cuts down on the cajoling and wheedling time.'

'Let's move,' said Hope. 'This table is about to come apart.'

The boy grabbed one of the table legs on his side. 'Keep sliding it back until we're over to where those hinges are in the floor. That's the trapdoor down to the cellar.'

She nodded, and the two began scooting the table back. More holes were appearing in the wood. Hope peeked through one and didn't see Drem anywhere. He had probably fled. The other gunmen didn't show any interest in advancing. They didn't need to. Huge pieces of the table were breaking off. It wouldn't hold much longer.

'Here we go!' The boy flipped open the trapdoor and jumped down into the hole. Hope crouched on the precipice, peered down into the darkness. She hated retreating like this. But more than anything, she knew she must avenge Carmichael. To do that, she had to bide her time. These men didn't matter. It was Drem she wanted. So she jumped.

She landed on a dirt floor in almost pitch-blackness. She nearly took the boy's arm off when he touched her hand.

'Piss'ell, you're jumpy.' He pulled her along by the wrist. 'This way.'

Normally, she didn't like to be touched, especially by someone she didn't know. But down here in this darkness, she could see almost nothing. She wondered how the boy was able to navigate through the stacks of crates and barrels. Perhaps he knew it well. Or perhaps his strange red eyes allowed him to see more keenly in the dark. Either way, he moved with confidence, and she allowed herself to be led through the cool cellar, the sound of gunfire growing fainter, until finally they came to a stop. She heard him wrestling with a lock. Then suddenly a hatch opened above them, and dim light spilled down.

'The brewery,' said the boy. 'It's across the street and the cellar runs beneath to connect them. They'll realize this is the way we've come soon enough, so we better keep moving.' He began to climb the narrow metal rungs.

'You're forgetting something,' she said.

'Oh?' He looked down at her, his expression slightly confused.

'Leaving the key. And the money. As you promised.'

He winced. 'Right. The downside of having a trustworthy person around. Follow-through.' He dropped back down, pulled out the key and the bag of coins, and placed them on the dirt ground. 'Happy?'

'Satisfied,' she said.

'I guess that'll have to do,' he said, and began climbing again.

When Hope emerged into the brewery, she let out a faint gasp. The space was like one giant machine, packed with towering copper vats, huge pipes, gears, pulleys, and other kinds of complicated mechanical apparatus that she could only guess the purpose of. She'd never seen anything like it.

'Amazing, isn't it?' His red eyes glinted in the dim moonlight that streamed through the windows. 'The resources and ingenuity that go into finding more efficient ways for folks to make themselves stupid.'

She smiled slightly, in spite of herself.

'I'm Red, by the way.' He held out his hand.

'My name is Bleak Hope,' she said, grasping it. 'Although most people just call me Hope.'

His grin returned. 'Red and Hope. That's got a nice ring to it, don't you think?'

Drem surveyed the wreckage of the Drowned Rat. There was a time when something like this could never have happened. He remembered when he was a young wag, still working his way up the ranks, that the Drowned Rat had been home to the fearsome Bracers Madge. He remembered her stalking the floor, ready to crush anyone who dared bring disorder into her establishment. But one day, a biomancer came with a squad of imps. He'd said he was fascinated by a woman with such natural power. He'd said he wanted to study her. Of course, Madge had told him exactly where he could shove his studying. It had taken the entire squad to subdue her. Madge had been a local celebrity. A hero, in a way. And for days after, there had been angry mutterings among the people. A few small riots had even broken out. But then people began disappearing in the middle of the night, and everyone knew what happened to people who disappeared. Drem remembered wondering, as a boy, how it was the biomancers could so easily take people from their own homes like that. Of course, now he knew.

Drem heard a groan coming from a few feet away. He walked over, his boots crunching on broken glass and splintered wood. He saw Ranking lying on the floor, clutching at the bloody stump where the bottom half of his right arm used to be.

'Drem,' gasped Ranking. 'Thank God you're okay. You've got to help me. I know things went leeward, but you've got the ship, and I can still captain it. You *promised* I could captain it. I'll be the best smuggler you've ever had, I swear.'

'Brackson,' Drem said to one of his men. 'Come here and bind up Rank's arm so he don't bleed to death.'

'Thank you, Drem!' wheezed Ranking. 'You won't regret it. I swear!'

Drem ignored him and said to Brackson, 'We'll give him to the biomancers.'

'No!' said Ranking. 'Please, God, no!'

'But boss,' said Brackson. 'We already gave them someone this month.'

Drem shrugged. 'Don't hurt to throw them an extra. It's important to stay on their good side. Especially lately.' He turned his flat gaze to the trapdoor in the back of the tavern. 'Who was it that helped the Southie girl?'

'I think it was Red, boss.'

'Really? Shame. I'd been thinking about inviting him to come work for me. Send some true wags over to the brewery. I want Red and that girl dead by sunrise.'

16

*I*t wasn't the first time Red had been chased through the narrow, mazelike streets of Paradise Circle at night by gun-toting gangsters out for blood. Or even the fifth time. But it was by far his favorite time. Mostly because of the view.

Hope ran in front of him, her legs and ass flexing beneath tight black leather in a way that made him want to believe in God just so he could thank him for making such a perfect molly.

A shot rang out behind him, and he heard a bullet whiz past his head. It struck the brick of a nearby building.

'Left!' he called to Hope. She pivoted with the grace of a dancer, not even losing momentum as she turned down the side street.

As Red made that same turn, he chanced a look back at their pursuers. *Six* men now? Drem really wanted them dead. They were being smart about it, too. Keeping their distance so they didn't end up with a yard of Hope's Vinchen steel in their bilge. With the guns they were packing, they didn't need to get close anyway.

Red toyed with the idea of stopping and fighting. Between the two of them, they could probably manage it. But while that would temporarily solve the problem, in the long run it would only make things worse. If they killed six of Drem's men, he'd just send twice as many next time. Drem had no problem throwing away men to get what he wanted or to make a point. They would need a more slippery solution to get out of this.

'Right!' he yelled and they turned down another street.

'Are we running somewhere specific or are you making it up as we go?' she asked over her shoulder, her pale cheek flushed.

'Most people won't hide us from Drem's men. He's too powerful around here. But I *do* know a person who'd shelter me from the emperor himself if it came to it.'

'That's a loyal friend,' she said.

'Well, I don't know if I'd call her a friend exactly . . .' He pointed at an unmarked door painted a dull pink. 'In there!'

Hope turned the knob, but it was locked.

'Right. Business hours.' Red knocked three times slow, then three times fast. As soon as the door opened, Red hustled Hope inside and quickly shut the door behind them.

'Is this . . .' Hope's eyes were wide as she took in the dingy velvet couches and chairs, the faded and torn drapes, and the women and men lounging around in their undergarments. 'Is this a *brothel*?'

'No. Yes. Depends on who you are,' said Red. 'They'll be here in a minute. We don't have time to discuss it now.'

'Red?' asked Tosh, the curly-haired woman stretched out on a moth-eaten green love seat. She sat up and looked at him curiously. 'What's going on? Who's that?'

'No time,' said Red. 'Is Nettles here?'

'First door on the right, cleaning up,' said Tosh.

'Thanks,' he said. 'We were never here.'

Tosh nodded, her forehead creased with concern.

Red didn't know how long Tosh and the others would be able to stall Drem's men. But he only needed a few more minutes. Unless Nettie was in a mood.

'Come on.' He climbed the wooden staircase. Hope looked like she had about a hundred questions on her mind as she followed, but for now she kept them to herself. He appreciated that.

When he opened the door to one of the bedrooms, he found Nettles on the floor, wiping up a pool of vomit. Next to the pool of vomit lay an unconscious sailor. Nearby, a naked man sat cross-legged on a bed, smoking a pipe.

'I don't see why I have to clean it up, is all,' said Nettles as she scooped up colorful chunks of what might once have been bread. 'You're perfectly capable.'

'I *told* you he'd been drinking too much. You shouldn't have kicked him in the stomach,' said the naked man, idly watching smoke from his pipe curl up toward the ceiling. He had long auburn hair, lightly curled, and a bit of powder on his long, finely pointed face. 'Besides, I won't get any clients if I smell all vomity.'

'Nettie,' said Red. 'I need you to drop us down the chute.'

Nettles turned and glared at him. 'Why? What have you done now? I swear, if you brought the imps here, I will personally—'

'It's not the imps,' said Red. 'Drem sent some men after us.'

'*Drem?* You pissing salthead, if it's not one thing, it's another.' She gestured to Hope. 'And who is *this* slice?'

'Can we not do this right now?' asked Red. 'Drem's got boots after us. They're only—'

The sound of the front door slamming open echoed up the stairs, followed by angry shouts.

Nettles scowled. 'You owe me. Keen?'

'Completely,' said Red as he closed and locked the door behind them.

Nettles moved over to the far wall and slid the battered old dresser to one side. Red hurried over to help her.

'Are you a prostitute?' asked Hope, looking very confused.

Red winced and waited to see how Nettles would respond. The naked man on the bed chuckled.

Nettles turned to Hope, her scowl deepening. She gestured to her thick gray wool jacket, grimy leather breaches, and knee-high riding boots. 'Do I pissing *look* like a whore? Just for that, you're going first, angel slice.' She gave the dresser one last hard shove, revealing a large hole in the wall.

'*I'm* the whore, blondie,' said the naked man. 'Nettie is security.'

Footsteps stomped up the stairs.

'Time to go,' said Red. 'Hope, slide down the chute. I'll be right behind you.'

Hope frowned, looking at the hole in the wall suspiciously.

He couldn't imagine what she made of all this. 'Look, you've trusted me this far. Just a little further to go.'

A fist pounded on the door.

'In a minute!' the naked man called, sounding petulant.

'Hope,' Red whispered. 'Please.'

'Don't make me regret this,' she said, then dove headfirst into the hole.

Red turned to Nettles.

'Nettie, I—'

'Save it. Go,' she whispered.

There was another knock on the door, louder this time.

'I said in a minute!' yelled the naked man.

As Red slipped down the chute, he heard a voice yell, 'Let us in or we'll break it down!' Then Nettles shoved the dresser back in place and there was nothing but darkness and the hiss of his leather coat as he slid down the metal chute, twisting and turning until he popped out into the night air and landed on top of Hope.

There was a moment when their bodies pressed together. Their faces were only an inch apart. Hope's lips were open and he could feel her breath on his lips. Her dark blue eyes seemed to tunnel directly into his head.

'Hi,' he said, smiling.

She grunted and pushed him off.

The two of them climbed to their feet. Hope looked around, her forehead furrowed. 'We're on the docks?'

It was the largest pier in New Laven, holding twenty merchant ships. It was late enough in the evening that most of the ships were dark. That was good. On the off chance Drem's men figured out how he and Hope had slipped away and came looking for them here, there'd be no one to say which direction they'd gone.

'What just happened?' asked Hope.

'Come on,' said Red. 'I'll tell you on the way. But go slow now so we don't draw attention to ourselves.' He glanced at her black Vinchen leather. 'Well, any more than we have to.'

'Where are we going now? Another brothel?' asked Hope as the two walked from the docks back into the muddy, cobblestone streets. After a moment, she said, 'That *was* a brothel, wasn't it?'

'Part of the income is from that. It's also a crimp house.'

'A what?'

'You don't have those in the South? Well, no, of course you don't. You're already there. See, a crimp house is a place where they drug or knock out sailors, steal their money, then sell them to a ship as a conscript.'

'Forced labor?' asked Hope.

'It's called southending, since mostly it's the ships bound for the Southern Isles that are desperate for sailors. Not a popular place to go.'

'Why not?'

'Oh, well, I mean, it's a little uncivilized down there, isn't it?'

Hope raised an eyebrow. 'If by uncivilized you mean there's rarely gunfire in the streets, or brothels that sell their clients as indentured servants, then yes, I suppose it is.'

'Sounds dull.' Red gave her a sly grin. That usually worked on the mollies, but she didn't seem to find it charming. Since his breakup with Nettles, he'd spent a lot of time making the rounds with the mollies and had a pretty good idea of his effect on them and how to get what he wanted. But none of his usual tricks seemed to be working on Hope. He decided to shut up for a bit as they walked through the dark streets until he'd figured out a new strategy.

'So, that slide we just went down,' said Hope. 'Normally they drop unconscious sailors down that?'

'And then the captains that need crew come and scoop them up,' said Red. 'Pretty efficient system.'

'What's to stop the captains from running off with their sailors without paying the brothel?'

Red gave a short laugh. 'Nettles, that's what. It happens now and then. But sooner or later, every ship has to make port here again. And when they do, Nettie is here to explain to them how things work in the Circle.'

'That was your friend? Or not-friend? She didn't seem overly fond of you.'

'Well, we used to be a couple.'

'Oh,' said Hope.

They continued to wind through narrow streets. Red purposely took the longest route possible. Partly to throw any would-be trackers off their trail, partly to get more time alone with Hope. He still wasn't sure what to make of her. She was a bit uptight and seemed to be pretty much innocent of the seedier side of life. But she was clever, which made her more fun to talk to than most of the wags he was around. And of course, she was very nice to look at. The great thing about a warrior woman, he decided, was that she could kill some gafs, crawl through tunnels, sprint halfway across the neighborhood, get tossed down a chute, and still come up looking fine as peaches. It was an unpretentious, practical sort of beauty.

'What happened?' asked Hope.

'Huh?' said Red.

'Why aren't you and Nettles a couple any longer? Didn't you love her?'

'Oh, uh . . .' Red wondered why he'd even said anything about that to begin with. It wasn't like him to bring up old history when he was in the middle of trying to convince a molly that he was the best wag she'd ever met. 'Well, I was young and stupid. You know how it is. Maybe they're not the person you convinced yourself they are.' He shrugged. 'We're better off as wags, that's all. And we still do love each other, I think. But it's different. More like brother-sister. You know how it can be.'

'No,' said Hope. 'I don't.'

'You never been in a couple?'

She blushed and shook her head.

'What?' he said, trying a gentler version of the grin. 'Too busy slicing off limbs to give a tom a chance to know you better?'

'Yes,' she said. 'A Vinchen warrior is dedicated to the order in body, mind, and heart. There cannot be room for anything or anyone else.'

'Ah,' said Red. 'Well, that's that, then. Isn't it?'

'Yes,' said Hope, giving him a strange glance. 'It is.'

He nodded and kept walking, playing it as pat as you like. But underneath, his plans for conquest crumbled. The first girl who'd really captured his attention since Nettles, one he might actually give a cup of piss about, and he *had* to pick a girl sworn to celibacy.

'It's for the best,' he said. 'Most toms talk nothing but balls and pricks anyway.'

'Do you?' she asked.

He shrugged. 'Come on. This way.'

'Where are we going?'

'Gunpowder Hall. Safest place in Paradise Circle. In a manner of speaking.'

Hope's eyes grew wide when they entered Gunpowder Hall. Red could see her struggling to keep her comments to herself, but finally she burst out, 'Those people are having sex over there! Right in front of everyone!'

'Not all whores are pretty enough to get accepted by a brothel,' said Red. 'Some have to just take a client where they can get them. Unfortunately, it's not so safe if you don't have someone like Nettles watching out for you. Never know when a client might turn mean.'

'You talk as if you know a lot about it. Are you a frequent client?'

'Nah. My dad was in the trade.'

'Oh.' Her whole face turned bright pink, her expression a mixture of embarrassment and confusion. It was so awkward and honest, he couldn't help but laugh.

Her eyes narrowed. 'Were you joking about that?'

'No, my dad really was a whore,' he said.

Her face got even redder and her expression even more embarrassed, which made him laugh again, even harder.

'You find my discomfort amusing,' she said.

'Yes. I do.' And he laughed again.

'I'm glad you're amused. Now, it's probably time I—'

'Hey, looks like Nettie's off work,' said Red, cutting off what was likely an attempt for her to leave him. God help him, doomed though it was, he wasn't ready to say good-bye to his angel in black leather quite yet. 'We better go fill her in before she comes looking for us. That always makes her grumpy.'

Maybe Hope wasn't quite ready to say good-bye either, or maybe she'd just gotten used to him dragging her around. Either way, she let him pull her over to the table where Nettles was sitting, cleaning blood from her chainblade.

'Saw some action tonight?' He nodded to the weapon in her hands.

'Less than you, I'll wager,' said Nettles. 'You only just getting here now?'

'Oh, uh . . .' said Red. 'I wanted to make sure we weren't being followed.'

Nettles glanced at Hope, then smirked as she coiled up her chain. 'Sure, that's it.'

'An interesting weapon,' said Hope. 'May I see it?'

Nettles looked skeptically at her, then at Red. He shrugged. 'Sure, okay.' She tossed the coiled chain to her.

Hope caught it easily and held it up for inspection.

'I've never seen anything like it. Part throwing knife, part chain mace. I hope I get the chance to see you use it.'

'You do, huh?' asked Nettles, squinting at her like she wasn't sure how to take that.

Hope handed it back to her. 'You take good care of it. As a warrior should.'

'Yeah, well,' said Nettles, looking a little uncomfortable now. 'It's important to me. I take care of the important things. And anyway, you think this is strange, you should see what Red uses.'

'Yes,' said Hope, turning to Red. 'I saw one for a moment in the tavern. It looked like a throwing knife, except I couldn't see the handle.'

'That's because there is no handle.' Red pulled open his coat to show the line of blades that went down the inside lining. He pulled one out. 'Thought it up myself.'

'With help,' said Nettles.

'I think best in a dialogue,' said Red. 'Anyway, it didn't make much sense having a throwing weapon that was only truly effective if it landed on one side. I like odds that are better than half. So I replaced the handle with another blade.'

'How do you throw them, then?' Hope was riveted by the throwing blade. Apparently all he'd had to do was start talking weapons to get her interested.

He pointed to the ring in the center. 'I just hook a finger in here. Watch.' He nodded to where a gray-haired wrink was sitting at the other end of the table, gnawing on a hunk of hard crust bread. Red snapped his hand, and the blade took the bread right out of the old man's grasp and nailed it to the table.

'Piss'ell!' The old man looked angry for a moment, then saw it was Red and eased back into mild irritation. 'Come on, Red. Like to give a wrink like me a heart attack.'

'Sorry, Nipper.' Red walked over, pulled the blade out, and handed the bread back to him. Quietly he added, 'Just trying to impress the mollies, you understand.'

Nipper chuckled and shook his head. 'That I do, boy. Many's a wag gone stupid for a bit of slice.'

Red winked at him, then walked back to Hope and Nettles.

'Shame on you for startling poor old Nipper,' said Nettles.

'He'll be alright,' said Red. 'Even a wrink needs some excitement now and then.'

Hope took the blade from Red and examined it more closely. 'How do you not cut your palm?'

Red held up his hands, still encased in the thick leather fingerless gloves. 'That's what these are for.'

'Also my idea,' said Nettles. 'He doesn't really need 'em anymore, though. Now he just wears 'em because he thinks they look pat.'

'They *do* look pat,' said Red.

'About as pat as your mole-rat jacket.'

'Deerskin.'

'*Anyway*,' said Nettles, turning back to Hope. 'I've never met a wag with better aim than Rixie here. It's uncanny.'

Hope was still staring intently at the blades, but her eyebrow shot up. 'Rixie?'

'Oh, didn't he tell you?' An evil smirk grew on Nettles's face. 'Red ain't his real name. It's—'

'Nettie, I know where you sleep,' said Red.

Nettles laughed. She'd given Red many opportunities over the past couple of years to regret telling her his birth name. Hope didn't seem to be paying much attention, though. Her pale brow was furrowed as she held the throwing blade up to Red. 'Have you . . . thought about putting another blade on it?'

'Eh?' said Red, taking it from her.

'Following your reasoning that the more blades, the better your chance at a perfect hit.'

'Well . . .' said Red doubtfully as he touched one of the empty sides of the ring. 'If I put another blade on, it wouldn't be balanced. And I don't think it'd fit four.'

'It would balance if you made it into a triangle shape.'

Red held it up and squinted, imagining three blades evenly space around the ring. 'Okay, that's brilliant.'

Hope's face flushed as she smiled shyly. 'I'm only building off your idea.'

'Still, I'm going to have to talk to Filler about this next chance I get.'

'Filler?'

'He's my best wag. We grew up on the streets together.'

'Sort of,' said Nettles.

Red gave her a sharp look. First the name, now this. What was Nettles playing at?

'Filler,' he continued, 'is a smithy. I come up with the idea, he makes it real. Did Nettles's, too.'

'You mean you actually have a friend with an honest profession?' asked Hope.

'Oh, well, I wouldn't go so far as to say "honest" . . .'

'Filler's got a bit of a problem with the imps,' said Nettles. 'He's a great big sugar lump of a wag most of the time. But he don't like the imps. If one even looks at him wrong, he's like to punch him in the bilge, or worse. Makes it hard to hold down a respectable smithy job.'

'So he works for the people now,' said Red.

'Meaning, he makes illegal weapons for all the wags and gangsters in the Circle,' said Nettles. 'That is, when he's not helping Red here with his latest bad idea.' She turned to Red and scowled. 'And speaking of which . . .'

'Here we go,' said Red.

'Henny's right. You must have a death wish. Getting on the hit list for Deadface Drem?' Nettles shook her head. 'That's crazy, even for you. Only one thing I can think of that would make you be such a salthead.' She looked meaningfully at Hope.

'Oh, now . . .' Red forced a little laugh. He needed a new subject, quick. His eyes scanned around and saw Backus picking his way through the hall, looking worried about something. 'Backus! You alright?'

Backus hurried over faster than usual.

'Red, you got the new batch of medicine? Sadie's . . . not doing so good.'

'What?' Red's gut suddenly went cold and tight.

'She's coughing real bad. Can't seem to catch her breath. I think . . . this might be it.'

17

*H*ope was beginning to understand that a large city like New Laven was more than just a collection of buildings or a place that people called home. It was like a world unto itself, the neighborhoods like towns, each with their own rules and codes of honor. In this world, gang leaders were brutal dictators, whores were friends, and smug boys with red eyes were full of surprises.

Hope watched him curiously now as she followed him across the hall, weaving in and out of people sleeping, drinking, playing games, and occasionally having sex. She did her best to ignore it and focus on Red. His whole demeanor had abruptly changed when the old man told him someone named Sadie was dying. All of his arrogance and forced charm had evaporated. *Everyone is afraid of something*, Grandteacher Hurlo had told her once. *What a man is afraid of will tell you much about his character*. The whole time Drem's men had been chasing them, Red hadn't seemed frightened at all. But what she saw in his eyes now was unmistakably fear.

The old man lifted up a hatch in the floor and, single file, they walked down a narrow wooden staircase into darkness. There was a spark, then a glowing lantern appeared in Red's hand. They were in some sort of underground basement

hallway that stretched far beyond the lantern light. There
were open doorways evenly spaced along both sides. Moans
and coughs came from some of them. And from everywhere
came the smell.

That had been another thing New Laven taught her. That
there were more unpleasant smells in this world than she
ever knew existed. She thought between the fishy docks, the
sewage in the streets, the ale-drenched tavern, the unwashed
bodies and vomit at the brothel, and the combination of all
those elements in Gunpowder Hall, that she had experienced
every terrible smell this city had to offer. But the stench that
now crept into her nostrils was at once terrible and familiar.
It was one she had not encountered in ten years: festering
death.

This was a place that people came to die.

As they walked down the long dark hallway, Hope leaned
in to Nettles and quietly asked, 'Who's Sadie?'

'Red's mentor,' she whispered back. 'His parents died
when he was eight. If Sadie hadn't taken him under her wing,
likely he wouldn't have lasted a year. The Circle can be a
vicious place for those who don't know its ways.'

'So I've discovered,' said Hope.

An orphan at the age of eight. It was a strange, sad coincidence that she and Red shared this misfortune. But that's all
it was. A coincidence. So why did it feel like more than that?
Grandteacher Hurlo had once told her that there was no such
thing as coincidence. That those who claimed to believe in it
simply refused to see the underlying connection between all
things. Captain Carmichael had once told her that anyone
who believed in fate was too cowardly to admit that everything was chance and there was no real meaning in life. Which
is it? she wondered. After all, they couldn't both be right.

Red stopped before one of the rooms. This boy who had
laughed while thugs rained gunfire on them now had to

muster his courage just to walk through the doorway. He
stood there, his face tight and his ruby eyes wide. Then he
tilted his head slightly so it gave a faint *crack*, squared his
shoulders, and walked through. Backus, Hope, and Nettles
followed behind at a respectful distance.

Hope decided that if there was a worst place to die, it
was this room. Dark, stuffy, damp, stinking, it was just an
empty, unlit space with a dirt floor. An old woman lay on a
rotting straw mat in the corner. She stirred slightly when
the group entered. Judging by the shallow rise and fall of
her chest, she couldn't manage much else. Her bloodshot
eyes rolled around in their sockets, pronounced in the
emaciated face.

'Oh, Red . . .' she wheezed.

Red's face showed a smile, but it was so strained that it
twitched.

'Well, now,' he said gently. 'I hear as how you've been
complaining about your accommodations, there, m'lady.'

'No jokes.' She paused to catch her breath. 'Nearly
time . . . to go . . .'

'No jokes?' He suddenly looked angry, although his voice
was still quiet. 'Fine, then. Serious. You aren't *going*
anywhere. Keen?'

She smiled weakly. 'Nobody . . . tells me . . . what . . . to
do . . .'

'Please,' whispered Red as he dropped down to his knees
next to her. He stroked her thin white hair. 'Please don't leave
me.' A tear ran down his cheek.

'There's that . . . soft artist . . .' said Sadie, laboring for
each word. 'Glad . . . I didn't . . . beat it . . . all . . . out of
you.'

Hope wanted to turn away. It was too much. Too close to
her own buried pain. This could be Carmichael, or Hurlo.
She wanted to run away from this suffering. But she forced

herself to keep watching, as she always did. To witness this, as she had witnessed every terrible thing.

'The medicine!' Red fumbled in his pocket and pulled out a small pouch. 'This time it will work. I know it.'

Sadie slowly shook her head but didn't say anything.

'Let me just mix it up for you.' He tapped some of the powder from the pouch into a nearby pitcher of water, and swirled the mixture around. Then he poured some into a small cup.

Hope frowned. 'What's he doing?' she whispered to Nettles.

'Weren't you listening? He's giving her the medicine.'

'But that's not . . .'

Then she saw him lift Sadie's head up. He was about to have her drink it.

'Red, stop.' She said it louder than she'd meant to.

'No,' he said without turning back to look at her. 'I'll do whatever I can for as long as I can.'

'But you're giving it to her wrong.'

He froze, the cup at Sadie's lips. '*What?*'

She knelt down beside them. 'May I see the powder?'

Red looked confused and frightened and suspicious and ever so slightly hopeful. 'Why?'

'It's your turn to trust me,' she said.

Reluctantly, he put down the cup and handed her the pouch.

Hope opened it and inhaled deeply. 'This is marsh blossom.'

'Eh, yeah . . .' he said. 'That's what the gaf said I'd need.'

Hope laid her ear on Sadie's chest and listened to the rattle of her breath. Then she pressed the back of her hand on Sadie's forehead.

'Stick out your tongue,' she told Sadie.

Sadie opened her mouth, and Hope moved the lantern to shine light down her throat.

'Tunnel lung,' she said at last.

'That's what he thought it was,' said Red. 'So it's the right medicine?'

'It is,' said Hope. 'But he didn't tell you how to give it to her? What kind of apothecary is he?'

'There aren't any of those in the Circle. He just sells the stuff. He knows some of the symptoms that match up with the medicines. That's about it.'

'No apothecaries in the entire neighborhood?' asked Hope.

Red shook his head.

'Why?' asked Nettles. 'Do *you* know about medicines?'

'All Vinchen warriors must learn how to heal as well as kill. Only then can they achieve balance.'

'So what do I need to do?' asked Red, his ruby eyes intense.

'First, if she has tunnel lung, this is the worst possible place for her. We need to get her out in the air, as high up as possible.'

'It's awful cold, though,' said Backus doubtfully.

'We'll need to keep her warm,' agreed Hope. 'Wrap her in blankets. But the cold fresh air should open her throat up a bit. Make it easier for her to breathe.'

'I know a place we can take her,' said Red. 'What else?'

'We'll need a thick cloth, like a towel, a pot, and something to heat the water to boiling.'

'Boil the medicine?' asked Red.

'Yes. That will turn it into steam. This is a lung ailment, so she doesn't need to drink it. She needs to *breathe* it.'

Hope wondered again at the shift in Red. Gone was the carefree charmer, but gone too was the fearful tender-heart. Now he seemed consumed with a calm, yet implacable determination to bring Hope's plan into action. He had ordered Backus and Nettles about like a ship's captain, and they scrambled to comply without hesitation. Nettles had gone to find a towel and a pot. Backus had gone to find Filler.

Hope and Red went ahead, with Sadie on Red's back. He led them to an unused church that had been left to crumble. Hope had been in the temple on Galemoor countless times, but never a proper church of the empire. It was much larger, able to hold hundreds of people. She knew from books that in an imperial church worshipers knelt throughout the service on cushions or blankets they brought with them, which explained why most of the space was empty. The only piece of furniture was on the high altar far in the back – a large, chipped, high-backed stone chair that loomed over everything. A few squatters lurked in the corners, but they seemed to know Red and allowed them to pass without comment.

There probably had once been tapestries depicting the early history of the empire on the walls when the church was in use. But the only evidence that they had ever existed was a slight discoloration in rectangular shapes on the stone walls. There would also have been stained glass windows, but those had all been broken, and the tall windows stood empty, letting in a cold wind from the sea. As she stepped, she felt a piece of colored glass crunch underfoot. It reminded her of sea glass, and her mother telling her that they didn't need such fancy northland frippery. The memory left a sudden hole in her chest. It amazed her that she could still hurt so much from something that had happened so long ago. She didn't know why it had recently become harder to push those feelings down. She wondered if the wound would ever heal. Perhaps once all the biomancers were dead.

She looked up then, and saw Sadie, her withered cheek resting on Red's shoulder as she dozed. Hope reached out and laid her hand on Sadie's back, feeling the faint warmth of her body through the blankets. For some reason, it gave her some small comfort.

At the far end of the church was a stone spiral staircase that she suspected led up to the bell tower. The staircase was narrow, and there were no railings.

After they had climbed a good while, Hope asked, 'Do you want me to take over?'

'No,' grunted Red, his face flushed and his temples gleaming with sweat.

'You don't have to be a hero, you know,' she said.

'I didn't say I was a hero. Just said I wanted to carry her. Let's keep moving. We've got a ways to go yet.'

Hope followed behind as they continued up the stairs, ready to grab either of them if he should slip. By this time, it was quite a drop down.

When they reached the bell tower, Hope saw that the bell had been removed. Now it was only an empty space. It was like the crow's nest of a ship that looked out over a sea of rooftops shining in the midday sun.

'She don't look half-bad from up here,' said Red, nodding toward the city stretched below them. 'Up close, she's all boils and pox. But from this distance, she looks a fine old lady.'

'Hey,' said Sadie, still draped across his back. 'Watch who yer callin' fine.'

Red gently laid her down on the weathered wood-planked floor.

'You,' he said, 'are heavier than you look.'

She grinned, showing her empty gums. 'It's me cruel, stony heart.'

Red laughed a short burst and turned to Hope, his eyes bright with gratitude. 'You were right. The cold fresh air is helping already.'

'It lessens the symptoms temporarily,' said Hope. 'She'll need to stay up here and take the medicine regularly for the next day and night. That should give the medicine time to kill the fungus.'

'Fungus?' Red looked alarmed. 'Like mushrooms?'

'More like mold, really. It sets up in the lungs, stopping them from using the air she takes in. If it spreads throughout, she'll suffocate.'

'We won't let that happen,' said Red.

'Of course not.'

'You there,' said Sadie, her voice gaining a little more strength. 'What's this? I got mold in my wheres?'

'Your lungs,' said Hope.

'The things you breathe with,' said Red.

'I breathe with my mouth,' said Sadie.

'After the air goes through your mouth, it goes down into your chest,' said Red. 'There are two air sacs in there called lungs. They collect the air for the rest of your body.'

'Piss'ell, where'd you learn a thing like that?' asked Sadie. 'In all those piles of books you read, I suppose.'

'You read?' asked Hope.

'Eh, sure,' said Red, looking uncomfortable.

'A lot?'

'I don't know.' He glanced around. 'I better go down and see if Nettie or Filler need help carrying anything up.' He turned to Sadie. 'You alright?'

'Getting there,' said Sadie.

'Be nice to Hope here. She just about saved your life today.'

'I'll do my best.'

Red turned to Hope. 'Which means she won't try to stab you or rob you. As for the rest, who knows? Just promise me you won't toss her over the side if she offends you, which she probably will.'

Hope smiled slightly. 'You have my word.'

Once Red was out of earshot, Sadie turned her bloodshot eyes on Hope. There was not a shred of weakness in her gaze. 'Well, now, molly girl, what's your story?'

'My story?' asked Hope, sitting down next to her.

'Everybody's got one. And a pretty little slice like you with such old eyes is sure to have a good one.'

'I told my story once, a long time ago,' said Hope. 'I swore I would never tell it again.'

'Ah,' said Sadie.

'I don't mean to be disrespectful. It's just—'

'I don't give a piss about respect. Or much else anymore.' Sadie squinted at Hope. 'But I do care about that boy. Under all that balls-and-pricks talk of his, he's got a heart like a rain song. And I don't want no Southie slice stepping all over it. Keen?'

'Oh, I think you misunderstand,' said Hope. 'Red and I are . . . well, friends, perhaps. Although even *that* seems a little premature. Certainly nothing more.'

'That what you think?' Sadie looked at her a moment, then shrugged. 'What does an old wrink like me know? Maybe you've got the right of it.'

'I do.'

'Sunny.'

They sat there for a bit, side by side, the wind whistling past as they stared out at the skyline of New Laven.

'Funny thing,' said Sadie. 'Red has a story, too. Terrible sad one. He only told it to one person.'

'You, of course,' said Hope.

'How'd you know that?'

'It's obvious. He treasures you more than anything or anyone on this earth.'

'Treasure? Me?' Sadie laughed, but that turned into a nasty wet cough.

'It's true,' said Hope. 'When we were underground in that awful place, and he thought he was losing you . . .' Hope stopped as she recalled the look of pain on his face. A pain she knew all too well. 'I didn't want to watch.'

'But you did.'

'I always do.'

Off in the distance came a low rumble of thunder.

'Where's *your* treasure?' asked Sadie.

'Gone,' said Bleak Hope, her voice growing distant. She thought of her parents. Of Hurlo. Of Carmichael. The darkness spread within her like the comfort of an old friend. 'I have no treasure now. Only vengeance.'

'On who?' asked Sadie.

'The list has grown long.'

While the fresh air had helped, Sadie was still weak and dangerously ill. Their brief conversation had exhausted her. Hope wrapped her up in blankets like the fish rolls her mother used to make her, then watched as the old woman nodded off.

Hope turned her gaze out over the skyline. As the storm clouds moved closer, she wondered why thoughts of her childhood seemed to be boiling dangerously close to the surface. Was it the feeling of unbalance she'd had since entering Red's world? Or was it his mother figure that made her long for one of her own? Whatever the reason, she didn't like it. She had much to do, and a head lost in the past could not tend to the present.

A short time later, Red returned, carrying a large cast-iron pot filled halfway with water. With him was a boy about their age. He towered over Red, however, easily six and a half feet tall. He had short brown hair that stuck out in all directions and a light shadow of beard. He was carrying a large cord of wood and a thick rough towel.

'This is the wag I was telling you about,' Red said to her. 'Filler, meet Hope.'

'Good to meet you,' said Hope.

Filler gave her a shy smile, then set to work arranging the wood for a fire.

'Where's Nettles?' asked Hope.

'I asked her to go back to Gunpowder Hall,' said Red. 'Like as not, Drem's men will come looking for us there eventually. I want a lookout in case this is their next stop.'

'Why would it be?' she asked.

'Backus might tell them where we are.'

'But you said he's been helping you take care of Sadie. Why would he do anything to endanger her now?'

'Because that's how it is in the Circle,' said Red. 'You do what you can for people when you can, but when the boss calls, you do what you're told.'

'That's wrong,' said Hope.

'Nothing personal. It's how you survive. Only a few people you're willing to cross somebody like Drem for. Me, Filler, and Nettles, and of course Sadie here. That's it.'

'You crossed Drem for *me*,' said Hope.

Red turned away from her, knelt down next to Filler, and began helping him arrange the wood and kindling.

'Anyway,' he said over his shoulder. 'I'm sure this isn't the first wrong thing you've seen since you've been hanging around me. Whores, drinking, gambling, and suchlike. Surprised you can even stand to be around street scum like us.'

'There's a difference between cultural values and blatant disloyalty,' said Hope. 'While I admit I'm uncomfortable having a conversation with a naked man in a brothel, I would not call him or how he chooses to make a living "wrong." But betraying someone you care about? That is wrong.'

'She talks kinda like you,' Filler said to Red.

'You,' said Red, shaking a finger at him, 'are not helping. Now let's focus on getting this fire started.'

Hope watched as Filler took a tinderbox from his pocket and laid some thin shavings of wood over the larger pieces. He then struck a flint, throwing sparks on the shavings.

Red had avoided the question about helping her, which made her even more curious. She felt she knew him well enough by this time to say that he was fiercely loyal to the people close to him. But they were all people he had built relationships with over a long period of time. So why would he include her in that group? Paradise Circle was his whole world, and Drem the most powerful man in it. He had risked so much to help her. Why?

Red and Filler had a nice small fire going. Filler seemed skilled with controlling the fire, probably thanks to his training as a blacksmith. While he set the pot on top to boil, Red moved over to Sadie and gently shook her awake. Her eyes fluttered open in a slight panic, but when she saw him looking down at her, she smiled and laid her thin, boney hand on his cheek.

Hope remembered how Sadie had mistakenly thought that she and Red were . . . a couple. When Hope had disagreed, she immediately backed off, which seemed out of character for the feisty old woman. What if Sadie was right? After all, she knew Red far better than Hope did. What if the reason Red had risked so much to help Hope was because he . . .

But that didn't make any sense. He didn't even know her. Not really.

'Water's starting to boil,' said Filler.

'What do we do now?' Red asked.

'Add the medicine,' said Hope. 'Have Sadie lean over the pot, then cover her head and the top of the pot with the towel to trap the steam. Sadie should breathe as deeply as possible for a few minutes, or as long as she can take it.'

Red carefully helped Sadie over to the pot. She was still so weak, he had to support her as she leaned in over the steaming pot. After a minute, Sadie began coughing in loud, wet bursts.

'What's happening?' asked Red, looking at Hope with alarm.

'Her body is trying to get rid of the fungus. Move her away from the pot.'

Red tilted her to the side just in time, as a glob of bright-orange-colored mucus hit the wooden floor.

'Piss'ell,' said Filler, his brown eyes wide. 'That was inside her?'

'That's not all of it,' said Hope. 'She should rest for a bit, but we'll need to do this several times before her lungs are clear.'

'How will we know when it's gone?' asked Red.

'When she isn't spitting orange anymore,' said Hope.

They repeated the process three more times. Each time, Sadie could breathe in the medication a little longer, and there was a little less orange in her phlegm.

By the time they had finished the fourth treatment, the sky was growing dark. As Red laid Sadie down in her blankets to rest and Filler stoked the fire, Hope sat back against one of the wooden support beams and closed her eyes. She breathed in deeply, enjoying the clean air the high tower provided.

'Hey.' Red's voice was right beside her.

She opened her eyes and watched as he leaned back against the same support post so that their shoulders were touching. It felt oddly comforting, so she didn't move away.

'Thank you,' he said. 'I think you probably understand how important Sadie is to me. And you've saved her life.'

'I'm glad I could help,' she said. 'That I could repay you for helping me escape from Drem's men.'

'You didn't owe me for that,' he said. 'I'm glad I did it. I'm . . . glad I met you.'

'Likewise,' said Hope. 'You are . . . interesting.'

'Interesting?' Red smiled wryly. 'I guess I'll take it. Better than being boring, anyway.'

'You are not boring,' she assured him.

'Yeah, I took you on a merry little run, didn't I?'

'Yes. I suppose it was . . . fun.' She felt guilty admitting that. A Vinchen warrior wasn't motivated by 'fun' or thrill seeking. But it was true. It had been fun.

'You probably have serious Vinchen things to get back to after this, I expect,' said Red.

'Oh,' said Hope, her guilt deepening. 'Yes. I'm afraid I do.'

'Of course,' said Red. 'And, eh . . . this Vinchen business of yours, it's probably something you have to do alone?'

'It's not something anyone would want to do with me.'

Red turned to her, his ruby eyes flickering in the firelight. 'You sure about that?'

Hope stared at him, unsure what to say. Unsure what he meant. In that moment, unsure of just about everything.

'Look bright, wags!' Nettles's voice cracked like a whip from the staircase. 'We've got company on the way!'

All three were on their feet by the time Nettles had reached the top step.

'How many?' asked Red.

'Maybe a dozen or so, all armed with revolvers.'

'They're fools to come here,' said Hope as she loosened the Song of Sorrows in its sheath. 'We have the high ground. They would have been doomed with twice that number.'

All of Hope's anxiety and confusion evaporated like fog in a sunbeam. This was something she *was* sure about.

18

*L*ife hands you a lot of disappointments. And sometimes it gives you things, only to snatch them away from you shortly after. Red knew this. It seemed to him almost as if it was by design, one cruel joke after another. But not this time. He would *not* have Sadie saved from sickness, only to be gunned down by Drem's men.

Still. Twelve boots with revolvers, and no means of escape. He wasn't sure how they were going to come out on the other side of this. Hope *seemed* good from the little Red had seen in the Drowned Rat. Really good. But if he was wrong about her, this whole thing would go leeward real quick.

Red moved Sadie as far from the stairs as possible and wrapped her in blankets so she didn't get a chill. Then he joined Hope, Nettles, and Filler at the top of the stairs. Nettles held her chainblade loosely coiled in her hands. Filler had his short mace. Hope held her sword in her hand, but it was still sheathed. Drem's men were slowly climbing the stairs, revolvers drawn.

'So should we wait until they get to the top, then start knocking them down?' asked Red.

'No,' said Hope. 'Too risky to let them get this close to Sadie. We meet them halfway, where the drop is still enough

to kill or incapacitate them, but we have room to fall back if
necessary.'

'And who put you in charge, angel slice?' asked Nettles.

Hope shrugged. 'Fine. Stay here and wait. But you'll miss
the fight, because I don't plan to let any of them make it to
the top.'

'What—' said Red. But then he watched as Hope, sheathed
sword still in hand, dove gracefully over the side and down
the center. The men on the stairs were not expecting that.
They shouted to each other and fired in wild panic. Hope's
drop was carefully angled so that she intersected with one
man about halfway down, using him to cushion her impact
as she slammed him into the stone wall. Her sword gave an
eerie hum as it slid from its sheath. Then she jumped across
the gap to the next level of stairs, cutting off the head of one
gunman and the arm of another.

'Piss'ell,' said Filler. 'She means it.'

Red grinned. 'We better get down there and take some for
ourselves before it's too late, then. The honor of the Circle is
at stake here, my wags.'

The three of them hurried down the steps like normal
human beings while Hope zigzagged back and forth across
the gap in the middle, never in one place more than a second,
never giving them time to aim, much less fire. The grace and
control he'd seen hints of ever since he first saw her were now
in full expression. She was like a force of nature, savage as a
storm and fast as fire. He had hoped she was good, and for
the first time he could remember, life not only avoided
disappointing; it delivered beyond expectation.

Of course, it *was* twelve of Drem's nastiest boots armed
with revolvers, and Hope couldn't avoid them all. But Red
was happy to watch her back, tossing blades at the ones out
of her reach. They dropped over the edge, clutching at
throats, or knees, whichever was more open. And as Hope

had predicted, the fall was just enough that no matter where they'd been wounded, they didn't get back up again.

With her impressive acrobatics and her flashing, humming blade, all eyes were on Hope. They didn't see Filler as he came barreling down into the largest cluster of them, laying about him with his mace, knocking several over the edge at once.

'Filler, look out!' called Nettles.

One gunman with a bit of distance had a clear shot on him. Nettles flung out her chainblade. The blade stabbed into the gunman's hand, and he dropped the revolver. She yanked back on her chain, jerking him off balance and over the edge. She stepped on the weighted end of the chain and braced herself. The chain went taut for a moment, then slack, as the blade ripped free from the gunman's hand and he fell to the bottom.

In a very short time, the sound of gunfire faded and only one of Drem's men was alive and conscious. Hope had him pinned down on the stairs at the waist, his arms windmilling as she held the upper half of his body over the edge.

'Please . . .' he whimpered.

'Tell me where to find Drem,' she said.

'He's at the Three Cups! He's always there. Everybody knows that!'

'*Where* at the Three Cups?'

'Th-third floor. He has it all to himself and his best wags.'

'Thank you.' Then she slammed the pommel of her sword into his forehead, knocking him out. She pulled him away from the edge, then stood up and surveyed the carnage, her expression unreadable.

'Well, that went well,' said Red. 'Thanks for leaving a few for the rest of us.'

A slight smile curled up around the corners of her mouth. 'I knew you'd catch up. Eventually.'

'Was that a *joke* from the great and serious Vinchen warrior?' he asked.

Her eyes grew wide, her smile vanished, and he knew he'd said exactly the wrong thing.

'Taking life is never a joking matter,' she said as she wiped the blood off her sword and sheathed it.

'Uh, right, of course,' he said.

'It won't take long for Drem to guess this didn't turn out his way,' said Nettles. 'We should get Sadie out of here as soon as she's ready to move. Then we should all disappear until this blows over.'

'Good idea,' said Hope. 'You should all stay hidden until this is done. I think it'll get worse before it gets better.'

'Sounds like you don't plan to join us,' said Nettles.

'She's going after Drem,' said Red.

'Ain't nobody *that* crazy,' said Filler.

'He had Captain Carmichael murdered in cold blood,' said Hope. 'A man I had sworn to protect with my life. A man who was as much mentor as he was captain. I cannot allow this to stand.'

'I hope you don't expect us to come on this death party with you,' said Nettles.

'Of course not. None of you took an oath.'

'All the same, I'll come along,' said Red.

'Don't be bludgeon,' said Nettles. 'Why in hells would you do that?'

'I got many reasons,' said Red. 'The most obvious of which is that without my help, Hope hasn't got a chance. And I'd rather the woman who saved Sadie's life have at least a shot of living a bit longer.'

'Red, I appreciate your courage, and your offer,' said Hope. 'But I don't think I will be doomed without it.'

'You sure about that?' asked Red. 'You heard what that boot just said about where to find Drem. That's not some secret. We all know where to look. So why do you suppose nobody's ever taken a shot at him?'

'He must be heavily guarded,' said Hope.

'He's got a pissing army,' said Nettles.

'Exactly,' said Red. 'Now, your skill is just about the most pat I've ever seen. But even still, there's no way you're getting through a hundred or more well-armed boots on your own.'

'And you think you would turn the tide?' asked Hope.

'Not by myself, no. But I could help you get an army of your own.'

'Such balls and pricks,' said Nettles. 'Where are *you* going to get an army?'

'Hammer Point. Big Sig has had a grind with Drem since way back.'

'No,' said Nettles. 'That's . . . You can't . . .' She shook her head, her mouth open.

'You're taking it outside the Circle,' said Filler.

It was more a statement than a question, but it hung in the air all the same. Nettles and Filler stared at him. Waiting for him to say it. Maybe they didn't believe he could. And until that moment, he wasn't sure he could either. The Circle had taken a lot of things away from him, it was true. But it had also *given* him so much. He was known. He was respected. If he wanted, he could have become one of Drem's lieutenants. Maybe even become as powerful as Drem someday. He felt in his bones that *could* happen for him. Which was why he could not let it.

Maybe Filler was right. Maybe it was his uptown blood that put crazy thoughts in his head. But being the leader of a garbage heap didn't change the fact that he and everybody else still lived in a garbage heap. He wanted better. He wasn't sure why Hope seemed like 'better' to him. Her education, her principles, the fact that she'd seen the world outside New Laven. Take your pick. And when she was around, he didn't

feel so crazy talking about wanting better. The idea of unit-
ing the neighborhoods seemed like more than just tavern
talk. It seemed possible. And that was all he needed.

'Yeah,' he said. 'I'm taking it outside the Circle.'

'Un-pissing-believable,' said Nettles. 'Come on, Filler.
Let's slide.' Without waiting, she started down the steps.
'Guess I shouldn't be surprised, since you weren't actually
born in the Circle,' she said over her shoulder, just loud
enough to make sure Red heard it.

Filler continued to stare at Red. Good old Filler, game for
any crazy adventure that Red could think up. But apparently
not this time. After another moment, he shook his head and
followed Nettles.

'Red . . .' said Hope. 'Are you sure—'

'Of course I am. Now let's get Sadie and find somewhere
safe for her to lie low.'

He started back up the stairs, and Hope followed quietly
behind. When they got to the top, he gently shook Sadie
awake.

'Where's Filler and Nettles?' she asked. 'They didn't get
hurt, did they?'

'No, they're fine,' said Red as he stoked the fire to get the
water boiling again.

'Then why do you look about like you're going to get the
weeps?'

'I, uh . . .' He stopped messing with the fire and turned to
face her. 'I'm leaving the Circle.'

'Hm.' Sadie tilted her head toward Hope. 'With her?'

'Yeah.'

'Good.'

Red gave her a startled look.

'You should get out of this slimy cunt of a place while you
can,' she said. 'And this Southie of yours has a better head
on than the rest of your wags.'

'But I thought you'd want me to—'

'Be a proper man of the Circle? Piss on that. Proper men of the Circle never got nobody nothing except dead early or old before their time. Rixidenteron, you were made for more and better. And I would take it as a personal insult if you didn't follow on that, after all those years I spent making sure you didn't starve or get knifed. Keen?'

'Sadie . . .'

'Don't "Sadie" me, you needle-pricked salthead. Do you *keen*?'

'Yes, Captain.'

And that was the end of it. They cooked up one more batch of medicine. After a solid minute of breathing, she spit out phlegm with only the faintest tint of orange.

'You're out of danger,' said Hope. 'But you'll still need to take it twice a day for the next few days to make sure it doesn't come back.'

'I'm good enough to travel, though?' asked Sadie.

'Yes. If you feel up to it.'

'Let's move, then. Can't imagine it will take Drem long to hear how you diced up his boots with that fancy blade of yours. And next time, he'll send a lot more.'

Sadie was breathing in harsh gasps by the time they got down to the docks. Red had offered to carry her part of the way, but she only glared at him and kept walking. She said she knew a wag near the boatyards who would put her up for a while.

'Missing Finn?' asked Red. 'I'm surprised you've kept a line on him.' Since the ship burned down, he'd stayed by the docks, taking honest jobs repairing ships and working the fishing boats.

'I've kept with all of that crew,' said Sadie. 'Happiest time of my life, so anyone who reminds me of it, I like to keep close.'

Missing Finn lived in a little shack along the wharf. He was sitting in front of it, threading a fishing pole with new line when they arrived. He looked about as worn and grizzled as Sadie. But when he saw them heading toward him, his one eye lit up and his ragged face folded up into a smile that showed the rot on his few remaining teeth.

'Is that the crown jewel of the Circle I see before me?' he asked, slowly standing up.

'Listen, you old sweet talker.' Sadie scowled at his smile. 'You've been begging me to move down wharf-side for years. I need a place to lie low. Maybe for a long time. You sunny with that, or have I got too old and ugly for your interest?'

'I don't know who's been tellin' you lies,' said Finn. 'But you ain't old or ugly. Me neither, truth be told. And lucky for you to have such a handsome wag to look at every day while you stay down here hiding from whatever serious badness that's deservedly caught up with you.'

Sadie turned to Red. 'Well, he's still a bit bludgeon, but he's got a way with words. And more important, he's safe.'

'You're sure?'

'Course I am. Stop being stupid.'

'Red.' Hope frowned as she scanned the docks, looking for something. 'Do you know where Pier Twelve is from here?'

'Sure. Why?'

'I should talk to the crew of the *Lady's Gambit*. They might not even know Captain Carmichael's dead. Those men have fought at my side. I should at least tell them what's happened.'

'Captainless ship, you say?' asked Finn.

'Gunned down by Drem's boots in the Drowned Rat yesterday,' said Red.

'Well, actually shot by Ranking, his first mate,' said Hope.

Sadie's eyes narrowed with interest. 'And what happened to the mate?'

'I'm not sure,' said Hope. 'The last time I saw him, he was bleeding all over the floor after I'd cut off half his arm.'

'You don't think the crew just elected a new captain and slipped away?' asked Finn.

'It needs a lot of repairs,' said Hope. 'I'm not even sure it's seaworthy.'

'Well, now,' said Finn, and gave Sadie a significant look.

'Why don't you show us this ship of yours,' said Sadie. 'I'm guessing you might, at some point, have a need to leave this place swiftlike. Good to have a functional ship on hand for that.'

'Perhaps,' said Hope, her eyes narrowing. She looked questioningly at Red, but he shrugged. He had no idea what Sadie's scheme was.

'Now, listen, it's not like what you're thinking,' said Sadie. 'Long as you're running with Red, you and I are old pots. What I'm thinkin' is this. Finn is good with ships. Got the *Savage Wind* up and seaworthy, and he's been workin' on them ever since. You kids do what you need to do. In the meantime, Finn and I will fix up your ship.'

'It's not my ship, though,' said Hope.

'Whose is it?' asked Sadie.

'No one's, really.'

'Then it's yours to take.'

'So what's the trade?' asked Red.

'Simple as sideways,' said Sadie. 'When you slide, you take us with you on the crew.'

Red was surprised. 'Really? That's what you want?'

'I only got so many years left, despite your best efforts. I surely wouldn't mind spending them at sea in the fresh air and sunshine. See a bit of the world before I go.'

'I'd as soon slip mooring as anything else,' said Missing Finn.

Red turned to Hope. 'What do you think? If we do somehow manage to pull this off, a boat might be a smart idea.'

'Let's see what's waiting for us before we make any decisions,' said Hope. 'The rest of the crew might have some objections to this plan.'

There were no objections to the plan. Because there was no crew. The *Lady's Gambit* had been emptied of both people and all supplies. Anything not locked or bolted down had been taken.

'As I thought,' said Finn. 'People got to eat. They ran out of provisions and patience, saw other ships around looking for crews, offering a meal and a bit of money. What would you do?'

'So we just . . . leave it here?' asked Hope.

'Well . . .' Finn turned toward the other end of the dock. A large man with a black beard was coming toward them. 'There's the dockmaster to deal with.'

'You! Southie!' the man yelled as he continued toward them. 'I don't know what happened to Carmichael and the rest of your crew, but someone owes me two days' docking fees. And if you don't pay me or get it off this dock by sundown, I'll have it sunk. Don't think I won't!'

'Now, now, my good wag,' said Red cheerfully. 'Let's leave off this talk of sinking ships. How much did you say it was per day to dock here?'

'A fiveyard,' said the man warily.

'Okay, then. So my maths aren't the greatest, but I think this' – he flashed two gold coins – 'ought to get us, what, a week?'

The man stopped short, eyeing the coins. Red made sure to turn them slightly so they gleamed in the sunlight.

'About,' admitted the dockmaster.

Red turned to Finn. 'That be long enough to get it shipshape?'

'Probably. Although judging by the lean of that foremast, might be more like two.'

'Well, then,' said Red. 'Better add two more, just to be safe.' He pulled out two more coins and placed all four in the dockmaster's hand. Then he held up a fifth. 'And this one is yours if no one other than us four goes near it without our leave. I come back in two weeks and find it still here and all of a piece, you can have it. Keen?'

The dockmaster smiled warmly, all chum and larder now. 'Yes, of course, Captain . . .'

Red pointed to Hope. 'There is the captain of the *Lady's Gambit*. Captain Bleak Hope.'

'At your service, Captain Hope,' said the dockmaster. 'Let me know if there's anything you need.'

'Thank you, Dockmaster, I will,' said Hope gravely. When the man had left, she turned to Red. 'Where did you get that money?'

'Could be I liberated a few from that bag before we left it to Prin in the cellar,' said Red. 'And aren't you glad of it now?'

Hope shook her head, but she was fighting a smile. 'Fine. It's too late now.'

'Sunny,' said Red. 'Now, shall we go find ourselves an army?'

'Before you head off on this slippy plan of yours,' said Sadie. 'You might want to consider filling your bilge and shutting your eyes for a bit.'

'The wisdom of years,' said Red.

*   *   *

Red wasn't sure how comfortable it would be for all four of them in Finn's wharf-side shack. But it turns out that when you've been trying to avoid death, both yours and others', for nearly two days without rest, you didn't much mind where you laid your head. Especially after a nice bowl of thick, hot fish stew.

So it was that he and Hope found themselves drifting off to sleep only an hour later as they lay on the shack's wood-planked floor. Sunlight streamed faintly through the wooden blinds over the one window. Sadie and Finn were outside, their conversation a lulling murmur in the background.

Red's eyes were beginning to close when he heard Hope's voice, soft and dreamy, say, 'What did she mean about you not being born in the Circle? Nettles, I mean.'

'Because I wasn't.'

'Where were you born?'

'Silverback. But that's not really what she meant. My mother was from Hollow Falls.'

'I don't know New Laven well enough to know what that means.'

'It means she was a lacy from uptown.'

'And that's . . . bad?'

'Around here? Yeah.'

'She thinks that makes you privileged.'

'Right.'

She opened her eyes and turned to look at him. 'Are you?'

'I could read by age five. Most wags in the Circle never learn. That alone gives me more than an extra share of fortune.'

'So they resent you.'

'Nettles resents everybody. I don't take that too personally. Not anymore. But as long as I've been here, I've had to compensate for it. Show 'em I wasn't soft. That I could handle things. The only one who never doubted me was Filler.'

'And now . . .'

'Yeah. Seeing him walk away like that . . . I'd rather be punched in the bilge.'

'That's the trouble with having people you care about,' said Hope. 'When you lose them, it hurts more than anything.'

They were silent for a while, interrupted only by Sadie's faint laughter outside.

'I feel I should warn you,' said Red. 'I don't know Hammer Point near as well as Paradise Circle. It's never been my turf. So I won't be able to come up with any clever escapes while we're there, or call upon the help of local wags who owe a favor.'

'Then it's a good thing,' said Hope, her voice sounding on the verge of sleep, 'you have other useful qualities.'

'You mean my undeniable charm?'

'I meant your impeccable aim.'

'Ah. Well. Yeah.' He was quiet for a minute. Then he said, 'You *do* think I'm charming, though, right? Hope?'

But she had drifted off to sleep.

19

*T*hey started out that night for Hammer Point. As Hope understood it, they were only going to the next neighborhood over. However, the gruff but heartfelt good-byes between Red and Sadie made it feel as if they were about to cross the ocean.

Now, as Hope and Red made their way through the streets lit with flickering gaslights, she noticed that he seemed on edge. His usual jaunty, carefree attitude felt forced. While Hope walked down the rough cobblestone streets with regular, even strides, he skipped, weaved back and forth, and at times even walked sideways, as if he couldn't regulate his own pace.

'Is it really so different in Hammer Point?' she asked.

He shrugged, his eyes darting all over. 'For you? Probably not. One urban Northern slum looks like any other. But for me, it's very different. Different buildings, different people, different ways of doing things.'

'Have you ever been there before?'

'Once or twice.'

'What were you doing there?'

He grinned. 'Nothing good.'

'Should we expect an unfriendly welcome?'

'There's no such thing as a friendly welcome in Hammer Point.' He picked up a few pebbles and threw one, knocking over a small bucket thirty feet ahead of them. 'They have a saying there, "It's hardest in the Hammer." And as far as I can tell, that's true.'

'Worse off than Paradise Circle?'

'Oh yeah. See, Deadface Drem may be a murdering, cold-blooded cock-dribble, but he keeps the Circle unified and orderly. There's no one like that in Hammer Point. Big Sig is the strongest right now. But it's always a hard scrabble between his gang and three or four others. Not even the imps can keep order in a place like that.'

'If Big Sig aligns himself with us, could it be enough to tip the balance of power in his favor?'

'That's what I'm hoping he'll decide,' said Red. 'Or he could decide that allying himself with us will only twist up the alliances he already has.'

'If that is what he decides?'

'Then he'll kill us.'

'He'll try.'

Red smiled. 'I love it when you earn your namesake.'

Hope wasn't sure exactly when it happened. But she gradually became aware that the streets around them were different. The cobblestones were not only filthy, but often cracked or broken. The buildings, too, seemed damaged, as if they'd been through a war. Shattered windows, splintered doors, chunks of stone and brick taken clean out of a wall. There were no streetlights either. The whole place was cast in gloom. 'We're in Hammer Point, aren't we?' asked Hope.

Red nodded. He was no longer bouncing around, but instead walked at her side, keeping perfectly apace. His hands were loose but ready at his sides, and his gaze scanned ahead of them.

'Do you have something that resembles a plan?' asked Hope.

'I know where to find Big Sig. The only trick is getting there without someone trying to roll us.'

'How likely do you think that is?'

'Not very.'

In fact, they were able to get several more blocks before three men stepped in front of them from an alley, and two more stepped out behind them.

'Good evenin', lovebirds. Going for a stroll, are we?' said one in a ragged top hat.

'Think they may have gotten lost,' said another with long hair past his shoulders.

'Maybe,' said a third with a thick scar on his cheek, 'after we get what we want, we should show them the way home.'

'That'd be real neighborly of us,' agreed Top Hat. ''Cept I haven't seen them in our neighborhood. I know I'd remember this Southie slice.'

Hope turned to Red. 'Do they think they're going to rob us?'

'Appears they do,' said Red.

'It hardly seems worth the effort,' said Hope. 'Are they even armed?'

'Oh, we're armed alright, you mouthy little slice,' said Scar. He drew a small knife that looked more useful for buttering bread than combat. The rest produced similarly pathetic weapons: a wooden club with a nail protruding from one end, a broken bottle, a brick, a leather sack filled with rocks.

'Be serious.' Hope began to walk, not slowing as she drew closer to them.

'That's it!' yelled Scar as he took a swipe with his knife.

Hope caught his wrist and twisted it so that he was forced to bend forward. At the same time, she brought up her knee into his face. With her free hand, she backhanded her fist into Top Hat's ear, sending him reeling. She let Scar drop to the cobblestones, and kicked Long Hair square in the chest, knocking him to the ground, gasping for air. Then she continued walking.

Behind her, Red said cheerfully, 'You see how it is, my wags. The lady likes things just so.'

The sound of rapid footfalls told her the remaining two had bolted.

Red caught up with her. 'Out of curiosity. Why didn't you take out your sword? You could have killed all three in one swing, I bet.'

'Killing unarmed, untrained people would have been an insult to the Song of Sorrows.'

'Sorry. The song of what?'

'That's the sword's name.'

'You named your sword? I mean, it's a great sword, but—'

'I didn't name it. This sword is centuries old, made with ancient arts lost to time. It was named long before either of us were born.'

'Sounds fancy.'

'It is a privilege to wield this blade. One that I hope someday to prove I am worthy of.'

'You aren't yet?'

'No,' said Hope. 'I haven't done anything truly worthy of it.'

'So how did you get it? I *know* you didn't steal it.'

'It was entrusted to me by my teacher. Just before he was murdered by his own brothers for teaching me the secret Vinchen arts.'

'Why in hells did they do that?'

'Because it is forbidden to teach those arts to a woman.'

'Why?' asked Red.

Hope glanced over at him, but judging by his expression, he genuinely didn't understand. 'Because women aren't supposed to participate in such things.'

Red frowned. 'Why not?'

'Because . . . I don't know, that's how it's always been.'

'Maybe elsewhere,' said Red. 'But here, being a tom or a molly don't matter much. If you can fight better than the next, that's all the argument you need.'

Hope tried to remember how it had been in her village. 'When I was very young, before I was taken in by the Vinchen monks, I lived in a small fishing village. I don't . . . remember a lot. But I know my mother did work. It was a hard life, but equally so for everyone, I think.'

'So it was those Vinchen who put this idea in your head? Were the boys there so much better than you?'

'No,' said Hope. 'I only fought one, but he wasn't much of a challenge. And I'd seen the others in their practice, and none seemed to possess any skills I did not.'

'Do you know what I think this is? Pure lacy nonsense. That's how they do it uptown, too. The men work, the women act all helpless. Load of balls and pricks. Downtown, everybody has to pull their weight. A molly does what she likes and a tom respects her for that.'

'I like that way of thinking,' said Hope. 'Perhaps in some ways, things *are* more civilized here.'

They didn't get waylaid the rest of their walk. Hope wasn't sure if it was coincidence or if word had spread that quickly.

'Well, here we are,' said Red, stopping before an unmarked warehouse. The windows glowed with light, and the sound of talking, laughter, and occasional yelling came from inside. He scrunched his nose up. 'Doesn't look like much.'

'You've never been here before?' asked Hope.

Red shook his head. 'Used to know a wag from Hammer Point. He told me about this place.'

'What happened to him?' asked Hope.

'Disappeared one night. Nobody knew for sure, but folks whispered it was biomancers.'

'Here?' asked Hope.

'Mostly uptown,' said Red. 'But sometimes they come down if they need fresh material. Or so people say. I knew this woman once. Little Bee's mom . . .' He shook his head. 'Anyway, it's hard to know for sure what's true and what's gossip.'

Hope had thought to leave New Laven after avenging Carmichael. But if there were biomancers gathered further uptown, she might need to stay longer. She wondered if Red would follow her there as well. She found herself hoping, selfishly, that he would.

'I guess we should knock or something.' Red pounded on the door with his fist.

A moment passed with only the muffled sounds from inside. Then a narrow slat opened in the door, and a suspicious pair of eyes peered out. 'What do you want?'

'To see Big Sig.'

'Yeah. And what makes you think you'll get to do that?'

'This does.' Red flashed a gold coin in front of his eyes. That was *another* coin he'd taken from the bag meant for the barmaid. Hope thought she'd watched him carefully when he'd put it down, but clearly his dexterous fingers were put to use for more than just throwing blades.

The eyes looked less suspicious now. 'Alright.'

The slot closed and the door swung open. A gaunt man with a pistol was on the other side. No revolvers for Big Sig's men, Hope noted.

'Very kind, my good wag,' said Red as he tossed him the coin.

The man caught it and held it up. 'This gets you in the building and past me. But it doesn't get you in with Sig.'

'Does it get me a tip on how I might arrange a friendly talk with him?' asked Red.

'He likes to play stones. There's a bunch of wags playing right now. You show yourself to have some skill, he'll probably want to play you.'

'Is that so?' Red flexed his fingers, his red eyes glittering. 'It happens I do have some small skill at the game.'

The man pocketed the coin. 'Well, good luck to you, then.'

'Oh, there's very little luck involved.' Red gave a quiet chuckle that sounded almost sinister.

They walked through a short hallway and into a large open space. It was mostly bare, except for ten tables spaced evenly in the center. Two people sat across from each other at each table. Hope didn't know how to play stones. She'd seen some of the crew playing on the *Lady's Gambit*, but she hadn't taken enough interest to try to figure out its rules.

Off to one side, next to a stone fire pit, was a man sitting in a chair with a metal lockbox. Red walked over to him and held up yet another coin. 'Pair me up the next game.'

The man looked warily at him. 'Not seen you around before.'

'Just got here,' said Red.

'Main rule is no drawing a weapon, even if you lose. Big Sig don't take kindly to rudeness in his gaming hall.'

'You don't have to worry about me, my wag. Especially since I don't lose.'

'That so?' The man grinned. 'Then maybe it's time you met Greeny Colleen. She's been pining for a respectable challenge.'

'I'm not respectable, but I promise you, I am a challenge.'

'Last table on the right.' The man traded the coin for a wooden chip. 'She should be cleaning up the current salt-head in just a minute.'

Hope and Red stood watching as a small, frail-looking woman of about thirty played with an older man.

'I don't really understand this game,' Hope whispered to Red.

'Each player starts out with twenty stones. You take the remaining ten stones from the set and line them up across the table. Now, each stone has a number from zero to nine on it. The idea is to get rid of all your stones. If you have the next number up from one in the center, you can put it above it. If you have the next one down, you can put it below it. Or if you have the same, put it on top. But once you start that row, either up and down or on top, you can't change it. Unless you take them all away again from that row and start back with just the original stone.'

'Why would you take any back if you're trying to get rid of them all?'

'Because if you run out of stones you can put down, you *have* to start picking them up until you can put one down again.'

'Still, it doesn't seem too complicated.'

'That's just the general idea. Things get interesting when you start to bridge between two or more rows by adding, subtracting, multiplying, or dividing the numbers.'

'Math?'

He shrugged and looked away. 'It's a hobby of mine.'

That morning, before they'd gone to sleep, Red had mentioned that his 'lacy' background made him privileged. But rather than be proud of his ability to read, or his interest in math, he seemed embarrassed by them.

'But how does that work?' pressed Hope. 'It's a fairly small number of options to work with if the answer must be in single digits.'

He struggled for a moment, as if he didn't want to get sucked into the conversation any deeper. But then he suddenly gave in and his face lit up with almost childish delight. 'Right, but when you combine two rows, you can make a two-digit number. Combine three rows at once, and you make a three-digit number, and so on. The bigger the number, the more stones you can put down.'

'Okay. I can see how that could get complicated.'

Red smiled at her, and it wasn't one of his smirks that he thought were so charming. It was grateful. 'Most people don't get it.'

And that was it. Other people might appreciate his charm or his aim, but Hope wondered if there had been anyone else since his parents died who appreciated his intelligence.

'Piss'ell!' yelled the old man at Greeny Colleen's table. 'Again, Greeny! How do you . . .'

The small woman smiled shyly. 'I like numbers, Cast. That's all. They're like friends to me.'

Cast grunted, shoved his last wooden chip into the stacks of stones on the table, and left.

'That's our cue,' said Red.

They walked over to the table. Colleen looked up at them, her brow furrowed. 'You're new.'

'I am,' agreed Red as he sat down.

'I don't usually play new people.'

'The guy over there.' Red nodded to him. 'He said you needed a challenge.'

'Are you any good?' She squinted at him, her lips pursed.

'Only one way to find out,' said Red.

'How do you play?' she asked.

'No digit limit. Is there any other way?'

Colleen gave another shy smile. 'Not if you love the game.'

*   *   *

They played for over an hour. Hope hadn't realized a game could even go on that long. There would be times when each was down to only a few stones. But then one would block the other and the next thing she knew, they'd both be forced to pull stones until it seemed they were starting from the beginning again.

At first, she followed the flow of the game easily. Sitting behind Red, she could see the numbers on his remaining stones and was even able to predict some of his moves. But as the game progressed, and the two players began to understand how well matched they were, things sped up until it was a rapid fire of clicks, as stone after stone was placed, removed, shuffled. This was about more than quick mathematical equations. There was something larger at play. It reminded her of the same inspired free flow that ran through her when she fought.

Other players left their own games to watch, whispering to each other as if afraid a loud noise would break the spell. Hope suspected that not even a thunderclap would break their focus. Sweat trickled down Red's temple, and Colleen's face was flushed. So much effort in such stillness, thought Hope. There was something to this. Some lesson she could learn. It flickered tantalizingly at the edges of her mind, but would not come. The more she reached for it, the more it eluded her.

And then she realized, all at once, *that* was the lesson. In stillness, there was no reaching. There was only observation, acceptance, and reaction, all without seeking to control.

'Well,' said Red, breaking into Hope's thoughts. A ripple of muttered comments worked through the crowd.

Hope looked down at his hands to see if he had played all his stones. He had something in his hand, but she couldn't see what it was.

Greeny Colleen had both hands splayed in front of her, and she was panting through a fierce grin. 'That . . . was worth it.' She lifted up her hands. Beneath one was her last stone. She held out a wooden chip.

Red shook his head. 'The pleasure was just as much mine.' He held up his own wooden chip. 'Keep yours and take mine, if you can get me a friendly introduction to Big Sig.'

Greeny Colleen's eyes went wide in surprise. She was about to speak, but a new voice cut in. 'You don't need to bribe any more of my wags. Your skill alone is enough to get an introduction with me.'

The crowd of spectators around them parted. Towering over them all was the largest man Hope had ever seen. His fists were as big as a child's head, his chest as thick as a bear's. He had close-cropped hair and a long beard, black but peppered with gray. His nose looked like it had been broken several times, and there was a hard glint to his eyes that suggested to Hope that he rarely lost his temper, and was all the more dangerous for that reason.

'Now let's see . . .' said Big Sig. 'Red, right? I heard of you. The clever thief with the red eyes.'

Red gave him a calm smile. 'You keen me.'

'Not entirely,' said Big Sig. 'Never knew you were also a master stones player.'

'Ah, that bit I try to keep quiet,' said Red. 'Otherwise, it'd be hells to get a game going. Most people don't care to play me once they find out how good I am.'

'I'll play you.' Big Sig nodded to Greeny Colleen, who gathered up her chips and stood aside respectfully. 'I doubt I'll win, mind you. But it's nice to have at least one activity I can participate in where losing doesn't mean death.'

'You like losing?' asked Red.

'It's instructive,' said Sig. 'Besides, while we play, you can explain to me why you're here in a way that convinces me you're not one of Drem's boots come to stick a knife in me. I'd hate to kill such a talented stones player.'

'With respect,' said Red as he set up for a new game, 'if I was here to kill you, you'd already be dead.'

'Hear you have remarkable aim,' said Sig as he pulled his twenty stones from the pile.

'You heard right. Although I'm not the truly deadly one.'

Big Sig glanced up at Hope. 'That your bodyguard?'

'Body and soul guard, you could say,' said Red. 'She's teaching me how to be a person who's worth more than some clever tricks.'

Hope was struck by that. She never intended to instruct him or anyone else in the right way to live. Perhaps she voiced her opinions about Red and his lifestyle too carelessly. After all, what was it to her how he lived?

'Remarkable woman,' said Sig.

'You got no idea.'

And yet, he insisted on being so rude at times. She couldn't help herself. 'Are you two finished talking about me as if I wasn't present?'

Big Sig nodded politely to her. Then he looked back at Red. 'Begin.'

'So it's like this,' said Red as he laid his first stone. 'My wag here needs Deadface Drem dead. Personal matter.'

'I see.' Sig placed a stone, his expression slightly amused.

'And in the spirit of someone who is trying to look beyond himself, I feel like the Circle could do without Drem. Might even improve the place.'

'Also, he has a price on your head,' said Sig.

'Getting rid of that would be included in the improvements,' admitted Red with no trace of embarrassment as he slid a stone into place.

Big Sig placed a stone of his own. 'And where do I come in?'

'Drem has an army to protect him at his club. So I thought—'

'You'd run on over to Hammer Point and get your own army. But what's in it for me and my wags?'

'Tell me you don't want Drem dead.'

'There's a lot of things I want,' said Sig. 'I'm accustomed to not always getting them.'

'Fair enough. But this could be about more than getting back at Drem. Once Drem's out of the picture, and things are more favorable toward you in the Circle, we could return the favor. Help you muscle out your competition here.'

All this time, Red and Sig had been placing pieces, almost indifferently. But now Red laid down a stone that seemed to block all of Sig's progress. He smirked slightly.

Big Sig nodded gravely as he surveyed the pieces. 'All that sounds quite sharp. Except there's a piece that you're missing.' Then he laid down a stone in a row that had appeared blocked because, up until that moment, he hadn't used a combination like that.

Red's eyebrow shot up as he assessed the changed situation. 'Oh?'

'Do you know how hard it is to consolidate power over an entire neighborhood?' asked Sig. 'Nearly impossible. I can't do it, and while I'm not as ruthless as Drem, I'm smarter and my wags are more loyal. It takes more than one person to gain that kind of power.' He laid another stone.

'You're saying he had help?' asked Hope. 'From outside Paradise Circle?'

'I am,' said Sig.

'From who?' Red looked skeptical as he took up a stone.

'Biomancers,' said Sig. 'Army or not, we're no match for them.'

'Biomancers?' Red snorted. 'That's a load of balls and pricks.'

'How do you know?' Hope asked Sig. She was not so ready to dismiss a potential lead to a biomancer.

'He doesn't know,' said Red. 'He's just repeating gossip.'

'I *know*,' said Sig, 'because they offered me the same deal they gave him. They told me they could give me the advantage over the other neighborhood gangs, put me in charge of all Hammer Point. In return, I would provide them with a new human subject every month.'

'To experiment on.' Hope's voice was flat. The tentacles of these biomancers reached even into the New Laven underworld. Yet there was something fitting about Carmichael's murderer having some connection to the other people she hated.

'Yes,' said Sig. 'That's when they told me that Drem had already taken the deal. They said if I didn't, eventually Drem would overrun Hammer Point.'

'And what did you say?' Hope wondered, if he admitted to joining them, would she kill him on the spot?

'I told them I would claim Hammer Point on my own or not at all,' said Sig.

Hope relaxed a little. 'Very brave of you.'

'Very stupid, too. They said to me, "You've bitten off more than you can chew." Then one of them, this cunt-dropping with a burn mark on his face, comes up to me and just taps on my jaw with his finger. That's it. But a sharp pain went through my face, and then my teeth crumbled in my mouth.'

Big Sig smiled. A big, wide smile that showed he had a full set of wooden teeth.

'This biomancer with the burn mark.' Hope's voice was barely louder than a whisper. The idea that this biomancer could be the one she'd been seeking for the past ten years sent her pulse racing, but outwardly she remained calm. 'Did he also have brown hair and a pointy face?'

'You've met him?' Sig looked at her with new interest.

'I've seen him from a distance.' There was nothing but darkness in her voice, and the way Big Sig looked at her, he clearly saw it. He nodded his head and did not press her further.

'How do we know this is all true?' asked Red. 'You could be lying to us. Or they could have been lying to you.'

Big Sig looked back at Red. 'I felt you deserved an answer as to why I won't help you take down Drem. I don't care if you believe it.'

'You should,' said Red.

'Why's that?'

Red stared down at their forgotten game of stones, almost as if he didn't know what it was. His eyes were somewhere else. His face was relaxed, almost smiling. But Hope could see a vein throbbing in his throat.

'Because,' he said at last. 'If you can prove to me that Drem has sold out all of Paradise Circle to the biomancers, I promise you, I will raise an army in the Circle to match yours. Together we will knock down Drem's door.'

He placed his wooden chip on the table and looked up at Big Sig.

'And biomancers or no, I will kill that traitor myself.'

PART FOUR

*The person you believe yourself to be is only
part of you, just as all truths are only partial
truths.*

— from *The Book of Storms*

20

Nettles wrapped her rough wool coat around herself more tightly. 'I don't like this, Red.'

'The ale tastes different here.' Filler wrinkled his nose at his tankard of dark.

'You two are my best wags, and you know it,' said Red.

'Do we?' Nettles glanced at Hope, the fourth and final person at the table.

'Of course you do,' said Red. 'Otherwise, you wouldn't have come with me to a tavern in Hammer Point.'

'It's only just over the line.' Nettles said it like it didn't matter, which was bludgeon because as they all knew, it *did* matter.

'Ale's not as good on this side of the line,' pronounced Filler. The poor wag looked more uncomfortable than Red had ever seen him, shifting restlessly in his seat, a thin sheen of sweat at his temples. This was the first time he'd ever been out of Paradise Circle.

'All the same,' said Red, 'I know I asked a lot for you to be here, especially after you made it clear that you didn't want to help us take down Drem.' He spoke quiet and low. They were outside the Circle, and the Point of No Return wasn't crowded. The taverns that bordered a neighborhood rarely were. But still, this was too grave to talk soundly on.

'Then what is it we're doing here, if not helping you with that?'

'You don't need to *do* anything.' Red couldn't blame her for being suspicious. 'You don't need to say anything or even think anything. All you need to do is watch and listen.'

Nettles leaned forward. 'And what is it we're supposed to see and hear?'

'I don't know, exactly. Big Sig has made some . . . accusations. He claims he can prove they're true. Tonight, with you two as witness, we'll see for ourselves.'

'You been reading them spy books again?' asked Nettles. 'What'd I tell you about all that reading? Makes you soft in the head.'

Red was about to reply, but then he saw Greeny Colleen enter the tavern. Such a small, mousy thing, practically invisible. He almost missed her, and for Red, that was a rare thing.

She came over to the table and eyed Nettles and Filler suspiciously. 'Who're these two?'

'I need trustworthy types to vouch for me,' said Red. 'If what Sig says is true.'

Colleen frowned. 'It'll be a tight squeeze. And you'll be there for a while. The meeting isn't for an hour, but we need to get you in there now.'

'We'll manage,' said Red.

Colleen shrugged. 'Come on, then.' She turned and headed toward the exit.

'You ready?' Red asked Hope.

'Hmm?' she said, blinking.

Red wasn't sure why, but she'd been withdrawn lately. He hadn't given it a lot of thought, though, because he'd been preoccupied himself while they were lying low down at the docks, sleeping on the *Lady's Gambit*, and helping with repairs. It felt like he'd been holding his breath for days, waiting to listen in on this meeting. If what Big Sig said was true, it changed everything. But he didn't say any of that. Instead, he said, 'Time to go lurk. Your least favorite thing.'

'Oh. Right.'

As they stood up to follow Colleen, Nettles put her hand on Red's arm. 'You *sure* about this?'

'I promise you, Nettles. One way or the other, this is something we need to know.'

'Fine. But you owe me.'

'I already owed you for getting us down the chute a few nights ago.'

'That's two, then.' Nettles gave him a tight grin. 'Maybe I'm saving up for something special.'

Colleen led them out of the tavern and into the cold night air. It was turning to the wet season, bringing with it occasional hard squalls of icy rain. Red pulled his leather coat tighter around him. The rest of the group braced similarly. All except Hope, who seemed completely unaffected. Red wondered how cold it actually got in the Southern Isles.

'The leaders will come through the main entrance,' said Colleen as she led them around the side of the building. 'They're meeting in the back room. No windows and only one entrance, which will be guarded. But there's a hidden crawlspace in the floor of that room, which you can enter from out here.'

The back of the tavern faced a dark alley, puddled with muddy water from the afternoon's cold rain. Icy water seeped into Red's boots as he scanned the back wall of the building. 'I don't see the entrance.'

'Of course not.' Colleen knocked on an old ale barrel that was propped up on the side of the wall. It reverberated with an odd echo. She lifted the lid. Red peered in and saw that a tunnel had been dug out beneath the barrel.

He grinned and turned to Nettles. 'Spy stuff!'

'Who knows about this crawlspace?' asked Hope.

'Big Sig, of course. And Thorn Billy, another leader who's allied with Sig. He knows you'll be there.'

'Can we trust him?' asked Red.

'To keep quiet? Yes.' Colleen looked irritated by the question. 'He doesn't want to see Hammer Point turn into another Paradise Circle either.'

'What does *that* mean?' Nettles rolled her shoulder like she was warming up for a punch.

Colleen ignored her. 'You'll be able to see and hear what's happening above from the crawlspace. Which means that if you move or make any sound, they'll be able to hear you, too. And if they do, Sig will act like he's never seen you in his life. He expects the same.'

Red caught her arm. 'Thank you for this.'

She nodded, suddenly looking shy. 'If you ever want a rematch on stones . . .'

He grinned. 'I know just where to find it.'

She smiled and hurried away.

They contemplated the barrel.

'Filler, my old pot,' said Red. 'You may lose a bit of skin in this venture.'

One at a time, they slipped through the barrel to the tunnel beneath, then shimmied on their stomachs for a few yards until the tunnel opened above into the crawlspace. True to its name, the space was so low that Red found he couldn't get his belly more than six inches from the ground. They slid in one at a time, then awkwardly rolled onto their backs to stare up through the floorboards. The room above them was still dark, so it was difficult to tell how much they would actually be able to see.

'Don't move, she says,' muttered Nettles beside him. 'Like there's any room to move.'

They were all mushed up together, lying side by side. Hope, then Red, then Nettles, and finally Filler. With his ex pressed up against him on one side and the celibate girl he could never have on the other, Red couldn't quite decide if this was Heaven or one of the darker sort of hells.

'Don't you go getting any ideas, there,' said Nettles, as if she could read his mind.

'I didn't do anything,' protested Red.

'I *know* you, and you're a leaky tom if ever there was one.'

'Furthest thing from my mind,' he lied. 'But clearly, it's on *your* mind. Who's leaky, then?'

'Shut up, you two,' said Filler.

'Thank you,' said Hope.

The minutes dragged by as they lay in the darkness. Finally, someone came into the room with lanterns, hung them from the walls, and left. Once there was light, Red was surprised at how much he could see. It wasn't perfect, of course. But it would be enough to see who was talking.

Several more minutes passed, and then four people entered the room. Red recognized Big Sig easily. There was also a short man with black hair that stuck out in many different directions like a hedgehog. Red assumed this was Thorn Billy. Those Hammer Point wags had a way of stating the obvious. With them was also an older woman with bone-white hair and an eye patch, and a man with skin even darker than Hope's Captain Carmichael.

'Surprised you came, Sig,' said the woman with the eye patch.

'Heard this wasn't one to miss, Sharn,' said Big Sig.

'I heard the same,' said Sharn. 'Although no details as to why.'

'Has it crossed anyone's mind that this could be a trap?' asked the dark-skinned man. He spoke with a faint accent.

'Of course, Palla,' said Sig. 'My people have orders to let in no one except Drem and one . . . guest.'

'Yes, this mystery person who will supposedly change our minds,' said Billy.

The four gang leaders waited a little longer, talking quietly. Red wanted to chance a look at Nettles after they mentioned Drem, to see her expression. But he resisted, unsure if even that slight movement would draw attention. Even his breathing seemed ridiculously loud, and his chest rose and fell far more visibly than he'd realized.

Finally, the door opened and Drem entered. Beside him was a man in a white robe belted at the waist with a gold chain. His face was hidden in the shadow of his white hood. Red knew that this was the uniform of the biomancers, though he'd never seen one himself. Nettles gave a sharp intake of breath, but it was okay because much louder things were happening above them.

Palla, Sharn, and Billy were demanding that Drem explain himself, looking somewhere between offended and alarmed. Only Sig, his face stony, remained silent.

'Now, now, you bunch of gafs, don't get all wobbly.' Drem held up his hands. 'Just hear us out.'

'I'm not interested in anything that man has to say,' said Sharn, her one eye blazing with rage.

'Drem, I'm sure I don't need to remind you that you are in the Hammer right now as our protected guest,' said Palla. 'If we were to withdraw that protection, things would not go well for you.'

'Right you are,' said Drem. 'Which is why I came here not as an enemy, but as a potential ally.'

'I'm listening,' said Palla, his eyes hard.

'Quickly, Drem,' said Sharn. 'Say your speech.'

'Thanks, kindly.' Drem's expression was oddly cheerful. 'As you know, I control Paradise Circle without rival. This is partly through hard work and quality, and partly because of the biomancers.'

Despite his insistence on getting proof, Red had known in his gut that it was true. But the sadness that welled up in his chest, hot and sharp, the sense of betrayal that a true man of the Circle could sell them out like that, was more intense than he'd expected. He wondered what Filler and Nettles were feeling, getting the whole thing all at once for the first time.

'In exchange for their help,' Drem was saying, 'the biomancers only want test subjects to work their trade on.'

'People, you mean,' said Palla.

'In the past, it's only been one a month. Very reasonable, I say. But, things are changing.' He glanced at the biomancer.

The biomancer pulled back his white hood, and he looked so normal, so unremarkable, that Red wondered if he was a real biomancer or just someone Drem had dressed up to get a rise out of the Hammer Point leaders. But then he spoke, and his voice was like something dredged up from the bottom of the ocean, grimy and rough like barnacles.

'The safety of the empire is in peril from enemies beyond the Dark Sea,' he said. 'The emperor has commanded that we increase our efforts to develop new weapons and strategies for defense. To do this, we need more test subjects for our research. You will provide them.'

'Like hells!' said Billy.

'Let's not get ahead of ourselves.' Drem gave the biomancer a look that said, *Let me handle this*. Then he turned back to Thorn Billy. 'Here's the length of it. We all come together, Paradise Circle and Hammer Point. Then we take Silverback. My friend here' – he gestured to the biomancer – 'assured me this won't be a problem. Then the five of us have complete control over half of New Laven. I'll share the docks, you share the mills. Everything south of Keystown is ours to do with as we like. Sounds sunny, don't it?'

Billy shook his head. 'You want us to give our own people to the biomancers?'

'Come now, Billy, old pot,' said Drem. 'Let's speak crystal. We all know there are some people out there who are just useless bottom-feeders. The world won't change a hair with them gone.'

'How *many* people are we talking about?' Palla asked the biomancer.

'The exact number may change over time,' said the biomancer. 'Twenty per month to start should be sufficient.'

'Twenty innocent people every pissing month?' asked Billy. 'I can't believe any of you are even considering this.' He looked at each of them in turn. They remained silent. 'Forget the scary bedtime stories. The biomancers are just people. Flesh and blood like us. They control through fear, intimidation, and the idle gossip of idiots.'

'Billy.' Sig laid a large hand on his shoulder. 'This isn't the time for—'

'It's exactly the time!' Billy shrugged Sig's hand off. 'We have to stop this now, before it goes any further. Before they destroy us all!' He turned desperately to the other leaders. None could meet his gaze.

'You misunderstand us completely,' said the biomancer, his low voice like an anchor dragging across coral. 'You think us cold? Cruel? Unfeeling?' He shook his head sadly. 'You were right before when you said that we are just people. We feel things deeply. We must. It is the curse of what we do. But while you only feel the small little corner of your small little neighborhood in your small little city, we feel the whole empire. We watch over it and care for it, just as it watches over and cares for you. Everything we are, everything we do, is given to this purpose. Can you not see this larger image?'

He placed his hand on Billy's and squeezed. He had tears in his eyes, his expression pleading. Billy had clearly not anticipated such an impassioned response and stared at him in bewilderment.

'If you cannot see it,' continued the biomancer, 'if you cannot feel as we do, perhaps it is *you* who are cold.' Then he turned away and walked back over to Drem.

The room was silent, the leaders all looking at each other uncertainly, even Big Sig. The only one who seemed unaffected was Deadface Drem. His expression was blank.

That's when Red knew.

Billy suddenly shivered. 'What is . . .'

His skin began to grow pale, the veins more pronounced – a spiderweb of blue that shot across his hands and face. His body grew rigid and shook. His eyes filmed over and turned to balls of ice. His black hair dropped from his head in chunks, and his fingernails dropped from his crooked fingers. He opened his mouth to scream, but his jaw cracked on one side so that it dangled from one hinge. His tongue was a dark frozen slab of meat that flapped up and down. Both jaw and tongue dropped to the ground and shattered. Guttural noises escaped from his mouth hole as his eyes slowly squeezed out of his sockets. The skin on his neck split, and first one arm broke off at the elbow, and then the other at the shoulder. Finally, his legs splintered and his body hit the floor, breaking into pieces. The chunks continued to shudder inside the clothes. Then everything was still.

Drem stepped forward, his face still expressionless. 'We'll give you a few days to think about it.'

'I'm trying to figure out the exact moment that my life went leeward,' said Nettles as she tossed a small crust of bread into the pond. Pale white fish with large, luminous eyes shot to the surface and gobbled up the bread. It was an underground pond and the fish in it didn't often get bread crusts.

Red, Hope, Nettles, and Filler had gotten the all-clear knock from Colleen an hour after the Hammer Point leaders had left the room and someone had come in and swept up the frozen pieces of Thorn Billy. Red told Colleen he'd get in touch with Big Sig in a day or two. Then the four had returned to Paradise Circle.

It was Nettles who had suggested Apple Grove Manor. The place sounded lacy, because once, a long time ago, it had been. This was back when the city of New Laven was only uptown, and the entire downtown area was nothing but small farms and orchards. Apple Grove Manor had been the only building for five miles in any direction. A lone mansion in a sea of apple trees, all owned by the Bulmatedies family. But that had been centuries ago. The apple orchard was gone, the last of the Bulmatedieses dead. The only thing that remained was the manor house itself, a crumbling beauty allowed to persist as the cobblestone streets and ramshackle houses were built up around it.

Apple Grove Manor had been many things to many people over the years. A squat house for the homeless, a drug house for the addicts, a sex house for the whores. One optimistic businessman even tried to turn it into a respectable hotel and boardinghouse. That particular enterprise lasted only a few months. Customers complained of midnight hauntings and missing items, such as a left stocking or half the buttons on a jacket. The owner had even brought in a necromancer to clean it out, but it didn't do any good. Within the year, the businessman gave up and moved back uptown to Keystown where he belonged.

The most recent tenant had been Jix the Lift, back before Drem used his innards as a cravat. Jix swore the whole time he and his crew were there, he never saw a single haunting or had the tiniest thing go missing. People said the house preferred a proper man of the Circle to an uptown lacy. It was easy to believe that. Like anything old and left too long on its own, the manor had grown strange. Among its many eccentricities was the fishpond in the basement.

No one knew how the pond got there or how it was filled with strange, ghostlike fish. Many muttered *biomancer* and steered clear, but many things were attributed to biomancers that probably shouldn't have been. Some people didn't like to think it, but the world was strange enough on its own and didn't really need much help in that regard.

The basement was a large room, and the pond took up all of it. The only thing left above the waterline was the top row of storage shelves that were bolted to the walls. By dropping down from the hatch above on the ground floor, and sliding carefully along, one could circle the entire room. It was dark and damp and smelled like rotting algae. That, combined with the biomancer and ghost rumors, made it an unpopular spot to visit. Red and Nettles had come out of curiosity back when they were together. It became a special place for them during that time. Neither had been back since they split. So Red was surprised when she'd suggested it.

Now the four of them sat on the shelving, feet dangling above the dark water.

'Did my life go leeward when I met Red?' Nettles mused, tossing another bit of bread to the ghost fish.

'That's when your life got *interesting*,' said Red. 'But I see how you might confuse that.'

'Maybe it was when the angel slice showed up,' she continued as if she hadn't heard.

'That's a load of balls and pricks if ever there was one,' said Filler.

They all turned to look at him in surprise, even Hope.

'Why do you say that, old pot?' asked Red.

'What's here ain't none of her doing,' said Filler. 'All she did was blow the dust off so we could see that there ain't no Circle. Ain't been one for a while.'

'You don't mean that, Fill.' Nettles looked at him pleadingly. Like she wanted him to take it back.

'I mean it more than anything I've ever said in my life. I wish I didn't, Nettie. But you saw the length of it. The biggest wag in Paradise Circle nothing but a pet monkey for the imps and biomancers. It makes me want to burn it all down. It would be better if it was nothing. Better than this lie.'

Red expected Nettles to argue. To disagree. But she didn't say anything, so he turned to Hope. 'What about you? You've been more quiet than usual.'

'It wasn't him,' she said, staring into the black depths of the pond.

'Wasn't who?'

'The biomancer. I hoped it would be the one I know. The one with the burn scar that knocked out all Big Sig's teeth.'

'Why?'

She turned to him, then, and there were tears in her eyes. It took Red by surprise. Up till that point, he hadn't been sure she was even capable of that kind of emotion.

'If there is one person in the world I long to kill more than any other, it is that man. The man who murdered my entire village.'

Again there was silence, broken only by the quiet splashes of the ghost fish sucking up the bread. Red wondered how the fish never fought over it. There wasn't much to be had, and he was sure that many of them never tasted a single speck. Weren't they mad? Didn't they think it was unfair? No, of course not. Because fish were bludgeon as they came. He thought they were probably blind anyway. So most of them never even saw when there was bread to be had. He wondered how things would be different if they could see. If some of the fish at the very bottom suddenly had a big light they could shine up.

'Still, you wouldn't be opposed to killing *this* biomancer, would you?' he asked.

'What do you mean?' Hope asked.

'Make you a deal. You help me not only take down Drem but this whole biomancer scheme, and I will help you take down this scar-faced biomancer of yours.'

She gave him a doubtful look. 'The biomancer I want may not even be in New Laven anymore.'

'Then it's a good thing we're getting ourselves a ship seaworthy as we speak.'

'Red, I don't give or accept promises lightly.'

'You're saying I do?'

Nettles coughed and raised an eyebrow at him. And Red had to admit that she had cause. He had a way of fudging things, of using the inevitable moral gray that came along with the hardscrabble life of the slums to his advantage. He generally liked it that way.

'I'm saying,' said Hope, her blue eyes sparkling, 'that if we agree to this, and you break your promise, I will kill you. And I don't want to kill you. So please, only make this promise if you truly mean it.'

The truth was, Red hadn't been sure before how far he'd go with Hope on her quest to kill Drem. To be sure, she was the most fascinating molly he'd ever laid eyes on, celibate or no, and in theory, he'd agreed with her cause. But in the end, if things had gotten too hot for his liking, if it had come down to dying, he probably would have slid. He could admit that all to himself now because it wasn't true anymore. The muddy gray was gone, and the choice before him was crystal.

'You heard the biomancer. Twenty true neighborhood wags every month just to start. And once they get that number, you don't think they'll bump it up to twenty-five? Thirty? Fifty people getting done like Thorn Billy every pissing month? There won't be nothing left of us in a year, and they won't even care.'

Red stared at the ghost fish and thought about shining a light into dark places.

'Bleak Hope,' he said finally. 'If you help me save the Circle, I will follow you across the Dark Sea if need be.'

Red knew there were only a few places where one could talk to a large number of people at once. The biggest and most obvious was Gunpowder Hall. What he didn't know was how to get everyone in the hall to stop eating and gambling and thieving and drinking and dropping coral spice and bending pricks and stretching cunts long enough so they would all listen to him. The chaos of the place made the idea laughable. Fortunately, Gunpowder Hall was not the only place neighborhood wags congregated. There was the Rag and Boards.

The Rag and Boards was not a tavern or gaming hall. It was a theater. But a theater as only Paradise Circle could make it. In Silverback, theaters were luxurious buildings that had seats with velvet cushions, chandeliers with gas lighting, majestic balconies, full orchestras, and the finest performers in the empire. The Rag and Boards, on the other hand, had no seats or balconies. The smoky torchlight made it difficult at times to even see the performers. That didn't stop the drunken, rowdy audience from shouting criticism and advice. At the Rag and Boards, such behavior was not only allowed but encouraged. Often the performers would even instigate it. The curtain, or rag, rose at six o'clock daily and hosted a rotating program of plays and performances until midnight.

Stories, folk dances, juggling, and clowning. For a fiveyard, it was possible you might see just about anything. But Red was sure no one had ever seen something quite like the night he took over the program.

It only required the right amount of money and knowing the right people for him to get a last-minute slot in that evening's program, especially after Bull-nose Nelly and her dancing bear suddenly fell ill. Finding one of the lead 'performers' proved to be tricky. But once he recruited Handsome Henny and the Twins as extra muscle, even that difficulty was resolved. The hardest part was convincing Hope that her small role was not simply important, but essential. Finally, with only minutes to spare, everything was ready.

Red let the audience wait until they were properly worked up and chanting, 'Hoist that rag!' When the curtain finally did come up, and it was only Red standing on a bare stage, they instantly fell silent. Red was known in the neighborhood for being a top-notch thief, a devious scoundrel, a tom with the mollies, a brutal stones player, and more recently, wanted alive or otherwise by Deadface Drem. This last one, he suspected, was what made the audience go quiet with equal parts awe and incredulity. It was a bold move. He could see a few people in the back shifting around, their hands slipping to sheathed knives or clubs, thinking they might slip around to the stage door and try to collect on Drem's price. But as he'd hoped, they didn't do it. Not yet, anyway. He'd have to talk fast.

'Toms and mollies! Neighborhood wags! Sorry for this last-minute substitution. I know you were all wanting your fill of bear dancing this night.'

'Bet *you* dance like a bear!' someone called.

'You flatter me, sir.' Red beamed. 'Anyway, I'm sorry to say, something of a bit more serious nature requires your immediate attention.'

'Spit it out, Red, you lacy ponce!' shouted Handsome Henny from the crowd.

'Henny, you never were one for long speeches,' said Red. 'Very well. The length of it is this: The Circle has been betrayed.'

Shouts came from all over. Red let it go awhile before he held up his hand to quiet them down. 'I could tell you the whole thing myself, of course. But then it's just me up here talking, and we all know how I like to talk.' A few chuckles in the audience. 'Plus, you paid your coin to be entertained, and I'd hate to deny you one of the few pleasures life has for us here. So instead, I'll have this old boot tell you.'

Red signaled offstage to Filler, who took one of the fly ropes and lowered a man slowly down to the stage next to Red. His feet dangled just above the boards. His hands were tied behind his back, and a dirty handkerchief was tied across his mouth. The shouts began again, some of them angry this time, some of them frightened.

'Judging by reactions,' said Red, 'I'm guessing some of you wags recognize Brackson, chief boot for Deadface Drem. I thought to myself, who better to break the news than someone who was partly responsible for it? Of course, he's a bit embarrassed about what he's done, and most like he's reluctant to speak of it. So I brought along a friend to loosen his tongue.'

Nettles walked out, her boots clacking sharply on the wooden boards of the stage.

'What tom wouldn't be a bit more talkative for such a lovely molly, am I right, wags?' said Red.

A few hoots and catcalls came from the audience, but those were silenced by one cold look from Nettles.

'Would you do the honors?' Red asked her.

Nettles nodded. She unhooked her chainblade from her belt and loosened the coil. Then she snapped her wrist, sending the blade out to slice off the gag and a fair amount of cheek as well.

Brackson screamed, 'Damn you all to every hell! Drem will have the lot of you for this!'

'And what will he do with us?' asked Red.

'Kill you in the worst ways he can find!'

'Will he really kill *all* of us?' asked Red. 'You sure he doesn't have another plan?'

'What?' said Brackson, brought up short. He looked confused by the question.

'Thought he might want to, oh, I don't know, give some of us over to someone.'

Brackson's face hardened. 'I don't know what you're talking about.' But he could have learned a thing or two from his boss, because it was plain to Red – and probably to everyone in that theater – that he was a terrible liar.

Red nodded to Nettles, who snapped her chainblade a second time. Now both of Brackson's cheeks dripped as if he were crying blood.

'Next one takes an eye,' said Red, no longer playing the smiling entertainer. 'Now, tell us all, nice and loud, what does Drem do with the ones he doesn't kill?'

Brackson looked first at Red, then at Nettles, who was carefully cleaning his blood off her chainblade. He looked to the audience, pleading. But Red knew he'd find no pity there. The wags of Paradise Circle were many things. Starry-eyed and innocent were not any of them. They seemed to be getting a sense that this was serious and affected them all.

Finally, Brackson dropped his head to stare at the boards beneath him. 'He gives them to the biomancers.'

The theater exploded with a roar of shouts and curses. Red waited while they got it out of their system. It took several minutes before he could get their attention again.

'Now, let me make sure I have this right,' said Red. 'Currently, he gives them one true wag of the Circle every month. Yes?'

Brackson nodded, and the curses from the audience rose again. People threw rotten fruit at him that they'd brought for the dancing bear.

Once things had settled down a bit again, Red said, 'I wish I could say that was all of it, but it's not. It gets much worse.' He told them everything he'd heard at the meeting, including how the biomancers were demanding twenty people a month from Paradise Circle, Hammer Point, and even Silverback. The shouts grew less enraged and more panicked. Red knew he had them.

'Make no mistake, the uptown lacies and their biomancers have declared war on the poor folk of downtown New Laven. They have decided we are no better than a shoal of fish to be caught and cooked. Circle or Hammer or Silver, they don't care. They mean to chew us all up until there aren't any left. And I ask you, do we accept that?'

'No!' shouted the audience.

'Of course not! Now is the time to lay aside old grudges with Hammer Point and join together to bring down the betrayer Drem and kick the biomancers out of our neighborhoods so hard they'll be pissing blood for a week. They need to know that we won't lie down for them!'

Shouts of agreement echoed around the theater.

'You're all pissing bludgeon!' shouted Brackson, thrashing on his rope, blood flinging from his face. 'Don't you get it? We're talking about pissing *biomancers* here! The right hand of the emperor himself. You haven't got a chance. I've seen them do things you can't even imagine!'

The audience grew quieter to listen.

'Yes.' Brackson nodded vehemently. 'You never met one, but you've heard the stories your whole lives. Even when you were just a child, your mom and dad told you, "If you don't behave, the biomancers'll get ya!" Oh, and they will! Let me tell you all, I have *seen* it with my own eyes, and every story you have ever heard is true. Why the hells do you think I went along with Drem? Because I was – and still am – pissing terrified of them. And you all should be, too.'

'It's true,' said Red, 'that we face the right hand of the emperor. But what if I were to tell you that *we* have the left hand? Toms and mollies, I give you . . . Bleak Hope.'

Hope dropped down from the flies, landing on one knee, the sheathed Song of Sorrows extended in front of her. A new surge of talk went through the crowd, but it was subdued and whispered.

'Yes, you see the armor and the sword,' said Red. 'You know who, or what, this is. A Vinchen warrior. It just so happens, she has sworn to end the life of any biomancer she can find. And we've all heard the stories about Vinchen and their oaths, haven't we?'

Red turned to Brackson. 'You're right about those biomancers. We were brought up to fear them, and with good reason. I've seen the awful things they can do.' He turned back to the audience. 'But if we were scared by stories of biomancers, weren't we inspired by the stories of the Vinchen? Warriors unlike any other, with a code of honor that protected all, not just the rich and noble. Remember Selk the Brave, who saved the village of Walta from a swarm of goblin sharks? Or Manay the True, who ended the Dark Mage's reign? Or Hurlo the Cunning, who singlehandedly defeated the brutal Jackal Lords? These Vinchen live as the poorest people in the empire, down in the Southern Isles, far from the splendor of Stonepeak. Why? Because they swore not to serve a single emperor but the whole of the empire. And last I checked, that includes us.'

He paused, letting that all sink in. There was complete silence and all eyes were on him. Even Hope's. He couldn't help but savor the moment.

'So let Drem have his nightmares. We have our hero.'

The audience exploded in a cheer that shook the boards beneath his feet.

'Tell everyone!' he shouted. 'Tomorrow at noon we march on the Three Cups! And we take back our home! Where it's cold and it's wet!'

'And the sun doesn't get!' roared the crowd.

'But still it's my home!' called Red.

'BLESS THE CIRCLE!' rang through the theater like a monsoon.

21

*H*ope stood on the grimy stage of the Rag and Boards and looked out at a hundred or more people who were cheering, in part, because of her. Because of what they *thought* she was. She stood silent and still, forcing herself not to cringe. She was not a true Vinchen. She had not passed the final ordeal or taken the final vows of chastity, poverty, and service. Without those, she could never truly call herself a Vinchen warrior.

But she understood why Red had said all that. These people needed to believe in someone or something that would be a match for a biomancer. Having grown up in the Southern Isles, she hadn't realized how much these Northerners idolized the Vinchen order. When she'd heard her own grandteacher's name called forth like a legend, it had flooded her with such pride and sadness, she had to fight to keep the grim, formidable poise she knew Red wanted her to maintain.

'Just do the pat hard molly look you do,' he'd said beforehand. 'They'll drain the bucket on that.'

And they had. Which made it all the harder to bear. But even if she was no true Vinchen, she hoped she could at least free them from the biomancer plot. The idea was almost beyond comprehension. All of downtown New Laven

– thousands of people – condemned to the same fate as the people of Murgesia. As her village. What sort of emperor would allow that? Would *command* it? She'd always agreed with Hurlo that it was best for the Vinchen order to remove themselves from the politics of Stonepeak. But she couldn't help wondering: If they had been closer, could they have curbed such excessive and cruel abuse of power before it reached this point?

It was too late for that now, though. She wished she could have brought more warriors with her. But, of course, they would never heed her call. If they came at all, it would be to kill her. She would have to make do without them. At least she could count on Red, Nettles, and Filler to hold their own. The rest of these people seemed more like an impulsive, disorganized rabble than the 'army' that Red had promised. She hoped Big Sig had a slightly more disciplined group.

The next day, Hope found out that 'slightly' was about right.

They had agreed that the Paradise Circle and Hammer Point armies would meet in front of the Drowned Rat. All the Paradise Circle people were there, restless, belligerent, many of them already drunk despite the fact that it was only noon. A few had knives or axes, and the occasional mace. But most were armed with lead pipes, broken glass, bricks, and other items that could barely be considered weapons.

'Finally,' said Nettles. 'Here comes the Hammer.' She pointed down the street at the mass of people coming toward them. 'Red, you better get over there so there's no misunderstandings here. I'd hate to waste all this fighting spirit on the wrong people.'

'Keen.' Red looked over at Hope. 'Coming?'

'Of course.' Hope had never been in a battle of this magnitude, but she had studied tactics and strategy extensively. She suspected none of the others had, although perhaps the Hammer Point leaders, with their endless infighting, had experience. Between the two, maybe they could come up with a workable strategy.

Hope and Red walked the slowly shortening gap between the mob of Paradise Circle and the mob of Hammer Point. When they got close, Big Sig held up his huge hands and shouted for everyone to stop. It took a little while, but eventually the mass of people ground to a halt.

Sig had absorbed Thorn Billy's gang. He had also been able to recruit the dark-skinned Palla and his gang. Hope wondered if Palla had come from across the Dark Sea like Carmichael's father. She hoped she'd be able to ask him when this was over.

They all stood in the cobblestone street. Great clouds of steam rose up from Big Sig's mob into the chilly, bright, midday air.

'Where is Drem holed up?' asked Palla. 'And does he know we're coming?'

'I'm sure he does by now,' said Red. 'With any luck, he didn't catch wind of it until you marched across the border this morning. That wouldn't give him much time to fortify the Three Cups and call in his people.'

'And without luck?' asked Big Sig.

'He heard about it last night as soon as I started recruiting, and the Three Cups is now a pissing fortress.'

'So it could turn into a siege, then?' asked Hope.

'Nice idea, but we won't have time to starve them out,' said Red. 'The imps won't like the rabble gathering in force like this, even if it's us fighting each other. It won't take them but a few hours after we engage before they bring a platoon with guns or worse down on our heads.'

'So what happens if we run into fortifications?' asked Palla.

'We break through them,' said Big Sig. 'Quickly.'

*　　*　　*

Nettles found herself at the front of the largest mob of wags she'd ever seen. They marched down the middle of the street, a wave of outrage set to crash against the Three Cups. Red led the way, with Hope at his side, her hand resting on the pommel of her sword. Behind them came Palla and Big Sig. And behind them, the two mob armies of Paradise Circle and Hammer Point, side by side.

There was some animosity between the two sides at first. A group of wags from each side that were a bit too drunk for their own good began trading insults, then threats. But Nettles snapped her chain-blade at both sides.

'Save the fighting for the betrayers!' Even though Nettles was the shortest by several feet, they backed away, mumbling apologies. She glared at them. 'This isn't some chum-and-larder japery for you to piss around with. This is New Laven justice. We all want the same thing today. Death to the biomancers and death to the betrayers!'

'Let me hear that last bit loud and strong!' bellowed Filler.

'Death to the biomancers! Death to the betrayers!' the group shouted.

'Louder!' yelled Filler.

'Death to the biomancers! Death to the betrayers!' This time the whole section picked it up.

'AGAIN!' shouted Filler.

'DEATH TO THE BIOMANCERS! DEATH TO THE BETRAYERS!' roared both armies with a sound like an avalanche.

'You go up and walk beside them Hammer Point leaders,' Filler told Nettles. 'Show 'em what it looks like to walk side by side.'

She gave him a sharp look. If she'd been the soft sort, it might have even made her catch her breath. 'Yeah, all right, Fill. You keep these wags in line for me.'

'Aye, general!' said Filler, smiling.

Nettles strode up to the short line and fell in next to Palla. 'Good idea,' was all he said, and continued walking.

Nettles had never been much interested in leadership or fame. But as she marched along with an army of true wags at her back, she had to admit that she could see the appeal.

Hope noticed people were starting to line the street on either side, watching as the army marched past, whispering among themselves. She knew Paradise Circle well enough by now that everyone they passed probably knew where they were going and why. Some joined in the march. Most stayed to the side, but followed – curious, concerned, or maybe just looking for a good show. By the time they reached the Three Cups, their army had grown and an even larger crowd of onlookers had gathered on the periphery.

'This many angry people is like a keg of gunpowder,' Hope said quietly.

'That's the idea.' Red winked at her.

Hope assessed their target. The Three Cups looked like any other building. Three stories, windows on each level. But they had all been boarded up, with only a few cracks open. 'They'll be shooting at us through those open slots in the windows.'

Red nodded. 'They can't shoot this many of us. We just have to find a way to get that door open.'

'And those first-floor windows, too,' said Big Sig. 'Can't squeeze a whole army through one door.'

'I think we have enough wags with axes. That won't be a problem.'

'Except they'll be shooting at us the whole time we're doing it,' said Palla.

'Why aren't they shooting at us now?' Hope mused. 'I would have thought as soon as they saw us, they'd open fire.'

'Feels like a trap,' said Big Sig.

'Well, we go home or we spring it,' said Palla.

'Is there a back entrance?' asked Hope.

'Yeah, but I'm sure it's sealed up,' said Red. 'And besides, it's in a narrow alley. We couldn't get many people back there.'

'I could take a few people and slip in the back way. We could take out the window gunners and cut down on your losses as you're breaking through.'

'I like this idea,' said Palla. 'I'll come with you.'

'Me, too,' said Nettles.

Hope was surprised. She'd assumed Nettles would stay with Red and Filler. 'We'll be significantly outnumbered. The risk will be high.'

'These full-frontal assaults don't play to my strengths.' Nettles had a brightness in her eye that Hope hadn't seen before. 'Sneaking around and stabbing people in the back is more my quality.'

'Is that it?' asked Red. 'Just the three of you?'

'Any more would get in my way,' said Hope.

'Fine,' said Red. 'Look . . . I know you want Drem. But—'

'Now that he's betrayed the Circle, so do you,' finished Hope. 'I understand.'

'You do?' asked Red, eyeing her suspiciously.

'We both have a just claim. So, whoever gets to him first.' She tried out one of those grins he was always giving her. 'See you inside.' As she turned and led Palla and Nettles toward the side of the building, she heard him laugh.

* * *

When Red let himself think too long and too deeply about the fact that hundreds of people had put their lives in his hands, his heart pounded in a really unpleasant way. So he tried his best not to think of it as he stood across the street from the Three Cups with Filler and Big Sig.

'Is this Vinchen girl as good as she seems?' asked Big Sig.

'Better, actually,' said Red. 'Modesty is one of those Vinchen virtues.'

'Don't you think we might need her up front?'

'We need her everywhere. But that's something she *can't* do. At least, I don't think so. And if we're having a small party infiltrate, I want her in it. She's practically an army on her own.'

'One thing we can do is make her job a bit easier,' said Sig. 'If we make a frontal assault, it will draw everyone in there up to the front. Give her some room to work.'

'The wags are getting impatient, too,' said Filler. 'We hold them back much longer, they're liable to charge on their own anyway.'

'But the gunners will still be in place,' said Red. 'I thought we were trying to prevent people from getting shot.'

'No, we're trying to *reduce* the people getting shot,' said Big Sig. 'People will get shot, no matter what. She said herself that it was high risk. We can't wait for a slim chance that they'll make it through. This whole time imps are getting wind of what's happening down here, so we're clocking now. Keen?'

'I don't like it,' said Red.

'It's leadership,' said Big Sig. 'You still want the reins, or you want to hand them off?'

'No, I keen,' Red said quietly.

Big Sig nodded, just a hint of approval in his hard face. 'Let's get on with it, then.'

Red turned to Filler. 'Give us a boost, old pot.'

Filler helped Red climb up onto his shoulders.

'Does everybody know why we're here today?' Red called to the restless mob.

'Death to the biomancers! Death to the betrayers!' they shouted immediately.

'We primed them a bit,' Filler admitted.

Red looked back at the crowd. 'Today the Circle and the Hammer join together against a common enemy. The biomancers have stolen our loved ones and subjected them to unspeakable horrors. It's time to show them and that betraying cock-dribble Drem that we will not allow it anymore!'

The mob roared, brandishing cleavers and knives, pipes and bats and bricks.

'So what are you waiting for, a pissing invitation?' shouted Red.

They surged forward. Red hastily dropped down from Filler's shoulders before he was knocked down by the tide of angry wags. They swarmed against the front of the building, hacking at the door and boarded first-floor windows with whatever they had to hand.

But even then, not a single shot was fired from inside.

'What's Drem waiting for?' Red asked.

Filler shrugged and unslung his mace. 'You complaining?' Then he headed toward the door to help with the dismantling.

Red caught a flash out of the corner of his eye in one of the windows of the building on the opposite side of the street. 'Wait!'

Filler paused and looked back curiously, his mace held loose in one hand.

'If I could just . . .' Red squinted, trying to look beyond the darkened windows. His vision gave a funny lurch. Then he saw that every window in the building across the street had a gun barrel in it.

'GET DOWN, EVERYONE!' he screamed.

The alley behind the Three Cups was so narrow that Hope, Nettles, and Palla had to walk single file.

'No wonder they weren't worried about a serious attack from the rear,' said Nettles.

'They did board up these windows, though,' said Palla.

'But not the top-floor windows.' Hope squinted as she gauged the distance between the back wall of the Three Cups and the building behind it. It was even better than she'd hoped.

'Because nobody's going to get up there,' said Nettles. 'Even if you had a grapple, there's not enough room down here to get a decent throw.'

'We don't need a grapple.' Hope jumped against the building behind, then to the back wall of the Three Cups, vaulting back and forth as she worked her way up to the top window. She broke the window with the pommel of her sword and climbed into the dark room.

She was surprised to find the room empty. It was a long space filled mostly with cots. This must be where Drem's men slept. It really *was* like a standing army. But where were they? All crammed up in the front of the building?

The cots gave her an idea. She quickly pulled off the thick blankets and tied them into a long line. She hadn't been sure how she would get Nettles and Palla up there. She'd thought there was a good chance she would have to leave them behind, which would have been very insulting. So she was glad this solution had presented itself. She tied one end to an iron cot as an anchor, then dropped the other end through the window. She wasn't sure the weight of the cot would be enough, so she braced her legs against the wall below the window and her back against the cot. The blanket rope went taut, and a few moments later, Nettles appeared in the window.

'Yeah, okay, I'm impressed, angel slice,' she muttered quietly as she climbed into the room.

The two of them braced the bed as Palla made his climb.

'From here we work our way to the other side of the building,' said Hope. 'The goal is to take out as many shooters as possible. But we need to do it silently. We make too much noise, and the whole building will be on top of us.'

'What if we run into Drem or the biomancer?' asked Nettles.

Hope smiled grimly. 'Then fortune has favored us.'

A roar of gunfire came from the front of the building. 'That sounds like a *lot* of guns,' said Palla.

'Let's go take care of that, then,' said Hope.

Red's face was pressed against the cobbles, Filler's massive body pressing down on him as gunfire thundered all around. When the first shots rang out, Filler had knocked down Red and rolled them both under a nearby horse carriage.

'You okay?' Red wheezed.

'Yeah.'

'Great, then please stop crushing the life out of me.'

Filler rolled over, which allowed Red to get a breath. He took in a couple of gasps, then looked out from under their shelter. Gunfire was coming from both the Three Cups and the building behind them. Drem had set them up in a meat grinder, and people were dropping all around them.

The gunfire paused as Drem's boots paused to reload.

Red climbed out from under the carriage and stared at the dead and dying all around him. 'Traitors!' he shouted to one building, then the other. 'Firing on your own people while their backs are turned!'

'Get down!' said Filler. 'They'll start again in a few seconds!'

Red wouldn't. He *couldn't*. He'd had enough of this.

'You broke the Circle, Drem! Sold out your own people for power and land.' He spit on the ground and held out his arms. 'Come out and fight me, man-to-man, you pissing coward!'

'Please, Red!'

Filler grabbed at his leg, but he kicked it away. He saw the rifle barrels return to the windows. Saw them all pointed in his direction. In that moment, he truly didn't care. Too many people had died. Too many. If he was to join them, so be it. If people like Drem got to rule it, this world wasn't worth a piss anyway.

'Red!' pleaded Filler.

Maybe it was his imagination, but it seemed like he could hear fifty gun hammers pull back with a *click*.

'Piss on you, traitors!' shouted a small boy who had been standing on the sidelines. He threw a glass jar at one of the windows.

A rifle from one of the windows fired, perhaps by accident, and the boy dropped to the ground.

There was a moment of total silence.

Then the entire neighborhood erupted in a fit of rage. Hundreds of people – old, young, man, woman – boiling over with an anger that had been simmering below the surface for so long that they'd all forgotten it was there until now. They rushed both buildings, wielding anything they could get their hands on.

There was some gunfire returned, though not as much as Red had expected. Perhaps some of them had grown a conscience. Or perhaps some of them had a yard of Vinchen steel in their backs by now.

Red drew throwing blades from his longcoat. 'Come on, Filler. Let's go find Drem before Hope gets to him first.'

Hope moved swiftly through the dim halls, her sword drawn and held in both hands. Nettles and Palla followed behind. They weren't as silent as Hope, but with all the gunfire, it didn't matter.

Up ahead, she spotted one of Drem's men hurrying past, his arms loaded down with ammunition. She glided up behind and slid her sword through the base of his skull so that the point appeared between his eyes. He shuddered, but made no sound as Hope withdrew the blade and watched him drop to the ground.

'I would have thought we'd encounter more people by now,' said Palla quietly. He had a thin spear with a flat iron point held loosely in one hand.

'Maybe Drem doesn't have as many people as we thought,' said Nettles.

'Or maybe the rest are somewhere else,' said Hope. 'Hurry, we're nearly there.'

They reached the front of the building. Three gunners at three windows died at the same time from sword, spear, and chainblade.

'We'll clear out each room on this floor,' said Hope. 'Then work our way down.'

*   *   *

As devastating as the two-sided attack had been, Red's last-minute warning had allowed many to find cover. Now with the unexpected reinforcements from the sidelines, they went back to their attack with a will, hacking at the door and boarded-up windows again. When one of them was shot, more took their place with even greater ferocity.

While Red pushed his way toward the door, he noticed no one was firing down from the windows on the top floor. He was sure that Hope, Nettles, and Palla were responsible for that.

'Remember when we tried to rob this place?' Filler shouted over the noise as he lagged behind. 'And we got banned for life?'

'I thought we'd agreed never to speak of it,' Red shouted back.

'Just saying. I bet you never thought we'd return with an army.'

Red stopped. 'Return . . .' He grabbed Filler by the shoulders and shook him. 'That's exactly what we're going to do, old pot. Return to the scene of the crime!'

Filler looked confused.

'We botched that job because we hadn't expected that safe to be big enough to have a guard *inside* it.'

'Sure, took us by surprise.' Filler's face was starkly pale, but Red was too caught up in his idea to notice.

'I'd bet every last tooth in Sadie's head that's where Drem is holed up right now. And if we kill Drem—'

'It's over and no one else has to die,' said Filler.

'Exactly!' shouted Red as he slapped Filler on the back.

Filler groaned. His leg buckled beneath him, and he fell to the ground. That's when Red saw the trail of blood behind his best wag.

*   *   *

Hope, Palla, and Nettles had cleared out the small rooms on the top floor easily enough. The second floor was more of a challenge. The rooms were larger, with more windows. Hope guessed they were used as gambling rooms. And there were anywhere from eight to ten gunners in each one. The first three went down easy, but then it was fighting in close quarters with the remainder.

Hope originally had doubts about Palla's weapon. Vinchen did not train extensively in spear fighting, believing it to be a less elegant weapon that was more suited to the common foot soldier. But they had never seen a spear in Palla's hands. Somehow, even in such tight quarters, he maneuvered his spear with a grace that was matched only by its sheer destructive force. The wood was soft and flexible, and he snapped it around almost like a whip, but with far more power. This was a technique that Hope wanted to learn. With it, even a common staff could be a formidable weapon.

The fighting was heated but over quickly.

'Anyone hurt?' asked Hope as she cleaned off her blade.

'Nobody worth worrying about,' said Nettles. 'Let's hit the next room. If we hurry, we can have this all cleaned up before they even break the door down.'

Blood had soaked through the thick wool of Filler's right pant leg at the knee.

'What happened!' said Red as he struggled to drag Filler out of the line of fire.

'Got shot. When I covered you.'

'You said you were okay!'

'I lied.'

'Piss'ell,' said Red. 'Okay. Tourniquet.' He cut a long sliver from the bottom of his leather coat.

'Hey, you're . . . messing your . . . nice coat.'

'Shut up, you.' Red tied the strip around Filler's thigh, just above the gunshot wound. 'I read about this. It'll stop the bleeding. But we'll have to loosen it now and then, or you might lose the leg. Don't you worry, my best wag. We'll have you shipshape in no time.'

Filler shook his head. 'You have to get Drem.'

'Fill—'

'*You* shut up now. I need you . . . to kill him. Stop . . . more of our . . . people . . . from dying. Promise me. Swear it. On your mother's art.'

'Filler, please—'

'Swear!'

Red glared down at his best friend in the world. 'I swear on the art that killed my mother that I will kill Deadface Drem for you. And you better still be pissing alive when I come back to tell you it's done. Do *you* keen?'

They cleared out the second floor and then headed down the stairs to the first. Hope wondered if this was almost over. And then they reached the bottom of the steps.

'Piss'ell,' muttered Nettles.

The bottom floor was a dance hall. It was one big room full of Drem's people, all staring at the front door, waiting for it to get smashed down.

'Behind us!' shouted a familiar wet and gravelly voice. Standing in the midst of the mob was the white-hooded biomancer that killed Thorn Billy. He pointed to Hope, Nettles, and Palla.

Palla's face was bleak as he readied his spear. 'There goes our advantage.'

Drem's people surged toward them. Fortunately, they

were only armed with knives, clubs, and bricks. Drem must have used up all his guns.

'Not our only advantage,' said Hope. 'Back midway up the stairs. They'll have to come up only two at a time, and we have the higher ground.'

They defended the stairs as best they could, finding a flow of slash, stab, chain. Hope had never had such a union. A perfect rhythm where no one got in another's way, and everything was balanced. They rapidly whittled down the numbers, but there were still so many of them that even Hope wondered if they would survive.

Then the door crashed down. Big Sig was through first, laying about him with a massive sledgehammer, knocking over several people with each swing. And behind him came a mob of people who seemed enraged to the point of madness.

Red went with the flow of the mob through the door. As they rushed into the massive brawl on the dance floor, he peeled off to one side and headed for the hatch down to the basement. He felt a pang of guilt, leaving them all to fight. But he had promised Filler he would kill Drem and end this as cleanly as possible. And there may have been just the tiniest little part of him that was pleased to see Hope all the way on the other side of the dance hall. Even if she knew where Drem was holed up, there was no way she could get to him before Red did. This one was all his.

He pulled up the hatch and dropped into the basement, the dirt floor silencing his landing. He crept through the near darkness. Barrels of ale, wine, and liquor were stacked along the sides. It had been only two years since he was down here, that night he first met Nettles. But it seemed like a lifetime ago. At the back was the massive iron door of the safe. The lock wasn't quite as easy this time, since it was older and hadn't been kept up well. But ten minutes later, he had it open.

He moved with the door as it swung wide, keeping it between himself and the opening. Sure enough, three shots fired in rapid succession, reverberating loudly in the closed space.

Red peeked through the crack between the top and bottom hinges and saw Drem inside, his eyes wide as he looked around. Red had always been able to see in the dark better than other people. Like his red eyes were better attuned to it. Judging by Drem's expression, he had fired blindly. To test it, Red pulled a wooden barrel down on its side and rolled it across the entrance. Drem fired two more shots. One missed. One struck the barrel.

'One shot left, Drem,' said Red.

'Red?' Drem squinted into the dark. 'Is that you, boy?'

'It's me. Promised a couple of friends you'd die tonight. Thought I'd try keeping my word for a change.'

'You clever old pot, you.' Drem's tone was light and waggish. 'It's a shame you got mixed up with that Southie slice. I was just thinking it was time to bring you on the crew.'

'I want no part of a crew that helps imps and biomancers,' said Red.

'Now listen, that's all a misunderstanding. You know how gossip in the Circle gets twisted around.'

'I don't need the gossip. I watched you with that biomancer when he killed Thorn Billy. I heard the whole pissing plan. You are no man of the Circle, betrayer.'

'You think that matters?' Drem's light tone went dark. 'You've lived in this gutter your whole life. The world is so much bigger than you could understand. The entire Circle could get wiped clean out tomorrow and nobody would even pissing care.'

'The people who lived here would,' Red said quietly. 'That's your problem, Drem. You think small equals worthless. We aren't worthless.'

'Oh yes, we pissing are, you bludgeon ponce. You have no idea how insignificant, how pathetic, how—'

Drem stopped talking as his throat filled with blood, a throwing blade protruding from his neck. He gasped and gurgled, firing his last shot uselessly into empty space. Then he dropped to his knees, gurgled one last time, and died.

Red had always wondered if he'd be able to make a ricochet shot. It worked out well enough. Although judging by the ragged wound, the side of the safe had blunted the blade. And he'd been aiming for Drem's gun hand, so clearly he needed practice.

The influx of people through the front door scattered the knot who had been trying to get at Hope, Nettles, and Palla. It gave them enough room to come down and enter the larger fight that was now raging on the dance floor.

Hope scanned the crowd, looking for that white hood. She found him in the center. He had no weapon that she could see. When an attacker came at him with a knife or club, he would hold up his hand, palm facing out, and the moment the weapon touched his hand, it would crumble to dust. If he touched the person, they would wither, decay, and crumble as well. It didn't take long for people to avoid him. Hope wasn't sure what she could do to beat him, but she knew that if she didn't try, no one would.

She hacked her way through the crowd, her eyes never leaving the biomancer. Most of her assailants were so unskilled, she only needed her peripheral vision to counter and strike. As she drew near, the biomancer's eyes widened with surprise. No doubt the strangeness of seeing a Vinchen warrior in this place – a female one, no less – was clearer to him than most. But as she rushed at him, he quickly recovered. He smiled coldly as he lifted his hand.

But the Song of Sorrows did not crumble. Its mournful tune continued as it sliced clean through the center of the biomancer's hand. There was a split second of both surprise and horror on his face, then the Song of Sorrows continued its trajectory and lopped off his head. A font of blood gushed up from the stump of his neck, drenching Hope in crimson. Then the body toppled over.

Hope stared down at the Song of Sorrows, wet from hilt to tip with blood. A blade that was immune to the power of biomancers. No wonder it was such a treasured weapon. And it was clear that Hurlo had insisted she take it so that she could fulfill her vow of vengeance on the biomancer who murdered her parents and her village.

'Thank you, Grandteacher,' she whispered.

Big Sig burst through a clump of people, his hammer slamming into a man's chest so hard, he flew back several feet. Sig stopped to wipe his sweat-, blood-, and grime-streaked forehead with his sleeve, and looked down at the beheaded biomancer.

'Nicely done,' he said.

Hope nodded.

'Shall we, then?' he asked.

The two of them turned back and continued to fight. Hope could tell Drem's men were losing their nerve after seeing their biomancer struck down. Their posture became more defensive, and they began eyeing the exits.

'STOP FIGHTING! DREM IS DEAD!'

Red stood on top of the bar, a body over his shoulder. Everyone backed away as he threw it on the ground.

Hope had thought that when she saw Drem dead, the pain of losing Carmichael would leave her. Or at least lessen. But she stared at his lifeless body, his eyes open and glassy, a gash in his throat, and all she felt was the darkness that always lingered on the edge of her awareness, still hungry. She wondered if it would ever be satisfied.

She turned to Drem's remaining men, her sword ready. But they threw down their weapons. The battle was over.

Then from the street came a thunderous boom, followed quickly by the sound of cracking stone and shattering glass.

Filler appeared in the doorway, leaning heavily on the frame. His face was ashen, but determined.

'We got a problem,' he said. 'The imps are here. And they brought cannons.'

22

Red had a vivid imagination. He'd thought of many different ways the march on the Three Cups could have gone leeward. What he hadn't thought about was how bad it might get even if they won.

When he stepped out onto the street, it looked like the whole of Paradise Circle had been consumed by one of the more terrible hells. The rage that he'd stirred up had grown, unchecked, and was now directionless. Buildings were on fire and people climbed out of broken shop windows, their arms full of loot. To make matters worse, every couple of minutes, the distant *boom* of a cannon would sound, and a barrage of shot would rain down on the block, smashing windows, shredding wooden signs, peppering walls, and occasionally ripping through someone not fast enough to find cover.

'This isn't what I wanted,' he said to Big Sig.

'I know,' Sig said quietly. 'But there isn't anything we can do to stop it. It's turned into a full-blown riot. I'm taking my people back to Hammer Point. I expect Palla will do the same.'

'You're leaving us like this?' Red said accusingly.

'What would you have me do? Have my people stop your people from looting and start a neighborhood war? Or would you rather I send my people into the face of imp cannon fire?'

'No, of course not,' said Red. 'I just—'

Big Sig put his massive hand on Red's shoulder, completely engulfing it. 'We did something good today. Whatever happens next doesn't change that. We stood up for ourselves. That scares them.'

'Shouldn't we take advantage of that?'

'A leader knows when to press forward and when to fall back. Many of our people have joined the looters. Others ran with the first cannon. Those who are left have been fighting for hours. They're exhausted, and many of them wounded. The imps are fresh and much better armed. The right choice is clear.'

'Red!' Hope yelled from inside the Three Cups. 'We need you!'

Red looked at Big Sig. 'Okay. Another day, then?' He held out his hand.

Big Sig gripped it. 'Count on it.'

Red nodded, then ran back into the building. Nearly everyone had cleared out, either to run and hide or to take advantage of the chaos to loot. Filler lay stretched out on the bar, his face pale and creased with pain. Hope and Nettles stood on either side of him. Nettles held a bottle of whiskey, and Hope held a large curved needle and thread.

'We need you to hold Filler down,' said Nettles.

'How is he?' asked Red as he moved down to Filler's feet.

'Weak from blood loss, but the bullet's out,' said Hope. 'We need to disinfect and stitch him up before he loses any more blood.'

'He'll . . . be alright, then?' asked Red.

Hope gave him a grave look. 'He'll live.'

'Is it the tourniquet? Did I tie it too tight? It was something I read about but never tried before, so I didn't know exactly.'

'It saved his life. And I don't think we'll have to lose the leg. But the bullet shattered his knee.'

'Won't it heal?'

Hope shook her head. 'I'm sorry. There isn't enough left. He'll need a crutch to walk for the rest of his life.'

'It's my fault,' Red said hollowly. 'It's just like Henny said. My best wag paid for my crazy scheme.'

'Balls and pricks,' Filler said faintly. '*My* choice to fight for the Circle. *My* choice to take a bullet for my best wag. Don't you take that away from me. Don't you *dare*.'

'Okay, Fill. Okay,' Red said quietly.

'We done with the poncey dramatics?' asked Nettles. 'Time to stitch this wag closed.'

'Do it,' said Filler.

Nettles took Filler's wrists, and Red took his ankles. Hope poured whiskey on the wound, and Filler's body involuntarily spasmed so hard, his foot nearly ended up in Red's mouth. Red had to lean his whole weight down to get his friend's legs flat on the bar again. Then Hope began to stitch up the wound.

'How bad is it out there?' asked Nettles as she held Filler's hands pressed to the bar above his head.

'Pretty bad,' admitted Red.

Filler grunted as Hope pulled the needle through the swollen flesh around his wound.

'We got uppity and complicated things for the powers that be,' Red continued. 'Now they're here to put us in our place. Meanwhile, whatever solidarity we had pissed off without so much as a good-bye.'

'I'm still amazed you pulled them all together as long as you did,' said Nettles.

Filler grunted again, this time long and low, almost like a hum. Or a whimper.

'Nearly done, Filler,' said Hope. 'You're doing great.'

Red watched as Hope's fingers flickered back and forth with the needle. 'You've got quality on that.'

'When I was younger, the Vinchen brothers would hold regular sparring matches. Often one or both would be wounded. It was my job to patch them up after.'

'You must have been popular, then,' said Nettles. 'Especially being the only molly.'

'No, they hated me,' said Hope. 'Only my teacher held any affection for me, and he had to withhold it while others were around, or they might have suspected that he was secretly training me in their arts.'

'How long did you live like that?' asked Nettles.

'Eight years.'

'Piss'ell, that must have been lonely.'

'I suppose,' said Hope as she continued to work the needle through Filler's wound. 'I didn't think much of it at the time. I had become . . . unaccustomed to warmth or companionship.'

'We made one hells of a team today,' said Nettles.

'We did,' said Hope.

'I can't promise much warmth, but you and me, we're alright.'

Hope smiled shyly as she continued to sew Filler's knee. 'Are we wags, then?'

Nettles grinned. 'You've got the length of it, angel slice.'

Hope tied off the thread. 'Okay, Filler, you're all patched up. That should keep the bleeding under control. Just be careful you don't tear those stitches.'

'Thanks, Hope,' Filler said weakly.

Hope nodded and stepped away from the bar, wiping the blood off her hands with a rag. Outside, the cannon fire was coming more frequently. Two or three shots a minute. 'We can't stay here, though. It sounds like they've brought in more cannons. We'll need to transport you somewhere safe.'

'Gunpowder Hall,' said Nettles. 'Everybody who's not already dead or caught up in the looting will go there.'

'It's the only place the imps have never been able to control,' said Red. 'But getting there is going to be tricky. Normally, I'd say we use the back alleys to avoid the cannon shot. But there's no way we can carry Filler all the way there. We'll need a wagon. Which means taking the main streets and putting ourselves right in the line of fire.'

'So we'll have to take out the cannons first,' said Hope.

'How do we do that?' asked Nettles.

'If we took the rooftops,' said Red, 'we could get to where the cannons are positioned without getting torn apart or detected. Nettles, you guard Filler, I'll show Hope the way.'

'Why don't *you* guard Filler and I'll take Hope,' suggested Nettles.

'Because you don't know the roofs like I do,' said Red. 'It's not going to be a straight line from here to there. Some of them are too steep even for me to cross, and I've been climbing them for years.'

'Let's get going, then,' said Hope. 'I think I know how we can get to the roof of this building, at least.'

Hope led Red up to the third floor into a room with two rows of sleeping cots.

'This is where we came in,' she said. 'Through that window.'

Red stuck his head out the window and looked down at the alley several stories below. 'How did you get up here?'

'The alley is narrow enough that I simply vaulted back and forth, working my way up,' said Hope.

'Simple as sideways,' muttered Red. He craned his head up. The roof was just out of reach, so he'd have to jump from the sill. He hadn't done something that foolhardy since he was a boy, but with Hope's talk about vaulting, he couldn't exactly beg off now. So he climbed out the window, stood up on the sill, and before he could think about it too deeply, jumped. He overshot the edge, but caught it on the way down. The leather of his fingerless gloves kept his hands from getting cut up by the jagged slate edge. He pulled himself slowly up until his elbows rested on the edge, then hooked a leg over and clambered up to the roof.

He stood for a moment, feeling pretty pleased with how that had gone. He leaned down over the edge. 'Are you coming?'

Hope's head popped through the open window, looking up at him. 'Be right there.' She grabbed the top edge of the window, then pulled up and out, flipping in the air and landing feetfirst on the edge. 'Ready?'

'Show-off.'

Red led her to the front edge of the building. Several blocks down, he saw a blossom of smoke in the fading light of day. A moment later he heard the shot whistle below as it scattered across the street. If they'd been in a wagon right then, they'd all be dead. He turned back to where the shot had originated, his eyes scanning the rooftops for the best possible route.

'Oh,' said Hope.

'You okay?' Red asked sharply.

'Yes.' Hope stared west out across the rooftops, her face serene as the red light of the setting sun tinted her yellow hair. 'The skyline is lovely, don't you think?'

Red felt a flash of irritation. 'Now's not really the time.'

'A Vinchen warrior strives to see the beauty all around him,' Hope said quietly. 'So that he knows the value of what he fights for.'

That brought Red up short. Had he really been bothered by Hope doing something he'd done countless times himself?

He recalled the day he'd brought Nettles to the roofs, excited to share its beauty with her. It had been wasted on her. And this had almost been wasted on him. He refused to let that happen. So he took a deep breath and stood with Hope. The two of them watched the sun drop slowly behind the uneven line of rooftops.

Hope turned to him. 'The cover of darkness should give us some advantage, too.'

'That's why you wanted to wait?'

She shrugged. 'They're both good reasons and I don't think they contradict each other.'

Red stared at her a moment, thinking nothing was ever simple with this molly. He realized that it was one of the reasons he liked her. 'True as trouble. Let's go.'

No one had lit the street lamps, so the block was unusually dark. But the lingering twilight drenched everything in a faint sepia. They moved from roof to roof, zigzagging gradually closer to the cannons. The cannon fire seemed to be coming more rapidly now. Red suspected they were trying to clear the streets as much as they could so that they could sweep in with a couple of squads of soldiers.

Night had fallen in earnest by the time they reached the cross street where the cannons were set. There were five of them, distributed evenly so that one pointed down each street. There were four soldiers stationed at each cannon.

'Our best chance of taking them all out quickly is to hit each one so fast, they don't have time to alert the next one in the line,' whispered Hope as they stood on a rooftop nearest the first group. 'Can you accurately throw two blades at once?'

'Two, but not four,' said Red.

'You take the two on the sides, I'll take the two in the middle.'

Red nodded and pulled his coat back so he was ready to draw.

'Now,' said Hope.

Red snapped a blade from each hand as Hope launched herself from the roof, drawing her sword in midair. She spun like a top, her blade flashing as it struck the two soldiers in the middle in rapid succession. At the same time, the soldiers on either side dropped to the ground, clutching at the blades in their necks.

Hope landed softly on top of the cannon. She signaled to Red to move to the building across the street.

Red gauged the distance to jump and winced. He wasn't at all sure he could make it, but he wasn't about to tell Hope that. He took a deep breath, got a nice running start, and jumped. It wasn't graceful, but he made it. His midsection slammed into the edge of the roof so hard, he had to pause a moment, clinging to it as he tried to get his breath back. Once he recovered, he slowly climbed to his feet. He saw Hope watching him, still standing on top of the cannon, her head cocked to one side curiously. He waved her on, feeling a little embarrassed.

She nodded. With her sword held low, she moved in a silent crouch toward the next cannon. Red saw that their best chance was for her to hit the two on the near side, while he hit the two on the far side. He hoped she would realize that, too. There wasn't really a way for him to get her attention without attracting theirs.

She ran between the first two, slashing right and left. She stopped when she saw the remaining two drop. She looked up at Red, nodded slowly in approval, and smiled. That tiny bit of acknowledgment sent a flush of satisfaction through Red. He allowed himself to bask in it for a moment, then muttered to himself, 'Do *not* get sotted with the celibate molly,' because Filler wasn't there to say it to him.

They moved on to each cannon the same way, taking them out as they went. The last one proved to be more of a problem, though. Next to the cannon and its operators was a squad of imps. Red saw them before they struck. He wasn't sure if Hope saw them, but he had no way to warn her other than to wave and point. She nodded tersely and waved for them to continue.

They took the four at the cannon as easily as the others, but then the shouts went out from the squad and they turned toward Hope, fumbling with their rifles. Red reached into his coat for more blades, but came up with nothing. He'd just thrown his last two. He started to scramble down the building, not sure how he could help, but not willing to just sit idly by as Hope was gunned down. But by the time he'd reached the ground, half the soldiers were dead and the other half had turned and run.

Hope stood for a second, breathing hard as she watched them go. Then she wiped her blade on the white tunic of one of the dead soldiers. 'Out of blades?'

Red nodded sheepishly.

'You'll have a chance to retrieve them,' she said. 'I want to go back and make sure that when the imperial reinforcements arrive, these cannons won't be much use to them anymore.'

Red had never seen Gunpowder Hall so crowded or so subdued. The combination was unnerving. When he arrived, lugging Filler with the help of Nettles and Hope, he found the hall nearly filled to capacity, and yet no one was having sex, or doing drugs. There was no drinking or rowdy laughter. Everyone sat and talked quietly, their faces drawn with worry.

'Piss'ell, this is eerie,' said Nettles as they laid Filler on a table that Handsome Henny and the Twins had staked out.

'You wags alright?' asked Red as he clasped Henny's hand.

'Better than Filler, it looks like,' said Henny.

'I'll be alright, Hen,' Filler said weakly. 'Hope patched me up good.'

'Thanks for that.' Henny tossed her an apple from a small sack. 'Red? Nettie?'

'God, yes,' said Nettles, gratefully taking a chunk of bread from him.

'I haven't eaten all day,' said Red, taking some bread for himself.

'You know, Red,' said Henny. 'When I saw you up there at the Rag and Boards, I thought you were bludgeon. I thought, here's another crazy scheme.' His eyes glistened in the torch-light. 'But it wasn't tavern talk, old pot. You pissing *did* it. Brought the neighborhood together, just like you said, and hit them imps hard enough for them to feel it.'

'Yeah, and look where it's gotten us,' said Red.

Henny shook his head. 'Nothing without cost, my wag. Nothing is ever free in the Circle, and you know that. But now *they* know it, too, those cunt-droppings. They can only push us so far before we push back.'

'But now what do we do?' Red asked.

'I don't know,' admitted Henny. 'I guess we wait and see if they plan to storm the hall.'

The windows were all boarded up, with just enough of a gap to keep an eye on what was going on out on the street. All of the merchants had pulled their wares inside. Those with food were sharing it among their neighbors. People with weapons were spreading them around, trying to arm as many able-bodied wags as possible. The Circle was often a cruel and selfish place. Red had heard about folks coming together in times of adversity, but he'd never seen it before and he'd had a hard time believing it. Now, as he munched on his bread and watched Paradise Circle slowly gather itself together, bracing itself for the inevitable fight to come, he'd never been more proud of his adopted home.

'I haven't seen Sadie.' Hope bit into her apple, looking concerned.

'She'll stay down at the docks with Finn. Probably hide on the ship. It's unlikely the imps will go that far down, so she'll be okay.' He looked at her. 'You know, if the ship was ready, you could just leave. Get away from all this.'

'Would *you* do that?' she asked.

He shook his head. 'It's not that I want to stay here forever. But leaving right at this moment, with things so uncertain . . . it just wouldn't feel right.'

'I feel the same,' she said.

It was a tense night. People slipped out now and then to get provisions and scout out the imps. A large force was heading toward the hall, but it was still some ways off. As the hours crawled by, the tension boiled over here and there, and small fights started to break out. To pass the time and keep people sunny, Red regaled the hall with a somewhat exaggerated account of 'The Storming of the Three Cups.' Many of them had been there, but none of them had known the whole story. When asked how he knew where Drem would be hiding, he then went into a highly exaggerated account of the attempted robbery of the Three Cups two years before. He decided to cut that story off before it reached the part where he kissed Nettles. Some things were better left to the past.

Once he had finished, applause rang out in the hall.

'Your gift for storytelling is as good as your aim,' said Hope.

'His gift of exaggeration, too,' said Nettles. 'I certainly don't remember taking down thirty boots in that alley with just a chain.'

'Now, now, Nettie,' said Red, his eyes sparkling. 'Just because it didn't happen, don't make the story less true. This wasn't for the history books, anyway. Just a way to take folks' minds off what's coming. Surely you don't begrudge that.'

'So long as nobody ever actually expects me to be able to take out thirty armed boots at once with a bit of chain,' said Nettles.

He grinned. 'You could always tell people you've gotten too *old* for that sort of thing.'

'Or I could break that pretty face of yours so it stops spouting lies,' offered Nettles.

Red laughed.

It was afternoon the next day that one of the scouts, a boy about thirteen, burst into the hall, his face flushed, his breath coming in gasps. 'Better lock the door! The imps are almost here!'

A murmur went through the hall. A few people slid the thick wooden bar into place across the door, and Red hurried to the boarded-up front window. Nettles, Hope, and Henny followed right behind him. They peeked through the cracks in the boards and watched as a full battalion of imps, ten wide and five deep, all armed with rifles, marched up to the hall.

'No cannons?' asked Henny in surprise.

'Hope and I blew them up before we got here,' Red said smugly.

A commander in a shining gold helmet with a white plume rode to the front on a fine white horse. He held one hand up and the soldiers immediately came to a stop.

'Very disciplined,' Hope said approvingly.

'Whose side are you on?' asked Red.

'A Vinchen warrior gives credit where it is due, even to his enemies,' she said.

'*Her* enemies,' muttered Nettles.

'PEOPLE OF PARADISE CIRCLE!' The commander spoke through a large metal cone that amplified his voice enough for the sound to filter into the hall. 'WE HAVE NO WISH FOR FURTHER BLOODSHED. HAND OVER THE WOMAN DRESSED AS A VINCHEN AND WE WILL ALLOW YOU TO RETURN TO YOUR HOMES UNHARMED.'

There was a moment of silence in the hall. Maybe the first true silence that Gunpowder Hall ever had.

'The choice is obvious,' Hope said loud enough for everyone to hear. 'One life for many. A Vinchen warrior must always be ready to give his life to protect the good people of the empire. And make no mistake. None of you are perfect, but all of you are good.'

'Hope, don't you pissing dare,' said Red.

Hope ignored him and turned to Nettles. 'I am grateful for your acceptance and your friendship. I have never had another woman as a friend before, and I am glad to have that experience.'

Nettles nodded.

Hope walked over to Filler, who lay unconscious on the table. She laid her hand on his sweaty forehead. 'Take care of this one. His loyalty is as great as any warrior I have known.'

'Hope, there is no way I'm letting you do this!' said Red.

Her face was tight, and her deep blue eyes were harder and colder than he had ever seen. 'Red, it has been an honor to fight at your side. And . . .' She hesitated. 'And a joy.' Then she turned toward the door.

'No!' Red grabbed her arm, but she moved so fast, there was only a blur, and then he was on the ground, dazed from the sharp rap on the head she had given him. He struggled to his feet, trying to gather his thoughts as he watched her walk through the door and shut it behind her.

He stumbled toward the door, but Nettles spun him back around to face her.

'And where do you think you're going?' she asked.

'After Hope, of course!'

'All by yourself?'

'If I have to.'

'Do you have to?'

That brought Red up short. 'What?'

Nettles turned to the rest of the hall. 'Well, don't you all look an inch tall. There she goes. Our Bleak Hope. Yes, *ours*, I say. She may not be from Paradise Circle, but she has risked her life several times over. For us. So I name her a Hero of the Circle. Would any of you disagree?'

Nettles's gaze swept the hall, and none spoke.

'And now,' she continued, 'this hero of ours has gone to die *for us*. And we're just going to let her? Is *that* how it is in the Circle now?'

23

*H*ope stepped out of the hall into the golden afternoon sun. She never would have thought the air of New Laven would seem fresh, but after nearly a day stuck in Gunpowder Hall, she breathed it in deeply. She looked up at the commander astride his horse. He looked down at her with mild curiosity. Behind him, fifty soldiers held rifles, all of them pointed at her.

'Will you kill me now?' she asked calmly.

'There is one who wants to speak with you first,' said the commander. 'Surrender your sword and I will take you to him.'

'And no one else will get hurt.'

'I will withdraw my men from this place,' he agreed.

Handing the Song of Sorrows to the imperial commander may have been the hardest thing Hope had ever done. Other events had been far more painful, but those she had been helpless to prevent. The act of relinquishing one of the most sacred items of the Vinchen order, entrusted to her by Grandteacher Hurlo, to a man who neither knew nor cared about it, was something she had to do of her own free will. With icy hatred blazing in her eyes, she held the sheathed sword up to him horizontally with both hands. He leaned over in his saddle and took it almost indifferently.

'Chain her,' he said.

Two soldiers hurried over and wrapped her wrists in a chain, securing it with a large padlock. One handed the padlock key to the commander. The other handed him the end of the chain, which he fastened to the front of his saddle.

'Come along, then.' The commander wheeled his horse around and gave the chain a yank as he led her away from Gunpowder Hall. The soldiers parted to let them pass, then closed ranks behind them. Hope glanced back, expecting to see the soldiers turn as well and follow them. But they remained with their rifles pointed at the hall.

'You said you would withdraw your men.'

'I know the Vinchen have an almost religious zeal concerning honor,' the commander said. 'But the thieves, cutthroats, whores, and traitors hidden away in that place are the worst scum in the empire. They have no honor and deserve none in return. I cannot allow them to think they have won a victory today, however fleeting. We'll keep them pinned down in there until we repair the cannons you disabled last night. By that time they might be so starved, they'll already have killed each other. If not, we'll sweep in and clean up that filthy hall at last.'

'You tell me this and still expect me to cooperate with you?' Hope asked quietly.

The commander chuckled. 'You are disarmed and in chains. What could you possibly do?'

A strange roar came from within Gunpowder Hall, like a hundred voices shouting in unison.

'What in God's name was—' began the commander.

Then the door burst open and Red and Nettles charged out, a mass of people behind them. The soldiers had not been expecting a frontal assault and fumbled with their rifles. But Hope knew they would recover before Red and Nettles reached them. It would be a massacre, unless someone stopped them from firing.

'This is what I can do.' She pulled hard on the chain, jerking the horse a little off balance. In the second it took the commander to steady his mount, she jumped up behind him. She pulled her chained hands over his head, pressing her upper arms against the sides of his neck, cutting off part of his airflow as she yanked the reins from his hands. She wheeled the horse back toward the soldiers, and snapped the reins on the horse's neck, sending the animal charging back into the battalion of soldiers. Their shots went wide, and they didn't have time to chamber another round before the people of Paradise Circle crashed into them.

Had the commander been able to speak, he might have kept his troops in line, rallying them to fight off the horde of thieves, cutthroats, whores, and traitors that descended on them. But at that moment, the commander could barely breathe, much less speak. He fought weakly for control of the horse as Hope grabbed the padlock key from his belt. He managed to take hold of the reins, but by then, Hope had opened the padlock. She shook off the chains, grabbed the Song of Sorrows, and pulled them both off the horse. She twisted as they fell so that the commander hit the cobblestones first, and she landed on top of him. She hauled him to his feet, but he had already been knocked unconscious by the fall.

'Hope!' called Red from the other side of the battle. 'You okay?'

She smiled as she drew the Song of Sorrows, then she threw herself into the thickest part of the fight. The soldiers were better trained, better disciplined, and better armed, but they were outnumbered and without their commander. They did not run, however, and for that reason, Hope gave each one she confronted a quick and honorable death.

It wasn't long before most of the soldiers lay dead or dying on the cobblestones. That was when Hope saw the man in the white robe standing on the other side of the street. She wiped her blade clean on a nearby soldier's tunic, then walked purposefully toward the hooded figure.

'When I first heard the report of a female Vinchen leading a rebellion at the Three Cups, I thought it a mistake,' the biomancer said with a voice that crackled like fire. His head was bowed so that Hope couldn't see his face. 'After all, women are no more allowed to join that order than they are allowed to join mine. But when I heard a second report of a female Vinchen disabling my cannons, I knew I must investigate.' He lifted his head to look directly at her.

It was the biomancer with a burn mark on his cheek. Hope had been so afraid that Big Sig had been wrong, or that there was another biomancer with similar features. But there was no mistake. He was older, the hair beneath his white hood mostly gray. But she knew at a glance that it was the man who had murdered her village.

'Even though I came to find this supposed female Vinchen,' continued the biomancer, 'I did not expect her to be wielding the Song of Sorrows. My great-grandfather helped forge it for Manay the True. How is it you come by that blade?'

A cold wave of wrath surged within Hope's body. Through gritted teeth, she said, 'This sword was entrusted to me by my teacher, Hurlo the Cunning. And it will be your doom.'

'Perhaps,' said the biomancer. 'But not today.'

He snapped his fingers and there was a sudden flash of light. Hope blinked back the spots as she lunged in his direction. But it was too late. Her blade met only emptiness. When her vision cleared, she saw him several blocks away, running away like a coward.

'No!' she snarled, and ran after him.

*   *   *

A Vinchen warrior was balanced in all aspects, at one with his surroundings and at peace with himself. When things became faster on the outside, he became quieter on the inside. He remained in the current moment, undistracted by memories of the past or thoughts of the future.

Bleak Hope was none of those things.

She sprinted after the biomancer, all the buried rage and pain of the past ten years burning through her system like lamp oil set ablaze. She was vaguely aware that a sound somewhere between a growl and a hiss was escaping from between her clenched teeth, but it was nothing compared to the roar of vengeance in her mind. This night she would do it. This night she would be free.

The biomancer led her through winding back alleys and crooked side streets. She wondered if he knew where he was going, or if he was randomly weaving from street to street. He had been smart to get away from the main roads. In these darkening skies, the gas lamps would have starkly illuminated his white hood. But even in those unlit back streets, the white on unrelieved gray mortar and brick was easy to spot. She would lose him for a moment, but a flicker out of the corner of her eye was all she needed to stay on his trail.

Still, it wouldn't be long before the sun was completely down. Then it would be too dark to even pick out white on gray. She needed to catch him before then. She could continue chasing him, hoping he began to tire before the sun set. Or she could try a different tack altogether. Captain Carmichael had once said to her, *Hope, my girl. Sometimes you've headed right into the wind and you make no progress at all. That's when you have to tack from side to side. Some problems are better to come at from an angle.* She needed a different angle now if she was going to cut the distance in time.

She jumped to a narrow awning above a door, then to a window ledge, and finally to the roof. Then, even though

every instinct in her cried out to run, she knelt down on the
hard wood slats. She closed her eyes and listened. She heard
her own breath and heartbeat, fast and hard from exertion
and anger. *Beyond that*, she imagined Hurlo saying. She
heard the coo of a nearby dove and the scritch of a rat. *And
beyond that*, Hurlo would have said. She heard someone
opening a window and dumping something liquid. She heard
a horse whinny. *Further still*. And there it was. Harsh gasps
of breath and soft leather shoes on cobblestones zigzagging
unevenly.

She launched herself across the rooftop to the next, and
the next. He didn't know she had stopped following after
him, so while he continued his circuitous route, she headed
straight as an arrow to intercept. Six blocks later, she landed
in front of him just as he rounded a corner.

He skidded to a halt. 'You are as skilled as any Vinchen I
have seen. But it will take more than skill to kill me.'

'What is your name, Biomancer?' hissed Hope through
clenched teeth.

'Teltho Kan,' he said, looking slightly amused. 'If you
think to report me to some authority, you are—'

She snapped her sword out so fast, it was nothing more
than a flicker. His eyes widened as a trickle of blood ran
down from a horizontal line freshly made on his forehead.

'Ten years ago, you massacred the village of Bleak Hope.
I am its vengeance.'

Teltho Kan sighed heavily. 'Vinchen and their precious
vendettas. It couldn't be helped. I was doing important work,
developing a new weapon to protect the empire. The para-
sitic wasp program is one of our most promising—'

'Any emperor who throws away the lives of his people so
carelessly is not fit to rule. Now, if you have a weapon, I
suggest you draw it. I will grant you every warrior's courtesy,
though you deserve none.'

Teltho Kan's eyes were looking increasingly uneasy. He glanced up at the setting sun and said, 'Even if you did manage to kill me, you would not last a day. They would hunt you down and kill you by some means too horrible for you to even contemplate.'

'That doesn't matter,' said Hope. And in that moment, it didn't. With the death of Teltho Kan, all debts would be paid, all oaths fulfilled. The idea of a life beyond vengeance was not something worth considering.

Teltho Kan's eyes narrowed. 'I see.' He pulled his hands inside his sleeves. 'It is a shame you chose to betray the emperor. Despite your gender, you would no doubt have been useful to him. Steadfast determination of this kind is rare. But I'm afraid I must deny you your life's ambition.'

He stretched out his hands, which were as burn-scarred as his face. A silver bracelet on each wrist gleamed in the fading light of the sun.

Hope raised her sword, unsure what biomancery he had planned.

But instead of attacking, he brought his wrists together sharply so that the bracelets gave a muted chime. The sound of the chime grew, and his hands and face began to shimmer. Hope thrust the Song of Sorrows into his chest, but it was too late. He was gone, leaving only the empty white robe, which now hung limply on the end of her sword. She stood there for a moment, staring dumbly at it. She had been close. If she had simply killed him on sight, it would all be over. But she had insisted on a warrior's courtesy: knowing his name, declaring her intention, and giving him a chance to fight, just as Hurlo taught her. Now she was back to the beginning, not even knowing his location. Worse, he knew she was after him now, and would no doubt be far more cautious.

She suddenly felt so heavy, so sick, and so tired. Even her sword felt heavy in her hands. She let the tip droop so that the robe slid off and fell to the cobblestones. It felt like the earth was pulling her down. She dropped to her knees and bowed her head until her chin touched her chest. The final light of the sun cast everything in sharp relief. The sounds of the city buzzed all around her, but in this empty alley, there was nothing. No light, no sound. No hope.

She looked down at the Song of Sorrows, gleaming even in the dim twilight, a small line of Teltho Kan's blood where she had nicked him along the edge. She had failed. She was not worthy of this blade or this life. She turned the sword so that the point faced her. She placed the pommel against the cobblestones, and set the point to her breastbone over her heart. She may not be truly a Vinchen, but she could die a Vinchen death.

'Never did knock you for a quitter,' said Red.

She looked up and saw him, arms folded, leaning against the wall. His attitude and voice were casual, playful even. But his eyes were crimson steel.

'I failed.' Her voice sounded as hollow as she felt.

'How's that?' he asked.

'He escaped.'

'So we'll catch him again. Can't very well do that if you've got a sword in your chest.'

'He knows I'm after him. My one advantage, the element of surprise, is gone. I'll never get close again.'

'Your *one* advantage?' he asked. 'Leaving aside the fact that you're the greatest warrior alive, what about your *other* big advantage?'

'Which is?'

'*Me*, you Southie salthead.' He walked over to her, rubbing his hands together. 'Now, let's see what we've got here. His robe, eh?' He knelt down next to it and turned the hood inside out. He pulled a few strands of gray hair out of it. 'This his?'

Hope nodded, her sword lowering slightly.

He pointed to the blade. 'That his blood on there?'

Again she nodded.

'Now all we have to do is find out his name.'

'It's Teltho Kan. He just told me.'

Red suddenly grinned wide. 'Then, my darling molly, we are all chum and larder here.'

'I don't understand.'

'You may not have noticed, what with running around like a madwoman, but we're not in Paradise Circle anymore.' He gestured around them like it was obvious at a glance. 'We're in Silverback.'

'So?'

'Biomancers aren't the only ones with unsettling abilities. There are people in Silverback who do many strange things. Fortune-telling, necromancy, and bloodwork.'

'I still don't see your point.'

'It has to be seen to be believed.' He held out his hand. 'Will you trust me on this and leave off impaling yourself? At least for a little while?'

He still believed she would fulfill her oath, even when she did not. Had she lost her resolve so easily? Sure, Teltho Kan knew she was after him, but that might even work in her favor. He might be running scared, more prone to rash mistakes. And it was true that Red was an important advantage. Not just because of his extensive knowledge of New Laven and his uncanny accuracy with a throwing blade. He had just bolstered her faith when it was at the lowest it had ever been. That advantage was immeasurable.

She took his hand and let him help her up to her feet.

'We will try this bloodwork of yours.'

'Sunny. Just have a care you don't smear what's on the sword. She'll need that.'

'Who?'

'Old Yammy. The wag who's going to get us on the right path again.'

The differences between Paradise Circle and Hammer Point had been one of degree. If Paradise Circle was poor, Hammer Point was destitute. If Paradise Circle was dirty, Hammer Point was a festering sinkhole. If the people of Paradise Circle were hard, the people of Hammer Point were stone and steel.

Hope had expected Silverback to fall somewhere on that spectrum, probably on the nicer side, since it was the neighborhood that stretched long and thin across the city, acting as a buffer between the downtown poor and the wealthy uptown communities. But as Red led her through the early-evening streets of Silverback, she saw that it was nowhere on that spectrum. Instead it seemed to exist purely in its own world. The streets were crammed with theaters, art galleries, craftsmen of all kinds. Brightly colored wares spilled out onto the streets, with people calling out sales and bargains.

'Silverback is an artistic community,' said Red. 'Some of the finest painters, musicians, poets, and performers in the empire call it home.'

'They certainly like dressing colorfully,' said Hope. It seemed everyone around her was a riot of colors, sometimes matching, sometimes conflicting, but always bright and vivid. Performers were on nearly every corner. Musicians, acrobats, and jugglers for the most part. Crowds gathered to watch, sometimes cheering, sometimes mocking.

'There's more street lamps in Silverback,' said Red. 'And there's street cleaners who take your garbage away for you.'

'Why?'

'The lacies like it pat when they come down here for a gallery showing or a play. And there's at least twice as many imps on patrol here. They don't bother protecting the artists, of course. Just here to make the lacies feel safe.'

'It must be a terrible thing for those lacies,' said Hope. 'To be so afraid of other people.'

Red gave her a funny look. 'That's an interesting way of looking at it. I suppose you're right.'

Hope and Red walked down the boisterous streets of Silverback for a while, a small island of quiet.

'Here we are!' said Red at last. 'Madame Destiny's House of All!'

'I thought you said we were looking for someone named Old Yammy.'

'Sure, but you don't bring in the customers with a name like that. Come on, I bet she'll do that thing where she looks at us like she knew we were coming. I can never tell if she's bluffing.'

He opened the door just as a woman came out. Hope had never seen anyone like her. Her long brown hair was tied up in a highly intricate series of braids. Her face was painted an unnatural shade of orange, and small flecks of gold had been somehow adhered to her eyelids, making them so heavy that her eyes were only half-open. Her lips were painted a bright blue. She wore a long blue silk gown that seemed to be interwoven with gold thread. She had gold jewelry around her slim wrists and long neck. Hope could only gape at this strange, impractical creature, dimly aware that the woman was staring back at her with unease.

Red yanked Hope to one side.

'Sorry, your ladyship,' he said, turning on a smile that gave off more light than the nearby street lamp.

The woman did not respond, but hurried past.

'What was *that*?' asked Hope.

'That was a proper lacy from uptown.'

'Do they all dress like that?'

'They do when they're down here,' said Red. 'I doubt they go in for that much bother if they're at home, just putting their feet up. But I can't say for sure.'

'Why was she painted orange?'

'How should I know? Just because I have some lacy blood doesn't mean I understand their fashion. Now let's go inside. We don't want to keep Old Yammy waiting.'

Hope wasn't sure what she expected to find in the House of All. Perhaps crystal balls, exotic tapestries, luridly colored rugs, and bits of bone hanging from the doorway. So she was a little disappointed when he led her into what appeared to be a normal kitchen, similar to the one back on Galemoor. Wooden cabinets with a thick butcher block on top, a basin, and an iron potbellied stove. The only obvious difference was the rows of glass jars, unlabeled, that were filled with leaves, powders, and other things she couldn't quite determine.

A woman stood in the middle of the kitchen. Hope had been expecting Old Yammy to be old, but this woman couldn't have been more than forty. Hope wondered if this was an assistant. But then Red smiled and walked over to her, arms outstretched.

'Old Yammy!' He wrapped his arms around her.

She gave him a level gaze, not so much hugging as allowing herself to be hugged. 'It's Madame Destiny while I'm working, Rixidenteron.'

'Right, and it's Red when I'm with my friends, keen?'

'Rixidenteron?' asked Hope.

'It's the name he was born with,' said Old Yammy. 'It no longer suits him, but I call him that out of habit, and perhaps nostalgia for happier times.' She squinted at Hope, brushing a lock of her black hair back behind her ear. 'But you would know something of that, wouldn't you?'

'Why do you think that?' asked Hope, her expression guarded. There was something about the way Old Yammy looked at her that made her feel oddly exposed.

'I am Madame Destiny. I know many things.'

'Yeah, yeah, enough with the japery,' said Red. 'We've got a serious thing to talk to you about.'

Old Yammy gave him a tolerant smile. 'You always do.'

'We need to find someone. We've got his hair, his blood, and his name. That'll work for a dowsing, right?'

'It will.' Old Yammy walked over to one counter, motioning for them to follow. 'Show me.'

Red held out the strands of hair. Hope had wrapped her sword loosely in the white robe instead of sheathing it. The sheath was a perfect fit for the sword and would have wiped the blood off. Now she carefully unrolled the robe, never letting it touch the end of the blade where the blood still darkened the edge.

Old Yammy sucked in a breath when she saw the Song of Sorrows. 'This sword! I have never seen its like.' She reached out hesitantly and touched the flat of the blade with her fingertips. 'It has a power all its own. Enmeshed into the steel itself.'

'It was forged with the help of a biomancer,' said Hope.

Old Yammy touched her finger to the blood, then brought it to her mouth, licked it, then spat. 'And you seek a biomancer as well.'

'Is that a problem?' asked Red.

'In finding him? Normally. But if we use this sword as the dowsing wand, it will magnify the bloodwork.'

'Will that harm the sword?' asked Hope.

Old Yammy laughed. 'There is no power you or I could conjure that would hurt this blade. It is safe. But know that the moment someone else's blood touches it, the bloodwork will be dispelled and you will no longer be able to use it to search for this man.'

'So you won't be able to use your sword to fight,' said Red.

'I can use it sheathed. Or I can use other weapons. If the need arises.'

'Likely it will.' Red turned to Old Yammy. 'Trouble seems to follow us.'

Old Yammy rolled her eyes. 'Can't imagine why.' She patted the counter. 'Lay the sword here.'

Hope felt uneasy as she set the sword down, as if she were a protective parent, despite Old Yammy's claim that they couldn't harm it.

Old Yammy laid the hairs on top of the blood, muttering something quietly under her breath. She took a bottle with a yellow liquid and sprinkled a few drops on the blood and hair. Then she took a jar of white powder and covered the blade liberally with a thick coating of it. 'When the flames appear,' said Old Yammy, 'call out his name.'

'The flames?' asked Hope, alarmed. But before she could act, Old Yammy struck flint, and a spark leapt onto the tip of the sword. The entire blade from point to hilt was engulfed in fire.

'Teltho Kan!' Hope called out, louder than she'd intended.

The fire went out as if snuffed, leaving the blade completely clean of powder, blood, and hair.

Red cleared his throat. 'Did it—'

'Shh!' said Old Yammy.

They stared at the blade for a moment. Then slowly, it began to move, as if being rotated by an invisible hand. It stopped once it was pointing in a northwesterly direction.

'That is your way,' said Old Yammy with absolute confidence.

'It will always point to him?' asked Hope. 'Even if he moves?'
'Until you dispel the bloodwork.'

Hope had been skeptical. But seeing the sword move of its own accord kindled a warm gratitude within her. 'How can I repay you for this?'

'Rixidenteron knows my payment.'

Hope looked quizzically at Red.

He rolled his eyes. 'A painting.'

'By who?'

'Me.'

'I didn't know you were an artist.' Yet another facet of him that she had uncovered.

He glared at Old Yammy as he said, 'I'm not.'

'Nonsense,' said Old Yammy. 'An artist is anyone who makes art. And that, you do.'

'Only when you ask me to.'

'It's a good thing I do, then. It's what your mother would want.'

Red flinched when Old Yammy mentioned his mother. 'Fine, okay, I'll do it.'

'Did you know Red's mother?' asked Hope.

Old Yammy smiled. 'I did. And it was a pleasure. The art the two of them made together . . . to this day, it has no equal.'

'Yammy, please don't,' said Red.

'There's a new exhibition of her work over at Bayview Gallery. Did you know that?' asked Old Yammy.

'Bayview?' asked Red. 'Seems a little lacy for her stuff.'

'Not at all. You should go see it, since you're in the neighborhood.'

'We don't have time,' he said curtly. 'Let's get this painting done with so we can start our search. What do you want this time?'

Old Yammy frowned thoughtfully. 'A portrait, I think.'

'Of who?'

Old Yammy pointed at Hope. 'Her.'

'Me?' asked Hope.

'Her?' asked Red.

Old Yammy nodded. 'That's my price.'

Red looked at Hope. 'Sorry. Do you mind?'

The idea of having someone stare at her in complete concentration like that for so long made her skin crawl. But any excuse she could think of sounded like childish vanity. If this was the price to pay for tracking down Teltho Kan, she would just have to endure it. Surely she had suffered worse. 'No, I don't mind,' she lied.

'Wonderful.' Old Yammy smiled. 'I'd like it with natural light, not lamplight. So you can get started first thing in the morning.'

Old Yammy lived above her shop in a small bedroom that afforded no room for Hope and Red. Instead, she laid thick quilts on the kitchen floor by the potbellied stove. The kitchen was dark except for the flickering orange of the stove. Hope could hear laughter and music from a nearby building. She wondered if the music in this neighborhood ever stopped. Oddly, she hoped not.

'This kind of reminds me of that first night, you and me sleeping in Missing Finn's shack,' said Red.

'It was actually during the day,' said Hope.

'Right. Then we headed to Hammer Point that night. And all hells came rolling in.'

They were silent a moment, lying side by side.

'Thank you for killing Drem,' Hope said quietly. His death still hadn't lessened the loss she felt for Carmichael. But she was grateful he was avenged, nonetheless.

'The pleasure was all mine. Although I wish you would have been there to see the astonishing bank shot I made. One for the storybooks.'

'I think Carmichael would have liked you. Despite your insistence on presenting yourself as a rogue and a thief.'

'I *am* a rogue and a thief.'

'You never spoke about Old Yammy before,' said Hope suddenly. It was a small detail, but it seemed significant to her somehow. Yammy seemed like the sort of person who might appreciate his more refined qualities like reading and math.

'I don't talk about her a lot. People from my past in general.'

'But you still visit her.'

'Well, sure. She's one of the most quality people I've ever known.'

'Do you talk to Filler and Nettles about her?'

'Not much,' he admitted.

'Have they ever met her?'

'Filler did the once. When she came down to Paradise Circle and found me.'

'You see, this is what I mean,' said Hope. 'You may be a rogue and a thief. But you're also a lot more than that. A scholar, a storyteller, and now I discover you are a painter as well? Why do you keep these parts of yourself separate?'

Red was silent for a long time. Hope began to wonder if he would even answer. If he even knew the answer.

'I guess because,' he said finally, 'I never met someone who could really see all the parts of me before.'

Hope thought back to when she'd first learned that Red became an orphan at the same age as her. Their lives had been so disparate, but this one similarity was like a spike driven into the center of their being, on which their dreams, fears, and desires all pivoted. She had never known she could be so different from someone, yet understand them so well.

'Hope?' asked Red.

'Yes?'

'Back in that alley earlier today. You wouldn't really have killed yourself. Would you?'

Hope sighed and closed her eyes. 'The Vinchen code says that the only true vengeance is the death of the offender. If the warrior fails in this, better that he die than live in such dishonor. I thought I had failed.'

'And your honor is worth that much to you?' he asked.

'No,' she said. 'My vengeance is.'

Teltho Kan awoke naked and shivering in a dark alley near the western coast of New Laven. His skin felt raw, as if he'd been scraped all over with a dull razor. The cold wind raked painfully at him as he got slowly and unsteadily to his feet.

That had been a bad jump. So little time to prepare. No buffers, no safeguards. And he wasn't getting any younger. Another one like that and he might leave his skin behind along with his clothes.

Still, it had been necessary. He'd never have expected a rule follower like Hurlo to do something as heretical as train a female in the Vinchen Way. Perhaps he'd gotten eccentric in his old age. Or senile. The reason didn't really matter. He'd trained her well. She would have to be dealt with.

Teltho Kan looked down at his naked, shivering body, rail thin and taut with stringy muscle. First things first. He needed some clothes.

He walked unselfconsciously out to the main thoroughfare. There weren't any street lamps in this part of town and there weren't many people about. It was somewhat amusing to watch the few people who walked past him pretend not to see the nude old man lurking in the shadows.

Finally he saw a man around his height and build. The man was wearing a white peasant shirt, breeches, and boots with barely a sole intact. It wasn't ideal, but he didn't have time to be picky. When the man walked past, he stepped out of the shadows and touched the man's neck.

'Hells to you,' growled the man, and stepped away.

Teltho Kan watched him take three more steps. When he brought his foot down on the fourth step, his leg broke with a loud crack. The man screamed and swayed on one leg. Then that leg broke. As he fell, the man put out both arms to catch his fall.

Those both broke on impact. The man lay there, all four limbs bent in unnatural directions. Teltho Kan continued to watch as the man wailed in agony, thrashing around, each movement breaking more bones in his body. Finally the man was only a quivering, whimpering mass of odd angles. Teltho Kan knelt down and tapped the man's forehead. His skull caved in, and he grew still.

Teltho Kan pulled the clothes off the body, which continued to make little pops and cracks at each movement. At last he was dressed and warm.

This girl of Hurlo's had sworn vengeance on him. If there was one thing Hurlo was likely to have burned into her brain above all else, it was fulfilling oaths. He'd always been implacable that way. If she was anything like her grandteacher, she would find his trail again, sooner rather than later. He needed to prepare. Next time, he would be ready for her.

24

*I*t would have been difficult for Red to explain to someone who wasn't an artist the strange intimacy he felt when painting a portrait. He didn't know if it was just him who felt it, or if all artists felt it to some degree. Not that he was an artist . . .

They got started on the portrait at first light. Hope sat on a tall stool over by the window. Her blond hair, usually tied back tight, had been loosened for the portrait at Old Yammy's request. The morning sun streamed through it, making her hair look truly angelic. Yet even so, while seemingly serene and completely still, she still looked dangerous. And that, he had to admit, was part of her attraction.

But as he painted in Old Yammy's kitchen, it became more than the impulses of a leaky tom. He found himself drawn to tiny details about her. Things he wouldn't ordinarily have noticed. The slight upturn of her nose. The curved bow of her lips. The faint line of her eyebrows, as pale as her hair. The light dusting of freckles across the bridge of her nose. The hard, clean line of her jaw. The graceful curve of her neck. And those eyes. So deep and blue, he felt dizzy if he looked at them too long. But he *had* to look. He had to do them justice on the canvas. If he got nothing else right, he wanted the eyes.

She shifted slightly and asked, 'How long will this take?'

'The more you move, the longer it'll take,' he said tersely.

'But how—'

'Talking counts as moving.' He was being unfair. He'd never painted a portrait where the subject was as still as she was. There were moments he wasn't even sure she was breathing. And later, when he asked if she needed a break, she said no. He'd never known anyone who could sit that still for that long. It was like she'd put herself into some kind of Vinchen trance.

But he was in a sort of trance himself. He knew it, even as he was in it. He always got that way when he painted. Time stopped, and all other thoughts and worries receded. There was only the canvas, the brush, the paint, and the subject. Her.

It was late afternoon when he came up for air and saw that he was done. 'Okay.' His voice was dreamy, like he was just waking up. 'That's it.'

Old Yammy scrutinized it. 'Your best yet. A portrait worthy of the subject.'

'Thank you.' He knew the warm buzz of euphoria would pass soon, as Red the pat tom from Paradise Circle reasserted himself. So he savored this moment.

'Let me see.' Hope stood up from the stool, seeming no worse off for having sat completely still for over eight hours. She came around and peered at the portrait over his shoulder.

'Hm,' she said and walked away.

A cold fist seized his gut. 'You don't like it?' he asked before he could stop himself.

'No, it's beautiful.' A slow blush crept onto her pale, freckled cheeks. 'You paint me flatteringly.'

'I paint you as I see you.'

'Hm,' she said again, then turned to Old Yammy. 'I hope the payment is sufficient?'

'Oh yes.' Old Yammy gave Red a mischievous look. 'It turned out just as I'd hoped.'

Red didn't like her expression. It reminded him of himself when he was pulling a con. That wasn't too surprising. After all, Old Yammy was one of his mentors. She'd tracked him down several years back. After his time as a pirate, but before he'd met Nettles. She'd wanted him to come back to Silverback, but by then, he'd become too invested in Paradise Circle. That hadn't stopped him from visiting now and then to learn what he could from her. While it was true she had formidable skill with blood magic and all sorts of medicinal remedies and poisons, fortune-telling was her most popular service, and anyone worth a fiveyard knew that stuff was nothing but balls and pricks. Deceit and chicanery were a necessary part of her business. She'd been the one to teach him that a clever mind could get you far more than clever fingers.

That didn't bother Red, of course. What *did* bother him was when he couldn't tell what con she was pulling, or on whom. Nine out of ten, that usually meant it was him. What it was this time, he couldn't say. At least, not yet. She was too clever for her own good, and Old Yammy's machinations had a way of revealing themselves, too late to be prevented, but early enough that you could recognize her handiwork if you were paying attention.

'Right . . .' he said, narrowing his eyes at her. Then he turned to Hope. 'You ready to go?'

'Nonsense,' said Old Yammy. 'You haven't eaten a bite all day. I can't send you back out into the world on an empty stomach.'

'We might as well,' said Hope. 'I hate to let Teltho Kan slip any further away. But neither of us have money. We don't know when we'll be able to eat again.'

Red flashed his grin. 'Money can always be got.'

'I would prefer not to steal whenever possible.' She glanced at Old Yammy, then smiled back at him. 'Besides, this may be my only opportunity to learn about Rixidenteron.'

'I'm suddenly not hungry,' he said.

As Red feared, the conversation over their meal focused almost exclusively on his early childhood exploits. They sat at the large table in the center of the kitchen and ate a thick vegetable stew as Old Yammy shared one embarrassing anecdote after another. Red wasn't sure which was worse, the smug relish with which Old Yammy told them, or the gleeful avidity with which Hope listened. Red imagined her saving up a hefty arsenal of details that she would judiciously deploy whenever she felt like making him squirm.

'So you've known him his whole life?' she asked Old Yammy.

'I didn't have this shop back then. His parents and I were neighbors for the whole of his childhood. I would have taken him in when his parents passed, bless them, but I was in prison that year.'

'Prison?' asked Hope. 'For what?'

'Devilry. That's what the biomancers call it. Of course, they can bend the laws of nature as they see fit, and it's for the good of the empire. But if someone does it who isn't in their order, especially a woman? Well, surely that must be an evil power granted by a demon. They sweep through every five years or so, looking for anyone with real ability. If you're a man, they may recruit you. But if you're a woman, it's a year on the Empty Cliffs or death. I've since learned to spot them coming and hide my skill. But back then I was young and stupid and eager to impress anyone who chanced by.' She turned to Red, her face growing long. 'I wish I'd been there. It was a hard year, so I'm told.'

'It was,' said Red quietly.

There was a moment of quiet, during which Red silently hoped neither woman would chase those particular memories into the light. He was grateful when Old Yammy then said, 'Fortunately, I found him a few years later. He was changed by then. Already going by Red, his head filled with the wild roguery Sadie the Goat put there, that old sturgeon.'

'You've met?' asked Hope.

'Of course. And for all the trouble she's wrought, I'll always be grateful to her for saving this one's life and keeping him more or less out of trouble.' She poked Red in the shoulder. 'But he's come by now and then to learn a thing or two from me over the years.'

'And what did you teach him?' asked Hope.

Old Yammy laughed, a rich throaty burst. 'Wouldn't you like to know.' Then she laughed again.

Red was surprised by her evasion. It hadn't been any remarkable thing. He'd had no real aptitude for blood magic, so she'd taught him her other trade. The subtle art of convincing people of things. But perhaps her reluctance to talk of it was no great mystery. As she'd said to him many a time, a magician never reveals her secrets, except to her apprentice.

Still, there were hints of some long game she'd been playing since the night before. Whatever it was, Red dreaded its inevitable revelation.

But perhaps he was too suspicious. Because they left Madame Destiny's House of All with no shocking turns. Either she was playing a truly long game, or Red had been wrong to worry.

'Will you get word to Sadie?' he asked her. 'She's down at the docks, working on a ship called the *Lady's Gambit* with Missing Finn. Just let her know we're okay, give her an idea what we're doing. Nothing too specific, though. I don't want her to worry.'

'I'll tell her what she needs to know,' said Old Yammy. Then she reached out and embraced him, something she rarely did. 'It'll be a while until I see you again. You'll have grown up a lot by then. Promise you won't forget your Old Yammy, keen?' She squeezed him hard.

'Yeah, alright,' he said, a little embarrassed.

It was shortly after sunset when they set out. Hope kept her sword at her side, her hand resting on the pommel so she could feel it move while keeping it from actually pointing.

'What did Old Yammy mean?' asked Hope. 'When she was talking about not seeing you for a while? Is she going somewhere?'

Red shook his head. 'She puts on that she has some sort of Sight, like she can see the future. It's all balls and pricks, though. Nobody can see the future, because we haven't made it yet.'

'It's said the Dark Mage could see the future. Some believe it was what drove him mad.'

'Could you blame him?' asked Red. 'I mean, *if* it was possible, which it isn't, then seeing the future but not being able to do anything about it? That would make anyone slippy.'

'What if they *could* do something about it?' asked Hope.

'Then it wouldn't be the future anymore, now would it?'

'Good point,' conceded Hope.

They walked silently down the main thoroughfare, each block bringing a different melody from a different musician: drummers, flautists, string players, singers, all of them performing for the few coins tossed into their hats. The lacies

tossed coppers, silvers, even the occasional gold piece. Red
wondered if there was some sort of competition among them
on who could be the most extravagant. If you could afford to
toss a gold coin to a string player just because you fancied his
tune, you must be wealthy indeed.

'The lights and the music and the colors . . .' said Hope.
'I've never encountered a place like this before. It almost
doesn't feel real.'

Red watched the lamplight play across her skin. Her hair
was pulled back again, but it still had a faint angelic glow to
it. The shadows and light flickered across her features in a
way that made his fingers itch to paint her again.

'What?' she said.

'Huh?'

'You're staring at me.'

'Oh. Sorry.' He hurriedly faced forward again. That's when
Old Yammy's long game hit him. She was playing pissing
matchmaker, trying to get Red hooked on Hope. Before, he'd
admired Hope's many attractive features, as any hot-blooded
tom with a fancy for mollies might. But he was no lovesick
piddle anymore. When he'd found out she was not for tossing,
he'd been fairly successful in realigning his view of her into
fellow wag and not a thing more. But now? He couldn't stop
noticing things. All the little details he'd painted kept catching
his attention. It was distracting, and it made his heart sick with
frustration. But what could he do except bear it? The only
other option was to get away from her as quickly as possible.
But the mere thought of that froze his insides. That's how he
knew Old Yammy's plan had worked, and he was well and
truly sotted. Of course, Yammy didn't realize that nothing
could ever come of it because of that pissing vow of chastity.

Hope lifted her chin and inhaled. 'I smell the sea. My
sword is pointing in that direction. Could he have left New
Laven?'

'That's Joiner's Bay up ahead. It cuts into New Laven pretty deep. On the other side is Keystown. He could be there.'

'Good.'

'Not really. First we have to go all the way around the bay, or else find a way across. We could get word to Sadie and ask her to bring up your ship, assuming the ship is ready. Even if it is, that would take a day for her to sail up the coast from New Laven.'

'We're already further behind than I would have liked.'

'You were the one who said we should stay for dinner,' Red pointed out.

'A Vinchen knows when the limits of the body should be considered.'

'Meaning, you were starving.'

'Yes,' she said without a trace of embarrassment.

'Well, no matter how we cross, once we get to Keystown, we likely won't find it a friendly place, since it's imp head-quarters. Teltho Kan is probably spreading your description all over. The imps around here may not have picked it up yet. But the ones up there will be looking for you, true as trouble. We'll need to disguise your more striking features before we cross the bay.'

She raised one eyebrow. 'Which features are those?'

'The blond hair and the Vinchen leather.' *And the unearthly beauty*, he thought to himself with a healthy amount of self-mockery.

'What sort of disguise did you have in mind?'

'If we're going uptown, it should be a lacy disguise.'

She wrinkled her nose. 'Do I have to paint myself orange?'

'They don't all do that. But many wear silly hats and big poufy dresses.'

'Wonderful,' she said without enthusiasm. 'So where do we get this disguise?'

'Need you even ask?' He pressed his hand to his chest, affecting a hurt tone.

Her eyes narrowed. 'You plan to steal it.'

'Naturally. Even if we did have money, it wouldn't be near enough for a whole lacy getup. Those cost more than you or I see in a year. We just have to find a lacy woman about your size.'

He began to look for a victim as they continued walking toward the bay. The street ended at the edge of a cliff. Far below, the moon glinted off the dark water. The reflection was blotted out here and there by the dark shapes of small leisure boats owned by lacies. He could faintly hear their wooden creaks as they moved with the water. Further up the coast, he caught the sound of classical music. Not earthy street musicians, but a proper twinkling lacy orchestra. He looked toward the sound and could just make out the source: a large building right on the edge of the cliff overlooking the bay.

He smiled wolfishly. 'Bayview Gallery. Come on. I have a sudden desire to reconnect with my childhood.'

Bayview Gallery was the most prestigious art gallery in Silverback, which made it the most prestigious gallery in New Laven and possibly the entire empire. It was four stories of gratuitous architecture. Arches, flying buttresses, domed balconies, and rotundas, just to name the more obvious. As he and Hope approached, its massive windows glowed like giant lanterns. It would have been enough to light up the entire block on its own. But of course there were street lamps, twice as many as any other block, and guttering torches as well, just for the aesthetics.

'I don't understand why you'd want to rob someone at your own mother's show,' said Hope.

'Mom hated this place, like any proper artist in Silverback does. She said you knew your art was no longer relevant when they hung it in Bayview.'

'Even if that's true, the people inside are there because they admire your mother's art. That has to count for something.'

'Why? Because they buy and sell her work for more money than she ever saw during her life? Someone's getting rich off the passion that killed her. If that counts for something, it's a place in one of the wetter hells.'

Hope said nothing more as they approached the gallery, and Red was glad. He needed to calm down. Quiet his mind so he could do this properly. Yes, rolling a lacy at his mom's gallery show had a certain self-indulgent flourish to it. But he was still a professional.

The place was too brightly lit to sneak into, and looking like they did, they'd get turned away by the two thick-shouldered boots guarding the front door.

Fortunately, there was brisk traffic between the small larder building and the gallery, as lacy servants hauled food and drink in a continuous stream for the insatiable rich. Red and Hope worked their way around to the larder and grabbed a cask of ale between them, then fell behind a harried, silver-haired servant with a smoked ham under one arm and a cheese wheel under the other. They followed him across an open stretch of grass to the servants' entrance on the side of the gallery. The entrance led straight to the kitchen, where Hope and Red were greeted by a vast banquet of food. Meat and cheese, fish and fruit, cut into tiny pieces and artfully arranged on huge silver platters. Even though he'd already eaten, Red stared at it all hungrily.

'Red, don't,' said Hope. 'You'll draw more attention.'

'More?' Red glanced around. Servants were staring at them and whispering. Of course, because everyone around them was in a servant uniform. 'Right. Time to go.'

Before anyone could stop them, they took the nearest door. It led out into a long hallway with arched ceilings. The floors were white marble, the walls had gilded wallpaper, and burgundy velvet drapes hung from the windows. It was empty of people and art, but the music sounded in full swing upstairs. Red guessed most of the 'art patrons' were up there right now. He hoped there were at least a few people down on this level looking at the actual art. So he could steal their clothes, of course.

He pressed forward. 'Come on, the main gallery must be this way.'

'You do have some kind of plan, right?' asked Hope as she walked beside him. She kept glancing around, looking even more uncomfortable than when he'd first taken her to Gunpowder Hall. Red wondered if she'd ever seen anything as luxurious as this place. Probably not. Just when she'd adjusted to the Circle, he'd dragged her somewhere even more alien. He had to admit, he took a certain perverse delight in that.

'Pfft, plans are for amateurs.' He kept his tone light and unconcerned.

'Actually,' she said, 'I'm fairly certain they're the mark of a professional.'

They crossed into a large room where two hallways intersected. Above them hung a massive crystal chandelier. 'How is it lit?' asked Hope, her eyes wide with wonder.

'Gas piped in through the walls.'

She shook her head. 'Amazing.'

'Yeah, yeah.' Red scanned the other hallways and found one of them had people. Now he needed to find a woman about Hope's size wearing a hat. He wasn't sure yet how he'd get her clothes, but he'd figure that part out later. Depending on her character, anything from guile to a blunt instrument might work.

As they walked past lacies staring at his mother's paintings, he couldn't help listening in on their comments.

'So striking!'

'Ethereal, wouldn't you say?'

'Captivating! I can't turn away.'

'This one's a bit lurid, don't you think?'

It set his teeth on edge. He didn't like these lacies staring at his mother's work like they had some right or claim to it. He hurried past them, fighting to stay focused and search for a thin woman with a hat. It was dawning on him that this whole thing was a terrible mistake. He shouldn't have come anywhere near this gallery. But it was too late now.

That's when he saw the painting. He hadn't meant to. In fact, he'd been doing his best to avoid looking at any of them, knowing their memories might throw off what little calm he was still clinging to. But his eyes were drawn helplessly to one particular canvas at the end of the hall. He stumbled over to it almost against his will. He stood there and stared, his fists clenched at his sides.

'Red?' Hope appeared beside him. He was dimly aware she was looking back and forth between him and the painting. 'Are you okay?'

No, he was definitely not okay. He was sinking into a maelstrom of images he hadn't called to mind in years. His mother, beautiful, with her gray eyes and curly black hair. She had a way of smirking, quietly, mischievously, that always made you think she knew something you didn't. He had tried all his life to emulate that smirk and hadn't yet truly succeeded.

He had adored her. Even later, when she couldn't stop her hands from shaking, when she couldn't even hold a brush. It was only at the end that things got hard. When her descriptions stopped making sense. She would grow frustrated and curse at him, tell him he was stupid and clumsy. He would cry, which would only make her angrier. But then his father would swoop in, his patient eyes and gentle smile soothing them both as he wrapped his long, strong arms around them, bringing them into a big family hug. Then everything would be okay again.

Until there came a time his father wasn't there to swoop in. Red knew he was out whoring to make money to buy those new paintings that nobody wanted. Red wasn't supposed to tell his mother, because it would make her sad. But without his father there to soothe them, her frustration and his hurt went unchecked until one night, after she had called him weak and talentless and the worst thing that ever happened to her, he couldn't hold it in any longer. He *wanted* her to be sad, to hurt like he did. So he told her what his father was doing. Without a word, she had lain down on the sofa and closed her eyes. Red stood there, horrified by what he'd said, so much anguished energy boiling inside him. He hadn't known what else to do with it, so he'd painted. The first and only painting that was all his own.

And that was the painting he stared at now.

'Fascinating piece, wouldn't you say?' asked a voice behind him. Older. Male. A lacy, by the sound and polish. 'Her final work before she died. It was a departure for her. Different from everything that came before it. One wonders if it was a sign of things to come? If she had lived, of course. Some people theorize it was a self-portrait of sorts. Painting herself as she imagined herself to look as she lay dying.'

Red had not turned his gaze from the painting. In swirls of muted browns and grays, with small streaks of beige, his mother lay on the couch, one arm hanging off the edge, a corkscrew lock of black hair falling across her face, gaunt but peaceful. Peaceful as Red had wanted her to be. As if in painting that, it would become true.

Red's voice was thick as he said, 'She didn't paint this one. I did.'

'What's this you say?' asked the man, his tone offended.

Red turned to the man, not trying to hide the tears that coursed down his cheeks. The man's distrustful scowl evaporated when he saw Red's face. He ran his hands through his thin gray hair, then pressed them to his plump lips. 'Those eyes!' he whispered. 'Those red eyes! You . . . you're the lost son, Rixidenteron.'

'Red, we should go,' said Hope quietly, her hand on his arm protectively.

'No, please don't!' The man reached his hand out to them. 'I'll do anything, only let me talk to you a moment.'

Even openly weeping, his heart torn and his mind reeling, the part of Red that had kept him alive all these years recognized that tone of desperation. It was the sound of opportunity.

'Why?' Red made a show of narrowing his eyes suspiciously, as if he was afraid of this well-dressed lacy wrink. 'What do you want to talk about?'

'Your mother, of course.' His hands trembled, and his brow was beaded with sweat. 'My name is Thoriston Baggelworthy. Perhaps she spoke of me?'

Red shook his head.

'Well, I *knew* her long ago, when we were children. We used to play ropes and sticks, she and I. I was terribly smitten with her, of course. But she was more interested in art than courtship. When she left Hollow Falls, I was despondent. I thought I'd never get over it.' He gave a strange chuckle. 'And perhaps I never did. After all, this' – he gestured around them – 'is all mine.'

'What do you mean, all yours?' asked Red. He didn't like

the man's possessive tone. And he didn't like that the few times he had come back to Silverback, he was inevitably sucked into the world of Rixidenteron and its memories. Probably the best thing about Paradise Circle was that nobody gave a cup of piss about famous artists.

'The collection,' said Thoriston. 'Every single painting she ever made is mine. I have hunted all over New Laven and brought them together at last. I will make your mother the most famous painter in the world! You'll see!'

Red wanted to tell him that fame had never mattered to his mother. He didn't know if that was true, but he didn't like how the man acted as though he was somehow entitled to his mother and her work. The survivalist part of him cautioned against that, though. Instead he asked, 'What was it you wanted to know about her?'

'Everything! I hope to write a biography of her life, you see. And it would be invaluable to my work and to her legacy if you could tell me as much as you remember about your early life with her.'

'We've got things to do, and we're in a hurry,' said Red, turning away. 'Besides, it would be too painful for me to talk about it.'

'Wait, I beg you!' Thoriston wrung his hands. 'I know I'm asking a lot for you to relive such troubling times. If there is any way I can repay you, name it, and if it is within my power, I will do it.'

Red pretended to consider it a moment. 'We need clothes. Proper clothes, like you're wearing.'

'Clothes?' He looked utterly baffled. Like they grew on trees and were there for the taking by anyone at any time.

'For both of us,' continued Red. 'And transportation across the bay to Keystown.'

Thoriston gave him a shrewd look. 'Oh, I see now. You're making your way to Hollow Falls to be reunited with your mother's family, and you don't want to present yourself in these old rags.'

'You *are* sharp,' said Red smoothly. 'I didn't expect you to work that out so quickly.'

'Ah, but do you know where to go once you get there?' asked Thoriston, looking very pleased with himself.

Red put on a sheepish expression. 'Not exactly . . .'

'Then I can give you even more than you ask for! I know your grandfather's address. I can give you directions right to his door.'

Directions to his grandfather's door was the last thing he wanted. But he forced himself to smile. 'That would be a great help.'

'Wonderful! Won't he be pleased to finally meet you!' Thoriston clapped his hands together in an oddly childish expression of glee.

'Undoubtedly,' Hope murmured.

'Now, let's see . . .' Thoriston scratched his smooth, round chin. 'My wife and I are staying next door at the Hotel Sunset for the duration of the gallery exhibition period. It may be a bit loose around the waist, but I think you can fit into something of mine.' He frowned at Hope. 'You might be more of a challenge, my dear. You're far too thin to wear my wife's dresses. They'd fall right off that boyish frame.'

Red felt Hope tense up. He nudged her with his elbow, and she nodded curtly. 'As you say, sir.'

He continued to stare at her. 'You *would* fit into her maid-servant's dresses. But I'm afraid the maid's mother just passed away, so all she packed was mourning clothes.'

'I prefer black anyway,' she said.

'Ah yes . . .' He eyed her black leather outfit. 'So I see.' Then he turned back to Red. 'Once you've both changed, I'll take you across the bay myself. That way you can tell me

about your mother while we travel, and you don't lose much
time in the telling.'

'Sounds perfect,' said Red, this time with sincerity.

Red tried not to gawk as Thoriston led them through the
hotel lobby, which was even more opulent than the gallery.
Gas-powered lights in every room, crystal chandeliers, silk
embroidered wall hangings, thick fur rugs. Every room
smelled like flowers and sweets. He glanced over at Hope and
saw her eyes nearly popping out of her head.

Thoriston led them into his lodgings, which were just as
fine as the lobby.

'Where is your wife?' asked Hope as her eyes scanned the
rooms.

'Oh, back at the gallery, I expect,' he called as he walked
into the bedroom and began to sort through the clothes in
his wardrobe. 'She's fond of that orchestra. That's why I
hired them. My deep, lifelong passion for Lady Pastinas's art
is sometimes difficult for her to appreciate.'

'I can't imagine why,' said Hope dryly.

Hope and Red waited in the sitting room while Thoriston
riffled through the clothes, leaving a mess in his wake. Red
suspected there were probably people who picked up after
him. He might not even be used to getting clothes himself.

'Here we are!' he said, beaming triumphantly as he
returned with clothes for Red. He turned to Hope. 'There's
the maidservant's quarters. I'm sure anything in there will
do.' He paused, suddenly looking unsure. 'Eh . . . do you
require assistance in getting dressed? I can call up—'

'We'll manage just fine, thanks,' said Red.

Once Red had finished dressing, he looked at himself
admiringly in the mirror. He had on a fine brown frockcoat

with gold trim and brass buttons, a waistcoat, trousers, and a silk cravat, which Thoriston had to help him tie properly. What would his old wags say if they saw him now? Handsome Henny would've pissed himself laughing. Sadie might have died in shock. Filler probably wouldn't have been able to look him in the eye. And Nettles . . . he would've never heard the end of it. But now, without their snide remarks and disapproving glances, he allowed himself to relish in this odd little fantasy while he waited for Hope to finish.

Hope was not nearly as enthusiastic.

'All this fabric swishing around my legs.' She clutched at the thick folds of black cloth. 'It's nearly impossible to move properly.'

'I think it's a significant improvement,' said Thoriston. 'It lends a great deal to accentuate your more feminine attributes.'

Red had to agree. Her pale, freckled shoulders gleamed in the lamplight, and the black corset pushed her small breasts together to offer a hint of cleavage while flaring out her waist at the bottom. But he was smart enough not to say anything out loud.

Hope grunted and tugged at the corset. 'It's impractical and uncomfortable. And I have nowhere to hang my sword.'

'I can hold it,' offered Red.

She placed the small, round black hat on her head. 'No. You can't.'

'Shall I have these . . . disposed of?' Thoriston pointed to their regular clothes.

'No!' both Hope and Red said at once.

'Ah, we'll just hold on to those, thanks,' said Red as he rolled them all up in his longcoat and tucked it under his arm.

Thoriston led them back out of the hotel and to the path along the cliff. The moon and stars were out, glimmering off the bay far below. After a short walk, they descended a narrow staircase that zigzagged down to the docks.

'I sail my own vessel,' Thoriston said proudly as he led them to a small sailboat. 'Not out into the ocean, of course. Just around the bay. My wife tells me I'm mad and refuses to get in it with me, but I find it quite invigorating.'

His small yacht looked much like the ones they used to raid on the *Savage Wind*. Red suppressed a smile as he imagined how Thoriston would have reacted to being boarded by Sadie the Pirate Queen and her crew. But Thoriston did, indeed, know how to handle the small craft. Soon they were under sail and gliding smoothly out into the bay.

'Now,' said Thoriston as he leaned comfortably back at the stern, one hand on the tiller. 'I want you to tell me *everything* about her.'

'Ah, the tragic tale of Lady Pastinas, is it?' asked Red, working into his storytelling tone. It helped him get some distance from it, and it made things more entertaining for his audience.

'Yes,' breathed Thoriston, his eyes wide like a child.

It was nearly sunrise by the time they reached the far side of the bay. The first streaks of red were just coming up over the square, orderly tops of the Keystown Imperial Garrison. Red had finished his tale a few minutes before, timing it perfectly. Thoriston was dabbing at his eyes with a handkerchief.

'Your poor family,' he muttered as he tied his boat to the docks.

'Well, you've done a great deal to mend things,' said Red, clasping his hand. 'Both in honoring my mother's memory and helping to reunite me with my grandfather.'

'It seems the least I can do,' Thoriston sniffled. 'Your mother's work has given my whole life meaning.'

'Truly said.' Red gave his best smile and patted the top of the old gaf's hand.

Thoriston gave them detailed directions to Pastinas Manor. Red took careful note so that he could make sure to avoid it. Then he and Hope disembarked. They stood on the dock and watched as Thoriston's boat glided back out into the bay.

'You didn't tell him everything.' Hope's tone was oddly subdued.

'Of course not,' said Red. 'A story is told as much by what you leave out as what you put in.'

'But if he's truly going to write it down and make a history of it, no one will ever know that you were the one that painted so many of her works.'

Part of him wished Old Yammy hadn't told her quite so much about his childhood. Although he was surprised to find that a part of him was grateful.

'Only one hero in a story, Hope, my old pot. And there's no sense bogging a fine tale down with the dreary truth. Besides, we all need to keep some things for ourselves.' He turned to face the hard, uninviting exterior of Keystown. 'Now, where does that sword of yours say we go next?'

25

*H*ope knew that dresses were something many women wore. She *knew* it. And yet, as she and Red prowled through the orderly streets of Keystown, she had a hard time accepting that fact. Simply getting the thing on had been an ordeal. Halfway through, as she nearly dislocated her shoulder trying to tighten the corset strings at her back, she understood why Thoriston had suggested someone help her. Clothing that was so poorly designed that one couldn't put it on alone? It seemed like a cruel joke. And once she had the corset tight enough, it was an uncomfortable joke as well. She understood now why women were always fainting in the imperial romances she'd read in her youth. It wasn't from shock or fear, but from simple lack of breath. And this was no minor detail. Breath, as Hurlo had told her many times, was at the root of who we were. Our very soul. Mastering one's breath was the first lesson she had to learn. To think that the women in the upper classes had this necessary aspect of themselves so restricted, it was no wonder men seemed to hold the advantage.

She had thought that at least there would be ease of movement below the waist. But these were not the simple loose peasant skirts her mother wore. These were tight, packed with redundant cloth, and then draped with even more redundant cloth. The slim pointed shoes didn't help. Walking was a challenge. Running, if it came to that, would be far worse.

But she was grudgingly grateful for the clothes. Keystown was swarming with imperial soldiers. The neighborhood seemed to be one vast barracks. The few non-imperial people she saw were either wealthy uptown residents or their clean and smartly dressed servants. Had Hope and Red shown up in their grimy, patched-up clothing, they would have drawn the soldiers' eyes immediately. Even dressed as they were, they were stopped at two different places by a soldier asking if they had seen a blond woman in black leather. Hope held her sword down at her side, concealing it within the ruffles of her ridiculous dress. Her round black hat didn't completely cover her hair, and she worried that one of them would notice the color. But none did. Perhaps it was the earliness of the hour, or perhaps the investigative training of the imperial troops really was as poor as Red claimed. As they continued through the broad, straight streets, she started to believe they might make it through Keystown without incident.

The third time they were stopped went a bit differently, however. The soldier wore the standard white-and-gold uniform like the others, and had that same bored expression as he stepped in front of them. 'Pardon me, good people. Have you seen a blond woman dressed in a strange black leather costume skulking about?'

'No indeed, sir,' said Red cheerfully. 'Is she dangerous?'

'Extremely.' The soldier's eyes passed over Hope without even a glimmer of interest. 'If you see her, don't approach. Just go find the nearest . . .'

He trailed off as he looked harder at Red. 'Do I know you?'

'I don't think so.' Red turned to Hope. 'Come along, dear, we must hurry on our errand.'

They tried to make their way around the soldier, when his face suddenly lit up. 'You! You're the one who stole the money off my cart! Got me demoted to foot patrol. I'm going to—'

He stopped short as Hope struck him between the eyes with the end of her sheathed sword. He crumpled to the ground in a heap.

'Is he dead?' Red peered down at him.

'Unconscious.'

'How long till he wakes up?'

'An hour at least,' said Hope.

'I could have talked us out of it.'

'I think your opinion of your own charm is a little inflated,' she said.

'But now we have the body to worry about,' said Red. 'And this place is crawling with imps. It won't be long before another one comes by.'

'True,' admitted Hope. She scanned the surrounding area, but there wasn't really anywhere around to stow the body. The streets were so clean, there wasn't even anything to cover it with. Then she took a closer look at the surface of the street itself.

'Is that some kind of hatch in the ground?' She pointed to a round iron disk embedded into the cobblestones.

Red frowned. 'I'm not sure.'

He bent down and slid his fingers along the edge.

'Heavy,' he grunted. 'You want to give me a hand?'

She tried to bend over, but the corset made that impossible. Instead she had to squat, straight-backed, until she was low enough to reach. And even then, she heard a slight tear as her thighs pressed out against the dress. Apparently, uptown ladies were not expected to pick things up.

'Let's open it slowly,' she said. 'We don't know what's down there.' But when they did open it, the stench made it clear precisely what was in there.

'It smells like the worst parts of Paradise Circle all in one place.' She wrinkled her nose and turned her head away as they slid the iron lid to one side.

'That's about what it is.' Red pointed down into the hole, where a shallow stream of excrement moved sluggishly along. 'No wonder the streets are so clean. They move it all underground. Kind of ingenious, really.'

'Also useful for us,' said Hope, nodding to the unconscious soldier.

'So right after I get him demoted, we knock him out and drop him in a puddle of piss and shit,' said Red. 'Maybe you should have just killed him.'

In other parts of New Laven, the transitions from one neighborhood to the next had been gradual. It had been difficult for Hope to tell where exactly one ended and the next began. But the transition from Keystown to Hollow Falls was so starkly abrupt, it seemed a purposeful declaration.

On one side of the street were the neat, orderly, tightly packed barracks of the imperial garrison. On the other side, the world opened up into rolling hills, charming wood fences, and clear trickling brooks with finely crafted bridges. Ornate mansions dotted the landscape, surrounded by vast spreads of green. Coming from downtown, where everything and everyone were piled up on top of each other, it struck Hope that in a place like New Laven, space might be the most precious commodity. To have this much open space, and to keep it without functional purposes such as farming or storage, was the height of decadence.

'You sure the sword says to go this way?' Red asked.

She nodded.

'Rich people aren't so scary,' he said, as if assuring her.

'I'm not frightened of them,' she said.

'Right. Well. Me neither.'

It was unusual to see his confidence falter like this. A few days ago, she might have found it amusing. But after the last few nights, learning more about his childhood and family, she understood far better what lay behind all his cavalier bluster. Now it pained her to watch him struggle.

'Let's continue, then,' she suggested gently.

'Of course!' His smile returned, but looked a little tight. 'If he keeps fleeing north, there's only so much further he can go before he runs out of land. We might even catch him before nightfall.'

'Unless he takes to ship,' said Hope.

'Don't you worry, old pot, we'll catch him before that.' He slapped her back like she was one of his wags. She wondered if he missed Filler. She could see how his tall, quiet presence might give Red some additional confidence right now. She was surprised to find that she missed him as well. And Nettles, too. If nothing else, it would have been nice to have someone else to share the misery of formal uptown dress with. She wondered if she would ever see either of them again.

'Let's be on our way, then,' said Red. 'Biomancers don't behead themselves, you know.'

They crossed the street into the wide, spacious neighborhood of Hollow Falls. It felt like a transgression to do even that small thing, and Hope half expected to see soldiers pop up from behind bushes to drive them back. But of course, nothing happened. In fact, as they walked down the side of the winding road that cut through the meadows, there were hardly any people at all. The few they saw were in carriages or on horseback, and nodded politely as they passed. Some even wished them a good afternoon.

After the drab grays and browns of downtown, the colors in this place were a welcome relief. Lush green grass covered the rolling hills. Pale green and yellow leaves covered the thin, elegant trees. Bright flowers in reds, blues, and yellows sprang from carefully manicured shrubs and bushes. Fences were painted a dazzling white that reflected the afternoon sunlight.

But even more striking than the space or the color was the quiet. Hope had grown up in quiet, both in her village, and later on Galemoor. Even on the *Lady's Gambit*, quiet had been fairly easy to find once she got used to the sounds of the sea. But since landing in New Laven, she had not had a single moment of true quiet. Whether it was people talking, shouting, music playing, carriages rattling, guns firing, or companions snoring, the silence was nonexistent. But now it was all around them, soaring out over a landscape so vast, sound seemed like an intrusion.

She could tell Red didn't find silence the same peaceful respite she did. He kept glancing around them, his eyes darting, his hands tense at his sides. He would try to engage her in conversation, but when she only answered in shrugs or quiet grunts, he seemed to take the hint and gave up.

They continued up the winding road, occasionally crossing side paths that were just wide enough to let a carriage pass. Those led up to mansions that stretched several stories and were surrounded by dense, complex gardens full of rare plants Hope had only read about. Though not quite as large as Bayview Gallery or the hotel, they were still big enough that Hope found it difficult to believe they were merely homes for a single family.

It was late afternoon, the sun low in the horizon, when the sword gave a jump in Hope's hand. She jerked to a stop, her heart suddenly pounding.

'What is it?' asked Red, breaking the silence for the first time in a while.

'The sword is pointing to that mansion.'

'Is he *in* the mansion, or *past* it?'

'Let's find out.' Hope continued walking past the mansion, but at a faster pace. Her pulse steadily increased with each step, and she felt a hot eagerness welling up inside. Hurlo would have chastised her and told her to stop and return to a place of calm before proceeding. But she couldn't help herself. If it weren't for her dress, she might have even broken into a run. She held the sword out before her, and as they moved past the mansion, it began to slowly twist in her hand, keeping its point toward the mansion.

She stopped and looked at Red. 'He must be in there.'

'Um.' Red squinted as he surveyed the place.

'Look for possible entry points,' said Hope. 'Probably one of the balconies. Those might not be locked. But there aren't any trees near the building, so we'll have to scale the side.'

'Um, Hope?' Red's voice was barely above a whisper.

'Of course that means we'll have to wait until nightfall. I hate to give him that time. He could easily slip away by then. We could try to find somewhere to keep watch, but there's so little cover around here. And he could wait until dark, conceivably slipping away at the same time we're breaking in . . .' She frowned. It was not an ideal setup at all.

'Hope,' said Red.

'What is it?' she snapped a little more impatiently than she'd intended.

'Judging by the directions Thoriston gave me, I think . . . that's Pastinas Manor.'

It took Hope a second to make the connection. The name Pastinas sounded familiar. It was his mother's surname.

'That's your grandfather's house?'

'Yeah,' he said quietly.

She tried to assess what it meant for him to be at his ancestral home, uninvited, and possibly unwanted. There was a faint look of dread on his face as he stood there with his eyes fixed on the mansion in the distance.

'Well?' she asked. 'What do you want to do?'

He turned to her slowly, as if coming out of a trance. 'What do you mean?'

'No oath made in friendship can override the familial bond. If your family is harboring the biomancer, they are in my way. It won't stop me, but I understand if it stops you. I . . .' She paused, selfishly not wanting to continue, but knowing it was the right thing to do. 'I release you from your oath.'

His brow furrowed as he looked at her. 'Family?' Then he spat. 'That isn't my pissing family. Sadie and Old Yammy are my family. Filler and Nettles are my family.' He held out his hand to her. 'You are more my family than any of these lacies, blood be damned. Keen?'

Unfamiliar emotions weltered up inside Hope. No one had called her 'family' in a long time. She looked into Red's fierce ruby eyes and realized that he was the best, most important person in her life.

She took his warm, gloved hand in hers and squeezed. 'Thank you.'

The two of them stood there, hands clasped, and stared at each other, neither able to find the words that might come next.

'I say, there, fronzies! Watch out!'

Hope and Red leapt apart as a large clanking jumble of metal and wood on wheels zoomed past. A young man sat on top of the pile, yanking levers and pressing down on pedals, a panicked expression on his face. The contraption continued on a little further, then spun around sharply and tipped over with a crash.

Hope and Red got to their feet, watching the pile of machinery warily. A moment later, the man jumped up from the wreckage, his eyes a little wild. He had long dark hair that was now only partly pulled back in a ponytail. The rest was a curtain that covered half his face. He wore the elegant finery of the uptown class, except the jacket was torn, and there were black smudges all over his pants. But the thing that struck Hope the most was that he looked so much like Red, he could have been his older brother.

'Is everyone alright?' he demanded, stumbling free of the pile. 'I have some slight medical knowledge. If I can be of any assistance, I should be very glad of it.'

Red seemed to assess the situation in a second, then his eyes locked on Hope's. 'Oh dear!' he said in a fairly good imitation of the young man's lacy tone. 'I fear my companion may have injured her leg in the fall!'

Hope had no talent for performance, but she did her best to look pained and hold on to her ankle.

'My goodness, but this is awful!' exclaimed the man. 'You must come inside at once so I can tend to your injury!'

'Very kind indeed, but we'd hate to be such a nuisance,' said Red, finding more confidence in the lacy speech.

'Nonsense, I insist!' He hurried over to Hope. 'My name is Alash Havolon, and it would be an embarrassment to my name if I didn't care for an injured lady. And may I have the honor of your name?'

'My name is Bleak Hope.' Only after she said it did it occur to her that she should have used a fake name. One that sounded a little more lacy and not known by Teltho Kan.

'A troubling name for such a lovely lady.' Alash reached for her right hand, but found that it was holding a sword. He stared at it for a moment, his expression openly shocked.

'And I'm Rixidenteron,' Red said quickly, grasping his hand and shaking it vigorously. 'Is this your estate?'

'Actually, my grandfather is the head of Pastinas Manor,' said Alash.

'Do tell!' Red's expression gave no indication that he'd just learned he was talking to his cousin. 'We were passing by and stopped to admire it.'

'I'm smitten you like it!' said Alash, brushing his hair back out of his face. Unlike Red, his eyes were a light gray.

'Oh yes. Clearly the finest in the area,' said Red. 'A pleasure to behold.'

'Perhaps once we have seen to Miss Hope's injuries, you would like a tour?'

Red smiled triumphantly. 'That would be marvelous.'

'Excellent!' Alash held his elbow out to Hope. 'Please permit me to escort you in, Miss Hope.'

'Sure.' She tentatively reached out and took hold of his elbow.

He gave her a confused look.

'Miss Hope is not familiar with our customs,' said Red. 'She's from the Southern Isles, you know.'

'Damned if you say!' gasped Alash.

'Have no fear of her, though,' said Red, really warming into his role now. 'Despite what you may have heard, the Southerners are not all cannibals.'

Alash laughed, his voice like a clear bell. 'I *had* heard such tales.' He took Hope's arm and slipped it through his so they interlocked. 'But I never believe such ignorant nonsense. I am a man of science, you see.'

He held his arm stiff so that she could put weight on it. That was a fortunate prompt, because after being nearly accused of cannibalism, Hope had almost forgotten that she should be limping.

'I will not make any more assumptions, Miss Hope,' he continued, 'but shall strive my utmost to make you feel as comfortable as possible, being so far from home.'

Hope glanced over her shoulder at Red, who wore an amused grin. There was something else in his gaze, though.

It seemed almost like jealousy. But he gave her an encouraging nod and gestured for her to go with it.

'You are very kind,' Hope said quietly as she and Alash began walking slowly up the path toward the manor entrance.

'Forgive me if this is too bold, Miss Hope,' said Alash. 'But is it customary for a Southern lady to carry a sword?'

'Yes,' she said, surprising herself with the easiness of the lie. Perhaps she was warming to her role as well. 'All Southern ladies of a certain age must be armed. The isles are not as peaceful as this place.'

'It seems cumbersome to always have it in hand,' Alash said sympathetically.

'We normally belt the sheath to our side. But your Northern clothes don't have a place for it.'

'So this is not even your native garb?' He seemed utterly fascinated. Hope suspected that Alash was starved for anything outside his own limited experience.

'No, it's not,' she said truthfully.

He frowned thoughtfully. 'Well, I think we should be able to figure some way for you to wear it comfortably. I'm quite clever, you see.'

Red made a quiet choking sound behind them.

'You said you are a man of science?' asked Hope.

'Indeed! It is my passion! Science of all kinds. Mechanical, natural, philosophical. I'm smitten with it all!'

'What was that machine you were riding?' asked Hope.

'Ah, that!' Alash beamed. 'I call it a pedal carriage. It relies on a system of gears, rather like a clock, only much larger. This system allows one to make the carriage move simply by pedaling, without any need of horses!'

'How's the steering?' asked Red cheerfully.

'Yes.' Alash's cheeks flushed slightly. 'As you witnessed, the steering is not quite ready.'

'Or the brakes,' said Red.

'That as well,' admitted Alash. Then he patted Hope's hand. 'But I assure you, Miss Hope, this is the way of science. Trial and error and refinement, day after day, until it is perfected!'

'That is the way of *all* things, not just science,' said Hope.

'Oh!' said Alash. 'You are clearly a practitioner of the science of philosophy! I did not realize they had such studies in the South, but I am glad to hear it. The world would be much improved if we all took the time for philosophical speculation.'

'I agree.' Hope found herself smiling. There was something artlessly charming about Red's cousin. A bright exuberance she had seen only in children. In many ways, he seemed the exact opposite of Red. Sweet, guileless, and without pretense.

As he led her across the rolling meadow to the stately Pastinas Manor, she felt a pang of regret that she was bringing violence within its walls.

No. They were harboring the vile biomancer, Teltho Kan. Alash might well be innocent. But someone in that place was not.

Alash led them through the lush gardens that encircled the home and up the imposing stone steps to the front door. 'Here we are, then. Welcome to Pastinas Manor!'

The thick, dark wood doors were carved with intricate designs of fish and otters painted with accents of gold. He threw them open to reveal a large room with gleaming white floors, thick rugs, and delicately decorated sculpture hanging from every wall. In the center of the room was a grand staircase that swept up to the next level. At the top of the stairs, a giant portrait of an old man with thin black hair and a neck like a lizard gazed down balefully at them.

'That's Grandfather,' said Alash. 'And yes, he *is* that dour, I'm afraid.' He patted Hope's hand, still hooked through his arm. 'Perhaps we should head to my workshop, where I can attend to your injury and fashion some small contrivance to hold your sword, Miss Hope.'

'That would be greatly appreciated, Alash,' said Hope.

Alash opened a small door off to one side that led to a narrow hallway. The plainness and economy of the hallway was in stark contrast to the front room, and Hope wondered why it was so different. At the end of the hall was a room with a bare wood floor and worktables along the walls. The room was strewn with metal gears, leather straps, sheets of waxed canvas, small pieces of wood, and odd little mechanical objects.

'Apologies for the mess,' Alash said absently as he bent down next to one of the piles and pulled out a wooden box. 'Miss Hope, I must ask you to sit on this stool. I'm terribly sorry I don't have anything more comfortable.'

'It's fine, thank you.' Hope sat on the short, wooden stool and watched as he pulled a bandage from his box.

'I confess, I am more at home with mechanical sciences than medical ones,' said Alash as he knelt down in front of her. 'But as you saw, my mechanical experiments frequently lead to injury. Usually my own. So I have some experience with a turned ankle.' He held up the bandage. 'If you will permit me to wrap this around the injured ankle, the additional support should give you some relief and speed up your recovery.'

Alash's hands were rough and calloused from his work with machinery. But his touch was gentle as he slowly wrapped Hope's ankle in the soft cotton bandage. Out of the corner of her eye, she saw Red shifting his weight back and forth. She wondered what he was feeling, now that he was actually inside his ancestral home.

'That should do it.' Alash stood up and packed his wooden box of medical supplies away. 'Now to find you a suitable means of securing your sword.'

'It really is a workshop,' remarked Hope as she watched him rummage around in the piles of material.

'Naturally.'

'I suppose I wasn't expecting to see something so . . .'

'Honest?' Red gave her a smirk.

She ignored him. She suspected he was making these little jabs at his cousin to relieve his own discomfort at being in this place. But if he wasn't careful, he might alienate Alash too much.

'Oh yes.' Alash chuckled good-naturedly. 'My family tolerates my passion, but only just. It is, as Rixidenteron suggests, a bit too much like honest labor for their tastes. I must confine it to this room, and I am never to bring guests . . .' He trailed off, looking suddenly first at Hope, then Red. 'Oh drown it all! What a terrible host I am! I rarely have guests. Well, never, actually. So I haven't had any practice at this. But of course you'd much prefer to see the nice parts of the house!'

'Actually, I think it's likely that this will be my favorite room,' said Hope. 'Southerners appreciate rooms – or anything, really – that have a purpose.'

'You are too kind.' Alash turned away, his face reddening.

'Right, well, shall we get on with it?' said Red brusquely.

'Even so!' said Alash, and went back to rooting through his piles of junk.

'Do you have any other guests here right now?' asked Hope in what she hoped was a casual tone.

'Oh yes.' Alash nodded absently. 'People come in and out all the time. My grandfather knows a lot of people. It's nothing to do with me, though, so I pay it little mind. Ah!' He held up a pair of odd-looking flat-nosed pliers and a few thin strips of leather. 'This should do nicely.' He walked over to Hope. 'Would you kindly lift your arms?'

She watched as he wove the thin leather straps into a long, narrow web, attaching it to a longer strip of leather that encircled her waist.

'There we are.' Alash stepped back and examined his handiwork. 'Let me know how it feels.'

Hope slid the sheath through the leather weave and let it hang at her side. 'It distributes the weight nicely. It keeps it at my side and out of the way without confining my movements.'

'If I had better materials, I could make it more ornate.'

'No, I prefer this.' She gave him a full smile. 'You are just as clever as you said.'

'Do you think so?' asked Alash, his face lighting up. 'Take a look at this, then! I've been longing to show it to someone who might appreciate it.' He picked up a leather sleeve with a metal tube attached to the bottom of it. 'This is something I recently completed. You strap it on like so.' He slid it over his hand so that it covered his arm up to the elbow. The metal tube ran along the bottom of his forearm. Hope examined it closely and saw that there were small springs attached to the sides and little wires and pulleys.

Alash held out his arm. 'Now watch. When I twist my wrist just so . . .' He rotated his hand at an angle. A small pole popped out of the tube, extending a foot past his fingertips.

'Very interesting,' said Hope.

'But wait!' said Alash, looking absolutely giddy now. He pulled a tiny lever on the side of the sleeve, and the pole retracted back into the tube. 'It resets itself so that it can pop in and out as often as you like.'

'Remarkable,' said Hope.

'Yes, indeed!' said Red, his enthusiasm sounding a bit sarcastic to Hope. 'But what is it actually for?'

'For?' asked Alash, blinking.

'Yes, as Miss Hope said, Southerners do like things to have a *purpose*,' he said lightly.

'Well . . . I hadn't really . . . The pole comes out with quite a bit of force. So I suppose you could use it to . . . poke holes in things? While building . . . things? Perhaps?' He smiled weakly.

'Regardless, I'm sure someone will find a use for it.' Hope gave Red an angry look. She was doing everything to make Alash feel inclined to help them, and Red seemed to be doing the opposite.

He winced, his eyes fixed guiltily on the floor.

'Right you are, Miss Hope. Such a clever design like that, I'm sure better minds than mine will have thought of ten different uses for it.'

'Do you think so?' asked Alash earnestly. 'I tinker around all day, never sure if anything I do will ever truly amount to anything. Mr. Kan says I should stop wasting my time and learn a practical skill.'

'Mr. *Kan*?' asked Hope, unable to prevent an edge coming to her voice.

'Do you know him?' asked Alash.

'Yes.' Her voice was as dark and thick as tar.

'Is he a . . . friend of yours?' asked Alash.

'No.' After Hope said it, she realized that if Alash liked Kan, everything she'd been trying to do up until now would have been for nothing. But there were some lies she simply could not bring herself to tell.

Alash smiled with obvious relief. 'Well found! Feels like spiders are crawling up my back every time I see him. He's forever trying to convince me to join the imperial administration in Stonepeak.'

'But you refused?' asked Hope.

'My father joined when I was ten years old. At Mr. Kan's suggestion.' He paused and began fiddling with the contraption still attached to his arm. 'We buried him a year later.'

'I'm sorry to hear that,' said Hope.

A bitter smile played across Alash's lips. All of his lacy frivolity had evaporated. 'They say it is a great honor to die in the emperor's service. But I saw nothing except the tears my mother and I shed for his loss. And when a man dies before he has served out his sworn tenure to the emperor, he has a debt, which must be paid in the money and property he leaves behind. We lost my father's fortune and estate. If Grandfather had not taken us in, I don't know what would have happened to us.'

It had never occurred to Hope that the rich could suffer from the cruelty of the emperor just like everyone else.

'I don't know why I told you all that,' Alash said quietly. 'I just . . . have so few friends. And you seem kind.'

Hope's heart went out to him. A beggar in a house of plenty, living in fear of the day his angry old grandfather tired of keeping him around. It seemed a lonely life, stuck in here with nothing but machines to keep him company. It made her feel even worse that they were lying to him. She found a strong urge to tell him everything. Perhaps she wasn't cut out for deception like this after all.

But then it was Red who put his hand on Alash's shoulder and said in his own voice, 'I misjudged you, my wag. That's a terrible sad story.'

Alash looked at him in surprise. He opened his mouth to say something, but then an older female voice came from a nearby room. 'Alash Havolon, what is that pile of rubbish doing out on the lawn?'

Alash winced. 'Coming, Mother!' He looked at them. 'Who *are* you people, really?'

'Why don't we go see your mother?' said Red. 'I'll bet she can tell you.'

26

*W*hen Red saw his aunt, it took his breath away. She looked so much like his mother. Older, of course. Neat and fine in her elegant lacy gown compared to his mother's flowing dresses and paint-stained smocks. And instead of his mother's mischievous grin, his aunt had a hard set to her face. But in a thousand little ways and mannerisms, she was exactly the same.

Alash had led them into a formal sitting room with plush sofas and tables made of gold and frosted glass. His aunt Minara sat in a chair, gazing disapprovingly out a window while she sipped her tea. He remembered when he was very young, she would sneak down to visit his mother, even though her father had forbidden it. She was the one who had brought the expensive medicine that had helped save his life.

'Uh, Mother.' Alash glanced nervously at Red and Hope. 'I have some guests I'd like you to meet.'

'Guests? You?' she asked, still staring out the window. 'I really wish you wouldn't leave your contraptions strewn across the lawn like that.'

'Their names are Hope and Rixidenteron.'

'Did you say—' She turned to face them. The teacup slipped from her hands and landed on the rug with a muted clatter. 'Those eyes . . .' She slowly stood up, her gaze never leaving him.

'Mother?' asked Alash. 'Are you okay?'

'It can't be . . . after so long.'

'Hello, Aunt Minara,' Red said quietly.

'Aunt?' asked Alash.

Red hadn't been sure how she would react. After all, he hadn't seen her since he was six years old. He'd considered outright rejection, of course. Ignorance, feigned or real. He'd even fantasized a restrained pleasure at seeing him. But the one scenario he honestly had never considered was a hysterical, sobbing, smothering embrace.

'You poor, cursed boy, where have you been, how have you survived, how did you find us, why have you come?' It came out in one long burst that he couldn't answer even if he wanted to because his face was mashed into her silk-covered shoulder. Finally she released him. 'You've gotten so big.'

'It's been a long time,' he said.

She put her ring-covered fingers on his cheek. 'You've become quite handsome. Just like your father.' She looked appraisingly at his clothes. 'It appears you've done well for yourself.' She frowned. 'Although you need to get a new tailor. The fit on this jacket is atrocious.'

'They're, uh, not actually mine,' he admitted. 'I borrowed them.'

'Borrowed clothes?' she asked, like it was the most bizarre thing she'd ever heard of.

'From some gaf named Thoriston.'

'Thoriston? Oh, dear God.' She rolled her eyes. 'Is he *still* obsessed with your mother?'

'He's hosting a show of her artwork at Bayview Gallery, so I suppose he is,' said Red.

'Why on earth did you borrow clothes from him, though?' she asked.

'Because my regular clothes wouldn't be fine enough for a place like this.'

She gave him a pained look. 'Did you become a whore like your father?'

'Uh, no.' Red was having a hard time keeping his composure. It was like she instinctually knew which questions were the most uncomfortable for him.

'Well, thank God for that.' But then she gave him another worried look. 'Oh, dear, you didn't become a *painter*, did you?' Red couldn't tell if that was better or worse than whoring in his aunt's eyes.

'Red – Rixidenteron is a well-respected and highly valued member of his community,' said Hope.

Aunt Minara's gray eyes focused on her. 'And who is this solemn creature? Your beloved?'

'A, uh, good friend,' said Red. It was just one sharp point after another with his aunt, though he was nearly certain she wasn't doing it on purpose.

Aunt Minara moved over to her. 'Yes, I can see why. But there's a great deal of potential in you, my dear. Really, brighter colors, a touch of makeup, and a more fetching hairstyle would work wonders to catch a man.'

'I won't need those things to catch the man I'm after,' Hope said grimly.

'Eh, Mother dear, Hope is from the Southern Isles. I don't think it's customary for them to wear makeup.'

'The Southern Isles!' Alash's reaction to the same information had been fascination. But Minara backed quickly away instead. Red was beginning to see why Alash spent most of his time hiding in a workshop with machines.

'She won't infect you with barbarianism,' Red said acidly.

'She's quite intelligent and sweet, I can assure you, Mother,' added Alash.

Red wasn't sure about the sweet part, but thought it best not to argue.

Aunt Minara didn't look completely convinced, but she cautiously approached Hope again. 'Yes, of course. The colorless hair. The pale skin. I should have known.' She looked Hope over more carefully. 'Are all Southern women as thin as you? You look as underfed as Rixidenteron's mother.' She sighed. 'I suppose that's why they call them starving artists, isn't it? You're not an artist, are you?'

'No,' Hope said quietly, her hand opening and closing next to her sword as if she longed to draw it.

'Yes, I expect they don't really have culture down in the Southern Isles,' said Minara.

'Mother dear,' Alash said quickly. 'Perhaps we should invite my long-lost cousin and his friend to dinner?'

She chewed worriedly on her lip. 'Did your grandfather say when he would be done with his meeting?'

'He said he didn't expect to be done until quite late.'

'I suppose it would be fine if they stayed for dinner, then. But they'll need to leave after that.' She turned to Red. 'I'm sorry, my darling boy. It would make your grandfather terribly cross to find you here. Now if you'll excuse me, I must go tell the cook to set a few more places.' She swept elegantly out of the room.

'Sorry about that,' said Alash as he settled into one of the chairs. 'She's terrified of Grandfather. Convinced he'll throw us out at the slightest provocation.'

'Would he?' asked Hope.

'I don't know,' admitted Alash. 'Honestly, I didn't even know I *had* a cousin until this moment.'

'But you're older than Red,' said Hope. 'Wouldn't you have heard of his birth at least?'

'I confess that all I've ever heard about Aunt Gulia is that she was wild and reckless,' said Alash. 'That she caused a lot of embarrassment for the family. Grandfather was greatly relieved when she ran away to Silverback to become an artist. And we never spoke of her again after that.'

Red moved to the window, not wanting to look at anyone else. He gazed out at the meadows, watching the fireflies light up as the sky darkened. 'After my mom died, a man came to visit. He was dressed in a nice suit. Like this one.' He plucked at his own clothes. Suddenly he didn't like them as much. 'The man offered my father money in exchange for signing a paper that said I was not related to the Pastinas family. That I was *not* the son of Lady Gulia Pastinas.'

'Damned if you say,' said Alash. 'That's horrible.'

'It was the only time I ever saw my father angry,' said Red. 'He didn't say a word. But his face twisted up and he punched the man in the face. The man left, clutching his unsigned papers in one hand, and his bleeding nose in the other.'

'And your grandfather sent that man?' asked Hope. 'Why would he do that?'

'When my mom died, old man Pastinas wanted to sweep all her mistakes away so none would come back to haunt him. And top of the list of mistakes was me.'

'You Northerners talk about being more civilized,' said Hope. 'But in my home village, a grandparent would never disown a grandchild.'

'It must be a kind place, your village,' said Alash.

'It was,' said Hope.

'Do you still have family there?'

'No. They're all dead.' Her voice was little more than a whisper.

Red didn't know how she was able to restrain herself from grabbing Alash and demanding to know where Teltho Kan was. He had to be somewhere in this mansion. Probably with his grandfather. Red couldn't help but admire her control.

He reached out and took her hand. She tensed up for a moment, but then nodded and gave his hand a gentle squeeze. It would be over soon. Then they could get out of this beautiful, airless house.

They sat down to dinner at a long table covered in a pure white cloth. Servants appeared as if out of nowhere and brought a steaming roast, platters of fresh fruits and vegetables, bread and cheese. The smell of the savory soup alone almost made Red swoon. It had been a day since he and Hope had eaten, and a lifetime since he'd had such fine cuisine. He and Hope attacked their plates with ferocity.

After a few minutes of shoveling in food, he noticed the silence from the other side of the table. He glanced up. Aunt Minara and Alash were staring at them in something very near disgust. Red nudged Hope with his elbow. She stopped and looked over at him.

'I think we're, uh, not using proper table manners,' he said under his breath.

'Oh,' said Hope. 'I read a book on upper-class etiquette, but it was a long time ago. I don't remember much. What should I be doing?'

'You think I know?' asked Red. 'Maybe if we just slow down.'

Hope nodded and sat up a little straighter in her seat.

'So, Rixidenteron.' Aunt Minara still looked a little put off, but was clearly trying to get past it. 'What *are* you doing here?'

'What, I can't visit my lacy uptown family now and then?' he asked. He kept his tone light, but there was a real challenge in it.

'Of course, my dear,' she said quickly. 'But after all this time, I just wondered if you were in trouble. Or perhaps needed money?'

'I don't want your money,' he said coldly.

'Miss Hope,' Alash said quickly. 'What brought you up from the Southern Isles?'

'I grew up in a very remote place. I'd read a great deal about the world, but that's not the same thing as experiencing it. So I joined a ship's crew and explored it for myself.'

'Marvelous,' said Alash wistfully. 'I would love to sail the seas. See the world.'

'Why don't you, then?' asked Red.

'It's not really possible,' he said.

'Why not?' pressed Red.

'Well . . .' said Alash, looking doubtful.

'What would be the point?' cut in Aunt Minara. 'Everything he needs is right here. His place is at Pastinas Manor. Someday he will be the sole inheritor of the estate.'

'I do have a responsibility to this place,' Alash said. 'And of course to my poor widowed mother.'

'I don't know, she seems to be getting on alright,' said Red.

'It's bad enough he spends all his time with those damned machines instead of participating in the social events of his peers,' said Aunt Minara. 'Please don't go filling his head with adventures at sea.'

'Furthest thing from my mind, Auntie.' Red gave her a winning smile.

Aunt Minara's stern countenance grudgingly melted into a smile of her own. 'You are so much like your mother. Charmingly incorrigible.' She dabbed at her eyes with a fine silk handkerchief. 'I'm . . . glad you came to visit.'

'Surely we're not going to send them out into the night after dinner, Mother,' said Alash.

'But your grandfather . . .' Her face creased with worry.

'You know how he is,' said Alash. 'He could be locked away for days.'

Minara chewed on her lip. 'I *suppose*. But we must put them in the north wing, so there's no chance of him coming across them.'

Alash looked apologetically at Hope. 'The north wing is a bit cramped, I'm afraid.'

'I can sleep on the floor if need be,' said Hope.

'Oh heavens!' said Aunt Minara. 'The floor? Perhaps that's what they do in the Southern Isles, but we are not barbarians. Alash just means there's no four-poster on the bed, and the bath is at the end of the hall rather than in your room.' She turned to Red, giving him a searching look. 'And unless you two are married, I expect different rooms.'

Red watched Hope blush, then grinned at Minara. 'Naturally, my dear aunt. Wouldn't want a scandal under the Pastinas roof, would we?'

She tried to suppress another smile, and shook her finger scoldingly at him.

'Excuse me, Lady Havolon,' said Hope. 'When you say "bath," do you mean a bathing tub?'

'Yes, of course,' said Aunt Minara. 'After all that travel, I expect you'll want an extra-long one tonight. I'll have the servants heat the water as soon as we've finished eating.'

'A *hot* bath?' asked Hope. It seemed to Red that she might be near tears.

'I certainly wouldn't expect you to take a *cold* bath, dear,' said Aunt Minara.

Hope gave an audible sigh. 'A hot bath would be marvelous, Lady Havolon.'

*   *   *

While Hope went up to enjoy her hot bath, and Aunt Minara retired for the night, Alash and Red sat in yet another finely furnished room, this one smaller and a little more darkly colored with stuffed leather furniture. A fireplace crackled in one wall.

'This is the manly lacy room, is it?' he asked as Alash handed him a small glass of something brown.

Alash smiled slightly as he settled into the chair across from him with his own glass. 'We must seem so terribly frivolous to you.'

'All lacies are frivolous,' said Red. 'Not your fault. It's just the way you were raised.'

Alash stared down at his glass, swirling the liquid in it. 'But at a certain point in our lives, we cannot passively allow our upbringing to define us. We must choose it or choose other.' He took a sip.

'More of that science of philosophy you were talking about?' Red took a gulp of his drink and found it much stronger than he'd expected. He forced a smile as his eyes and throat burned.

'I wish I could go on adventures with you and Miss Hope,' Alash said quietly.

'You really could, you know,' said Red. 'But it's not all like it is in books. It can be hard and painful and exhausting. Sometimes you just want to give up.'

'But you don't,' said Alash.

'Because, cousin, the alternative is death.'

They sat for a moment, both of them staring into the fire.

'Still,' said Alash. 'You said it's not all like it is in books. Does that mean sometimes it is?'

Red had intended to make Alash feel better about being cooped up in this rigid, humorless place. But sometimes he was a weak man. Especially when the temptation was to tell a good story. So instead of begging off like he should have, he allowed himself to smile wide, that old gleam in his eyes.

'Would you like to know the story of how Hope and I started a gang war in downtown New Laven?'

When Red retired for the evening to the north wing, he discovered that what Alash had called 'a bit cramped' was nicer than any room Red had ever seen. The bed had a wrought-iron frame and a thick mattress, a pile of blankets, and so many pillows, Red wondered if there was some danger of suffocating among them. Near the bed was a window that overlooked the grounds, and a small writing desk complete with paper and ink. Red thought it would be funny to write a note to the wags back in Paradise Circle. *Hello, fronzies! Just taking a quick break from things downtown. Pastinas Manor is simply delightful!*

But since none of them could read, he realized it would only be funny to him.

There was a knock at his door. He opened it and saw Hope. Her hair was wet and hung in thick clumps to her shoulders, and her pale face and neck were scrubbed clean. She wore a long red silk robe even more elegant than the maidservant dress she'd worn that day.

He grinned. 'That color suits you.'

She gave him a tolerant smile. 'Your aunt gave it to me.' She sat down at the edge of the bed. 'How long do you think we should wait?'

'For your biomancer to show himself?' asked Red. 'Hard to say. I know this can't be easy for you. Honestly, I'm amazed you're even sane by this point, having to make polite dinner conversation while the man who murdered your parents is under the same roof.'

'It wasn't easy,' she admitted. 'But the bath helped.'

'I never pegged you for one of those bathing zealots,' said Red.

'There was a hot spring at the monastery, so we bathed nearly every day. It became a very soothing activity for me, especially when I was bruised and sore from my training. You should try it.'

'What, tonight?' he asked.

She shrugged. 'The water is still warm. It would be a shame to waste it.'

'I'll think about it,' he said. 'Anyway, back to your biomancer.'

'Teltho Kan.' Her face hardened immediately. 'We can assume he is meeting with your grandfather?'

'I'd say so. We either wait until they're done, or we go looking for them, with or without the help of my aunt and cousin.'

'I would prefer not to upset them or put them in danger,' said Hope. 'It might be better if you keep them occupied while I go searching for Teltho Kan on my own.'

'Without my help?' Red tried to keep the hurt out of his voice, but judging by the way she looked at him, it didn't work.

'You have helped me so much already.' She reached out and laid her pale hand on his. 'This fight is mine alone. I will try to keep your grandfather safe as well.'

'I'm not too worried about that part,' said Red. 'I just . . .' He put his hands on her shoulders, feeling the taut muscles through the thin silk robe. 'You can't leave me behind.'

'I don't plan to,' she said.

'Not even to death. Keen?'

'I can't promise that.'

'You can promise you won't do the deed yourself.'

'Red, I—'

'It's not that hard a thing I'm asking.' Red pulled her closer, his eyes boring into hers. 'Don't pissing kill yourself.'

'But what if—'

'You won't fail. Because if this doesn't work, we'll find another way. We'll just keep trying. Me and you, Red and Hope. No matter what, we won't give up. Ever.'

Hope looked like she was about to say something, but it died in her throat. She nodded her head. 'I promise.' Then she wrinkled her nose. 'As long as you promise to take a bath. Right now.'

The next morning Red put on his regular clothes with relief. There was little point in the pretext, and if things went leeward, he might have need of his throwing blades. He found that sometime during the night, someone had washed his shirt and breeches and left them hanging up next to his bed. At first he found that a little alarming, but he had to admit there was little point in taking a bath, then putting on dirty clothes. The bath he'd taken the night before hadn't been too bad either. It seemed like a lot of trouble, though, just to soak in some hot water.

He also found a tray with breakfast next to his bed when he woke. Warm bread, sausage, and a boiled egg. Eating this early seemed a bit unnatural to him, but he wasn't sure when his next meal would be, so he wolfed it down anyway.

When he went down to the sitting room, he saw Hope had put on her leather armor. It looked clean of bloodstains, and shinier than before, though. He wondered if she'd somehow gotten ahold of leather polish.

Aunt Minara came in, wearing a large poufy green gown, followed by Alash in a more understated gray frockcoat and cravat. Minara eyed Hope and Red. 'Is this what you usually wear *downtown*?'

'Style is a bit different down there,' said Red, turning up the collar on his leather longcoat.

'Yes, of course.' Aunt Minara walked over and pulled his collar back down, then buttoned his shirt all the way up. She turned to Hope. 'Not even a dress, dear? I can certainly find one that should fit you.'

'Thank you, Lady Pastinas,' said Hope. 'But this armor is far more practical for my purposes, and it was crafted by the man who raised me from girlhood, so it holds a great deal of meaning for me.'

Aunt Minara sighed. 'I trust you've eaten?'

'Yes, thank you,' said Hope.

'Then I think we've tempted fate long enough. You should be off before my father discovers you.'

'Discovers who?' came a weak, nasally voice behind Red.

Aunt Minara froze for a moment, then a smile popped onto her face. 'Why, hello, Father!' Without moving her mouth, she hissed only loud enough for Red to hear: '*Close your eyes. Keep them closed.*'

Red closed his eyes, and she spun him around to face the voice.

'This poor blind boy that Alash found wandering around outside,' said Aunt Minara. 'Isn't that right, dear?'

'Right it is!' said Alash. 'Sorry, Grandfather. I injured his caretaker with one of my confounded machines, you know. Felt terrible about it and brought them inside.'

'Yes, and I know how you *hate* to be in the presence of those with afflictions,' said Minara. 'I thought he might upset you. I was just telling Alash to get rid of them so you wouldn't have to look upon him.'

'I see. How considerate of you,' said Grandfather Pastinas. The old man's tone was so careful, Red couldn't read a thing into it. If he could just see the wrink's expression, he'd know. Until this moment, he'd never realized how much he'd relied on visual cues to gauge people.

'It is ever a daughter's duty to consider her father,' said Aunt Minara. 'Now, Alash, why don't you take—'

'And who is this . . . striking young woman in black with him?' asked Pastinas. 'Judging by her coloring, I would guess she is from the Southern Isles.'

'Oh yes, Grandfather!' said Alash. 'She is the boy's guide and protector. Did you know, Southern ladies are expected to wear swords? And that they are not in the habit of wearing dresses?'

'So I see,' said Pastinas. 'That would explain why the young woman is wearing a sword in my home.'

'Of course, Father,' said Aunt Minara. 'We didn't want to offend her.'

'Again your consideration becomes you,' said Pastinas. 'However, what has *not* been explained yet is why you think I wouldn't recognize my own daughter's bastard simply because I cannot see his telltale red eyes.'

Red's eyes snapped open and saw his grandfather for the first time. A gaunt wrink with watery eyes and a sneer on his thin lips. His white hair stuck up in odd places, and he had a slight tremor in his hand. Red was still waiting for the scary part.

'This son of a whore is not welcome in my house, or on my property, or within a hundred miles of me!' said the old man, his face screwed up petulantly. 'I have allowed him to exist as long as he did not trouble me. It seems I have been too lenient!'

'No, Father! Please!' begged Aunt Minara as she clutched Red to her. 'He's just a boy.'

'Don't hurt him!' pleaded Alash.

'Silence!' yelled Pastinas. '*I* will decide his fate, now that he dares to come here and make some claim to this family. Punishment—'

'I'm sorry, can we go back a moment?' asked Red, stepping away from his aunt's embrace. 'What was that bit about you deciding my fate?'

'*I* am the—'

'Rhetorical question,' said Red. 'There is only one wag in all the world who decides my fate and that's me, keen? Furthermore, there is nothing in this family I want to claim. The only useful thing I've witnessed here is my clever cousin, who seems to get nothing but jape for his quality. I've made it this far without your pissing money, and I don't reckon I need it now.'

The old man stared at him in such shock that Red suspected no one had ever talked to him like that in his life. Maybe it was petty, but that made him feel real sunny.

'Then why,' Pastinas said through gritted teeth, 'are you here?'

Red saw Hope put her hand on the pommel of her sword. Did she think it was going to come to that? Surely she didn't expect this old man to attack them. He was nothing but bluster. But then he realized her eyes kept darting to the hallway behind the old man, and that the pommel of the sword was quivering faintly on its own.

'Drown it all, Pastinas!' A voice that crackled like fire came from the hallway. 'We have precious little time! Must you get bogged down in family bickering right at . . .'

A man in a hooded white robe with gold trim stepped into the room. He had his hood up, but Red could see that he had a burn mark on his face. He was focused on Pastinas at first, but when his eyes swept the rest of the room, he froze.

Red heard the hiss of steel as Hope drew her sword.

Teltho Kan grabbed Pastinas roughly by the arm and pulled him in front as a shield. He held his bare hand next to the old man's withered face.

'One touch, girl.' The biomancer's eyes were locked on Hope. 'You well know that's all it would take to send this man to a painful and lingering death.'

'To answer your question, Grandfather,' said Red dryly. '*He's* the reason we're here.'

'Let him go, Kan.' Hope's sword quivered, the tip pointing at him as if straining to leap from her hands. The blood magic hungered for its target.

'Mr. Kan, I demand to know the meaning of this!' screamed the old man shrilly.

Teltho Kan ignored him, keeping his gaze focused solely on Hope. 'I confess, while I expected you to track me down again, I did not think it would be *this* quickly. I have underestimated you once again. But I assure you, it will be the last time I do so.'

'Because there won't be another time,' said Hope, inching closer, her blade gleaming in the sunlight that filtered through the window. 'You can't hold him and make another jump at the same time.'

'True,' admitted the biomancer. 'But I have something else in mind. Something I've prepared expressly for you.'

He whistled shrilly. It was answered by a strange clicking roar from outside the mansion. Hope's eyes narrowed suspiciously.

Teltho Kan smiled. 'An old friend of yours, I think.'

Red saw it a second before it hit – a dark, massive shape outside the window. He had just enough time to pull his aunt to the ground before the glass exploded in a storm of shards. The shape launched through the window and into a sofa, breaking it to pieces. It lurched to its feet, and Red saw that it was Ranking, the wag who had sold out Hope and her captain. Or it used to be him. The last time Red saw him, Ranking had been writhing on the floor of the Drowned Rat, clutching at the stump where his hand used to be. Now, instead of a stump, he had a thick brown claw like a scorpion's. He was bigger, too. His skin looked like ill-fitting clothes, baggy in places, torn in others. His eyes were a shiny black, and beneath the long mustache, his mouth was only a ragged hole from which hairy mandibles protruded.

Aunt Minara screamed.

'How dare you bring such a creature into my home!' Pastinas yelled at Teltho Kan.

The biomancer laughed and shoved the old man to the ground.

'Until next time, girl!' he said to Hope. 'Enjoy your playmate.'

'No!' howled Hope. But before she could run after him, the creature was upon her. She had just enough time to slam the sword back into its scabbard before blocking its attack. The claw crunched into the scabbard's wood, inches from her face.

'Draw your pissing sword!' yelled Red.

'I won't lose his trail!' said Hope as she fought off the creature.

'He won't get away.' Red pulled his aunt to her feet, then turned to Alash. 'Get your mother to safety.'

Alash nodded, his face pale as he took his mother's hand.

Red ran for the hallway, leaping over the fallen Pastinas.

'Stop, Red! He'll kill you!' Hope shouted.

But Red was already out of the room. He saw a flicker of white disappear around the corner of the hallway and sprinted after it. As he ran, it dawned on him that he was chasing after a biomancer. As he rounded the corner, he thought, *Am I completely slippy?*

The biomancer was waiting, his hood shadowing his face, his white robe luminous in the dim hallway. Red skidded to a halt.

'Your end is now, fool,' said Teltho Kan as he reached for Red.

But just before his fingertips touched Red's forehead, he stopped.

'Can it be? A survivor?' He slowly drew back his hand. Then he smiled in a way Red did not like at all.

'We will meet again, boy. For now, sleep.'

He blew a puff of air into Red's face, and everything went dark.

27

*F*or the first time in her life, Hope stared into the face of someone she hated and felt pity. Ranking had been many things, most of them bad. But even he didn't deserve being turned into this mindless monstrosity. His dripping mandibles stretched toward her as he pressed his crooked, uneven weight against her. His black, glassy eyes seemed completely devoid of humanity or even thought. The kindest thing she could do for him was put her sword through his head. But she refused to risk losing her one sure way of tracking Teltho Kan.

As she used the sheathed sword to hold back his claw, he pushed her against the wall. She kicked him in the groin, but it didn't feel like there was anything down there, and he didn't react. She punched his bare stomach, but it felt hard and the skin tore away, revealing chitinous insectile armor beneath.

She ripped her sheathed sword free from his claw and slammed the flat wooden end into his eye. The eye caved in with a soft crunch, and dark fluid leaked out. His mandibles clicked furiously, and he took another swipe with his claw. She blocked it again with her sheathed sword, thinking how each moment this creature occupied her, Teltho Kan was farther away. And Red . . .

He'd never have done something so reckless in Paradise Circle. She suspected it was being in this place that had unbalanced him. Surely he knew that he was no match for Teltho Kan. Hope needed to finish this creature quickly so she could save him. But if she drew her sword and stabbed him, would she even be able to find them?

The creature gave another clicking roar and pushed hard against Hope. Her arms were tiring, while the creature seemed to grow stronger the longer they fought. Hope cast around for another weapon, but there was nothing in this fine sitting room that would pierce his hide.

He bore down on her, forcing her to the ground. Then he put his full weight on her. Her arms shook with the strain, and she began to think she would need to unsheathe her sword simply to save her own life.

Then there was a sharp *clang*, and a steel pole protruded from the creature's forehead. Alash stood behind him, his hand stretched out to the back of the creature's head. Alash pulled the lever at his wrist, and the pole retracted back into the pipe on his forearm. The creature shuddered once, then collapsed. Hope rolled the body off her.

'There's a use for it,' she said, then headed for the door.

'Wait, Miss Hope!' said Alash.

As she stepped over the stunned Pastinas, she felt a pang of sadness for Alash, trapped here in this luxurious prison where no one appreciated him. She wished she could have stayed a little longer to be the voice of encouragement he seemed so desperately to need.

'Keep heart, Alash,' she said, then left.

Alash checked on his mother, whom he'd laid down on a sofa in the next room. She was still sobbing and wouldn't speak. Then he went back to the sitting room. He surveyed the wreckage for a moment, taking it in slowly. He had lived in this house since his father died. He had been in this room nearly every day since, and it had never changed. Until today. He found it shocking, not because of the mess, but because in his heart, he had never truly believed that real change of any kind was possible. Until today.

He walked across the room, his half boots quietly crunching on glass. His grandfather seemed to be recovering. When Alash offered his hand, he sneered and batted it away.

'Well, Grandfather,' he said quietly. 'Now who is the one who brought something vile and threatening into this house?'

'How dare you show me such disrespect, boy! It is still my house and my money—'

'Respect?' mused Alash. 'I have always loved you, because you are my grandfather. But I have never respected you. Please take care of Mother. She's always been the one most loyal to you.' Then he stepped over his grandfather and walked toward the doorway.

'Where in all hells are you going?'

'It's time for a change, Grandfather. I'm going to see the world.'

Hope didn't get far before she found Red lying on the hallway floor. Her heart gave a lurch when she saw him there on the rug, motionless. It was everything she feared in one image. The most important person in her life, killed by a biomancer.

But then his chest rose and fell, and she knew that he was still alive.

Of course the biomancer had left him alive. It was a smart delaying tactic. Had Red been dead, Hope would have pursued even faster. But she couldn't simply abandon him here in this house, lorded over by a frightened old man who hated him.

She picked him up and slung him over her shoulders. She'd frequently had to carry a pair of large buckets filled with water on a yoke when she lived at the monastery. Red was heavier, though. It was slow going as she trudged out of the mansion and into the bright grassy meadow, still wet with morning dew.

She didn't know how long she stumbled in the direction her sword pointed, Red draped around her neck like a millstone. The sun blazed down from the bright blue cloudless sky, and the meadows seemed to stretch on forever. Her breath hissed painfully through clenched teeth, and her hair was soaked in sweat.

She imagined she was hearing someone calling her name. She ignored it at first, but it grew louder and more insistent until she began to wonder if it was real. Then Alash ran up from behind, puffing and red faced.

'Miss Hope . . .' he said between gasps of breath. 'May I please . . . accompany you?'

'Why?'

'I want to sail the seas! See the world!'

Hope thought about telling him the world was a terrible place and the seas more deadly than he could imagine. That he would be insane to throw away his life of luxury.

'Perhaps I could carry my cousin for a while?' he suggested.

But *that* sounded to Hope like the best idea ever conceived. She practically threw Red at him.

But Alash groaned under his weight, and his knees immediately began to buckle. 'Oh God, is he ever heavy! I don't . . .'

He looked both pained and ashamed. 'I fear I'm not as strong as you, Miss Hope. I've never been one for athletics.'

Hope sighed. 'Let's try splitting his weight between us, then.' She hooked one arm around her neck.

Alash hooked the other arm around his neck. 'Oh, that's much better, thanks.'

'Then let's go,' grunted Hope. 'We can't let Teltho Kan get away.'

Alash glanced worriedly at Red's lolling head between them. 'Will he be alright?'

'After how long I've carried him? He better be.'

They walked on in silence for a while, broken only by their harsh breaths. After some time, Hope asked, 'Do you know what lies in this direction?'

'A few more homes similar to my grandfather's.'

'That's it?'

'Well, and after that Radiant Harbor, of course.'

'A harbor?' asked Hope, adrenaline wiping away her exhaustion.

'Oh yes. The second-largest port in New Laven.'

'We have to hurry, then.' She picked up their pace.

Alash groaned and the two hurried on.

Teltho Kan was gone. Hope knew it before they even reached the docks. The Song of Sorrows gave an odd shudder, then slowly grew less insistent, as if the target was moving rapidly away. But Hope refused to acknowledge it. She forced herself and Alash to continue onward until they reached the sprawling port of Hollow Falls just before midday.

Merchant ships packed the docks. Sailors were at work, loading and unloading crates. Hope recalled the job Drem had wanted Carmichael to do, and she wondered if there were drugs in any of those crates. Perhaps the drug trade had stopped with Drem's death. Or perhaps someone else had already stepped in.

She lifted her sword, and it pointed unwaveringly out into the harbor and the open sea beyond. The exhaustion came crashing back down on her like a heavy blanket. 'Let's stop for a moment.'

They found a stack of crates and laid Red across them. Alash dropped down to the dock, wheezing and streaked with sweat. Hope tried to wake Red, but he barely stirred. 'Do you have a boat we can use?' she asked Alash.

He shook his head, still trying to catch his breath.

'Any money we can use to get passage on one?'

Again he shook his head.

She stared out at the ships, her jaw clenching and unclenching with a frustration that was turning slowly to impotent rage.

Then she saw her. Three piers down. The *Lady's Gambit*.

'Get up!' she shouted at Alash.

He looked up at her in something close to horror. 'But Miss Hope—'

'Now!' She propped up Red and took one arm.

'Yes, Miss Hope,' Alash said meekly as he took the other arm.

Alash seemed barely able to stay on his feet, but Hope pulled them in an awkward, unsteady gait down to the pier where the *Lady's Gambit* was tied.

Sadie stood at its bow, lit by the morning sun as she gazed out over the water. When Hope saw her, a warmth flooded her chest and she found herself near tears. 'Ahoy!' she called in a trembling voice. 'Captain Sadie! Permission to come aboard!'

Sadie didn't turn to look at them, but she cocked her head to one side and smiled her toothless smile.

'Captain? Not I. You're looking for someone altogether younger and paler than me.' Then she did look down at them and gave them an expression of mock surprise. 'Why, and there you are, Captain Bleak Hope!'

'I don't think I should be the c—'

'Is that my Red there on your arm?' asked Sadie.

'He'll be fine,' said Hope. 'But he's heavy.'

'Well, come on up, then.' She slid the gangplank down to them, squinting as they came aboard. 'And who's that with you? Looks oddly familiar.'

'Red's cousin,' said Hope.

'A pleasure to meet you, madam,' said Alash, mustering up a smile.

'He's a proper lacy sort, ain't he?' Sadie patted his sweat-slick cheek. 'Don't worry, wag, it's all chum and larder for anyone who shares Red's blood.'

'How did you know we'd be here?' asked Hope.

'Old Yammy sent word. She's got the Sight sometimes. A bit vague, though. Just said to come up here, and you'd be along eventually. We've been here nearly two days.'

'Red said she can't really tell the future.'

'Red says a lot of things, don't he? Some of 'em's even true,' said Sadie. 'Now, I assume you're in a hurry?'

'We're chasing a biomancer.'

'You best get Red into the cabins. I'll rouse the rest of the crew.'

'Crew?' asked Hope.

Sadie grinned. 'Oh yes, girl. You don't think I could sail this ship on my own, do you? It's a small crew, to be sure. But me, I always prefer a few reliable wags to an army of cunt-droppings.'

Hope felt as if she were in a dream as she and Alash carried Red's unconscious body along the deck toward the cabins. To be back on this ship was more comforting than she'd expected. As they walked the length of the ship, she noticed many improvements. It was cleaner, all the little cracks had been tarred, and the corroded iron had been burnished until it was shiny once again. Over at the helm, she saw the man whom she guessed was responsible for most of it. 'Missing Finn!'

The old man looked over at her with his one bright eye and smiled with a few more teeth than Sadie.

'Ahoy, Captain Hope!' he called. 'Sadie already told me you was aboard. I'm making the wheel nice and smooth for you!'

'For me?'

'Of course. We've too light a crew to spare you a helmsman.'

'I'm really not sure I'm the best choice for captain.'

Missing Finn held up his big, scarred hands. 'I'm just following orders from the first mate, Captain. You'll have to take it up with Sadie.'

'Do you think we could find a place to put Rixidenteron first?' asked Alash plaintively.

'Yes,' said Hope starting to move toward the cabins again. 'But you should call him Red.'

'He doesn't go by his birth name?'

'No.'

'Why not?'

Hope didn't reply at first. Then she caught sight of a familiar face emerging from the cabins, and she smiled. 'Because that's how it is in the Circle.'

Nettles walked toward them, grinning broadly. 'Hey, angel slice. What's he gone and done this time?'

'Tried to chase down a biomancer.'

'Will he be okay?'

'I think he's just unconscious.'

'Then let me give you a hand with the old salthead.'

As the three of them walked the rest of the way to the cabins, Hope asked, 'How are you? I'm sorry I left when I did.'

'We managed alright. After you chased off that biomancer, the soldiers ran. We braced for another raid, but none came. I expect things are getting back to normal. Or near enough.' She looked at Alash. 'And who's this?'

'Red's cousin,' said Hope.

'Alash Havolon,' he said, smiling more brightly now that some of the load had been taken from him. 'Miss . . .'

'Call me Nettles. I'm no miss or missus neither. Just Nettles. Keen?'

'Keen?' he asked.

'She wants to know if you understand her,' translated Hope.

'Oh. Yes. Well, I suppose I must seem terribly formal to you.'

'Nah, you're alright.' Nettles turned to Hope. 'Not bad on the gander, is he?'

'She thinks you look handsome,' Hope told Alash.

'Oh, er, thanks? And you as well, Miss, er, I mean Nettles.'

'Don't get any ideas, though,' said Nettles. 'Or I'll shove that lacy cock of yours up your own ass.'

Alash only stared at her.

'You get used to it,' said Hope.

They carefully walked Red down the narrow stairs into the cabin.

'What happened?' Filler limped over, leaning heavily on a crutch.

'How is your knee?' asked Hope.

Filler shrugged. ''Bout the same.'

'You'd think he'd want to sit this adventure out. But he wouldn't hear of it,' said Nettles.

Filler looked embarrassed. 'You needed the hands to crew this ship. My leg ain't working, but I can haul on a rope alright. So what happened to Red? Will he be okay?'

'I *think* so,' said Hope. 'I didn't see what Teltho Kan did to him. It seems he just knocked him out to slow me down so he could get away.'

'Which worked,' said Nettles.

'For now. But I have a way to track him, no matter where he runs.'

'So Red'll just wake up and be good as new, right?' asked Filler.

'Probably.' Hope smiled. That's one thing her time on New Laven had taught her. How to lie and smile while doing it. But in this case, it was a kindness. There was no sense in worrying poor Filler any more than necessary. Perhaps Red *would* be fine. Although in Hope's experience, interactions with biomancers were never so simple or so clean.

'Well, Captain, we're ready to set sail,' said Sadie.

She and Hope stood at the helm, the sun shining on the water.

'I think you would be the better choice for captain,' said Hope. 'You've done it before.'

'The time I've been on a boat wouldn't add up to half a year. And I've never been on the open sea. It's yours by right and by plain common sense. If you want to give chase to this biomancer of yours, we're with you. But it's you that's got to take the lead.'

'I've never been a leader.'

'It's not a big group. And you might surprise yourself. Here.' She gestured to the wheel. 'Why don't you take hold of the helm? Maybe the feel of it in your hands will inspire you.'

Hope gripped the wooden pegs like she'd seen Carmichael do countless times. 'I feel foolish.'

'That's just other people's voices in your head tellin' you a woman's got no place as a captain.'

'*You* did it. Red told me the story.'

'And you don't think I felt foolish? That's how it *always* feels when you do something new and bold. You feel as fake as a whore in a temple.'

'So how do you stop feeling that way?'

'You don't at first. You just feel like a fake and do it anyway. But you do it long enough and you don't feel like a fake anymore because you're *not* anymore. Keen? Now, let me hear you call it.'

'Now?'

'Of course.'

Hope took a deep breath. She remembered the way Carmichael would do it. A sound that bellowed from deep within his gut and a tone at once serious and fiercely joyful. 'Look alive, wags! Cast us off! Set sail!'

'Aye, aye, Captain!' called Missing Finn, bless him.

Hope guided the ship through the harbor, and it was as if she could hear Carmichael's voice overlaying her own, his hands guiding hers. Drem and Ranking, the two men who had caused his death, were now dead. But oddly enough, it wasn't their deaths that gave her peace. It was this moment. Sailing his beloved ship, the wind at her back and the sun in the sky. This was what he'd loved best, and she knew he would have been pleased.

As much as the Vinchen code spoke of vengeance for the dead, she wondered why it never mentioned honoring their life.

'Give me full sail!' she called. The *Lady's Gambit* headed out to the open sea.

* * *

The sun still blazed overhead, and the wind tossed Hope's hair as she stood at the helm alone. It was late afternoon, and she'd been at the wheel for hours, gradually feeling more comfortable with it.

'Well, now, haven't you put on the lords?' said Nettles, coming over.

'Put on the lords?' asked Hope. 'You just made that up.'

'They don't say that down south?' Nettles looked genuinely surprised. 'Like putting on airs, acting all important?'

Hope smiled and shook her head.

'Huh.' Nettles leaned her elbows on the rail and tilted her face up to the sky, closing her eyes against the sun. Hope noticed that it had lightened streaks in her dark, curly hair, and her complexion was brown and rosy.

'The sea agrees with you,' said Hope.

'You think?' asked Nettles, keeping her eyes closed. 'I never expected to leave the Circle. Never even thought about it. It was my whole world. But when Sadie asked if I wanted to come up with her, I found myself saying yes before I even realized it.'

'Because you were worried about Red?'

'That's some of it, I suppose. I've spent years expecting to find him dead in the street or else just vanished, so it's habit if nothing else. But this was more than just that. After all, he's got you to keep an eye on him, and you're nearly as sensible as I am.'

'Thank you.'

Nettles nodded. 'No, I reckon I started seeing things different that night you and me and Palla worked over Drem's crew. We was quality.'

'We were,' agreed Hope. 'How is Palla?'

'Back in the Hammer, still fighting with Big Sig and Sharn for control. Although now that Sig's absorbed Thorn Billy's share, I'd say he's like to come out on top. Anyway, after that

night, the Circle started to seem . . . small. I went back to my
job – which I'd always been grateful to have, you understand.
But there I was, beating on some tommy who don't know
how to treat a whore, and it just felt so bludgeon. Like, what's
the point? Keen?'

'You wanted more,' said Hope.

'Yeah. More world. More life. More *me*.' She looked at
Hope then, her eyes squinting in the glare, and smiled. 'And
drown it all, more pissing sunshine!'

The *Lady's Gambit* sailed into a storm just after sunset.
Thick black clouds swept over them, flickering with lightning. Thunder cracked like a giant whip in the sky. The wind
blew stinging sheets of rain sideways into their faces. They
rode up and down swells that were twice as high as the ship.

Hope had been in worse storms. But her crew was inexperi-
enced. Carmichael hadn't had to say much in a storm because
his people knew what to do. But Hope had to dictate every
action. To complicate matters further, Filler wasn't very
mobile, and Nettles and Alash didn't know the terminology.
So Hope had to rush around the ship, skidding on the rain-
slick deck as she ran from one station to the next, shouting her
commands in detail over the roar of the waves.

When the storm finally slackened, and the murky purple
clouds dispersed to reveal a bright crescent moon, she was
bone weary and hoarse.

'Well done, Captain,' said Missing Finn as the two stood
at the helm.

'Thank you. We'll get better at it the more we do it.'

'That we will, Captain. You look dead on your feet. Why
don't you let me take the helm for a bit and turn in?'

'Good idea,' said Hope. 'The helm is yours, Mr. Finn.'

Finn grinned as he took the wheel. 'You was trained by a proper man of the sea.'

'Captain Carmichael was a great man,' Hope said quietly. 'Perhaps not a perfect man, but a great one.'

'Ah, if that's all anyone says of me, I'd be content.'

Hope gave him a tired smile. 'I suppose you're right.' She turned and headed toward the cabins in the bow.

'Shouldn't you take the captain's quarters?' asked Finn, nodding toward the stern.

'I don't like separating myself from everyone like that.'

'Be a waste, don't you think?'

'You take it, then.'

'Not me, Captain. Wouldn't be proper. I reckon your Captain Carmichael would have agreed.'

Hope sighed. 'Fine. But I'm going to check in on Red first.'

When Hope came down to the cabins, it was dark and quiet. Everyone else was still topside. She was happy to be with them all again. More so than she would have expected. But at this moment, she was grateful for the silence and solitude.

She stood over Red, who was wrapped up in his hammock so that only his face was visible. His breathing was strong and regular. He looked peaceful, almost innocent.

Perhaps Hope had been wrong to worry. After all, he seemed fine. Better than Hope in some ways. At least he was getting some rest.

As if the thought reminded her body, a wave of exhaustion swept over her. She should retire to her cabin before she fell over. But she wasn't quite ready to leave Red's side. Last night, sleeping in separate rooms, she'd found it difficult to relax. She had grown so used to him that even in sleep, his presence comforted her. What a strange thing. Maybe she would just sit with him a bit longer.

Yes, that sounded reasonable. She sat sideways in the hammock across from him. It was far more comfortable than she remembered. Had Finn set up new, better hammocks? It seemed unlikely. And yet, there was no denying how nice it felt to sink into it. So much so that she thought it would be even nicer to lay her head in it. Just for a moment, of course. And then she would go to her own cabin. Which was on the other side of the ship. That sounded like a very long journey all of a sudden. Whereas this hammock was very comfortable and had the added advantage of already being underneath her.

She watched Red breathe gently in and out, finding the rhythm of it soothing. A slight smile curled up in the corners of his mouth, and the sight of it spread a gentle warmth through her.

'Me and you,' she whispered, and gently stroked his cheek. 'Hope and Red.'

In that moment, with no one around to see, and too tired to fight it any longer, she allowed herself to enjoy the sight of this boy – no, this *man* – who had followed her so far and so faithfully. He had proved his loyalty, his skill, and his courage, yes, but also his generosity and kindness. Her feelings for him were as strong as those she felt for Hurlo and Carmichael, but he was no mentor, no teacher, no captain. He was something altogether different. She did not know what, exactly. All she knew was that when she looked at him, she felt something she had never expected to feel again. She felt home.

28

*B*rigga Lin's time had come. Tonight, her two years of training, study, and sacrifice would at last bear fruit.

She stood in the antechamber, waiting to take her turn before the council. She gathered her thick white robe around her, her hood concealing her face. It wasn't just her breasts and genitals that had changed. Her features had softened and refined, becoming more feminine. And after some debate with herself, she'd even decided to allow her hair to grow long. She looked very much like the woman she had chosen to become, and she had to be careful that she did not reveal that prematurely, or else there would be . . . misunderstandings.

But she was not concerned. So far, her timing had been impeccable. Soon after she completed the final phase of incorporating her new abilities, she'd received the summons for the annual biomancer council meeting at Stonepeak. It had been an obvious sign that the council and the world were ready for what she would reveal to them.

What she was bringing to the council was not merely a weapon, but a means of strengthening the entire order of biomancery. Granted, her methods were unorthodox. But once they saw what she was capable of, she was sure the council would brush aside such provincial, antiquated concerns. They might even invite her to join the council. And at such a young age, wouldn't that be something? Her parents would rue the day they disowned her. When she had revealed herself to them, her father had said, 'My son is dead. I have no child.' They had been incapable of listening to her explanation once they had seen her transformation. As painful as the exchange had been, it taught Brigga Lin a valuable lesson. She could not reveal herself to the council until after she had explained the new abilities she had unlocked for biomancers. Once they were awed, perhaps even humbled, by what she could do, they would surely see her transformation with a more equanimous eye.

So Brigga Lin waited in the dimly lit antechamber, forcing herself to remain still, to not pace or wring her hands or show any outward sign of anxiety.

A novice entered the antechamber from the hallway, his hood back, his eyes wild, his robes flapping around his ankles as he walked quickly past her.

'*I* am next before the council!' she growled, grabbing his shoulder.

'I was instructed to bring urgent news to the council from Teltho Kan.' The novice's eyes were fixed on the thick wooden door to the council chamber.

'Kan is not a council member.' Brigga Lin forced her voice to remain low and gravelly. That had also changed to a woman's.

'Even so, I have been instructed,' said the novice.

His gaze began to shift toward Brigga Lin, so she let him go. It was too soon for anyone to look at her closely. 'Fine. But be quick.'

She watched the novice pull open the door and enter the chamber. Whatever Teltho Kan's message was, she was confident it couldn't possibly overshadow her own discovery.

* * *

'Brigga Lin,' called Ammon Set, chief of the biomancer council, in his dry, dusty voice. 'You may present your findings.'

Relief swept through Brigga Lin. The novice had been with them only a few minutes, and then left. She had expected to be called shortly after. But she had been waiting in the antechamber for hours while they discussed whatever news Teltho Kan had sent. It had been so long, Brigga Lin began to worry they would adjourn for the day. She would have to endure another night of concealing herself from her fellow biomancers. But now, at last, she could show the council, and everyone else, just how far she was willing to go to achieve greatness.

The thick doors opened to reveal the council chamber. It was a large room, mostly bare, with the sandstone floors and walls that comprised the building material for much of the palace. At the far end stood the council, the twelve wisest and most powerful men in the empire. They were all in a row, their hands joined, their faces hidden in the shadows of their hoods. Their white robes were lined at the hood and cuffs with gold thread, the mark of their high status.

Brigga Lin quelled her anxiety and walked to the center of the room. She bowed low to them. 'Masters, thank you for hearing me,' she said, trying to keep her voice as low as possible. It came out oddly raspy.

'Why do you not lower your hood before us, Brigga Lin?' asked Chiffet Mek in his voice like rusted metal.

'My apologies, masters. You will know the reason shortly. I beg your indulgence for just a few moments.'

'Your voice seems changed, Brigga Lin,' said Ammon Set.

'A result of my experiments, masters.' She had expected them to remain passive while she presented her findings, not this immediate questioning. Perhaps keeping her hood up had drawn their curiosity and they were eager to hear what she had to say.

'It happens to us all eventually,' said Progul Bon with a voice like cold oil. 'Our work scars both our skin and our voices. If you fear to show us your face because of this, trust that there is no deformation incurred from your work that would horrify us.'

'Thank you, masters. I am here to tell you that I have found the solution to our problems. Not simply a new weapon, but a means of making biomancers themselves more powerful.'

The council members did not outwardly react, but Brigga Lin had not expected them to. As long as their hands were linked, each of their thoughts were immediately known to the others.

After a pause, Ammon Set said, 'Indeed? Please elaborate.'

'If you may recall, masters, two years ago you granted me permission to explore the ruins of the temple of Morack Tor.'

'You wanted to bring soldiers,' said Chiffet Mek.

'Yes, and you wisely decided against it,' Brigga Lin said quickly. 'I see now how foolish my request was. Soldiers would have only been a hindrance to my search.'

'So you did find something?' asked Progul Bon.

'Indeed, masters. Hidden away in a secret place was an ancient copy of the *Biomancery Praxis*. It was identical to our edition in every way, but there was a final chapter that we have never seen. A chapter which instructs a biomancer how to unlock more power than we have ever known before. And with this newfound power, not even the might of Aukbontar will be able to stand against us!'

Brigga Lin hadn't meant to raise her voice. Now, when she stopped talking, the silence that followed was all the more palpable. Of course they were telepathically discussing this shocking revelation among themselves. She stood and waited patiently, ready to give them as much time as they needed. After all, the revelation of a lost branch of biomancery was earthshaking news. Let Teltho Kan try to top that.

'Approach the council, Brigga Lin,' said Ammon Set.

Brigga Lin could hardly believe what she was hearing. Her heart raced as she moved to stand directly in front of the chief of the biomancer council. She had thought she'd at least be expected to furnish some proof of these new abilities before they invited her to the council.

Ammon Set held out his right hand. 'Give me your hand, Brigga Lin.'

She was being allowed to join the silent telepathic conversation. This was even more than she had hoped for. In a moment, her thoughts would be joined with those of the greatest men in the empire.

She took a slow breath and willed her hand not to shake as she placed it in Ammon Set's dry, wrinkled hand.

'Even your hands have become fine and smooth,' said Chiffet Mek, his rusty voice suddenly grating with disgust.

'Masters?' Then Brigga Lin's body froze in place. She could breathe and she could blink, but no more.

'We knew of this final chapter in the *Praxis*,' said Ammon Set. 'Because it was Burness Vee who wisely excised it from the book. We know the power a female biomancer could obtain. But no power is worth degrading the order with such vileness by allowing women to join. Others have discovered this knowledge, but none ever became so depraved that they did what you have done.'

He reached out and pushed back Brigga Lin's hood to reveal her face. The features had become finer, her skin smooth and soft. Her lips had become fuller and more expressive. Her long black hair was thick and glossy as it spilled onto her shoulders.

'Disgusting,' said Chiffet Mek.

'Let us see how far you have gone,' said Progul Bon.

Ammon Set held up one finger and touched her robe at the collar. He slowly traced a line from her left collarbone, down across her left breast, all the way to her thigh. As his finger traveled down her body, it cut through cloth and into flesh, so that the white robe split open and revealed a red line on her bare skin, welling up with blood. He then did the same thing down her right side, so by the end, her robe was in tatters, exposing her naked, blood-streaked flesh. Her breath came out in harsh gasps, since she could not even cry out.

'You did a thorough job of it.' Progul Bon drew back his hood to reveal a face melted like softened candle wax as he gazed at her with watery eyes. 'A complete gender change from head to foot. It's impressive.'

'It's an abomination.' Chiffet Mek pulled back his hood to reveal a face threaded and patched with bits of metal. He spat on Brigga Lin's bare breast, the saliva mixing with the blood as it ran down her abdomen.

'It is heretical,' said Ammon Set. 'An example must be made so that no one else is foolish enough to repeat these loathsome actions. Take this . . . creature to the dungeon to await sentencing.'

Brigga Lin didn't know how long she'd been in the dungeon. They'd thrown her in an unlit cell just large enough to let her sit, but not lie down. The tattered remains of her white robes stuck to fresh wounds with newly dried blood. Every time she moved, the fabric tore open the wounds.

She didn't know why they hadn't already executed her. The Iron Spider seemed a likely candidate. Or the Mountain Seat. But perhaps they wanted to invent an entirely new means of execution, just for her. She'd witnessed that happen once before. A classmate of hers during her novitiate named Speld Mok had lied about his lineage in order to get accepted into the order. When the council found out, they severed his legs at the knees, to illustrate how much lower born he was than they were. Then they made him walk through the rocky paths of the palace gardens on his ragged stumps until he died of blood loss. They'd named this new form of execution Mok's Journey. Brigga Lin wondered if there would be a form of execution named after her.

But so far, it seemed they were content to let her rot down in a dark hole beneath the palace. Perhaps they would starve her to death. It seemed almost too much to hope for. Starvation was a gentle death compared to typical biomancer execution techniques. But Brigga Lin hadn't heard a single soul since she'd been locked up. Not even other prisoners. Perhaps that had been on purpose. After all, they knew what she could do. And she'd been so sure that would convince them. She had been a fool.

No, *they* were the fools. Foolish, cowardly old men whose time had come. She would make them pay for what they had done to her. Somehow. She would escape and grow stronger. Then she would return to wreak vengeance on the council. On the entire order.

She repeated this vow to herself many times. She didn't know how many, exactly. Or how long she'd been locked up. More than a few hours she was sure. But a few days? She had no idea. Unable to lie down, she'd only dozed here and there. But for how long? She had no way of knowing. No daylight reached her cell. No warden came to deliver food. There was no light and no sound. Nothing changed.

Then, finally, she heard something. At first the sound alarmed her, although she couldn't say why, exactly. Perhaps any sound would have. Gradually, she realized that it was footsteps. Two pairs of footsteps.

'Do you think they really found a survivor?' came a wheezing voice.

'I think *they* think so,' said an amused-sounding second voice. 'But whether Teltho Kan is right, who knows?'

They were getting closer.

'We'll know soon enough, anyway,' continued the second. 'Kan's due to arrive at any time.'

'Already? Wasn't he coming from New Laven?'

'I heard he's being chased by some Vinchen who's vowed to kill biomancers. A female, no less.'

'A female Vinchen?'

'That's what he said in his message.'

'Can't be all that dangerous, then. Only a female.'

They were definitely coming closer. And after making statements like that, their deaths would not weigh much on her conscience.

A light appeared, painful and blinding after her prolonged darkness.

'Alright, you. Time to eat.'

All she could see were two shadows cast by a blazing torch. She heard a panel slide open in the door and felt a tray press against her leg. She needed to be able to see them. If they left before her eyes adjusted, it would be too late. She took a slow breath, forcing herself to remain calm as she waited for her vision to clear.

'What's this one in for?' asked the amused one.

'No idea,' said the wheezy one.

'Wonder why she's wearing a biomancer robe.'

'Part of one, anyway.'

'I'm not complaining.'

They both laughed. Brigga Lin's eyes had adjusted by now, and she could clearly see the leering, lascivious gaze of the two men as they looked at her through the bars.

'I'm so cold,' she said meekly.

The two men looked at each other. Then one of them grinned down at her. 'We'll warm you up, girl.'

Brigga Lin forced herself to retain her confused, innocent look when she heard the door unlock. Only her hands moved, weaving, twisting, and flicking silently just out of the torchlight. She could strike anytime now, but she wanted to savor this. She waited until the door was wide open. Both men tried to get through the narrow opening at the same time.

'Me first,' said the amused one. He grabbed Wheezy's hand and tried to pull him away. But when he did, their hands stuck together.

'Let go!' said Wheezy.

'I can't!'

They struggled to pull their hands apart, but their flesh began to melt together, mingling and dripping down between them like candle wax.

'What in all hells . . .' said the no-longer-amused one, his eyes wide with fear.

Brigga Lin forced herself erect, though her body ached from lack of use. 'Only one hell for you,' she said. 'Me.'

The men continued to melt into each other like two lumps of wax being slowly heated. They struggled and flailed with their free limbs, but it did them no good. Both screamed as they continued to merge, even after their eyes and ears had sunken into the rest. Finally it was only the two mouths in a shapeless mass of oozing flesh. Then even those caved in, and there was silence in the dungeon again.

Brigga Lin picked up the tray and ate the food. She was starving, after all. Then she fished through the lump of flesh until she found the metal keys. She stepped over the lump and strolled down the dark hallway. As she walked, she thought about what the guards had said. A female Vinchen who had vowed to kill biomancers. A plan began to form in her mind.

But first, she needed a change of clothes.

29

*I*t wasn't a dream so much as it was a gradual awareness of going from absolute impenetrable darkness to a blinding white light. The light grew so strong that it was painful to look at. Then, just when he couldn't bear to look at it a moment longer, Red opened his eyes.

The first thing he saw was Hope, asleep in a hammock next to him. In sleep, she had an openness that never showed when she was awake. The sunlight streamed in through the portal to rest on her smooth, freckled cheek. Her lips were slightly parted, soft and dry like pink silk.

He was also in a hammock. He hadn't been ready for that, so when he leaned toward Hope, it rolled and dumped him on the ground with a loud thud.

Hope sat up. 'Red? Are you okay?' She looked around, like she hadn't noticed he was lying on the ground.

'Ouch.' He pushed himself up.

Other people sat up in their hammocks, and Red was not at all prepared to see so many loved faces in one place. 'Nettie? Filler? Sadie, too?' He frowned. 'Hold on. Am I dead?'

'You're alive,' said Hope.

'Surprisingly,' Nettles told him.

'What's that mean?' asked Red.

'Trying to take on a biomancer all on your own?' said Sadie. 'Thought I raised you with better sense than that.'

'Oh. That.' The memories of his confrontation with Teltho Kan began to surface. 'He was going to kill me.'

'But he didn't,' said Hope.

'He stopped right at the last second when he got a good look at my face. Called me a survivor and said I'd see him again soon. Then I was out.'

'When he saw the color of your eyes, perhaps?' asked Hope.

'Could be,' said Red. 'But the red comes from me being a coral spice baby. Why would a biomancer care about that?'

'I don't know,' said Hope. 'I'll let you ask him before I kill him.'

'Anyway, you're feeling fine now, right?' asked Filler.

'I'm sunny,' said Red. 'But what about all of you? Sleeping in the middle of the day?' He looked around. 'Are we on a boat?'

'It's the middle of the night, Red.' Hope's tone was careful.

'This bright? Not possible.'

'See for yourself.' Hope pointed to the steps that led up to the deck.

'Sure,' said Red, not liking the neutral look she was giving him.

He climbed the steps quickly. He felt better than sunny. That enforced rest had done him a world of good. He stepped out onto the deck and looked around the ship. Missing Finn had really put a shine on the *Lady's Gambit*. And Red had been right about it being day, of course.

'See?' he said to Hope, who had come up behind him. 'Bright as day.'

Wordlessly, she pointed up to the sky.

He craned his head up, and it took him a moment to understand what he was seeing. A light blue sky, with stars that shone as bright as moons, and a moon that shone as bright as the sun.

'What is wrong with the pissing sky?' he demanded.

'Nothing,' said Hope.

Nettles was beside him, looking uncharacteristically concerned. He pointed at the blazing sky. 'Nettie, you see it, right?'

She exchanged a worried look with Hope. 'Seems normal to me, Red.'

Sadie was up now, with Filler behind her, hobbling on a crutch. 'What's he seeing, then?' she asked.

'Red, come over into the light,' Hope said, her voice still unsettlingly calm.

She led him over to the helm, where there was a lantern hanging. It was so bright that it made Red squint. Looking past the light, he saw Missing Finn at the wheel. And someone else beside him. 'Alash? What are *you* doing here?'

'Seeing the world, cousin!' said Alash. 'Seeking my own path! Finding my purpose!'

'You've been talking to Missing Finn, then,' said Red.

'Red,' said Hope. 'Step closer to that lantern.'

'It's piss'ell bright, Hope. Isn't this close enough?'

'Just a little closer.'

He reluctantly moved closer, shading his eyes against the glare with his hand. 'This close enough for you?'

They were all staring at him. Not in a good way.

'Your eyes,' said Nettles. 'You look like you've got red cat eyes.'

His stomach went icy. 'How is that even possible?'

'Teltho Kan's biomancery,' said Hope. 'But the real question is, why?'

*   *   *

It was weird, of course. But being able to see in the dark didn't seem like a bad thing, really. Not until the next morning, when he went into the sunlight.

'Rot and damnation!' He stumbled back into the dim cabin. The sun had felt like needles in his eyes. The rest of them were just getting out of their hammocks again, after trying to catch a few more hours of sleep. 'It's all too bright out there! Like my eyes can't adjust.'

'I was wondering if that would be a problem,' said Hope.

'Does this mean I can't go out in the sun anymore?' he demanded.

'I might be able to figure something out,' said Alash.

Hope nodded. 'Get to work on that. I need to relieve Finn. The rest of you, grab some food and then to your stations.'

As they all started for the steps, Red said, 'What, you're leaving me down here all alone?'

Hope turned to Filler. 'Would you mind?'

'Course not.' Filler settled back down, laying his crutch across his lap.

'Thanks, old pot,' said Red. He watched the rest of them follow Hope up to the decks. Once they were all gone, he said, 'Our Hope sure has taken to captaining.'

'Weren't her idea,' said Filler, almost defensively.

'No, it was mine.' Red grinned. 'I didn't expect it to come quite so naturally to her.'

'The Circle wasn't really something she knew. Seamanship she knows pretty well. Better than me, anyway.'

'Yeah, but here you are, and not doing too bad with it yourself, all things considered,' said Red.

'I suppose.'

'What brought you out here, Filler? Not that I'm complaining.'

Filler shrugged. 'Without you, Nettie, and Sadie, it just didn't seem like the Circle anymore.'

'How was it back there when you left?'

'The same. Nothing ever changes in the Circle.'

'Did you expect it to?'

'Nah,' said Filler. 'But we changed.'

It was after midday when Alash came back down to the cabin. He had a pair of spectacles in his hands with dark lenses.

'They're stained with smoke,' he explained as he handed them to Red. 'Sorry they aren't more attractive. And they're a bit heavier and thicker than I would have liked. But I was a bit limited in materials. Anyway, I think they should allow you to bear the sunlight until I can make you a better pair.'

'Or until we force that biomancer to fix me.'

'Or that,' agreed Alash.

Red put the spectacles on and turned to Filler. 'Well? How do I look?'

'Not bad,' said Filler. 'Kind of pat, actually.'

'You should try them out in direct sunlight,' said Alash. 'Make sure I've darkened them enough. Or, you know, if they're too dark for you to see.'

Red cautiously edged toward the opening. 'So far so good.' Then he took a deep breath and climbed up to the deck.

'Well?' called Alash anxiously.

Red poked his head back down into the cabin, grinning. 'Cousin of mine, I may not have stolen even a fiveyard from Grandfather, but I took the most valuable thing at Pastinas Manor all the same.'

*   *   *

The dark spectacles allowed Red to spend the rest of the day topside, getting himself familiar with the *Lady's Gambit*. He'd spent a fair time helping to fix it up, but knew almost nothing about the sails and rigging.

He also enjoyed watching Hope settle into her role as captain. Red couldn't explain the deep warmth he felt when he saw her like that. Pride, maybe? Now that he'd stopped pretending to himself that he wasn't sotted with her, it was all a lot easier. Not that he let it show to her. No point in that. But he would look over at Sadie now and then and catch her giving him a knowing glance. The same kind of glance Old Yammy gave him. Two meddling old wrinks if ever there were.

As wonderful as the dark spectacles were, Red was relieved when the sun set and he could remove them. He hadn't understood at first what Alash meant about wanting them to be lighter. But after wearing them for half the day, he now understood perfectly. His ears and the bridge of his nose ached.

Now it was night, and they were all gathered at the table in the galley, lingering after dinner with a bit of rum that Missing Finn had thoughtfully brought along.

Filler and Alash were working on some kind of metal brace for Filler's leg. Between Alash's mechanical skills and Filler's experience of working with metals, they were making rapid progress. At the moment, they were tinkering with a hinge to the brace that would serve as Filler's knee. It would lock when he was walking but bend when he wanted to sit, so he didn't have his big old leg sticking out all the time.

On another side of the table, Sadie and Finn were talking quietly. There was no mistake in either of their eyes that each had found something in the other. Red wondered why it had taken them so long. But more than that, he was just glad for them.

Over in the corner, Hope and Nettles were talking. Whatever animosity they'd had between them seemed long gone. He found it at once comforting and inexplicably unnerving.

He leaned back in his chair, letting the rum warm his veins. He stared out the porthole. He still hadn't gotten used to the night sky being so bright, but he had to admit, it had a strange, almost otherworldly beauty to it. It occurred to him then that he was no longer on New Laven. Not even close. For the first time in his life, he was somewhere else. Yet he didn't feel at all homesick. Maybe because just about everyone he cared for had come with him. Maybe that's all he needed to feel at home.

'You know.' Alash set aside the hinge and followed Red's gaze out the porthole. 'Being at sea like this makes me think of all those old pirate tales my father used to tell me when I was a boy.'

'Lacies know pirate stories?' asked Filler.

'Certainly! Leadheart, Strawbeard. All of them.'

'And of course Dire Bane,' said Nettles.

'Who?' asked Alash.

'Never heard of Dire Bane?' asked Sadie. 'The greatest, most fearsome pirate that ever lived?'

'I'm afraid not.' Alash looked like he was trying to figure out if they were all teasing him. It probably wasn't easy being the only lacy aboard.

'It's no great surprise,' said Red. 'After all, most pirates were just lacies looking for a bit of thrill and fame. But Dire Bane was the champion of the common people. They say he sank more imperial ships than anyone else in the history of the empire. They say the mere mention of his name would make imp officers piss themselves. They say he was taller than any man alive, with arms thick around as most men's chests. His voice alone was enough to send a pack of killer seals on the run. They say he never lost a sea battle. That he could not be killed because his hatred of the empire burned so fierce, it would instantly seal up any wound he sustained.'

'Here we go,' said Nettles. 'He's warming up to a tall tale now.'

'Ah, but the tales of Dire Bane are irresistible!' said Red. 'One of my favorites was when an imperial ship came alongside his vessel, the *Kraken Hunter*. They tried to board her and things were in a bad way because they outnumbered Dire Bane's crew three to one. So what did he do? Ripped his own mast out by the roots and laid about him like it was a club. Knocked each and every imp into the ocean. Then he planted his own mast back where it belonged, took what he liked from the imperial ship, and sailed away.'

'That's not even possible,' said Alash.

Red shrugged. 'It's what they say happened.'

'What about that time with the cigar?' asked Filler, his eyes eager.

'There's another beauty,' agreed Red. 'One night he was landed at Paradise Circle, his favorite port, naturally. And he heard tell that an entire armada of imperial ships was sailing down from Keystown with enough cannons and pitch to raze the Circle to the ground, if that's what it took to make an end of Dire Bane.'

'Imperial soldiers were willing to slaughter an entire neighborhood of innocents simply to kill one man?' asked Alash doubtfully.

'Well, to be fair,' said Red, 'there are very few who are truly innocent in Paradise Circle. But set your mind to rest, because they never got the chance. Dire Bane walked out to the edge of the pier where the armada was to land. He took one of his cigars, which, by the way, I have heard tell were as long as a normal man's arm. And he blew a puff of smoke from it so mighty that the entire armada was lost in the cloud and pushed out to open waters. They got so turned around that they nearly set fire to Keystown before they realized how far they'd gone off course. And by that time, Dire Bane was long gone.'

'These stories are ridiculous,' said Alash dismissively. Then after a moment, almost guiltily, he asked, 'So . . . did they ever catch him?'

'Not the imps,' said Red. 'Finally, the emperor himself entreated the greatest Vinchen warrior of his generation to bring Dire Bane to justice. A man by the name of Hurlo the Cunning.' He frowned, then turned to Hope. 'Wasn't that . . .'

'It was my teacher who finally captured Dire Bane,' she said.

'Well, then, *you* tell us how it ended,' suggested Red.

'My telling won't be as colorful as yours.'

Red shrugged. 'I'm curious to hear what really happened.'

She looked strangely sad as her eyes surveyed them all. 'He was just a man. A brilliant, passionate man who cared deeply about his principles. He believed the empire had become corrupt. That it no longer cared about the people. So he determined to destroy it.'

'The *entire* empire?' asked Nettles. 'That's slippy.'

'Dire Bane was brave beyond measure,' said Hope. 'Anyone willing to challenge the entire world out of a sense of honor deserves the deepest respect. But you're right, it *was* an impossible task. And he was no giant or immortal. In fact, he was getting old. Slowing down. He knew his days were drawing to an end. Still he did not give up. My teacher, only a young man then, cornered him in the Painted Caves on the island of Pauper's Prayer. They fought honorably, and my teacher defeated him. The emperor wanted Dire Bane's body lashed to the masthead of his ship and paraded all over the empire as an example of what befell anyone who challenged him. But my teacher said it was dishonorable and refused.'

'He could do that?' asked Alash.

'Since the days of Manay the True, the Vinchen have vowed to serve the empire – the greater good – and not to be beholden to any one man.'

'So what did your teacher do with Dire Bane's body instead?' asked Nettles.

'He put it aboard the *Kraken Hunter*, covered the whole thing with pitch, and lit it on fire. They said you could see the column of smoke and flame for miles around. In the end, there was nothing left of man or ship but ash and scorched metal at the bottom of the sea.'

'You're right,' said Red. 'My ending was better.'

The next morning when Red stepped out onto the deck of the *Lady's Gambit*, he saw an island looming in the distance.

'Stonepeak.' Missing Finn stood at the helm.

Hope stood next to him and said nothing, her face set.

Red didn't know what he'd expected it to be like. The great capital city of the Empire of Storms, its largest and northernmost island, nothing beyond but the endless expanse of the Dark Sea. It was said to have the highest mountain in the empire, and the imperial palace was at its peak so that the emperor could literally look down on all of his subjects. But beyond that, Red knew nothing. If he'd given it any thought, it was just to imagine it as New Laven, but with a big mountain plopped in the middle. Maybe with fewer neighborhoods like Paradise Circle and more neighborhoods like Hollow Falls.

He'd been right about the mountain, at least. A mass of jagged rock sat right in the center of the upper half of the island, its base taking up nearly a quarter of it. But the rest of the city didn't look anything like New Laven. Or no, maybe there was one neighborhood that it looked like. Keystown. Stonepeak appeared to be one vast Keystown, just as orderly and clean, but on a scale Red couldn't quite believe. The midday sun gleamed off its beige walls and polished windows with a harshness that made Red wince even while wearing his dark spectacles.

'Piss'ell but that's a lot of drudgery,' he said.

'Looks like,' said Missing Finn.

Hope still said nothing, but Red noticed her knuckles were white as she gripped her sword.

'We've nearly got him,' Red assured her. 'It's almost over.'

'Really?' she asked. 'As far as I can tell, we've nearly *lost* him. There's only one place a biomancer running for his life is likely to go on Stonepeak.'

'The Council of Biomancery?'

'Which is behind the palace walls. If we don't get to him before he gets there . . .'

Red understood. Behind those walls lived nearly every biomancer in the empire. And, of course, the emperor's personal honor guard. Once Teltho Kan reached that haven, he would be untouchable.

'I should have guessed this is where he would go,' she said quietly.

'And how would that have made any difference?'

She didn't respond, but he knew her well enough now to guess that she was silently berating herself for her 'laxness' or something like that.

As soon as they were at the dock, she called, 'Sadie, you have command of the ship!' Then in three long, graceful strides, she was over the side and running down the pier.

'Hope! Wait!' called Red as he took off after her.

It was clear she was not waiting for him. Or even slowing down. She sprinted through the streets, which were crowded with carts, horses, and people. She dodged and shifted around them effortlessly, like it was a dance. But Red was keeping up just fine. In fact, he found it surprisingly easy to follow her. It was as if he could see everything at once, take it all in, and make his decisions in a split second. He'd always been coordinated, but this was something new.

He chased her for a while through those crowded streets. He wondered how any city could be this busy. He didn't have much opportunity to examine it in more detail, though. He had to stop Hope from doing something slippy.

He finally caught up with her at the palace gates. She was on her knees in the middle of the street, her head bowed, her sheathed sword pointing unwaveringly toward the high white walls before her.

'I failed them,' Hope said quietly as she stared at the sword in her hands. 'I swore vengeance on the man who murdered my village. And now he's beyond my reach.'

Red crouched down next to her, keenly aware that a guard on top of the palace walls was watching them, a rifle in his hands. 'Maybe we can . . . sneak in somehow?' he whispered. 'Get some disguises and slip in through the kitchens like we did at Bayview.'

'This isn't an art gallery, it's the imperial palace.'

'Okay. Well. Then we'll wait until he comes out.'

'*If* he comes out.'

'Of course he will. He can't stay in there forever.' Red looked up at the massive palace. There was an outer wall, then an open garden courtyard space of some kind, then the palace proper, which rose up slowly as it clung to the mountain. It soared higher than any building he had ever seen. Higher even than he'd imagined a building could go. 'Uh, can he?'

'Have you never read the histories of the emperors? That palace could outlast a ten-year siege.'

'Come on, Hope. There has to be a way,' Red said desperately. The look in her eye was one he had seen only once before. When he'd talked her out of falling on her own sword. 'We always find a way.'

'Do we?' she asked, still staring at her sword.

'Of course we do! Me and you! Red and Hope! We're unbeatable!'

'We just got beaten.'

'No, don't say that.'

'Why not? It's true. Another one of my true stories you'd like to make into one of your tall tales.'

A desperate thought popped into his head. It was at once crazy and the most reasonable thing he'd ever considered. 'What if . . . we chose to walk away from all this? Start a completely *new* story.'

'What?' Hope looked up at him for the first time. He took that as a good sign.

'What if we let go of vows and vengeance and all that rot and started fresh?' The more he said it, the more he liked it. 'Stonepeak seems like a nice clean place. A place where we could start nice clean lives. Proper lives that don't involve killing or stealing or anything like that.'

'Proper lives?' Hope looked bewildered.

'Or, hey, if that doesn't suit your fancy, we could go somewhere else. *Anywhere* else. We have our own pissing ship, after all. We could be whatever we like.' It was all so clear to him now. They didn't have to be a thief and a warrior. They could be anything they wanted. 'The only thing holding us back is our past. But what if we just chucked the whole thing? No revenge, no biomancers, just you and me. Together. Forever.'

His hand reached out to her. 'There is only one thing in this whole world I want. And that's you.'

'I . . . I don't know if I can do it.' Hope's deep blue eyes
were shot with red veins. 'Let it all go? Abandon my vows?
My purpose? It's the only thing that's kept me going for the
past ten years. I can't just throw it away.'

'But it's eating you from the inside. This obsession with
vengeance. It's slowly turning you into . . . I don't know
what, but it's not too late. I see it in you. The person behind
the vengeance trying to get out.'

'That's what you painted.' She finally took his hand in
hers. 'That part of me.'

'You are more than a biomancer hunter. You are more
than a killer.' He pressed her hand against his chest. 'Please,
Hope. Let me help you.'

'You want to help her?' came a voice from behind them,
feminine but not soft. 'Then stop holding her back.'

They both turned to see a woman standing over them. She
was taller than any woman Red had ever seen. She had long
black hair and piercing brown eyes. She wore a fine white silk
dress tight at the bodice, but with long billowing sleeves that
hung below her hands, and a white hood thrown back. It was
an odd look, but somehow elegant.

'What do you want?' Red asked, his eyes narrowing.

The woman nodded toward the soldiers at the palace wall.
There were two of them now, talking to each other. One
pointed down at them.

'If you want to get in there,' said the woman, 'come with
me.' Then she turned, her white dress flaring out, and walked
toward a nearby tavern.

Hope stood immediately and followed the woman.

Red was about to call to her, but he glanced at the wall.
There were three guards now. So he hurried after them.

The woman led them into the tavern, which was much
cleaner and better lit than any tavern in New Laven. The
tables were all well scrubbed, with a potted plant in the

center of each. She pointed to a table over in the corner. 'Get
comfortable. I'll order us refreshments.'

Hope sat down at the table.

'This seems like a really bad idea,' said Red as he sat down
beside her.

'If there is even a chance this woman has a way of getting
into the palace, I will hear her out,' said Hope.

'It could be a trap.'

'Set by whom? We are no longer a threat to Teltho Kan,
and we don't know anyone else in this city.'

'Exactly!' said Red. 'We don't know this woman. We don't
know a pissing thing about her.'

'My name is Brigga Lin.' The woman placed three wooden
goblets filled with red wine on the table. 'And anyone sworn
to vengeance against a biomancer is a friend of mine.'

'Why is that?' asked Hope.

'Because,' said the woman as she took a seat, 'I have vowed
to take revenge on the entire order.'

'You?' asked Red.

Brigga Lin smiled at him, bright white teeth behind red lips.
'I don't look like much, do I?' She took a delicate sip of her
wine. 'But a master of biomancery can look any way they
choose.'

'Wait, are you saying you're—'

'A biomancer. Yes.' She rolled her eyes. 'Or I was until
recently.'

Hope frowned. 'I thought they didn't allow female
biomancers.'

'And I thought they didn't allow female Vinchen, yet you
certainly are dressed as one.'

'How do we know you really are – or were – a biomancer?'
asked Red.

She touched the plant in the center of their table. There
had been only one flower in the pot, a wan, semi-wilted

chrysanthemum. As she leaned back and smugly took another sip from her goblet, the pot burst with blossoms.

'Okay. If you are a biomancer,' said Hope, 'why do you want to destroy the order?'

'*Were*,' said Brigga Lin. 'Let's not forget the all-important tense, there.'

'Why did they kick you out?' asked Red.

She arched one thin black eyebrow and gestured gracefully to her breasts as if formally presenting them. 'Why do you think? Because I'm a woman.'

'But if being a woman is against their laws,' said Hope, 'how did you—'

'Become a biomancer in the first place?' asked Brigga Lin. 'Simple. I was a man then.'

'Sorry,' said Red. 'What?'

'Not the most manly of men, it must be owned. But, I had the proper equipment. I studied and trained for years as a biomancer, and I was . . . mediocre at best, honestly. But I wanted to be more. So much more. Then a few years ago, I was exploring the ruins of the temple of Morack Tor, where I found one of the original sacred texts. It revealed that there were some branches of biomancery that were completely closed to men, and could only be mastered by women. I thought this was an astonishing discovery. It would revolutionize the order. But I would need to prove that it worked.'

'So you used biomancery to turn yourself into a woman?' asked Hope.

Brigga Lin shrugged. 'It was either that or spend years training a real girl in the basics of biomancery. And who has the time or patience for that? Also, and I'll only admit this to you now after I know better, I honestly wasn't sure a woman was smart enough to learn biomancery.' She smiled faintly at Hope. 'I hope you will forgive that. Like most men, I was an idiot.'

'So it was true?' asked Red. 'You can do things the rest of them can't?'

'Oh yes. That right there?' She pointed to the overflowing pot. 'They could never do that. The masculine biomancery can change living matter, but it cannot create it. Only feminine biomancery can do that. And if that's not a sign they're doing it wrong up on that mountain, I don't know what is.'

'And you thought you could convince them of that?' There was sympathy in Hope's eyes.

'I was a fool.' Brigga Lin's face grew dark. 'They called me a heretic. Spit on me. Cut me. I barely escaped with my life.'

'My teacher trained me in secret for eight years,' Hope said quietly. 'When his brothers found out what he was doing, they attacked us. He made me swear not to fight them. He said it was the natural consequence for his actions, and he accepted it with peace in his heart.' She put her hand on Brigga Lin's arm. 'I am sorry for your suffering. But it was you who were in the wrong, just as I was, by transgressing their rules. And this was your consequence.'

'Transgressing *their* rules?' Brigga Lin's eyes blazed. 'It is they who have transgressed the rules of life. When I told them women could become even more powerful biomancers than men, it was not a surprising revelation to them. The council already knew. But they would rather forgo that power than let women into the order. The Council of Biomancery is weak and stupid and conscienceless. Surely you know this. You must have seen what they do out there in the world to innocent people, or you would not have sworn vengeance on them. They are a blight on the entire empire.'

'You're just going to kill them all, then?' asked Red. 'Every biomancer in the empire?'

'If that is what it takes to change things,' said Brigga Lin. 'Adapt or die. *That* is the rule of life.'

'And how in hells do you plan to do it?'

'They are all gathered in the palace as we speak for the annual council meeting. That's why I was here. To present my findings.' She turned to Hope. 'The meeting ends tomorrow and they scatter back out into the empire. But if we strike tonight, we have a chance of wiping out every last one of them.'

'Hope, you're not actually listening to this talk, are you?' demanded Red. But he could see it in her eyes. She was listening.

'Centuries ago, Burness Vee and Selk the Brave worked together, biomancer and Vinchen.' Brigga Lin leaned closer to Hope. 'They *built* this empire. Together, they were unstoppable. Between us, we have a chance to take the palace. To correct the course of the empire. To make it *better*. Tonight!'

'It's suicide, Hope,' said Red.

'No,' said Brigga Lin. 'At best, it is a chance at glory and righteousness. At worst, it is a just and honorable death. And what do you offer? I heard you trying to convince her to relinquish her vows. You would advise acquiescence to their corrupt power? Or cowardly retreat? Those are but the shadows of a life, base and unworthy.'

'Hope . . .' Red was losing this argument. Against all reason and logic, the most important argument of his life, and he was losing. 'Please . . . I'm begging you. Come away with me. Come back to the ship with me and Sadie and Nettie and all the rest. We love you. Isn't that enough?'

Hope stared at him, and her deep blue pools truly opened. For the first time, he saw just how far down they went.

'Red, I know this is hard for you to understand, because this isn't how it is in the Circle. You talk as though my life were my own. But it has not been mine for many years. I have pledged it to uphold the honor of the empire and the Vinchen order. I must put that honor before my life. Before everything.' She reached out and pressed her hand against his cheek. 'And everyone.' She let her hand drop. 'I ask you to respect that.'

And that's when he knew for certain that he had lost her. Or maybe he'd never truly had her at all.

'I have always, and will always respect you.' He forced his voice to be quiet and even. 'But I can't be chum and larder with you walking purposefully to your own death, no matter how just or noble. I won't.'

He stood up slowly, giving her every possible moment to stop him. To ask him to stay. Or to go with him. But she didn't.

And really, he hadn't expected her to.

30

*T*hey stood before the white walls of the palace, which shone luminous in the moonlight.

'Do you wish he came with us?' asked Brigga Lin.

'No.' Hope didn't want to think about Red right now.

'He looked like he would have been helpful.'

'Yes.'

'You care for him that much?'

The question took Hope by surprise. It had been so long since she'd talked to someone who understood her formal code of honor. She'd more or less resigned herself to having her motives opaque to everyone she knew. But Brigga Lin understood. The biomancers seemed to have their own code of honor, twisted and poisonous though it might be. Brigga Lin understood why Hope hadn't asked Red to stay, though she knew he would be a valuable asset in this fight. If she had, and he said no, then she would have lost respect for him. And if she asked him and he said yes, then she would be dooming him to the same dark fate that was in store for her. She would rather reduce her own chances of success than suffer either of those two things.

'Yes, I suppose I do,' she said finally.

They stared at the guards on top of the wall, who were beginning to notice the unusual pair of women looking up at them. One with black hair and dressed all in white, one with nearly white hair and dressed all in black.

'I never asked your name,' said Brigga Lin.

'I don't remember my real name. My village was massacred by a biomancer. When Hurlo the Cunning took me in as his student, he named me after my village, so that I would never forget it, or the fate that befell it.'

'What was the name of your village?'

'Bleak Hope.'

Brigga Lin laughed, a rich, throaty sound that brought even more attention from the guards along the wall. 'I realize this is scant comfort, but I cannot think of another living soul I'd rather die with than someone named Bleak Hope.'

She pulled up her hood so that it shaded her eyes. The guards appeared to be alarmed by that. With the hood up, her flowing gown looked at once like a biomancer's, and yet not at all. One of the guards said something to the others. They lifted their rifles and took aim at the two women.

'Disperse at once!' one of them shouted.

'They're preparing to fire,' said Hope.

'I'll handle it,' said Brigga Lin.

'From so high up? I thought biomancers could only transfer their power through touch.'

'Yes,' said Brigga Lin, a smile flashing beneath her hood. 'I remember when that limitation was mine.' She wove her hands in an elegant pattern, the long sleeves swirling almost as if she were dancing.

'This is your last—' began the soldier.

Brigga Lin lifted her arms, splaying her fingers wide, and the rifles exploded. The soldiers screamed as they clutched at their powder-burned faces.

'Gunpowder is so nasty. I wish they wouldn't use it.' Brigga Lin moved smoothly toward the gate. She turned to

regard Hope. 'Once I take down this door, we will be wading
upstream in a river of soldiers. More than I can possibly
handle on my own. Are you ready?'

Hope looked up at the soldiers on the wall. They wailed in
pain, their faces a mess of burned and smoking flesh.
Something flickered within her. Pity, like she'd felt toward
Ranking at the end. Victims of a biomancer. This time, a
biomancer on her side . . .

But these men wore the same uniforms as the men who
had slaughtered her village. She focused on that, and the pity
was drowned out by that old, familiar darkness. So she made
the choice she'd always made.

'Yes,' she said. 'I am ready.'

'You made the right choice,' said Sadie after she'd let Red
cry awhile. As soon as he'd come to the ship, without Hope
– his face pale, his glinting cat eyes haunted – she'd shooed
everyone else away. Now the two of them sat in the captain's
quarters, which Hope still hadn't used. And it sounded like
she might not ever.

'It doesn't *feel* like the right choice,' said Red. 'It feels like
I left my heart back there in that tavern.'

'I know. You're young yet. And you got that soft artistic
side that'll never let you be. Can't help that. Nothing for it
but some pain, I'm afraid.'

He wrapped his arms around his torso, his shoulders
hunched and his head low. 'It's never been this bad before.
Not even with Nettie.'

'I know, boy. I know.'

They were silent, with only the occasional sniffle from
Red. That sound, and being on a boat, brought old memories back to Sadie. Bittersweet thoughts of times gone by. It

was surely a sign that she was getting soft in her old age, but she didn't mind. She was just glad her boy was alive. 'She made the right choice, too.'

'What?' Red's eyes widened. 'She's got a pissing death wish!'

'I mean about not asking you to stay with her. I'm sure she wanted to. If you're going to die, who wouldn't want to do it side by side with your own tom, right?'

'I was never her tom.'

'That so?'

'Yeah. We never tossed.'

'And you think that's what seals it? Wet bits of meat pressing on each other?'

'Well . . .'

'No molly I ever knew needed to get her cunt stretched to know she was sotted with her tom. Comes from deeper in, that sense of knowing.' She shrugged. 'Don't get me wrong, it's sunny. I've bent many a cock in my day, and rarely regretted it. But it ain't necessary to calling something between two people love.'

'No. I suppose not.' His eyes turned to the window like they could pierce through all the buildings between them and the palace.

'If she'd asked, you would have stayed. I know it. She knew it. And when it came down to it, she loved you so much, she let you go.' She patted his back. 'That's a special thing, Red, my wag. You best not forget it ever.'

They were silent again. Sadie noticed he wasn't sniffling anymore. Maybe what she said had comforted him. Maybe after years of mostly failing, she was getting good at this parenting thing.

He stood up, his shoulders back, head high. 'You're right, Sadie. It's too special to leave behind.'

'Now wait, there, Red, I didn't—'

But he ran out of the cabin, and a moment later she heard his boots hit the dock.

Okay, so maybe she still mostly failed at parenting.

It was difficult to know sometimes if the choices you made were truly right. It was tempting, for example, to see early signs of success as God or the universe (the Vinchen did not differentiate) showing approval by opening the way before you.

That was how Hope felt as she and Brigga Lin made their way through the gate, across the courtyard, and into the palace keep. Soldiers by the score rushed at her, and she struck them down as if they were merely grass in the rolling meadows of Hollow Falls. The Song of Sorrows echoed in the white halls of the palace, and it wasn't long before soldiers shied away from its sound. She'd lost the blood magic on the first strike. She'd felt the sword shudder, and the gentle but persistent tug dissipate. But it hardly mattered now. There was nowhere for Teltho Kan to run.

At her side, Brigga Lin stalked like a vengeful ghost, her hands constantly weaving, her sleeves whirling, as one by one she brought death from afar. One soldier fell to the floor screaming as his rib cage burst from his chest, splaying out like a blooming red, pink, and white flower. Another could not scream at all as his entrails turned inside out and spilled from his mouth onto the floor.

Was this the right choice? The question popped into Hope's mind as she hacked off one man's head, then disemboweled another. All this horror and death they were sowing? Was it right? In the distance she saw a man try to claw out his own eyes because they had turned to boiling pitch in his head. And she did not know the answer to her question.

But then in her mind's eye, she saw fat white larvae burst from her father's skin. She heard her mother calling out a name that to this day she could not remember. She saw Ontelli from Murgesia, an owl's beak emerging from his mouth, and heard his bones cracking as he became a beast before her eyes. She saw Thorn Billy turn to ice. She saw the people of Paradise Circle turn to dust.

So she hardened her heart and fought on.

Despite Stonepeak's luxuries of cleanliness and underground sewage, there were hardly any gas lamps lit. Compared to New Laven, the streets were eerily empty after sunset. The taverns, though occupied, were not spilling over with the rowdy enthusiasm of Paradise Circle or the passionate expression of Silverback. Everyone seemed subdued. Red wasn't sure if it was like that every night, or only on those nights the biomancer council was in town.

Either way, it freed up the path for him. He thought he had gone fast during the day, but it was nothing compared to his speed now. In the dark, his vision opened even further, allowing him to not only take in everything around him but also to calculate and plan his route several blocks ahead. His eyes seemed to absorb the darkness. He wondered what he must look like to those few people he passed in the street. A red-eyed demon? At the moment, he didn't care. He only cared about getting to Hope before she was killed. Maybe this fight of hers was impossible. But maybe his throwing blades could be the thing that tipped the scales into possible. One thing he was sure of: He couldn't live the rest of his life wondering about it. He would find out tonight, right or wrong. That resolution filled him with burning exuberance, and he ran on.

When he neared the palace wall, he saw that the gate had been broken into pieces. The metal was corroded through with rust that had not been there that afternoon. No doubt Brigga Lin's doing.

The courtyard was strewn with the bodies of soldiers, some horribly disfigured, some hacked to pieces or run through. There was so much to take in, even his new vision had trouble processing it all. So he didn't notice the two soldiers off to one side, still alive and armed with rifles. One of them took aim, but as Red's gaze finally turned toward them, the other soldier's eyes went wide and he knocked the rifle aside, sending the shot into the night sky.

'That's *him*,' said the second soldier. 'Look at the *eyes*!'

'Oh, piss!' said the rifleman.

'We survived those two horrors, and you almost got us worse than killed anyway,' said the second.

Red reached for his throwing knives, not sure what was going on. But they both threw down their rifles and raised their hands in the air.

'Spare us, please!' the first one begged. 'I've got a little girl at home!'

Red's eyes swept through the piles of bodies in the courtyard again. Whether it was right or wrong, he couldn't add two more, especially unarmed. 'Don't follow me.'

'On my honor!' the man said.

Red turned and entered the palace. They'd identified him somehow. There was another plan at work here. He would need to go carefully from this point. Stealth was really more his thing anyway.

When things had been going well, Hope was tempted to see it as a sign that she had made the right choice. Now that

things were turning against them, did that mean her choice
had been wrong? Did one cancel the other out?

These thoughts flitted through her mind as she and Brigga
Lin fought their way up the staircase, level by level, waves of
soldiers pressing down on them from above. The soldiers
were desperate now, driven by the biomancers, who had
finally joined the fray.

They'd come first singly or in pairs, looking flustered and
disheveled, as if roused from sleep or meditation. Those first
biomancers did little more than add to the chaos, shouting at
the soldiers to stand their ground even as Hope cut them
down.

But once enough of them had arrived, they organized
and formed a plan of sorts. They didn't have Brigga Lin's
ability to cast at a distance, and they seemed unwilling to
come within range of Hope's blade. Instead they began to
change individual soldiers into mindless beastlike people
with fangs or claws or pinchers. Those creatures were much
harder to put down, continuing to attack even after
mortally wounded.

Hope noticed that the beast people didn't seem to care all
that much whom they attacked, though. They would bite or
slash at whatever was moving in front of them. So rather
than fight them, she spun them around and shoved them
back up the stairs at the soldiers. It was not precise, but it
cleared the way to wet her blade with biomancers. And that
was why she'd come, after all.

The two women continued to climb with slow but relent-
less progress. When they finally reached the tenth level
where Brigga Lin said the biomancer council was supposed
to be convened, Hope was surprised to see moonlight
streaming in through the windows of the vast, open chamber. Was it still the same night they had begun this fight?
She was bleeding from at least twenty different wounds,

and every muscle in her body screamed. Brigga Lin did not look much better. Her beautiful dress was more red than white. A steady stream of blood leaked from her nose, most likely the constant efforts of her biomancery, and her skin was ghastly pale.

But the tide of soldiers had finally turned. Hope and Brigga Lin killed the few who remained in the hallway, and when they reached the council chamber, they found it nearly empty. Hope had lost count of how many white robes she had cut down. They had seemed endless. But now she wondered if they might actually be close to accomplishing their goal.

'Where is the council?' Brigga Lin raged at the lone biomancer in the chamber. Her hands swept sideways, and his legs broke outward at the knees. He dropped to the floor and when he screamed, his hood fell back and Hope saw his face. It was Teltho Kan.

'Wait!' said Hope. 'That one is mine!'

Brigga Lin's hands froze in mid-gesture. 'This is the one who murdered your people?'

'Oh yes, I am!' shouted Teltho Kan, his voice constricted with pain. 'I used them as incubators for a breed of giant wasp I was perfecting.' He laughed, a desperate, high-pitched sound.

Brigga Lin stepped back a few paces. 'He's yours, then. But make him tell you where the council members are hiding.'

'None of the others we killed were council members?' asked Hope.

'They were only novices,' hissed Teltho Kan. 'Unimportant and easily replaced. In fact, you did us a favor, thinning out their ranks like that. Most of them were barely worthy of the order. Those few who survived will be the stronger for it.' He laughed again.

Perhaps it was just the pain of having both legs shattered, but he looked quite mad with that grin on his face.
Again Hope felt a curl of pity around the edge of her
vision. It had been creeping up all night, and each time she
fought it off. But it was hard, now, to truly know what was
right. When witnessing the horror of what the biomancers
did from the outside, it had been easy to point to them and
say, *You are wrong*. But now that she had her own biomancer
– her own horror-maker – it was not so easy. She looked
down at herself and saw that her black leather armor
gleamed wet with blood. Her hands were sticky with it.
How could any choice that was truly right bring so much
death and pain?

'Where is the rest of the council, Kan?' asked Hope, her
voice weary.

'Where is your red-eyed lackey?' He looked around.

'He isn't here.'

He nodded. 'You're a good liar. Especially for a Vinchen.
But we both know that couldn't be true. He could no more
leave your side than you could abandon your oath.'

'Truly, Kan. He isn't here.' Hope didn't know what Teltho
Kan had planned for Red, but she was grateful he wasn't
there to find out.

A look of dread swept across Teltho Kan's face. He shook
his head vehemently. 'No, no, that can't be. He *must* be here.
I *told* them he would be here. I *swore* it!' He glared up at her.
'You knew, didn't you? You cunt, how did you know? How
did you . . .' He turned desperately around, scanning the
room. His broken legs cracked further, but he didn't seem to
notice. He looked lost. Terrified. Pathetic. 'How could I be
wrong . . .'

'Anyone can be wrong.' Even as Hope said that, she realized she was telling not just him, but herself. She had been
fighting off the doubts since they began this night, but seeing

the man she hated most in the world rendered broken and helpless before her gave her the courage to finally let them in. To a Vinchen warrior, carrying out vengeance was the most important thing he could do. The Vinchen code was quite clear on that point. But it had been celebrating Carmichael's life, not his death, that had felt right to her. Would she be honoring her parents and her village by all this death? Thinking back on it, Hurlo had never explicitly condoned her thirst for vengeance. Perhaps even he had doubts that the code was always right. After all, he broke it when he accepted her as a pupil.

'I thought swearing vengeance on you was an honorable oath,' she said quietly. 'I thought your death would somehow bring meaning to the meaningless waste of life you caused. But now I understand that it wouldn't make any difference. That neither my parents nor my teachers would have wanted me to squander my life to take yours.'

'Bleak Hope?' asked Brigga Lin, looking confused.

'This oath I made was the selfish and vindictive wish of a hurt child. Understandable, but not honorable. And I am no longer a child.'

She lowered her sword.

'No! Wait! You *must* kill me!' said Teltho Kan. 'Don't you see? I have failed them! You don't know what they will do to me, how they will make me suffer!'

'It is not my purpose to punish or save you,' said Hope. 'My life has intertwined with yours long enough. Here is where we part.' She turned away from him.

His face twisted in fury. 'No . . .' He lunged out, reaching for her sword hand.

'Hope!' Red's voice rang like a bell.

In the same moment that Teltho Kan's fingers grazed Hope's knuckles, a throwing blade embedded itself in his eye and he dropped to the ground.

Hope looked down at her hand and saw the knuckles withering, shrinking, desiccating, turning to rot. Her sword clattered to the floor.

She could hear Red calling her name. He had come after all. By his own choice. Even as the pain twisted in her hand, a part of her felt joy that he had chosen to join her on his own. And a part of her was terrified of what sort of trap Teltho Kan had laid for him.

But then pain took over her body, wiping out thoughts of anything else. Red's blade had killed the biomancer, slowing down the process a little, but not stopping it. The rot spread to Hope's fingers. She felt them dying one by one, each death sending a blast of agony up through her arm and into her skull.

Red was running toward her. Brigga Lin, too. But the rot was fast. It would finish her first. And even if they did reach her in time, what could they do? What could *she* do? She swayed, and her vision began to dim. She felt herself slipping away as the pain and rot traveled up into her palm.

'Hope!' screamed Red.

But she had made a promise to Red. Not to give up. Ever. That, she decided, was a vow worth keeping.

She forced herself to concentrate. She looked down at her hand. It was a curled and blackened thing, oozing pus. The rot was reaching up toward her wrist. She dropped to her knees and picked up the Song of Sorrows with her good hand. Then she brought the blade down, cutting off her rotting hand just above the wrist.

The rot was gone. She no longer felt its slow, withering death. Instead, there was a bright, hot pain, as blood poured from the stump of her forearm. The floor around her was suddenly slick with it. She pulled the strap tight on her sleeve to slow down the flow. Then she stared at the empty space where her hand used to be. That was when she finally screamed.

Then Red was there and she sank back into his warm embrace.

'Oh, God, Hope, I'm so sorry, so sorry!' His sweaty hand pressed her cold cheek as he held her. 'It'll be okay, we're going to make this okay.'

'You came,' said Hope, fighting to stay conscious.

'I'm here. I couldn't stay away. No matter what.'

She smiled faintly. 'Like we promised. You and me. Hope and Red. No matter what.'

'That's right,' he said, grinning through his tears.

'I can fix you.' Brigga Lin cradled Hope's stump in her hands. 'Let me seal this now, and I'll fix it later when I have materials.'

Hope nodded, too weak now to speak.

Brigga Lin brought the bleeding stump up to her lips. She kissed the white gleam of bone in the center gently, almost reverently. Immediately, the wound closed. Hope shuddered as the pain left her body, replaced by something cool and soothing.

'Well,' came a voice that sounded as old as dust. 'It appears that Teltho Kan was right after all.'

Hope weakly lifted her head up from Red's lap and saw a fresh troop of soldiers come boiling into the chamber from the stairs. They formed a ring around the three, rifles pointed inward at them.

'Welcome to the Council of Biomancery,' said the voice. Hope followed the sound to the far side of the council chambers, where a line of men in hooded white robes stood motionless, their hands joined, their faces hidden.

*   *   *

Red held Hope tightly to his chest, his arms protectively around her, as soldiers pointed rifles at them. He had been too slow to save her hand. He would save the rest of her, whatever the cost.

'There you are.' Brigga Lin glared at the biomancers on the far side of the room. She wiped the line of blood from her nose and slowly stood. 'Don't worry, Bleak Hope. I'll finish this.'

She raised her hands and began a series of fluid gestures so rapid, even Red's eyes could barely follow them. Then she swept her arms out toward the line of biomancers.

The air rippled around them, but nothing else happened.

'Did you really think we would have let you live if you posed a true threat to us?' asked the one in the center in the same dusty voice they'd heard before, now with just a hint of amusement.

Brigga Lin stepped back, all of her dark arrogance evaporated.

'Let me live?'

'Of course. Those poor souls we sent down there to feed you only knew that we wanted them to mention the female Vinchen within your hearing. We knew you wouldn't be able to resist. That you would kill them, make your escape, and seek her out. That with you egging her on, the female Vinchen might grow bold enough to attack us directly. And Teltho Kan was certain that the red-eyed youth wouldn't be able to let you attempt such a thing without him. It's a shame Teltho Kan didn't live long enough to see that he had been correct after all. This success would have finally brought him into the council.'

'Well, you got me.' Still cradling Hope, Red reached down and pulled out a throwing knife. 'But I reckon you'll be sorry you did. You might be able to block magic, but let's see you block steel.'

'You cannot kill all of us.'

'You're going to kill us anyway, so I might as well take down as many as I can.'

'On the contrary, we do not wish to kill you. And if you agree to surrender yourself to us peacefully, we will even set your Vinchen free.'

'You're lying.'

'We are incapable of perjury.'

Red looked at Brigga Lin.

'Biomancers cannot lie,' she conceded. 'Making untrue statements would weaken our power.'

Red turned back to the biomancer council. 'You'll let Hope go free? No restrictions? No hunting her down later?'

'If she leaves Stonepeak and never returns, for as long as you cooperate with us, we will never harm her directly.'

'Why?' asked Hope, her voice hoarse. She struggled to sit up, her stump tucked under her other arm. 'What will you do to him?'

'Train him. Help him realize his full potential,' said a different biomancer, his voice like dripping oil. 'He will be an essential element in saving our empire.'

'What's so special about me?' asked Red.

There was a pause.

'Perhaps he will be more willing to comply if he knows the whole truth,' said the biomancer with a voice like oil.

'Or he will become even more unwilling,' said another like rusty metal.

'We shall see,' said the dusty voice. 'Young man, you are the culmination of an experiment that has lasted almost twenty years. We developed a substance that caused feelings of confidence and sexual arousal in those who inhaled it. It was also highly addictive and, after repeated use, fatal. Its name was *Coractulous spucaceas*. But you would most likely know it as coral spice.'

'Wait,' said Red. '*You* invented coral spice? The drug?'

'It only behaved like a recreational drug. Its true purpose was to alter the unborn children of female users while they were still in the womb and vulnerable to such drastic changes.'

'Alter?' asked Brigga Lin.

'It would improve their reflexes and hand-eye coordination to performance levels well beyond a normal person. It would also mark these children with red eyes so we could readily identify them. But every one we found did not live longer than a month. We thought none had survived, so the experiment was considered a failure. Until Teltho Kan saw you.'

'You're saying that countless lives were ruined on the off chance someone like me might come along?' demanded Red.

'We did not force people to take the drug. One of our number was most insistent on that point.'

'There must always be an element of choice,' said the oily voice.

'So my whole life, the reason I've always been so clever with my hands and good with my aim? That was the coral spice.'

'Correct.'

'And Teltho Kan,' said Hope. 'He intensified it.'

'Yes. The subject's full ability lay dormant until unlocked by a biomancer.'

'Why do you need him?' Hope struggled to her knees. 'What is he saving the empire from?'

'That we will not tell you. Suffice it to say, it is a threat greater than even our power alone can face.'

'So if I agree to help you,' asked Red, 'you'll let Hope go free?'

'Yes.'

'What about Brigga Lin?'

There was a pause.

'She should be disciplined for her heresy.'

'You mean tortured to death, right?'

Another pause.

'Yes.'

Red's face set. 'Then I want you to let her go along with Hope.'

'Why? What is she to you?'

Red turned to Brigga Lin. She stared back, looking baffled. Perhaps even shocked. Red didn't blame her. After all, it was partly her fault they were in this mess. But that wasn't the most important thing right now. That was in the past and couldn't be changed. But something else could be changed.

'You fix her,' he said quietly to Brigga Lin. 'You *help* her. From now on. You have to be there for her when I can't be. Keen?'

'I . . .' She looked at him with something close to awe. 'Yes. I will. I swear it on the truth of the universal God that I will serve her until my last breath.'

'Good,' said Red.

'Red, no, please don't do this.' Hope struggled to her feet, her face pinched and wan. She swayed and Red caught her. 'Please don't leave your fate in their hands.'

'Listen, old pot,' he said quietly, forcing a smile as he held her in his arms. 'This is all crystal. We either both die today. Or we both live apart.'

'Red . . .' Her face twisted up. 'I wish I had—'

'Hey, just for a little while.' He didn't know what she'd been about to say, but he could barely hold on to this brave face as it was. One more thing might tip him over.

He gently handed Hope to Brigga Lin. 'Her ship is called the *Lady's Gambit*. Get her to our people. And fix her up.'

Brigga Lin drew herself up to her full height and nodded curtly. 'I will.'

Red turned back to the biomancer council. The biomancer in the center raised his hand, and the soldiers shifted to either side, leaving the doorway to the stairs open.

Hope drew herself up and shook off Brigga Lin's support. She gave Red one last look, then turned and walked slowly down the steps. Brigga Lin followed closely behind, her hands outstretched, ready to catch Hope if she stumbled. And it was that last sight that gave Red some tiny bit of comfort that they would be all right.

He watched until they were completely out of sight. Then he turned back to the line of hooded old men. 'Alright, you creepy gafs. I'm yours.'

31

*I*t was a long walk back to the *Lady's Gambit*. The sun was already in the sky by the time they arrived. Hope had insisted on leaving the palace without help, but now she leaned heavily on Brigga Lin, a sheen of sweat on her forehead.

It seemed the crew had been up all night waiting, because the moment she was in view, they jumped off the ship and rushed down the dock toward her, talking over each other.

'Where's Red?' asked Sadie.

'Where's your pissing *hand*?' asked Nettles.

'I-I can fix her,' stammered Brigga Lin, looking oddly intimidated by the cluster of concerned people around them. 'Red made me promise to fix her.'

'Where in piss'ell is *Red*?' Sadie said again.

'They took him, Sadie,' said Hope, her voice weak. 'They took our Red.'

Sadie's face went pale, and her mouth set. 'That stupid, stupid boy.'

'I didn't want . . . him . . . to come . . .' Another wave of dizziness swept over Hope, and the ground rushed up. But she heard a *clank* of metal, and two strong hands caught her. She looked into Filler's big, open face.

'I've got you, Captain,' he said.

'Filler . . .' Her voice broke. Her fingers moved lightly across his hairy cheek. 'He saved us. He traded himself.'

'Then we'll just have to steal him back, won't we, Captain?' He carried her onto the ship and back to the captain's quarters. Every other step was a clank, and Hope realized he was wearing the metal brace that he and Alash had constructed. He laid her down on the bunk.

'How can you possibly fix her?' Alash asked Brigga Lin.

'I am – I *was* a biomancer.'

The group erupted in angry shouts.

'But *now*' – Hope cut in, her voice hard as she mustered enough strength to sit up on her own – 'now, she's one of us. Keen?'

They all fell silent.

Then Missing Finn said, 'You heard the captain. That's how it is now.'

Hope put her hand on Finn's shoulder. 'Thank you, Mr. Finn.'

'So how *are* you going to fix her?' Alash asked.

'I just need a limb to replace it,' she said. 'Perhaps an animal limb . . .'

'No! No beast parts!' snapped Hope, thinking of Ranking, of the owl people, of those soldiers who had been transformed. She wanted nothing to do with that. She pointed at Filler's metal knee brace and turned to Alash. 'You make me something.'

His eyes widened and then his face grew serious. 'Right away, Captain. I should have thought of it myself.'

'Think of it now,' she said.

Over the next few days, Hope slipped in and out of consciousness. Brigga Lin came in frequently to push foul-smelling potions on her, saying it would help restore her after the blood loss. Filler and Alash would come in now and then to take measurements or discuss some element of the prosthesis design with her.

Once she was feeling well enough, she told Sadie and Nettles every detail of how Red had saved her not once, but twice in a single night.

'So you're sure they won't kill him or torture him?' asked Sadie.

Hope shook her head. 'They spoke as if he was one of the most important people in the empire.'

'But you know what those biomancers are capable of,' said Nettles. 'They'll do something to him, true as trouble.'

Hope did know, but it was abundantly clear she could not defeat the biomancer council.

After they left, she lay in her bunk, the yellow light of the fading sun spilling through the porthole. She'd always avoided staying in the captain's quarters before, and now she knew why. Sitting here in this small, neat room reminded her of loss. Carmichael, of course. But that in turn made her think of Hurlo, and her parents. And now Red. She could still see him in that last moment, giving her a grin as if she didn't know him well enough by now to see it was forced. A pain welled up inside that she'd never felt before. She missed him already, and it hurt more than any loss before it.

Filler's words came back to her: *We'll just have to steal him back, won't we?* And he was right. This was one person the biomancers had taken that she could still take back. She just needed to figure out how.

A short time later, Brigga Lin came in with another of her unpleasant tonics. This one made Hope drowsy, and soon she drifted to sleep. In her dreams, she and Red were back outside the palace walls. He was looking at her with that sweet, agonized expression and he said, *We have a choice. We can be whatever we like.*

When she woke, she knew what she must do.

The next day, Alash and Filler gathered everyone in Hope's cabin and proudly presented the prosthesis. They had converted the leather arm sheath from the pole mechanism and installed a hinge above that where her wrist had been. Then they fixed a clamp at the end of the hinge, big enough to hold her sword.

'Now we get to the complicated bit,' said Alash. 'The hinge has full rotation, as you requested.' He demonstrated by rolling the clamp around. 'And it can also lock into place when necessary, also as you requested.'

'Sounds good so far.' Hope watched Filler carefully slide the sheath over her stump and strap it in place.

'Here's the part you won't like,' said Alash. 'We can use the same catch-and-release system that Filler and I designed for his knee, but you'll have to operate it with your other hand.'

Hope shook her head. 'I'll need the other hand. Find a different way.'

'There *is* no other way.' Alash's face flushed with frustration.

'Perhaps I can help?' asked Brigga Lin.

'No beast parts,' said Hope.

'No,' agreed Brigga Lin. She held out her hand to Filler, who wordlessly handed Hope's sheathed arm to her. She pointed to the metal wires. 'Let me make sure I understand this mechanism correctly. It appears that if there was adjustable flex tension along this line, that would lock the hinge when and where necessary, at any point in the rotation?'

'Yeah,' said Filler. 'But how would you set that tension without using the other hand?'

'By fusing it to her tendons. Then she would control it with the same reflex she would normally use to rotate her wrist. A comparable motion.'

'Combining man and machine?' whispered Alash, looking at once shocked and fascinated.

'Do it,' said Hope.

'The procedure will be intensely painful,' said Brigga Lin. 'Perhaps we should wait until you've had more time to regain your health.'

'Do it now.'

She looked at Filler. He looked back at her helplessly. 'You heard the captain.'

'Fine,' said Brigga Lin, crisp and businesslike. 'Give her a strip of leather to bite so she doesn't break her teeth or chew out her tongue.'

Filler pulled off his belt, folded it in half, and held it out to Hope. She bit down on it, then nodded to Brigga Lin.

The pain was twice that of cutting off her own hand. It burrowed in deep beneath her flesh and coiled up until it felt like metal wires were being inserted into every muscle in her arm. She screamed through the belt until her voice was hoarse. But she didn't pass out. She refused to pass out. She would see this through as she had seen every terrible thing. The fact that she was the one suffering made no difference. She would never look away.

Finally, Brigga Lin stepped back, dabbing at her nose, which had started to bleed again. They let Hope catch her breath. Nettles forced her to drink some water. Then Alash and Filler completed the mechanical portion. And it was done.

Hope rose slowly from the bunk, steadying herself on the edge with her regular hand. She lifted up her new hand and gazed at it with satisfaction. 'I need room.'

She walked slowly toward the doorway. Filler offered to help, but she shook her head and continued on her own. Once she was out on the quarter deck, she said quietly, 'My sword.'

They had all followed cautiously behind her. Nettles handed her the sword, then stepped back with the others.

Hope fastened the hilt to her clamp. She twisted her arm, and the Song of Sorrows cut through the night sky. It still sang, but the tone was different now. Darker, yes, but smoother as well. She snapped it one way, then the other, in a smooth figure eight movement that made one long, mournful hum. Then she twisted her wrist, and the sword locked into place, pointing upward. It felt more a part of her than ever before. She smiled and held the blade up close to her face. In its reflection, she saw her crew standing behind her.

She lowered her blade and turned to them.

'I dedicated my life to avenging those who were already dead.' She shook her head. 'It makes so little sense to me now.'

They looked at each other, not grasping where she was headed with this. She didn't blame them.

'I will get Red back,' she continued. 'I cannot beat the Council of Biomancery head-on. Not yet. So I will attack their extremities. I will hack them apart, bit by bit, one biomancer or imperial ship at a time. If I must, I will tear this empire down until there is nothing left standing except Red, free. I will be a dark wind of chaos that wipes it all away so that something better can take its place.'

'Hope . . .' said Sadie.

'There is no Hope. Not anymore. From now on, they will know me as Dire Bane.'

She looked at each of them in turn. Sadie, Missing Finn, Filler, Nettles, Alash, and Brigga Lin. 'Are you with me?'

It was Nettles who dropped to one knee first. 'Dire Bane, champion of the people and scourge of the empire, I'm with you.'

Filler quickly followed, his metal knee squeaking as he knelt. 'I'm with you.'

'I abhor violence,' said Alash as he knelt, 'but if it saves my cousin, I'm with you.'

'I was hoping for a quiet retirement,' said Sadie. 'But I reckon I'd get bored of that fast anyway. I'm with you. I ain't going to kneel, though. I wouldn't be able to get back up.'

'If Sadie's with you, then so am I,' said Missing Finn. 'Besides, I've gotten a little sotted with this ship. And if it's pirating we're to be doing, she'll need to be refitted with cannons.'

Hope turned to Brigga Lin, the newest member of the crew.

'Red made you swear to help me. And you have. This course we plan to follow will be hard. If you want to leave now, I will consider your oath fulfilled.'

Brigga Lin's dark eyes were unreadable. 'Red's generosity in bargaining for my life when he hardly knew me – indeed when he had cause to hate me – is more kindness than I have known in my life. I will not consider my oath fulfilled until Red is free or I am dead.' She curtseyed low.

Hope swiveled her sword to point down and set the tip on the wooden deck. 'We'll be pirates, then. And woe to any who cross our path.'

Red stood at the window, gazing out over the building tops of Stonepeak. He had not realized until now just how far he could see. He watched as the *Lady's Gambit* glided out to sea, no imperial ships in pursuit.

'Alright, I reckon you made good on your promise,' he said.

'Do you think that you will remember her when we are done with you?' asked the dusty voice. 'Do you think you will even be *you*?'

Red turned to look at the hooded figure who hadn't left his side and didn't seem to need food or sleep. 'What else would I be?'

The biomancer pulled back his hood to reveal a face as hard and jagged as the rock on which the palace stood. With stone lips that barely moved, he said, 'When we are finished with you, you will not even be a man. You will be a shadow of death.'

Look out for

BANE AND SHADOW

The Empire of Storms: Book Two

by

Jon Skovron

With New Laven as her base of operations, Hope terrorises imperial ships as the pirate Dire Bane. Her fame spreads throughout and many who are dissatisfied with the emperor and his biomancers flock to her banner.

Red struggles to keep his sanity as the biomancers try to turn him into a cold-blooded assassin. He finds comfort in palace politics and befriends the son of the emperor and an ambassador from Aukbontar, a country located across the Dark Sea.

The new Grandteacher of the Vinchen has joined with the biomancers and they have a common enemy: Hope.

orbit

www.orbitbooks.net

A Cursory Examination Regarding the Common Folk Slang of New Laven

By Thoriston Baggelworthy

Reprinted with kind permission from the *Hollow Falls Gentleman's Quarterly*

It is true that the youth of the upper classes have developed the odd slang word here or there. For example, in Hollow Falls I hear them call each other 'fronzies' instead of friends. And rather than being pleased with something, they are invariably 'smitten' with it, regardless of the actual degree of pleasure they feel. But I recently spent a great deal of time in downtown New Laven where the lower classes reside. I was there to collect art and information concerning the great proto-Passionist painter and subject of my forthcoming biography, Lady Gulia Pastinas. During my time in the neighborhoods of Silverback, Hammer Point, and Paradise Circle, I encountered a folk slang so bewilderingly complex and pervasive, at times it seemed like they were speaking another language.

For your interest and amusement, I have recorded some of the more popular words and phrases of this curious and sometimes lewd slang of the lower classes. I have endeavored, to the best of my ability, to set down what I believe to be the meanings for these words, as well as theories regarding their etymological origins. Some meanings were fairly obvious, but I confess that with some I am merely taking a stab in the dark, based on the contexts in which I heard them.

What follows is not the sum total of the New Laven folk slang, but a sampling of the popular words and phrases I encountered during my time there.

Balls and pricks: Nonsense or foolishness. Both 'balls' and 'pricks' derive from the more universal slang for the male genitalia (the scrotum and penis, respectively), although why such words would imply foolishness is unclear.

Bilge: Stomach. A great many slang words are taken from sailing and ship vocabulary, which is curious, since the majority of inhabitants have never set foot on a ship.

Bludgeon: Stupid. It is worth noting that while we would typically use this word as a noun (e.g. a club or cudgel) or as a verb (e.g. to bludgeon someone), the lower classes use this word exclusively as an adjective.

Boot: Thug or gangster who serves a crime boss. While general criminal activity is rampant in the neighborhoods of Paradise Circle and Hammer Point, the organized crime element is strong enough to nearly be considered a form of neighborhood governance. To be a 'boot' for a powerful crime boss is considered a position of power and respect and often elicits fear in those not affiliated. At the same time, the 'boot' must give complete allegiance to his boss, including laying down his life in service if called to do so. In this respect, they remind me a great deal of our own imperial soldiers, who work tirelessly and selflessly to ensure the safety of our empire.

Cock-dribble: A loathsome, useless person. 'Cock' is another universal slang word for male genitalia. The 'dribble,' I suspect, refers to ejaculate. One might infer, then, that the meaning derives from ejaculate that escaped outside of copulation, something which would indeed be useless.

Chum and larder: Friendly or personable. While it is clear that 'larder,' or food pantry, is a pleasing thing, especially for those for whom healthy sustenance is difficult to obtain, I confess I have been unable to determine the sense in using the word 'chum,' which to my knowledge only means inedible bits of fish dropped into the water to encourage larger fish to approach and be more easily caught. I suspect there may have been some intermediate usage of the word that has been lost to memory.

Cunt-dropping: An idiot or ignorant fool. The word 'cunt' is derived from the more universal slang for the female genitalia. The implication, I suspect, is either that the recipient of the label has acted so stupidly, it is as if they had just been born, or that the speaker believes them to have been dropped on their head as an infant. So far, I have been unable to determine which is meant.

Drain the bucket: To love or enjoy something. I believe this phrase derives from the more universal slang phrase 'To eat it up.' Again, it is worth noting that lower classes, for whom sustenance can be difficult to obtain, place a great deal of value in food and drink.

Gaf: Person or acquaintance. This is one of the most slippery words I encountered. At times, the word signified only someone the speaker did not know, or did not know well. But at other times, there was an inflection to the word which indicated a mild distaste for the person.

Go leeward: Something that goes wrong or turns out poorly. Here is another example of a sailing term used in a new context. Traditionally, 'leeward' refers to the side of something (usually a ship or coastal land) that is not facing the wind. Why the leeward would be considered negative in this case is unclear.

Grave: Serious. It seems highly likely that the word derives from the more literal meaning of a place where the dead are buried. It is curious they would use or even know this word, considering there is no land in downtown New Laven for burial. The inhabitants either cremate their dead, or simply throw them into the ocean.

Imp: Imperial police. I suspect it is not a coincidence that the lower classes use a nickname for the imperial police that is also the word for a troublesome demon or spirit. The distrust of imperial power is so pervasive in the lower classes as to be assumed by all.

In a drop: In a second or without hesitation. The origin of this phrase confounds me. My current hypothesis is that at some point in the distant past, there was a method of time keeping that involved water or liquid of some kind and this phrase is the only surviving record of it.

Keen: To understand. Like 'gaf,' the usage of this word is somewhat fluid. Depending on context, this word can either be used in a sentence, as in 'Do you keen?' or on its own, as in simply 'Keen?' In either case, the speaker wishes to know whether the listener grasps their meaning, either direct or implied.

Lacy: An upper class or rich person. It should be noted that almost without exception, a strong negative opinion is implied.

Leaky: To be sexually aroused. Although the original meaning may have derived from the secretion of vaginal fluid during female sexual arousal, the present day use seems to be nonspecific regarding gender.

Molly: Young woman. This, along with its counterpart (see 'Tom'), is one of the few gender-specific titles used. There is generally a suggestion that the young woman is attractive or desirable in some way, although sometimes a more neutral meaning is implied. The difference is suggested in both context and tone.

Nearly choked on the gad: To laugh really hard. While the general idea of this phrase is somewhat obvious, of laughing so hard one coughs or chokes on their own saliva, I have been unable to find a specific meaning or origin for the word 'gad.'

Not for tossing: Someone who does not like or is not interested in sex (see 'Toss'). It is interesting to note that there is no negative meaning implied in this phrase. Indeed, both times I had occasion to hear it used, there was a measure of respect implied, which was surprising, given the generally liberal sexuality that is rampant among the lower classes.

Nothing but jape: To tease or give someone a hard time. Derived from the word 'jape,' which, along with 'japery,' is employed far more frequently by the lower classes than it is by the upper classes.

Old pot: A good friend. I have been unable to determine why a 'pot' should inspire such an affectionate title. Perhaps it again goes back to the idea that the lower classes place far more value on food and drink than we do. Simple pleasures for simple folk, as it were.

Pat: Popular or appealing. I confess the meaning of this word somewhat eludes me. I was never able to predict when something looked 'pat' or was 'pat,' yet every person I spoke to considered it so obvious, they had trouble explaining why it was 'pat.'

Piss: This is an all-purpose curse word. I have heard it used as a noun, verb, and even an adverb. Rarely is it used for the more universal slang for urine.

Pissed and peppered: To be upset. I have been unable to determine (or even conjecture) how these two words came to be used together. And yet, there is something that feels wholly appropriate that they are. Though coarse and vulgar, there is at times an undeniably poetic quality to this common folk slang that defies analysis.

Piss'ell: A contraction of 'piss' and 'hell,' used as an exclamation of an unpleasant surprise.

Ponce: Someone who is soft or weak-willed. Although the more universal use of this word refers only to men, the usage among the lower classes seems to be gender neutral.

Roll: To steal from someone. Usually in a physically violent manner. My hypothesis is that the word derives from the act of knocking the victim unconscious, then rolling their inert body over for easier access to any money or goods they might be harboring.

Salthead: Affectionate insult for someone exhibiting stupid behavior. I have been unable to determine when to use this word and when to use the more insulting 'bludgeon.' At times, it seems to be the severity of the stupidity. At other times it seems more to do with the relationship between the speaker and the subject.

Simple as sideways: Easily accomplished. What most confounds me about this phrase is just how unnecessary 'as sideways' is, when simply saying it is 'simple' would get the meaning across just as easily. As far as I can tell, it does not add in any way to the meaning and exists simply for alliteration.

Slice: Derogatory term for a woman or a vagina. I did note that while both men and women use the term, men invariably use it as a serious insult, but women sometimes employ it more as good-natured banter with no real offense meant or taken. I have come to suspect this disparity has something to do with the noted liberality concerning gender among the lower classes.

Slide: Leave or escape. The choice of the word 'slide' I think originally suggested that the person was leaving in a smooth or artful manner, but modern use seems to have expanded to a more general meaning.

Slippy: Crazy or unpredictable. Most likely this a shortening of the word 'slippery' and originally meant that the meaning of a person's words or actions was difficult to understand.

Sotted: To be in love. This is possibly my favorite word in the common folk slang of New Laven. To me it suggests that the speaker is saturated with feelings of affection for another person.

Soundly: Loudly. When I first heard this word, I thought it was one of those rare times in the folk slang of New Laven where the relationship between the word and its meaning was abundantly clear. But then I spoke to several native speakers, and they all agreed that 'sound' did not derive from the word for 'noise' in this case, but from 'sounding,' the act of measuring the depth of the ocean or other body of water. The lower classes of Paradise Circle have a rich, earthy sense of humor, and I confess that I could not determine if they were teasing me or not.

Southend: The act of selling an unwilling person to a ship's captain as an indentured servant. Other than robbery, this is perhaps the biggest danger to any visitor to Paradise Circle. There are inns and brothels which drug unsuspecting lodgers with a mild narcotic called black rose and sell them to ship captains. The victim usually wakes up the following day many miles out to sea, where they are given the option to either work on the crew or be thrown overboard as a stowaway. Most frequently this practice is undertaken by ships heading for the Southern Isles, which are said to be cold, inhospitable, and barely civilized, and therefore not a popular destination.

Southie: Mildly derogatory term for someone from the Southern Isles. The Southern peoples are a hard, taciturn lot with yellow hair and pale skin. They are a rare sight in New Laven and stand out in the predominantly dark-haired population. I have given some thought to their notable physical disparity and believe that their ancestors migrated from another country many centuries ago. If not for the difficulty in crossing to the Southern Isles, I suspect they would have blended with the rest of the population some time ago.

Speak crystal: To be truthful or to speak clearly. Again, the meaning shifts, depending on context. While discussing this widely used phrase with a native speaker, he was surprised to learn that 'crystal' is a naturally forming substance that has been discovered on certain islands of the empire, most notably the Painted Caves of Pauper's Prayer. He had been unaware that the word had any meaning outside the context of the slang phrase he used so frequently.

Sugar lump: A nice person. It is important to note that both 'niceness' and sugar are rare commodities in both Paradise Circle and Hammer Point. Niceness is greatly valued, as long as the person in question is not weak-willed or soft (see 'Ponce').

Sunny: Something good or pleasant. As a life-long inhabitant of Hollow Falls, this word makes perfect sense to me. The amount of rainfall per year on New Laven is more than twice that of Stonepeak. The sun is something we see all too rarely, and is one of the few hardships we share with the lower classes.

Tom: A young man. As with its female counterpart (see 'Molly'), the meaning varies somewhat in context. Generally the assumption is that the young man is virile, handsome, and sexually active, although sometimes a more neutral meaning is implied.

Toss: To have sexual intercourse. This term does not differentiate male or female, heterosexual or homosexual, oral, vaginal,

or anal, but encompasses all of it. The sexual liberality of
the lower classes is well known, but I cannot emphasize
enough just how little shame or discretion they have. In
Paradise Circle, I once witnessed two people 'tossing' in an
open alley for all the world to see, and no one but myself
seemed to remark on it.

True as trouble: Something that is certain to happen. While
there is still the same alliterative nature found in other
phrases (see 'Simple as sideways'), it seems appropriate,
and perhaps even poetic, that the lower classes of New
Laven equate certainty with trouble. For all their sexual
liberality and criminal activity, they did not choose the
difficult, often life-threatening conditions found in
Paradise Circle and Hammer Point. Death from starvation and disease are common occurrences, and violence
a necessary part of survival. As I sit here writing this in
my warm, comfortable study, it gives me pause to
wonder if there is not something that we, the upper
classes, could do to alleviate some of their suffering.

Wag: This title is gender neutral. It can refer to a friend or
acquaintance, or even to someone not known personally
to the speaker. One of the few things I can say defini-
tively is that it is always in reference to a fellow member
of the lower classes. If someone is a 'true wag,' it means
they exemplify the qualities of bravery and loyalty, both
to friends and to the neighborhood, that are prized by
the community above all else.

I hope you found my cursory examination of the common
folk slang of New Laven both educational and entertaining.
One component that I feel I should note is the musicality. It is
impossible for me to capture in mere words the shifting quality of the speech, which is at once earthy and lyrical. As such,
for those of you who wish to learn more about this fascinating

and unpredictable folk slang, I strongly recommend you
venture to Silverback, or even better, all the way down to
Paradise Circle. The inhabitants there have an almost child-
like fondness for coins. A handful of silver will encourage a
great many of them to discourse at length on the subject of
both their slang and the culture of their neighborhood. For
my part, I plan to return after I complete my biography of
Lady Gulia Pastinas, perhaps with the intention of expand-
ing this small work into something larger, if there is enough
interest among the upper classes to warrant it.

Acknowledgments

I was six years old when the sea took a finger from my left hand. It was an experience that could have frightened me off of boats and sailing forever. But my grandfather, John Kelley, wouldn't hear of it, and instead imparted upon me such a fierce love of the ocean that, to this day, no matter what troubles me, when I am on a boat of any kind, I am always able to find some peace. It feels like a gross understatement to say that this book would not have been possible without him, as well as my aunt Laura, uncle Peter, and cousins, Alex and Liz, who continue on in the fine tradition of sailing, while I sit here, much too far from the sea, and only dream about it.

It feels equally inadequate to thank my friend and fellow writer, Stephanie Perkins, who has been a champion of this book from the very beginning. Whether as cheerleader, critic, or savvy business advisor, I am grateful for everything she has contributed.

I want to thank my agent, Jill Grinberg, who was completely game when I said, 'Hey, I'd like to write a book for grown-ups!' She and the rest of the staff at JGLM continue to amaze me, and I am so grateful to have them in my corner. Thanks also to my editor, Devi Pillai, who consistently demands more from me. I know she hopes someday to make me cry, and I cherish her all the more for it.

I would be remiss if I didn't acknowledge the excellent book *The Gangs of New York: An Informal History of the*

Underworld by Herbert Asbury, which inspired a lot of the gang culture of New Laven, and in particular the character of Sadie the Goat. By all accounts (some of them even semi-credible), Sadie was a real person who truly did terrorize the Hudson riverbank, if only for a brief time. Whether fact or folktale, I am indebted to that 'artist of mayhem.'

extras

orbit

www.orbitbooks.net

about the author

Jon Skovron is the author of young adult novels *Struts & Frets*, *Misfit*, *Man Made Boy* and *This Broken Wondrous World* from Viking Penguin. His short stories have appeared in publications such as *ChiZine* and *Jim Baen's Universe*, and more recently in anthologies like *Defy the Dark* from HarperCollins, and *GRIM* from Harlequin Teen. He lives just outside Washington, DC, with his two sons and two cats.

Find out more about Jon Skovron and other Orbit authors by registering for the free monthly newsletter at www.orbitbooks.net.

if you enjoyed
HOPE AND RED

look out for

SNAKEWOOD

by

Adrian Selby

Once they were a band of mercenaries who shook the pillars of the world through their cunning, their closely guarded alchemical brews and stone cold steel. Whoever met their price won.

Now, their glory days behind them and their genius leader in hiding, the warriors known as the 'Twenty' are being hunted down and eliminated one by one.

A lifetime of enemies has its own price.

Chapter 1

Gant

My name's Gant and I'm sorry for my poor writing. I was a mercenary soldier who never took to it till Kailen taught us. It's for him and all the boys that I wanted to put this down, a telling of what become of Kailen's Twenty.

Seems right to begin it the day me and Shale got sold out, at the heart of the summer just gone, down in the Red Hills Confederacy.

It was the day I began dying.

It was a job with a crew to ambush a supply caravan. It went badly for us and I took an arrow, the poison from which will shortly kill me.

I woke up sodden with dew and rain like the boys, soaked all over from the trees above us, but my mouth was dusty like sand. Rivers couldn't wet it. The compound I use to ease my bones leeches my spit. I speak soft.

I could hardly crack a whistle at the boys wrapped like a nest of slugs in their oilskins against the winds of the plains these woods were edged against. I'm old. I just kicked them up before getting my bow out of the sack I put it in to keep rain off the string. It was a beauty what I called Juletta and I had her for most of my life.

*　　*　　*

The boys were slow to get going, blowing and fussing as the freezing air got to work in that bit of dawn. They were quiet, and grim like ghosts in this light, pairing up to strap their leathers and get the swords pasted with poison.

I patted heads and squeezed shoulders and give words as I moved through the crew so they knew I was about and watching. I knew enough of their language that I could give them encouragement like I was one of them, something else Kailen give me to help me bond with a crew.

'Paste it thick,' I said as they put on the mittens and rubbed their blades with the soaked rags from the pot Remy had opened.

I looked around the boys I'd shared skins and pipes with under the moon those last few weeks. Good crew.

There was Remy, looking up at me from his mixing, face all scarred like a milky walnut and speaking lispy from razor fights and rackets he ran with before joining up for a pardon. He had a poison of his own he made, less refined than my own mix, less quick, more agony.

Yasthin was crouched next to him. He was still having to shake the cramp off his leg that took a mace a month before. Saved his money for his brother, told me he was investing it. The boys said his brother gambled it and laughed him up.

Dolly was next to Yasthin, chewing some bacon rinds. Told me how her da chased her soak of a mother through the streets, had done since she was young. Kids followed her da too, singing with him but staying clear of his knives. She joined so's she could help her da keep her younger brother.

All of them got sorrows that led them to the likes of me and a fat purse for a crossroads job, which I mean to say is a do-or-die.

Soon enough they're lined up and waiting for the Honour, Kailen's Honour, the best fightbrew Kigan ever mixed, so the best fightbrew ever mixed, even all these years later. The boys had been talking up this brew since I took command, makes you feel like you could punch holes in mountains when you've risen on it.

Yasthin was first in line for a measure. I had to stand on my toes to pour it in, lots of the boys taller than me. Then a kiss. The lips are the raw end of your terror and love. No steel can toughen lips, they betray more than the eyes when you're looking for intent and the kiss is for telling them there's always some way to die.

Little Booey was the tenth and last of the crew to get the measure. I took a slug myself and Rirgwil fixed my leathers. I waited for our teeth to chatter like aristos, then went over the plan again.

'In the trees north, beyond those fields, is Trukhar's supply caravan,' I said. 'Find it, kill who you can but burn the wagons, supplies, an' then go for the craftsmen. Shale's leadin' his crew in from east an' we got them pincered when we meet, red bands left arm so as you know. It's a do-or-die purse, you're there 'til the job is done or you're dead anyway.'

It was getting real for them now I could see. A couple were starting shakes with their first full measure of the brew, despite all the prep the previous few days.

'I taught you how to focus what's happening to you boys. This brew has won wars an' it'll deliver this purse if you can keep tight. Now move out.'

No more words, it was hand signs now to the forest.

Jonah front, Yasthin, Booey and Henny with me. Remy group northeast at treeline

We ran through the silver grass, chests shuddering with the crackle of our blood as the brew stretched our veins and filled our bones with iron and fire. The song of the earth was filling my ears.

Ahead of us was the wall of trees and within, the camp of the Blackhands. Remy's boys split from us and moved away.

Slow I signed.

Juletta was warm in my hands, the arrow in my fingers humming to fly. Then, the brew fierce in my eyes, I saw it, the red glow of a pipe some seventy yards ahead at the treeline.

Two men. On mark

I moved forward to take the shot and stepped into a nest of eggs. The bird, a big grey weger, screeched at me and flapped madly into the air inches from my face, its cry filling the sky. One of the boys shouted out, in his prime on the brew, and the two men saw us. We were dead. My boys' arrows followed mine, the two men were hit, only half a pip of a horn escaping for warning, but it was surely enough.

Run

I had killed us all. We went in anyway, that was the purse, and these boys primed like this weren't leaving without bloodshed.

As we hit the trees we spread out.

Enemy left signed Jonah.

Three were nearing through the trunks, draining their own brew as they come to from some half-eyed slumber. They were a clear shot so I led again, arrows hitting and a muffled crack of bones. All down.

In my brewed-up ears I could hear then the crack of bowstrings pulling at some way off, but it was all around us. The whistle of arrows proved us flanked as we dropped to the ground.

The boys opened up, moving as we practised, aiming to surprise any flanks and split them off so a group of us could move in directly to the caravan. It was shooting practice for Trukhar's soldiers.

I never saw Henny or Jonah again, just heard some laughing and screaming and the sound of blades at work before it died off.

I stayed put, watching for the enemy's movements. I was in the outroots of a tree, unspotted. You feel eyes on you with this brew. Then I saw two scouts moving right, following Booey and Datschke's run.

I took a sporebag and popped it on the end of an arrow. I stood up and sent it at the ground ahead of them.

From my belt I got me some white oak sap which I took for my eyes to see safe in the spore cloud. I put on a mask covered with the same stuff for breathing.

The spores were quick to get in them and they wheezed and clutched their throats as I finished them off.

I was hoping I could have saved my boys but I needed to be in some guts and get the job done with Shale's crew.

Horns were going up now, so the fighting was on. I saw a few coming at me from the trees ahead. I got behind a trunk but I knew I was spotted. They slowed up and the hemp creaked as they drew for shots. There were four of them, from their breathing, and I could hear their commander whispering for a flanking.

I opened up a satchel of ricepaper bags, each with quicklime and oiled feathers. I needed smoke. I doused a few bags with my flask and threw them out.

'Masks!' came the shout. As the paper soaked, the lime caught and the feathers put out a fierce smoke.

My eyes were still smeared good. I took a couple more arrowbags out, but these were agave powders for blistering the eyes and skin.

Two shots to tree trunks spread the powders in the air around their position and I moved out from the tree to them as they screeched and staggered about blind. The Honour give me the senses enough to read where they were without my eyes, better to shut them with smoke and powders in the air, and their brews weren't the Honour's equal. They moved like they were running through honey and were easy to pick off.

It was then I took the arrow that'll do for me. I'd got maybe fifty yards further on when I heard the bow draw, but with the noise ahead I couldn't place it that fraction quicker to save myself. The arrow went in at my hip, into my guts. Something's gave in there, and the poison's gone right in, black mustard oil for sure from the vapours burning in my nose, probably some of their venom too.

I was on my knees trying to grab the arrow when I saw them approach, two of them. The one who killed me was dropping his bow and they both closed with the hate of their own fightbrew, their eyes crimson, skin an angry red and all the noisies.

They think I'm done. They're fucking right, to a point. In my belt was the treated guaia bark for the mix they were known to use. No time to rip out the arrow and push the bark in.

They moved in together, one in front, the other flanking. One's a heavy in his mail coat and broadsword, a boy's weapon in a forest, too big. Older one had leathers and a long knife. Him first. My sight was going, the world going flat like a drawing, so I had to get rid of the wiser one while I could still see him, while I still had the Honour's edge.

Knife in hand I lunged sudden, the leap bigger than they reckoned. The older one reacted, a sidestep. The slash I made wasn't for hitting him though. It flicked out a spray of paste from the blade and sure enough some bit of it caught him in the face. I spun about, brought my blade up and parried the boy's desperate swing as he closed behind me, the blow forcing me down as it hit my knife, sending a smack through my guts as the arrow broke in me. He took sight of his mate holding his smoking face, scratching at his cheeks and bleeding. He glanced at the brown treacle running over my blade and legged it. He had the spunk to know he was beaten. I put the knife in the old man's throat to quiet my noisies, the blood's smell as sweet as fresh bread to me.

I picked up my Juletta and moved on. The trees were filling with Blackhands now. I didn't have the time to be taking off my wamba and sorting myself out a cure for the arrow, much less tugging at it now it was into me. I cussed at myself, for this was likely where I was going to die if I didn't get something to fix me. I was slowing up. I took a hit of the Honour to keep me fresh. It was going to make a fierce claim on the other side, but I would gladly take that if I could get some treatment.

Finally I reached the caravan; smoke from the blazing wagons and stores filled the trees ahead. The grain carts were burning so Shale, again, delivered the purse.

Then I come across Dolly, slumped against the roots of a tree. Four arrows were thrusting proud from her belly. She saw me and her eyes widened and she smiled.

'Gant, you're not done . . . Oh,' she said, seeing the arrow in me. I might have been swaying, she certainly didn't look right, faded somewhat, like she was becoming a ghost before me.

'Have you a flask, Gant, some more of the Honour?'

Her hands were full of earth, grabbing at it, having their final fling.

'I'm out, Dolly,' I said. 'I'm done too. I'm sorry for how it all ended.'

She blinked, grief pinching her up.

'It can't be over already. I'm twenty summers, Gant, this was goin' to be the big purse.'

A moment then I couldn't fill with any words.

'Tell my father, Gant, say . . .'

I was raising my bow. I did my best to clean an arrow on my leggings. She was watching me as I did it, knowing.

'Tell him I love him, Gant, tell him I got the Honour, and give him my purse and my brother a kiss.'

'I will.'

As I drew it she looked above me, seeing something I knew I wouldn't see, leagues away, some answers to her questions in her eyes thrilling her. I let fly, fell to my knees and sicked up.

Where was Shale?

My mouth was too dry to speak or shout for him, but I needed him. My eyes, the lids of them, were peeling back so's they would burn in the sun. I put my hands to my face. It was only visions, but my chest was heavy, like somebody sat on it and others were piling on. Looking through my hands as I held them up, it was like there were just bones there, flesh thin like the fins of a fish. My breathing rattled and I reached to my throat to try to open it up more.

'Gant!'

So much blood on him. He kneeled next to me. He's got grey eyes, no colour. Enemy to him is just so much warm meat to be put still. He don't much smile unless he's drunk. He mostly never drinks. He sniffed about me and at my wound, to get a reading of what was in it, then forced the arrow out with a knife and filled the hole with guaia bark while kneeling on my shoulder to keep me still. He was barking at some boys as he stuffed some rugara leaves, sap and all, into my mouth, holding my nose shut, drowning me. Fuck! My brains were buzzing sore like a hive was in them. Some frothing liquid filled up my chest and I was bucking about for breath. He poured from a flask over my hip and the skin frosted over with an agony of burning. Then he took out some jumpcrick's legbones and held them against the hole, snap snap, a flash of blue flame and everything fell away high.

There was a choking, but it didn't feel like me no longer. It felt like the man I was before I died.

Kailen

'Let's see it.'

Achi flicked it across the table, a pebble across wood, but this stone was worked with precision, a stone coin, black and thick as a thumb. There were no markings on it, a hairline of quartz the only imperfection of the material itself. The ocean had polished it, my face made a shadow by it. It was the third I'd seen in the last few months.

'The Prince, from your old crew, his throat was cut,' said Achi.

Achi drained his cup, leaned back in his chair and yawned, the chair creaking, not built for such a big man still in his leathers. He was filthy and sour-smelling from the weeks sleeping out.

'How are the boys?' I asked.

He opened his eyes with a start, already drifting away to sleep. I smiled at his irritation.

'Sorry, sir, all good. Danik and Stimmy are sorting out the horses, Wil went looking for a mercer, wants to get his woman something as we been away a while.'

'Stimmy's boy is on the mend, I had word from the estate. Let him know if you see him before me.'

Achi nodded and yawned again.

I looked again at the black coin in my fingers. Such coins were given to mercenaries who betrayed their purse or their crew. But who had The Prince betrayed?

We had called him The Prince because there was a time when he was in line for a throne, last of three, least loved and cleverest. His homeland chose its emperors in a way as ridiculous as any; which of the incumbents best demonstrated martial prowess. His sister won their single combat on the day their father died and was thus made queen, but his sword wasn't what made him worthy of the Twenty.

The Prince did the politics his sister could not. War allows only two perspectives, yours and theirs, a limit his sister was not capable of seeing beyond. Nations require the management of more factions than cut diamonds have facets and I met nobody that could exploit his empire's *politic* more adroitly than The Prince.

I plucked a white grape from the bowl, milky and juicy as a blind eyeball. Achi peeled eggs, head bowed. The bargirl came in and cleared away my plate. She offered a quick smile before retreating to the noise of the inn below us.

I recalled the two other black coins I'd seen recently, as perfect as this one. The Prince had shown them to me in his cabin aboard one of the Quartet's galleys only a few months ago. The Quartet were an influential merchant guild across most of the Old Kingdoms, and it was as fine a cabin as I'd ever seen him in, satin cushions, exquisitely carved chests and lockers, some of them the work of masters I had had the good fortune to commission myself at my wife Araliah's recommendation.

I'd travelled to see The Prince after he'd sent an escort bidding me to return with him.

'These coins were found with Harlain and Milu,' he said. 'I will try and find out more.'

'How did they die?' I asked.

'Harlain returned to his homeland, Tetswana, became their leader, the Kaan of Tetswana no less. It was the gathering before the rains. Leaders and retinues of nine tribes. Seventy or so dead, the black coin in his hand only.'

Harlain would not join us at Snakewood, the last time any of the Twenty were together. He had wanted to leave us some time before the end. Paying the colour had taken from all of us, but it took his heart. It was only as we embraced for a final time and I helped him with his saddle that I realised I hadn't heard him singing for some months. I was glad he made it home.

'Milu?' I asked.

'He became a horse-singer out in Alagar. They found him lying at the side of a singer's pit. Someone had been with him, footprints in the sand around his body, the coin in his hand.'

'Poison?' I asked.

'Almost certainly. No way of placing it.'

Milu had also been at Snakewood, but stayed only for a drink and to buy supplies before leaving with Kheld. They had lost heart as much as Harlain had; no talk of purses or where in the world was at war; they did not discuss, as did Sho or Shale, how my name could be put to work to bolster the gold of a purse.

I never tired of watching Milu work, his grotesquely big chest and baggy jowls filling with the songs that brought the wild horses to his side, training them to hold firm in the charge. It seemed that he, like Harlain, had been able to let go of the mercenary life before the colour took everything.

'Their deaths are connected, Kailen. It must be the Twenty.'

'You've heard from nobody else?'

'Only that Dithnir had died. He went back home to Tarantrea; one of their envoys that negotiates with the Quartet I represent knows me well and shared the news with me. I asked about a coin but there was none. Apart from that I keep in touch with Kheld when I'm in Handar, but the rest, no word.'

I breathed deeply of the morning breeze that blew across the deck and slapped at the fringes of the awning we were beneath. Dithnir was a bowman, almost a match for Stixie, shy and inadvisedly romantic with whores, cold and implacable in the field.

'I remember Snakewood,' said The Prince.

Our eyes met briefly. 'No. That was dealt with.' I'd said it more sharply than I'd intended. Why did I feel a thread of doubt?

He reached across the table, took the carafe and refilled our glasses with the wine I'd brought for him.

'Your estate is improving,' he said, holding up his glass for a toast.

'Yes, these vines were planted two winters ago; they'll improve. I only wish for Jua's cooler summers, perhaps an estate nearer the hills. How is the Quartet? I hear you have brokered a treaty with the Shalec to cross their waters. Not even the Post could manage it. Have you considered lending them your talents?'

'Why would I toil through its ranks to High Reeve or Fieldsman when I can be a Partner with the Quartet? The Post – The Red himself – could learn something from the Quartet regarding our softening of the Shalec, but I'm glad he hasn't, I'm lining my pockets beautifully. Remarkable as the Post runs so much trade elsewhere. They can bid lower than us at almost every turn; we can't match the subs, but we can work with lower margins, give Shalec a fee on the nutmeg, a pittance of course. But every investor north of the Gulf believes the Post controls the winds.'

'While the Post can sub dividends over fewer summers than anyone else, the flatbacks will flock,' I said, 'but enough of trade: congratulations, Prince, I'm glad to see things are going well; being a Partner suits you. Will you get a message to me if you find Kheld? It would be good to know he's still alive.'

He nodded.

The Prince had been the difference at Ahmstad, turning three prominent families under the noses of Vilmor's king, extending the borders and fortifying them in a stroke. The mad king is still being strangled in the noose The Prince tied. His death proved that whoever of us was alive was in danger. I signed our purses. This could only be about getting at me.

Achi had fallen asleep.

I poured him some of the dreadful brandy that was the best The Riddle had to offer.

Shale and Gant were taking a purse only weeks south. If they were still anything like the soldiers of old I would have need of them. Achi's crew would be glad to be going back to Harudan. I needed good men with my wife, Araliah. Still, there was one more thing I needed to ask of Achi himself, one person I needed to confirm was dead.